CIRCLE TIDE

Rebecca K. Rowe

EDGE SCIENCE FICTION AND FANTASY PUBLISHING
AN IMPRINT OF HADES PUBLICATIONS, INC.

CALGARY

Circle Tide
Copyright © 2011 by Rebecca K. Rowe

EDGE

Edge Science Fiction and Fantasy Publishing
An Imprint of Hades Publications Inc.
P.O. Box 1714, Calgary, Alberta, T2P 2L7, Canada

Edited by Matt Hughs
Interior design by Janice Blaine
Cover Illustration and Design by David Willicome
ISBN: 978-1-894063-59-3

EDGE Science Fiction and Fantasy Publishing and Hades Publications, Inc. acknowledges the ongoing support of the Alberta Foundation for the Arts for our publishing programme.

Alberta Foundation for the Arts

Library and Archives Canada Cataloguing in Publication

Rowe, Rebecca K., 1965-

Circle tide / Rebecca K. Rowe.
ISBN 978-1-894063-59-3
(e-book ISBN: 978-1-894817-92-9)

I. Title.
PS3618.O965C57 2011   813'.6   C2011-901622-2

FIRST EDITION
(F-20110714)
Printed in Canada
www.edgewebsite.com

DEDICATION

For Craig and Mas
My Heroes

Acknowledgements

I am indebted to my mother Mary Jane Rowe and my sister Jennifer Rowe who taught me storytelling and who have always been there for me. I'd also like to express my gratitude for the incredible emotional support of the Willis family, Bert Lewis the world traveler, Emita Samuels who brings light into every room she graces, Benilda Samuels, the Rehors, the Griffiths, the Grouts, the Maslowskis, Rose Beetem, Rob Cordingley and of course, Chi Yang.

Sergio, Seth, Sasha, Sarah, Anna, Patrick, Connor and Allison Keiko continue to inspire me with their delight in the written and spoken word. They are our future.

For the talks, the hikes and their sheer mastery of the craft, special thanks must go to Helen Thorpe, Janis Hallowell, David, Peter Heller, Lisa Jones and Tory Read.

This book wouldn't have been possible without the invaluable counsel, good humor and patience of my editor Matt Hughes, and the generosity and exuberance of Brian and Anita Hades at EDGE Science Fiction and Fantasy Publishing.

Lastly, this story is dedicated to two great heroes, E. Thomas Rowe and Craig Willis, for their inspiration, their logic and their love.

CHAPTER 1

Family, his ultimate ruin or his saving grace: it had provoked Noah's withdrawal into the wilderness and was the sole reason for his return.

Noah stepped off the elevator into the darkness of Senator Mari Ortega's outer office suite. The odor of acrid sweat pervaded the room. He could hear muffled conversation. The inner office doorway formed a rectangle of light at the far end of the enormous, pitch-black room.

Across that island of light, a man and the senator danced. Noah stared at their silhouettes, defined by the luminous inner office behind them. The stranger had one arm wrapped tight around the senator's waist lifting her from the ground. Only the tips of her shoes graced the floor. As quickly as the couple had appeared, they spun out of Noah's field of vision.

This is awkward. She's the one who insisted we urgently meet, Noah thought. *Did she forget?*

A gut-wrenching wail issued from the other room. A second cry ended abruptly.

The illusion of the dance evaporated. Noah sprinted through the gloom into Ortega's inner sanctum. She had fallen to her knees. Doubled over with her arms around her stomach, the senator gasped for air. A man with arms as thick as tree trunks stood over her.

"Why don't you take on someone your own size?" Noah shouted.

The attacker turned toward Noah. His face had a distinctive half-smashed, crooked nose and his skin was the unmistakable ashen color of a Heartlander. In his right hand, he gripped a long, narrow-bladed knife. Blood trickled in rivulets over his fingers, dripping off the hilt onto the white marble floor. The man took a step toward Noah.

As Noah glanced around for something he could use as a weapon, he wondered, *How did this man get through MAM security and past the guards? And why hadn't his biostats registered on my visual overlays?*

The attacker might as well be a ghost.

Noah grabbed a small table, hoisted it in front of him, and thrust its legs into Ghost's chest. The man fell backwards, momentarily off balance. The knife sailed out of his hand and clattered across the marble floor, out of reach beneath the sofa.

Cursing, Ghost violently yanked the table from Noah and threw it against the wall. One of its legs snapped, and it clattered to the floor. In a few audible clicks, the pieces were drawn to each other, and the leg repaired itself.

If only it were so easy for humans, Noah thought, stealing a quick glance at Ortega. She hadn't moved. Blood stained her white robes. Ortega looked seriously wounded although Noah didn't dare go near her with this thug on his heels. He wanted desperately to contact the Order for help. Closing his eyes to make contact right now might get them both killed.

"How did you get past security?" Noah demanded. His voice trembled more than he would have liked.

Ghost lunged toward him. Noah scrambled backwards.

Unable to locate the knife, Ghost focused his attentions on Noah, aiming his punches at his skull, chest and liver. Without losing his balance, Noah bent back, over and to the side as flexible as a boiled noodle.

Ghost struck out, missed and feinted a blow. Noah moved sideways directly into a right hook. Blood arced from his mouth in a fine spray across the white cushioned furniture. He tumbled back from the force of the blow and his shoulder hit the coffee table. It overturned, and a heavy crystal vase toppled over onto an ancient throw rug. Noah landed wedged between coffee table and sofa.

His world went dark for a moment. The fly gamer came to with fragrant peonies under his nose and water in his ear. The empty vase lay beside him on the rug. Noah's jaw ached. He tasted copper and swallowed hard.

Turning his head toward the sofa, he located the knife. Pressing against the sofa, he stretched his arm and succeeded in wrapping his fingers around the hilt.

The sudden pulverizing grip on his ankles made him groan. Ghost dragged Noah out from under the sofa. Still slightly dazed, Noah lashed out with the knife. Each strike met air. Ghost pinned the gamer on his back and forced the knife from Noah's grip.

Noah grabbed the vase with his free hand and slammed it into his attacker's temple. Without the smallest gasp, Ghost collapsed out cold against the ottoman. Noah struggled up from beneath the heavy body and pried the weapon from the attacker's hand.

With Ghost temporarily knocked out, Noah staggered around the overturned furniture to Ortega. For the first time, he noticed the far walls had "Traitor" and "Heartland=Underground" scrawled across them.

Ortega remained on her knees. Noah eased himself down beside her, but kept a wary eye on the back of the sofa where Ghost lay out of view on the other side.

"Senator Ortega," Noah's voice caught in his throat. "May I take a look at your wounds?"

With her chin down and her black shoulder-length hair forward, she sat motionless except for her labored breathing. He couldn't see her face and worried that she had lost consciousness. Noah blinked to reset his visual overlays and closed his eyes to contact the Order through Citizen Emergency:

<Senator Mari Ortega has been knifed and seriously wounded. She needs help. The assailant is still here!>

<Noah of Domus Aqua, stay calm. The Order with medics will be there in five minutes.>

Startled by an external sound, Noah opened his eyes and refocused on the room. Ghost was no longer on the floor against the sofa. Torn between chasing down Ortega's attacker and protecting the senator, Noah jumped up and started for the doorway.

"Noah," the senator said quietly.

Immediately, he returned to her side.

"Medics will be here in a few minutes," he assured her.

"Are *you* hurt?" asked Ortega. With a trembling, blood-soaked hand, she pushed her hair back from her face and inadvertently smeared red across her cheek and ear.

"No, but your attacker got away," Noah said.

"Never mind him," she said. "He was only a messenger."

"What do you mean?" Noah asked.

"I need your help," she replied, ignoring the question.

"Anything."

"Take this locket from around my neck. It contains a datasphere. Deliver it personally to Goth."

"Goth."

"Gothardi Lotte, the Minister of Internal Affairs. You'll do this?"

"Of course. Is this why you wanted me to come tonight? Does it concern my brother?"

"Your brother..." she trailed off, pausing for a moment. Her face contorted in pain. She took a few shallow breaths before continuing, "You promise on the honor of your domus that you'll deliver the datasphere?"

"Yes ... upon Domus Aqua." He slipped the unusual piece from around her neck. The intricately designed silver sphere felt warm in his palm. Noah carefully slid the locket and chain into his pocket, and sealed it closed.

"You can't trust anyone with that — especially not the Order. They've been infiltrated, but that won't matter if you get the data to Goth. The truth will come out." She paused again and coughed. "Leave before the Order gets here."

"I'm not abandoning you. I'll wait until the medics arrive."

"You promised." Her voice grew weaker. He could barely hear her.

"Yes, but—"

"Underneath my desk ... there's an emergency exit."

Noah nodded, and she continued.

"The locket will allow you access. Go." Her voice had become so soft that he bent close and put his ear to her lips. "The Order. They're here."

"Keep the knife for protection," Noah said, pressing the hilt into her hand.

Noah rushed to Ortega's desk and crawled under it.

He pressed the locket against an access point and the floor opened beneath him. His heart skipped a beat as he free fell several feet. The trapdoor shut above him. Dragline-silkita mesh sprang down under his weight and lit its silver tendrils with the energy of his impact. It tossed him up again so that for a brief moment he remained airborne with the silver silkita threads illuminating the walls they covered. He'd landed in a room no bigger than an elevator with only one door.

The room zoomed abruptly downward, shifted laterally, travelled horizontally, and finally skidded to a stop, tossing him every which way against the silkita. Regaining his balance, Noah placed the locket against the door, which he thought of as the cab-hatch of a secret rollercoaster. Since it wouldn't open with the locket, he threw his full weight against it. The hatch remained shut.

"Come on," Noah said. "*Move!*"

Nothing. Seconds passed. He worried that the cab had malfunctioned or no longer had power. Trapped inside a undocumented, broken-down rollercoaster, he might as well be a rat trapped between the floorboards found only after his body began to smell. He pounded frantically on the wall, and the mesh lit up.

The cab arbitrarily jolted back to life. He felt the pull as it headed down and was glad of the protective mesh when it once again lurched to a stop. The door opened on a solid wall. Again, he held up the locket and the opening became visible. He stepped through into an old service tunnel in the Underground. Behind him the wall returned to its solid state.

Peering down the dim tunnel, Noah muttered, "Terrific."

In this city's labyrinth of arcane service tunnels unknown to groundsiders like him, Noah could easily become lost. Not far above him on the other side of the wall, he heard voices: orders being issued and acknowledged. His heart pounded in his throat.

Choosing the better-lit path, he bolted left down the tunnel. As he ran, disturbing images of the wounded senator kept popping into his head.

If only I'd moved more quickly, I might have saved her from getting stabbed, Noah thought.

Flashes of her pooling blood, her labored breathing, weak voice and pained smile haunted him. Her attacker's ghostly face was etched in Noah's memory. As he ran, his thoughts skipped from Ghost to worrying about whether the senator was going to be all right, to what he had to do next.

Focusing on the immediate, he kept a fast pace down the tunnels, periodically ducking under low-hanging ceiling pipes. All he had to do was get groundside and deliver the datasphere. After that, he'd turn himself in as a witness and explain what had happened. Of course, the senator would ensure he didn't get into trouble for running away from a crime scene. Even if she didn't want anyone to know about the datasphere, she'd figure out an excuse for him having left her.

Every time he came to a fork in the tunnel, he turned right. That way, he figured he could retrace his steps if necessary. The times he'd been lost in a game, he'd followed the same pattern. In many ways this night felt like a Seven Walls gaming scenario. None of it seemed real, except for the wounded senator.

Suddenly, Noah heard footsteps behind him. He looked back over his shoulder, but couldn't see anyone. At a curve in the tunnel, a narrow shadow flit across the wall beside him. Noah picked up his pace.

When he heard the familiar sound of the Underground Rapid Transit, he searched for an access point to the URT tunnels. It didn't take long to find a large vent grate that overlooked the station. Through the vent, he could see Order regulars stationed along the platform. They were, no doubt, looking for him. He squatted down for a better view. He'd have to wait until the platform below cleared. Alternating his focus between the tunnel and the platform, he sat back on his heels.

A fugitive from the Order hiding in the Underground, it was hard for Noah to believe that only hours ago he'd arrived in Los Angeles feeling carefree, fresh from tracking the once extinct (newly re-introduced from genetic archives) *Chelonia mydas* in the Revillagigedos Islands far to the south.

For the past eighteen months, Noah had indulged his wanderlust. He had donated all of his property to the Diversity Club, save for what remained in the Novus Orbis gaming worlds he frequented. At home among the nomadic group of biologists and astrobiologists, like them, he was dedicated to ridding Earth of off-world invasive species and bringing back those that were extinct. That is, until Senator Mari Ortega had summoned him to her Los Angeles office. The cryptic, urgent message said only that she wished to discuss his eldest brother Daniel and that Noah must tell no one.

Ortega was an old friend of Noah's family, and his intended mentor, if he ever bowed to his mother's demands and took up a career in politics.

Upon receiving her message, Noah immediately made up an excuse to the crew of scientists he was working with in the remote bays far to the south and flew north. He'd done as Ortega asked, telling no one he was headed for L.A., particularly not his brother, Daniel.

Sporting a midnight tan, relaxed and fit with his thick dreds cropped short, Noah had arrived in L.A. with two women on his mind: the senator and his ex-girlfriend Beatrice. True to the senator's request, he hadn't even told Beatrice that he was coming to the city. Since Beatrice lived in a penthouse not far from the Council Tower, he had planned to surprise her.

Now he was here, in Los Angeles, running from the Order like a criminal. He stared through the grate. The squad of regulars monitoring the crowd had been reduced to one.

Restless, Noah examined the elaborate silver locket. He clicked the latch open and Ortega's family popped up in 3D. Hidden within that familial data lay the encrypted datasphere. He tilted the locket, dropped the datasphere into his palm, and immediately felt the burn of a data link across his hand.

Despite the danger, Noah closed his eyes to access Novus Orbis, activating his user preferences where he stored his own memorabilia. He downloaded several short takes of his mother, Lila the Domus Aqua Master, as a substitute wraparound for Ortega's data. And then, he dropped the newly wrapped datasphere duplicate off at his estate in Seven Walls and updated every piece of data he had there with extra junk. It would take a while to sort through and find the real data he'd added. Exiting Novus Orbis, Noah checked to ensure an image of his mother had replaced that of the Ortegas. He clicked it shut and slipped its chain over his head. That was the best he could do for now: a backup in Novus Orbis and Ortega's datasphere hidden in plain sight.

As soon as the remaining Order regular boarded the train and the platform emptied of commuters, Noah removed the grate and jumped down to the platform. Glancing around, he quickly moved out of the light and into the shadows. When the next train arrived, and the platform filled with Los Angelinos, Noah walked out with the crowd and emerged from the Underground.

Pedestrians swarmed the sidewalks, and cyclists filled the road. At a distance past the no-fly zone, air traffic formed light patterns across the dark sky. Noah stopped briefly to study the Council Tower. It remained dark and quiet as though it'd joined the other living offices finally emptied of their occupants and self-optimizing in preparation for the morning influx.

The senator must not have been as badly injured as I thought. Otherwise, emergency heliovehicles would have swooped in. The area would be lit up and cordoned off.

Although no Order regulars were visible in the crowd, Noah noticed that a skinny kid, in roof gardener browns, was following him. When he finally thought he'd lost the kid, a crow buzzed his head. A few blocks later, the roof gardener showed up again. Still, the kid hadn't checked his biostats to identify him, or done anything threatening.

Noah was simply dressed without anything besides his ring to betray his domus and could be mistaken for a late-night service professional on his way home. As far as he could tell, he passed through the crowd unidentified.

Around him the pedestrians drew each other's attention with their elaborately coiffed hair, their lizard skin, their furry MAM embraces or their propensity for revealing flawless ample breasts no matter their true age. Even Noah noticed the yellow-spotted and orange-chested women — especially when they sported an extra breast. With their cloying scents, the forever youths' beauty-glow captivated everyone. They afforded him anonymity. Still, he knew he had to get off the street.

Noah paused to contact his ex-girlfriend, blending in with a group of pedestrians mesmerized by a street busker who kept turning himself into a leaping flame. Her face resolved on the back of his eyelids. She sported a feline MAM embrace replete with cat ears and whiskers — a favorite party-look of hers.

<Beatrice, I'm so relieved you answered. I'm here in Los Angeles. Are you home?>

<Noah?! … I'm home, but it's past midnight.>

<I knew you'd be up. May I stop by? I'm in a bit of a fix.>

<Look, I don't care what kind of girl trouble you've gotten yourself into this time … Don't tell me she's married.>

<This isn't about a girl. You don't understand.>

<Hm. That's the beauty of being the ex. I don't have to understand.>

Beatrice smiled sweetly and abruptly ended their communiqué. He let out a long sigh. Hearing her voice renewed his determination to see her and he continued toward her place. To be safe, he'd slip in through the little-used back service entrance of her building. After this past misunderstanding, he needed to explain himself.

Besides, from Noah's vantage, the office buildings around him were ominous crouching giants only a little blacker than the sky. He couldn't bring himself to enter another office complex tonight for a hideaway, assuming he could find a way past its security. Pushed up against every office tower, crowded residential palaces glowed and spiraled toward the stars or stretched sideways and curled around in what appeared to be impossible architectural feats. Los Angeles always embraced impossibilities.

Toward one such unlikely structure, Noah wove as quickly as he could through the throngs of no-goods, do-gooders and everyone-else-just-out-for-themselves.

Turning down an alleyway emptied of pedestrians and bikes, he approached the back of the pantheon-esque living building. It reflected the personalities and characters of its residents, one of whom was his ex-girlfriend.

Closing his eyes to contact Beatrice again, Noah heard, "Target identified." The next moment his legs collapsed. He lay convulsing on the ground.

"Target down," the Order regular said. From Noah's vantage on the ground, the regular's hands looked disproportionately large. *Big hands,* Noah thought.

"Good work," said another regular.

Then, just as Noah stopped convulsing uncontrollably and had a second to breathe, Big-hands placed his glock-goku against Noah's temple and hijacked him again.

"That should take care of him for..." Noah never heard that last part.

When Noah came to, he found himself curled up in the shadow of Beatrice's building with the Order regulars arguing over him. His vision had turned a grayish, green hue. Big-hands still had his glock-goku drawn. Noah, unable to move, warily watched them. The other regular looked extra wide with a smallish shaved head. *A pinhead.*

"It's Noah of Domus Aqua. Can you believe it? This is a guy who's got everything, and he's involved in this mess," Big-hands said. "We should at least search him."

"No, absolutely not," Pinhead replied.

In response, Big-hands bent down and frisked Noah. He felt the locket and yanked it from Noah's neck, flicked it open with his thumb, and bent down to view the images.

"Would you look at this? What a momma's boy," Big-hands said in disgust.

Big-hands offered the locket to Pinhead, who shook his head in refusal. Big-hands shrugged and pocketed it. Noticing Noah's domus ring on his pinky, the Order regular struggled to remove the engraved ruby ring. Since Noah never took it off, he wasn't surprised it wouldn't budge. The man would have to cut it off.

"I'm out of here," Pinhead warned.

Noah cleared his throat, but could do no more than glare up at Big-hands who'd gokued him so hard that he might as well have been observing the Order regular from another planet. Big-hands met his gaze and smirked.

This time, the glock-goku hurled Noah back with such force, his world cracked.

CHAPTER 2

Rika Musashi Grant swerved the heliovan into the no-fly zone.

"Downtown central, here I come," she said.

Her hands flicked across the controls making minute adjustments as she steered the heliovan over the green, undulating rooftops that together formed a vast Zen sky-garden of vegetable-scapes across living roofs.

Unfortunately, Rika couldn't enjoy the early-morning view. She had Angela's jarring communiqué on repeat in her head: *Yori is in trouble.*

Her boss at the Institute of Extended Cognition had forwarded Rika a two-word communiqué from Yori, "Send backup."

Despite Rika's repeated attempts to contact him, Yori remained unresponsive. Angela had told her that Yori entered the building when it began sucking power from its neighbors — including the Council Tower. While the residents evacuated, he had reported an invasive fungus and had managed to take the building off the MAM network, disengaging it from the grid. After that, he went silent.

Rika optimized her course. On several of the roof heliopads below she identified light-absorber Order vehicles. To her, they looked like miniature black holes. She half-expected them to take her down.

Luckily, they remained stationary, which meant that Angela had ensured Rika's clearance. Rika took a deep breath and forced herself to relax.

Minutes later, with a hiss and a thump, the heliovan landed on a lower rooftop's mini-tarmac nestled between tiered tomato vines, squash and daikon. Throwing open the door, Rika hopped out lugging a knapsack that rattled as she moved. Rika was tiny, little more than a sliver in her Institute-issued gray jumpsuit which contrasted with her deep caramel skin tone, her shock of long blue hair and her symmetrical features. Until she'd worked for the Institute, she'd always wanted to be tall with long legs, but being short meant she could maneuver places others would never fit, which had proven useful in her current position. Besides, before the Institute had chosen her for intensive cognitive enhancement, Rika couldn't get a job doing anything. She'd been mentally below average. Worse, she'd been an Undergrounder; one of the ostracized who lived in poverty beneath an opulent Los Angeles. As such, she would have been as unlikely to win a professional's status, as she would have been to sprout wings and fly.

Dropping her knapsack, Rika pulled out a tool-laden strap and wound it over her shoulder, down in front and around her waist in a folded infinity loop. Certain that Yori had only equipped himself with standard-issue Institute gear, she ran her fingertips along the strap-holds as she headed for the rooftop entrance. She double-checked her Undergrounder weapons — dark green "glass" chips, ToxSporeBlaster, ratcum-rodentstun, PestBane and portable Snuffire — as well as her climbing equipment.

Lately, her work had involved more pest control than her formal job description as a DeeJee had suggested. Rika was a _D_ata _G_atherer and a patterns-recognition specialist employed by the Institute of Extended Cognition and charged with correcting MAM imbalances. Rika didn't mind pest control. It got her out of the office. Fieldwork had proven more interesting, although she hated these crises. They meant that good scientists like Yori got hurt following outdated protocols that now rarely applied. Institute management always failed to understand. If anything went wrong, management looked for whoever had violated one of its rules.

Inside the building, Rika met sudden darkness. Light from the rooftop exit filtered in around the door, illuminating the top stairs. The stairwell had an odor like damp laundry that had been rolled up and left in some nearby corner to rot. She coughed and activated her hazmat anzug. The protective garment's hood stretched itself over Rika's face and grew from beneath her sleeves over her hands. It was skintight beneath her jumpsuit and had a breathing apparatus. Its quasi-permeable coating guarded against hazardous ingestion, inhalation or absorption, but remained forgiving so that Rika could breathe and speak.

"Emergency lights on," ordered Rika, hopeful the backup power might work.

She remained surrounded in inky blackness. Yanking her headlamp from its strap-hold, she slipped it over her forehead and activated it. The interior walls were low and rough, mimicking cutaways in the Underground tunnels. She recognized the architecture as the latest caricature of life Underground. It smacked of a groundside architect's rendition of what would make a Heartlander — the latest euphemism for Undergrounders like herself — feel at home, even though these residents had chosen to move above ground.

Accessing the building's sensors felt like communicating through water. Data transfer was slow and oddly distorted. Rika searched for her friend. Yori's biostats displayed at several floors below: on seven, on six and on five. Not good. She couldn't trust building data that reported Yori alive, but in three parts.

She took the stairs in twos and then threes.

Without even the building's anterior solar microharvesters to provide electricity, Rika wished Yori had waited for her. Sure, Sundays and Mondays were her days off, but that had never stopped Angela from contacting her. It shouldn't have stopped him. Yori always acted as though he could do everything on his own — especially when he was supposed to be teamed up with Rika. She didn't understand it.

Angela had admitted to Rika that Ortega had personally requested that Yori handle this mission. While Rika had only met the senator once, the woman had impressed Rika. Yori had consulted with the Senator many times on the environmental hazards that the Heartlanders faced living in the Underground or in the new groundside housing.

On the seventh floor, Rika found the stairwell access door. She tried it, but it was jammed. After several attempts and lots of cursing, Rika managed to wedge the door open wide enough to squeeze through. Consulting the building sensors led Rika straight to the elevator shaft. Yori's Institute bag and several sample kits lay beside the pried-open elevator door. A single rope, still secured to the doorframe, disappeared over the side.

Crazy Yori, she thought. *You better be okay.*

With the senator involved, this building was considered a high-profile case, more important than an isolated MAM imbalance that resulted in an extra bedroom suddenly becoming self-assembling from the kitchen floor or an apartment overrun with pests.

Leaning into the darkness, Rika saw the glint of green-black fungus on the walls as far as her light could reach. She sat back and wondered how a residential building in central Los Angeles had ended up with an odd-looking fungus thriving in its elevator shaft. Maybe the building tenants had brought in some exotic tropical fungus hoping to cultivate a new food source.

"Yori?" she yelled, and waited. And then as loud as she could, "Yor-ee!"

The rope moved ever so slightly.

"I'm coming down," Rika said. She meant to be reassuring.

Rika tested his rope: secure and weighted down, so he must still be hanging there.

She set up her own line and attached her descend-ascender on the far side of the door. Since she preferred not to slam into him on her descent, she headed down slowly. The building sensors still showed him on all three floors so she couldn't be certain precisely where he'd gotten in trouble.

The shaft sides felt slick, like oil, as she inched her way down. The fungus had grown thick enough to narrow the space. Passing the sixth floor, she noticed a large protrusion that she took for Yori. She hesitated, leaning against the wall of oily sponge and pivoting downward like an upside-down bat to get a better look. She could see an opening in the globular mess, a bit of sheer anzug-hood and the glint of an eye.

"Yori!" she said.

She heard a grunt.

That's when she realized the fungus turned glue-like with prolonged contact. Her one foot had adhered to the wall. She struggled and the black-green fungus engulfed her ankle.

She reached for her ToxSporeBlaster and released a cloud of it. It dusted the fungus a bright orange, but otherwise it remained unaffected. The fungus crawled up her calf. Taking a glass chip in each hand, Rika started hacking at it. The Pedralbes stained-glass chips with their fungal-growth inhibitors seemed to work. The mass visibly shrank away. She managed to hack herself free.

Once unstuck, she relied on the rope. Yori had become a gloppy obstruction beside what had once been the building's manual override controls. Carefully placing the chip's sharpest edge against the fungus she delicately sliced at it. She didn't want to compromise Yori's hazmat-anzug.

"I'm giving you a body haircut, razor-style," Rika told him, but he didn't laugh.

"Tell me they sent more than you," Yori croaked.

"I'm not good enough?"

"You've noticed I'm four times your weight and wedged in here like a sardine."

"I warned you to stop popping caramels, big brother," Rika said and grinned. He'd survived under all that muck. These hazmat anzugs were more reliable than she'd calculated.

"Hurry," Yori said, his voice hoarse. He moved his head around. "I followed all the protocols and used our fungicides. What new Institute tool did they give you to remove this fungal mess?"

"I'm using my own tool, glass chips imbedded with fungal growth inhibitors from the Underground."

"What? Are you kidding?" Yori said. She'd freed one of his arms and handed him her glass chip so that he could help cut himself free. She unclasped another chip from its strap-hold.

"Yep, I had the inspiration as soon as Angela mentioned fungus and gave me the address," Rika said, working as fast as she could to free him before the fungus reattached itself.

Yori fiddled with the glass and dug deep. He was perilously close to piercing his own hazmat-anzug.

"Let the glass do the work. The fungus is repelled."

"Repelled?"

"Okay Mr. Scientist, on contact the chip stops the enzymes in the spores' surface from releasing, among other processes," she said, waving her hand around to indicate further complexity, "So the fungus can't spread across its host."

"Rika, I must admit only you'd think up a correlation between fungus and Underground glass chips that is actually effective," Yori said, working to free his other arm while she cut the fungus from his back. "How your mind works is beyond me."

"It makes perfect sense. In the old days, these chips were developed for cutting blackbase. Since the crackdowns there's no blackbase, but the chips are still useful, especially in a Heartlander building."

"I get it," Yori said. "Treat an Undergrounder's building with Undergrounder tools."

"That's right. I figured this building is by design culturally predisposed to Heartlanders, and to our ways of dealing with organic malfunctions like fungal overgrowth, because it's been imprinted with its residents' biases."

"So that's your theory about why your commonplace Underground chips work, but not my state-of-the-art scrapers or fungicides?"

"Yep."

Yori shook his head and took one last swipe at the fungus. He swung free with such force that he nearly adhered himself to the wall on the other side. "If I keep following your logic, I'll end up thinking like you."

"Now that's a scary thought," Rika said.

"Let's get out of here. Do you mind carrying a couple of the samples?

"No problem," Rika replied, slipping the containers into specially reinforced pockets inside her strap-holders. She let Yori climb up ahead of her to make sure he made it. The way he swung back and forth, she worried he'd get stuck again. He hauled himself up out of the elevator shaft, and his foot disappeared over the edge. Only then did she ascend.

Cresting the seventh floor, Rika sighed in relief. She sat with her back against the wall next to the elevator while Yori tested the air. She moved her head back and forth to shine light on different parts of the hallway. The walls showed no signs of fungus, neither did the floor or the ceiling — not even in the corners. Besides the elevator shaft, the seventh floor appeared perfectly normal.

"It's strange," Yori said. "The fungal invasion is extremely aggressive yet highly localized. For some reason, our equipment detects no spores in the air right outside the open elevator shaft. It doesn't seem possible. Still, give me all your equipment and strip down to your hazmat suit. We don't want to spread this stuff."

Unfolding a contamination bag, Yori placed all their equipment and outer clothes inside and sealed it while Rika set up a temporary dry shower. They took turns dry showering in their hazmat suits to prevent any possibility of spreading the fungus.

"Thanks for saving my butt down there," Yori said at last, while Rika repacked her bag. He loaded his sample kits under one arm and slung his bag over his shoulder.

Seeing a loose corner of anzug material torn open and revealing a sliver of his neck, Rika gasped. "Yori, your anzug!"

"It's a small tear. No worries. We'll dry shower again before we go outside on the rooftop," Yori said, shrugging it off. "Keep those extra samples with you for now."

"I put the samples here," she said, tapping the strap-holders. "They're safe."

They mounted the stairs to the roof. Before opening the outer door, they took the time to dry shower again. Yori scanned their bags and sample containers to ensure they were clean.

In the light breeze, Rika retracted her hood. She gulped in air as though she'd been holding her breath the whole time. It took her a few seconds to process that she was staring directly at the black light-absorbing exterior and white crane insignia of an Order heliovan.

Suddenly Rika smelled ozone, as if lightning had struck nearby. Her skin buzzed with tiny repeated shocks. Puzzled, Rika rubbed her arms to reduce the tingling and studied the cloudless sky, blue except for a murder of crows. They swirled up and around the building clearly upset about their invaded garden. She turned and watched them circle. Their agitation matched her own. The crows were not simply circling; they focused on the five humans in their territory. With each wheel of their flying mass, the crows swerved nearer, almost striking the intruders. As they made their closest pass yet, Rika ducked.

The captain shifted her gaze to Rika and then up at the sky. She showed no concern.

"We'll take those samples off your hands," the Order captain told Yori. She was tall and blonde with piercing steel-colored eyes. One of her men stepped up to Yori, and he reluctantly held out his samples. The regular had to yank them from Yori's grasp.

"That's the evidence for a case we're working on," Yori explained, his voice still hoarse. "Senator Mari Ortega requested we take independent samples to discover how this MAM imbalance occurred."

"The Order has everything under control," the captain reassured him. She gave no hint that having Yori mention the powerful senator's name made any difference to her. "Let your superiors know that your samples will be of great use to us, and that we are deeply appreciative."

"And you are Captain Lynnfield," Yori said, reading her bio-stats.

"Yes." The captain's attention shifted to Rika.

"Rika Grant is a DeeJee and my colleague at the Institute of Extended Cognition," Yori explained.

"Watch it!" Rika yelled and pointed skyward. Only the captain and she ducked as the crows swooped down. Arms over her head, the sheer number of birds diving toward them made Rika crouch low so the crows couldn't peck her face.

Yori bent down beside Rika. Forcing her to stand, he wrenched her arm so hard she cried out. All the birds flew off in different directions. Except one, which landed nearby.

"How did you do that?" Captain Lynnfield asked Rika. "That was a private memory event, *my* private memory event!" To Yori, she said, "You should have your DeeJee examined. She's illegally accessing private memories."

Turning on her heel, the captain left with the two Order regulars falling in step behind her. Rika wondered why Lynnfield had saved such a disturbing memory event. Maybe it was the woman's personal reminder to stay on guard against crows or more symbolically Undergrounders like Rika. The thought made her shiver. Yori stood there, gripping Rika so tightly that she couldn't budge. He released her only after the black heliovan had shot straight upward and away from the building.

"What in Thesni's name was that all about?" Yori asked. "You could have gotten us arrested."

"The crows," Rika mumbled.

"What about them?"

"They dove at us."

"The crows flew nowhere near us." Yori said, as they headed toward the Institute heliovan. "What do you think you saw?"

Had she accessed the captain's M. E. like the woman had accused her of doing? Rika wondered and massaged her arm where he'd grabbed it. With a resentful glance at Yori, she said, "Never mind."

Yori took the driver's seat of the heliovan, and she jumped in beside him. He must have come via Underground Rapid Transit. It occurred to her that he'd had a premonition the Order would show up. "Did you suspect the Order would take our samples? Is that why you had me carry some?"

"Perhaps," Yori said. "Let's just say Senator Ortega made me cautious. She told me to trust no one with our findings, not the Order, not anyone else at the Institute — not even Angela. We're to report directly to the senator. Okay?"

He took the vehicle up into the air and headed toward the ocean and the Institute.

"Sure, that's okay with me," Rika said with a shrug. "It's unusual, maybe a bit paranoid, but—"

"The senator is in the middle of a big investigation — an important one. It's all very hush-hush. She even sent me her personal decryption key, but I haven't received anything encrypted from her or anyone else."

"Who else is in on the investigation?" Rika asked.

"There's an ex-Order private investigator named Sakoda who has an entire team of sleuths asking questions, although I've no idea how the fungus factors into it all."

"I knew this assignment would be different as soon as Angela said the senator specifically requested you," Rika said. "It's more significant than the MAM imbalances we usually fix."

"True," Yori said and pointed down toward a squat residential building. "Remember the hoarder over there on Broadway?"

She remembered. The hoarder had kept dinner leftovers in the weirdest places like his closet, his desk drawers, his hat, anywhere except the refrigerator, which was too far to walk to when he needed a snack, or so he'd told them. Over time, the living building had become attuned to him and misinterpreted his needs.

"He was a real loner," Rika commented.

"That Broadway Manor sure solved his problem, didn't it?" Rika nodded.

"I've never seen so many rats," Yori said. "Supposedly tame rats are good companions."

With the sudden precise memory of the rats and the man, Rika shifted uncomfortably in her seat. The rats had been wild — a detail the living building's MAM neural network, its built-in smart intelligence, categorized as "irrelevant." After catching all those big, aggressive vermin, adjusting the Broadway Manor's MAM imbalance had seemed like the easy part.

"From the little research I did before I entered the building, this fungus case is peculiar. Usually, I discover a clear cause-and-effect, but not this time," Yori said.

What Rika found more puzzling was that the fungus grew so aggressively without spreading beyond the walls of the elevator system.

"Tell me, have the residents admitted to any knowledge of how the fungus might have gotten there?" Yori asked.

Rika let her mind go blank for a moment, issuing the MAM query and then said, "Residents have reported they first noticed a bad smell near the elevators that became worse after the elevator stopped operating. That's when they discovered the fungus growing. No one admits to any prior knowledge of the fungus or its origins. Two people lied, according to their biostats. The results of their interrogation by the Order are currently classified."

"Very strange." Yori shook his head.

"You'll find the cause," Rika said.

"At least the senator is backing this investigation. Ortega told me she'd keep her suppositions to herself until after I delivered my analysis. She doesn't want to bias my findings whatever those turn out to be."

"That's a surprise. Most politicians tell you what they would prefer to hear. Ortega is different. I like this woman," Rika asserted.

"I'm partial to her, too," Yori said, nodding. "Sunday afternoon when she called requesting my help, I told her about you and that I'd need your help on this. She mentioned that she'd make sure we'd be recognized for our excellent service in return for us keeping everything confidential until she puts together the full report."

"What does getting 'recognized for our excellent service' mean?"

"You know the senator got me promoted to senior scientist the last time I came through for her."

"So," Rika said slowly, trying to sound casual and not show her excitement. "If I chose to forego all this testing mumbo jumbo the IEC insists on and skip to the next stage of mind enhancements, she'd arrange that for me?"

"Absolutely," Yori said with a grin. "But you could aim a little higher than that."

"That's all I want," Rika said.

Still feeling a little tingly after accessing the captain's memory event, Rika knew the only way she'd pass the Institute mental health tests would be to get them waived.

"Rika," Yori's grin faded. "I've been thinking."

"That's a mistake."

"You had a hallucination back there on the rooftop, didn't you?"

"No, not a hallucination," Rika said. To avoid further discussion, she instantly became enthralled by the air traffic.

Hallucinations weren't Rika's problem. The phenomenon that plagued her was recent, also sporadic and unpredictable. Other people's private memory events had begun poking into her consciousness. In the early months after her enhancements, she had learned to design specific queries in order to access any historical information, including her own. She had only been able to have data that the Institute formally gave her permission to access.

Unfortunately, and this was her real quandary, she was picking up the recorded, most highly protected memory events of people who were in close physical proximity to her. If someone was agitated and called up a private M. E., it overtook her mind as though she'd specifically requested it. If she admitted to such frequent and accidental data theft, her admission would only lead to her immediate internment at the Institute. She'd seen worse things happen to her colleagues.

A year had passed since her brain had been neural-knit with the MAM, giving her open access to its neural networks, its vast archives, its instantaneous data feeds — and providing the MAM in turn access to her experiences and her cognitive processes. Rika felt lucky to be able to remember her own name some days. Her identity had become as fluid as her access to others' memories — and increasingly less real. She found it ironic that her unintentional theft of the captain's few-second memory event about a crow attack might be the thing that finally gave her away.

"We should have you checked out by the Institute medics," Yori concluded, following her long silence. And then, he coughed, a harsh, hacking sound from deep inside his chest.

"It's you who needs a medic," Rika replied.

He gestured with his middle finger, and she laughed.

Détente, for now. And yet, she had an uneasy feeling that medics were destined for her near future unless she proved invaluable to the senator on this project. At least, Rika could count on Yori, and because of him, on the politician's help. Ortega had enough connections and influence to keep any DeeJee from becoming another failed experiment at the Institute.

CHAPTER 3

Sunshine through the window, too bright against Noah's sore eyes, meant it was morning. His mind and body had finally reconnected. He sat hunched over in a high-backed ornately carved armchair with a bitter-smelling concoction shoved under his nose. Beatrice's feline party face bent down so close to his, he could have kissed her.

Unfortunately, kissing wasn't an option. His head pounded so hard he'd have sworn his heart had taken residence there. He had spent the night with his mind and nervous system hijacked after some Order schmuck had glock-gokued him three times. Once would have been enough to give Noah a lasting, full-body muscle chopper. After getting three, he couldn't recall how his ex-girlfriend, the future Domus Phrack master, Beatrice had managed to get him up to her top-floor penthouse.

Once Noah had his eyes open and a strong grip on the cup of evil-smelling brew, Beatrice began talking. His ex wore a skimpy toga over a MAM embrace that coated her skin to look like silver fur as she moved, as well as sporting a temporary furless, catlike face. Although she'd been at home when he contacted her, Beatrice still wore her party-going MAM embrace. Under normal circumstances, he'd have been jealous. She paced in front of him like a caged animal while she spoke. Noah had never seen her this agitated. Following her movements made him dizzy. Something had her genuinely worried.

It's seeing me like this. The thought came to him from a distance sifted down through red-black waves of pain. Her words reached him from that same faraway place.

"Order regulars came to my door last night before you arrived," Beatrice was saying. "They asked all sorts of strange questions about your relationship with Senator Mari Ortega. They were waiting for you. What were you thinking to show up here?"

What was I thinking? Noah echoed. Nothing came to mind.

"You've been sleeping off their brutality ever since. I'm thinking of filing an official complaint. You've been out cold for hours. Just look at what they've done to you!"

It was just like his ex to demand the impossible. He couldn't look at what they'd done unless he first figured out how to make his legs move. Plus he'd need to find a mirror. Maybe she planned to bring him one.

The crawlies had definitely set in. He wanted to dig out whatever was moving beneath his skin. His head felt as big as a ship, an unmanned one at that.

"The Order is after you because of The Diversity Club," Beatrice guessed. "You've got to distance yourself from those radicals. Even Senator Ortega has come out against TDC in the last couple months."

Noah winced when she again mentioned the senator, but Beatrice was wrong about his involvement in The Diversity Club. He clung to her wrongness as though his sanity depended on it. Beatrice noticed his expression.

"Ha! I knew it. Your face says it all. TDC has gotten you in trouble."

You're wrong about The Diversity Club.

Yes, he was a card carrying member, but he had been inactive since Anatole, the charismatic founder issued his new manifesto — condemning humans on earth. The Diversity Club's leader not only wanted the rebirth of all extinct species stored in the genetic archives, he also called for the end of human civilization.

"Answer me," Beatrice said. "At least nod your head."

I'm trying to ignore what's crawling beneath my skin.

Noah clutched the cup and stared at his ex. This lovely, exaggerated creature was his only anchor to reality.

The Diversity Club. No, that's not why the Order hijacked me.

"Noah? Hello! You realize you've made yourself my problem. I'm an ex-girlfriend. Got that? You shouldn't have come here." More pacing. "Are you listening to me?"

Noah groaned and resisted the urge to dig holes in his arms and face with his fingernails. There'd been talk of a mirror, TDC and his coming here last night.

It's Monday morning already! I need to deliver the datasphere.

"Finish that drink, it'll reduce the crawlies so you can speak," she said and left the room. He glanced down at the bitter concoction and then gingerly sipped it.

Moments later, she returned with a man who looked more like a thug than a medic for Domus Phrack. The medic proceeded to scan, poke and needle Noah into better condition. Noah was used to rough medics. After almost every fly game, he had to see a medic. This time though every jab was amplified a thousand times.

"Late last night when Beatrice had me work on you," the medic told Noah when he was done, "I worried you might suffer real damage. You have a concussion probably from convulsing into the wall." The man stood and stretched after having been hunched over Noah, jabbing him with an elaborately curled needle. Beads of sweat rolled off the medic's brow. "You'll suffer various neurological symptoms for the next twenty-four hours, but you won't form lesions or those subcutaneous traveling fibers. That only happens when the hijacked are left untreated."

"Is he in pain?" Beatrice asked.

The medic turned to Beatrice and his tone softened. "Let's put it this way; in every case I've treated, the patient is howling and trying to scratch his skin off. Your boyfriend here is the toughest I've seen."

"He's not my boyfriend," she said. "Will he fully recover?"

"Like I said, give it twenty-four hours. While I can't eliminate all the pain, lasting damage is unlikely."

"Thank you," Beatrice said. She led the medic through Greek-themed columns into an adjacent room. For the first time since opening his eyes, he took in his surroundings; the plush chairs, the brocaded hangings depicting Domus Phrack's legendary fly games, and the ornate side table, empty except for a man's emerald ring. Noah picked up the jeweled band and saw the inner engraving. Like his ring, it had the Domus Aqua emblem stamped in the gold and read: *from Mom and Dad.* He recognized his eldest brother's ring. Beatrice might as well have left Daniel's dirty undergarments lying on the table for Noah to find. Noah had come back to the city because Senator Ortega had implied his avaricious brother was involved in a scandal. *Was this what she'd meant?* Noah thought. He couldn't be sure, and the senator wasn't going to be able to tell him in the near future. He found he had been squeezing the ring so hard, the faceted stone had cut into his palm. Opening his fist, Noah slid the emerald ring with its drop of blood onto his pinky and made his decision.

Once he had control of his legs, he staggered toward the outer door while Beatrice and the medic talked in the next room. Noah hated owing her his life. Luckily, the medic had diminished his crawlies to no more than a constant itch. Noah felt like he had a case of invisible hives — itchy, but bearable. Most importantly, the roar in his head had been reduced to a dull throb.

Ignored by everyone on the busy sidewalks, Noah hobbled slowly to the closest Novus Orbis café, rented a private cubicle and sat down. Beatrice had saved his life, but left him a bitter old man, at least temporarily. Closing his eyes, he heard the familiar whoosh and felt sudden vertigo as he entered Novus Orbis and engaged all his senses.

In the virtual universe, he wanted to land directly on his estate in the Seven Walls world, but received an unusual message: "Area Restricted." Since Seven Walls was a place he typically went to spar, he accessed the game the way he would if he wanted to fight an adversary. Immediately, he received a challenge.

At the craggy mountaintops, down by the sea or in its surreal city centers, he had met mind-benders, mavericks and innovators who challenged him. They prepared him for fly-gaming championships in ways that his own domus could rarely dream up. Domus Aqua and other top economic domus sponsored the fly games for positive publicity and to strengthen allegiances. Fly gamers played for the endorphin high and the joy of pushing their own extremes. In short, they made life interesting.

Today was different. Noah turned down the first match and the next, as he headed across rugged terrain toward his estate; an island at the confluence of two rivers where he'd hidden the senator's datasphere. When he got there, he stood on the shore beneath the trees and stared at the rushing water.

His island had disappeared.

"You get hijacked?" a silvery voice said, followed by several strange clicks.

His hand went to the hilt of his long sword as he surveyed his surroundings. Whoever had spoken was very close. The only movements he noticed were the boats on the water.

Suddenly, a pair of odd-looking spectacles dropped from the tree limb above him. He jumped back, catching the spectacles in midair.

"If you want to see me, you'll have to put those on."

After inspecting them closely for hidden dangers, Noah slid the spectacles over his eyes. Instantly, a bloated blue rectangular bug came into focus on his arm. It waved. Except for its flashy wings and black-pearl eyes, it might have passed for a dust mite.

"Get off me," Noah said. He shook his arm, swiped at it with no impact. It waved again. "Who gave you permission to hitch a ride?"

"Nice to meet you, too," said the microscopic bug, its mandibles giving the words an odd after-click. "What makes you such a nice guy?"

"My estate's vanished," Noah said.

"The spooks have it," said the bug.

"Have what?" Noah asked, thinking of the datasphere.

"Your property, idiot. Look, the rivers are patched over, but not quite seamlessly."

Shifting focus to the river, the spectacles zoomed out for him and then in; Noah could see the slight misalignment in the river and a lot of other troubling Seven Walls microscopic parasites that he never knew existed. They appeared to be hitching rides on just about anything that moved. "Yuck."

"You see the seam?" said the bug.

"Yes."

"Your Novus Orbis properties are in spookdom, expropriated for the 'common good.' I'd say you were in a lot of trouble, except that you're still free to walk about. Why's that?"

I wish I knew, Noah thought. He answered with a shrug and studied the river while his heart raced. He had his biostats on hidden, but Noah had a feeling this critter read whatever it liked.

"The question is do you have anything worth retrieving from there," the bug said, gesturing toward the seam under which Noah's island apparently still existed. "Before the Order destroys it."

"What's it to you?" Noah asked.

"You really are new to the dark side. I'm the mercenary Hrafn, at your service. That is to say: you pay me. I get you what you want."

"Oh. Really," Noah said. "Why don't you show me how to be like you, a microscopic bug, small enough to slip through those seams?"

"So there *is* something worth retrieving. I knew it," the bug said smugly. It turned toward the uneven seam in the river where Noah's island had been. "How much would you pay for what's now in spookdom?"

"Show me how to become a bug," Noah countered.

"Not a chance," Hrafn said.

Noah would never trust this Hrafn with the location of the senator's datasphere. It might go flying off with the data.

Hrafn launched itself off Noah's arm and said, "If I find what you're looking for, Noah of Domus Aqua, I'm charging you extra to buy it back from me, or it goes to the highest bidder."

"Hey, wait a second," Noah said. The bug ignored him and flew toward the seam. If the insect made it past the Order, it would have little problem locating the datasphere.

In a rush to protect the senator's data, Noah had logged on to Novus Orbis from an Underground service tunnel and hidden the datasphere in plain sight. It hung in a nook full of other glowing spheres that periodically displayed images of his experiences in this gaming world. As a precaution he'd updated everything he'd ever uploaded to Seven Walls. At first glance, an intruder might miss what he'd changed. Any hacker good enough to get past Order security would eventually figure it out.

To observe the bug's flight pattern, Noah kept the spectacles on. When the bug landed on the seam, Noah zoomed in as close as he could. As its head disappeared from view, Noah saw a thin line of smoke replace Hrafn.

So much for the bug, Noah thought. In trouble with the Order, he planned to go for help to the only brother he trusted, Jeremiah.

Chapter 4

Late morning clouds of fog rolled in from the ocean, insulating Rika from all but the closest pedestrians and cyclists. Above her, hidden by the fog ceiling, morning heliotraffic created a pitch-perfect "Om" that reminded her of monks chanting.

It was well past ten and, with two kilometers between her and the Institute of Extended Cognition, she used her organo-pumps to sucker-kiss the corners, curbs and anything else that dared to get in her way. Still, it took five minutes to reach the Institute.

The guards at the front gate eyed her with fleeting interest. They were busy: arguing over whether Noah of Domus Aqua would return from his hiatus in Earth's wildernesses to take the Fly Game Championships as his older brother Daniel and his father had done before him. With or without them, MAM security recognized her and allowed her to pass through the gates. She made a final sprint for the labs and bounded headfirst into a man just slightly taller than she, but seemingly built of granite.

Surprised, she instinctively checked his biostats and found she'd just head-butted Sebastian of Domus Restitio in the chest. His age read forty and he was in perfect health. Of course, with new genetics and a robust medical establishment, few ground-siders faced aging — unless they were poor Heartlanders or chose to age — until after their first century. His welcoming green eyes and wide smile gave Rika the impression she'd just done him a favor by slamming into him. He bent down and lifted her to her feet.

He opened his mouth as if to speak, but another voice issued from behind him, the harsh tone of Rika's team lead, Angela.

"Rika Musashi Grant," Angela enunciated, striding up beside them, "Why were you charging across campus? You could have injured Domus Master Sebastian."

"Nonsense," Sebastian said with a wink. "I'd be surprised if she weighs forty kilograms."

A twig had lodged in Rika's blue hair. It wavered from the top of her head like a bug antennae. Sebastian plucked it out.

"You're wanted in IEC Silver on Third," Angela said, making a face at Rika as though she'd just tasted something bitter. IEC Silver was the management building, nicknamed the "Silver Bullet" after its distinctive shape and metallic sheen.

"I should be more careful," Rika said, bowing low in deference to Sebastian and added, "Pardon me."

"No harm done," Sebastian replied. Turning to Angela, he said, "This must be the exceptional DeeJee I've heard so much about—"

"It is," Angela said with a smile that disappeared as she turned to Rika, "IEC Silver on Third, Conference Room 310. Now."

"How about I swing back to IEC Silver later?" Rika countered. "Yori and I worked on that offsite case this morning and we have a deadline to deliver samples and analysis to Senator Ortega, as soon as possible."

Both Angela and Sebastian visibly tensed at the mention of the senator, but Angela asked, "What part of *now* don't you understand?"

Rika bowed low again to Sebastian who nodded sympathetically and told her, "I look forward to meeting you again."

Curious about what Management needed from her, Rika entered the silver bullet. Inside, its wide arches, elaborate vaulted ceiling, modern moving frescos and enormous windows gave IEC the feel of a magical villa. Everything about it welcomed newcomers. Rika took the narrow backstairs, for employees only, to the third floor and found the windowless conference room labeled 310. It was empty. She sat and waited.

The room responded to her stressed biostats with chamomile and lime blossom aromas. Within a few minutes, Rika not only felt less anxious, but became obsessed with the notion that she needed a treat, specifically a shopping spree. Not a shopper, she wondered whether the subliminal images flitting across the

walls or the undefined chemical scents beneath the chamomile
fueled her desire more.

After a few minutes, Vasil, her advisor and medic, walked
into the room and sat down across from her. His black hair was
slicked back and he wore a crisp, creaseless Institute suit. Rika
never understood how the IEC matched its mentors to mentees.
Rika was as disheveled and rebellious as he was neat and
staunch in following Institute policies.

"It's ridiculous to have us meet on the third floor," Vasil said.

Rika inclined her head in greeting. "I assumed someone here
needed my assistance. It's my first time on this floor since I was
recruited to become a DeeJee."

"The Institute has had a problem on sixth," Vasil explained.
"We've been relocated temporarily to Sales on Third while it's
fixed."

"Do you need my expertise?" Rika asked.

"Oh no, you haven't been assigned," he said. "They'll come
up with a solution, although they had no success using override
commands yesterday."

"So it would violate protocol if I helped out," Rika said and
scratched her head.

"Precisely. You understand. We must follow established protocols. My colleague doesn't comprehend that. That's why we're
in this mess."

"What mess?"

"My colleague revived an ancient therapy which increased
blood flow to the brain by administering neurocognitive sessions
upside down. He then persuaded me to adopt the therapy. IEC
Silver on sixth responded by growing furniture from the ceiling.
I came to work yesterday to find my desk overhead."

"Gravity being what it is, that might be a bit of a work hazard,"
Rika said, coughing to hide a grin. "I wonder if communicating
your maintenance request for a reversal to right-side-up while
at your desks sitting upside down might help? After all that's
where the IEC Silver building has grown to expect you, right?"

"Reverse logic: interesting, it might be effective," Vasil said
tapping his cleft chin, something he did when thinking, "It
couldn't hurt to try upside-down therapy on the building to
return everything on sixth to right side up. I would suggest it, if
it were my problem to fix."

"I should leave you to your work." Rika stood and bowed.
This was her chance to escape.

"Rika," Vasil said, motioning for her to sit. "You're here to answer a few questions."

"I'm not scheduled for an evaluation," Rika blurted out. She silently cursed Yori, guessing he'd reported her strange behavior in front of the Order.

"Relax." Vasil said, "I'm not testing your intelligence. We understand your severe limitations."

Every time she met with Vasil, he gave her new reasons to dislike him.

"We simply want to make sure you're maintaining a healthy sense of self," he continued and then launched into his questions. "First of all, have you experienced any unusual visual or auditory images?"

Rika paused to rationalize seeing the crow attack. On the one hand, the crows hadn't actually swooped down on her. On the other hand, within Captain Lynnfield's memory event into which she'd inadvertently tapped, crows were definitely "usual images." Every garden rooftop housed crows. She could not lie, for fear her biostats would betray her, but it was always convenient to find a loophole.

"No, I haven't seen any *unusual* images," she said.

"Hallucinations? Unicorns?"

"Unicorns?" Rika asked. "No, never unicorns."

Vasil continued with straightforward questions, like when was she born. It wasn't that she still remembered her birthday, but the information came to her when she queried it, just like Vasil's or anyone else's birth date. The mind enhancements permanently linked her cognition with the MAM so that she had direct access to vast data collections. Unlike most DeeJees who focused on some niche data set, her mind enhancements made her into a generalist, the kind of data cataloguer who got access to just about anything — even highly classified data.

"My birthday is on the fourteenth of June, 2127."

"Correct. So how old does that make you now?" Vasil asked.

"I'm twenty-two," she answered with the number that the MAM provided.

"You mean twenty-three, don't you? It's August of 2150."

"Well, of course," Rika stammered and then rushed on, "that would be true if I hadn't expired last June, 2149."

"Excuse me?" asked Vasil, his eyes narrowing.

Rika bit her lip to keep from blurting something even more ridiculous. The information in her head was wrong. For the first time ever, the MAM had fed her false data, and she needed to find out the reason.

"Just kidding," Rika recovered, forcing a giggle that sounded more like choking. "I must stop pretending to be younger than my age. I'm twenty-three."

Vasil studied her for a moment from beneath raised brows, before returning to his questions. He focused on her emotions surrounding key events in her life, specific personal memories they had on file from her childhood and as a teenager. He then moved on to ask about more recent experiences.

Recalling all these memories proved easy, but she no longer felt they were uniquely hers. The associated emotions had definitely fallen away. She could only guess at her emotions during those moments and guess she did, especially when he asked her to recount one of her most embarrassing moments. Qualitative rather than quantitative questions threw her. Profoundly shaken, she responded, intuitively grabbing the closest memories from the MAM archive filed under "humiliating."

"Well," she told him, her heart beating so fast now she sounded breathless. Even the room failed to calm her. "One time I was the guest lecturer at a conference, and someone I'd secretly adored for years showed up. When she winked at me as she sat down in the front row, I lost what I was saying. She kept crossing and re-crossing her long legs in a short skirt."

Vasil's face visibly changed color, turning a flushed blotchy pink. His frown made Rika speak so quickly that every three or four words were strung together as one.

"After the lecture, I rushed down to sit beside her and asked her if she wanted to stay for the next talk or go out for drinks or dinner. I touched her knee. She pulled away and informed me in a confused tone that the next lecturer was her husband. She wasn't there to see me at all."

Given his glare and frown, Rika double-checked her data source too late. In her anxiety, she'd accidently accessed and substituted one of his most embarrassing private moments.

"Do you think this test is a joke?" Vasil asked. "How did you gain access to my memories!?"

"You looked so bored," Rika passed it off. She'd relied on the MAM to supply her with data while she forced herself not to panic about possibly failing this test. Rika replayed in her mind what she'd just said and flinched. She had access to a lot of information she shouldn't, including his private memory events. Vasil's reason for privately saving that embarrassing event escaped Rika, except that she noticed he'd saved many earlier memory events with the same woman when they were both much younger.

"Simply answer my questions," Vasil ordered.

She avoided telling him a truth that had become apparent to her: other individual's M. E.s carried the same level of brilliance and detail as her own memories, which she covertly stored in an illegal site in Novus Orbis called Jaa City. And then, he had complicated her usual pathways to data by asking her to reach them via emotional linkages that, for Rika, no longer existed. When the Institute enhanced her cognitive functions, they had simultaneously taken from her almost all personal memories of who she had been before the procedures, except those she'd deliberately recorded by the MAM as memory events.

Now, asked to provide memories, her unique brain accessed the MAM and picked up the strongest pathway that emerged. With Vasil sitting across from her, the strongest thread was his set of memory events.

His thick dark brows locked into a "v" as she answered. Flailing about mentally, she took back some things she'd said or reframed how she might have felt, all in an effort to weave a coherent emotional tableau of her life, to convey to him a stable sense of self. In short, she made a mess of her responses.

After several more of her agonized ramblings, Vasil interrupted her, "There's no point in continuing."

"I was just getting started," Rika muttered.

"Hmm," her advisor said. "Either you're humor escapes me or—"

"Or what?" asked Rika. Her breakfast rose toward the back of her throat and her stomach tightened.

"Do you want me to be frank?"

"Frank is good."

"Your mind appears to be rejecting the enhancements. You're aware of possible physiological incompatibilities. Isn't that right?"

"I suppose so," Rika admitted. "What happens if I keep failing these tests?"

"You know what'll happen. You have been permitted access to every case of failure at the Institute."

"Tell me," Rika said and placed both hands on the table between them. "You'll make an exception in my case."

"We don't make exceptions. Failing these tests isn't the end of the world. You will undergo our newest and most promising cognitive therapies. You'll have time off to spend here on campus under my care and expert supervision. I'll personally make sure you're fully stabilized before you have to return to your daily stresses."

"After I'm 'stabilized,' I'd return to DeeJeeing."

"No, you could never return to DeeJeeing. On the bright side, as long as you stabilize, the Institute will find you a place in Collections or Reception or even as a Recruit, assuming you keep your positive attitude."

"I've gone into serious debt to get these. If my neural-knits fail, is there any chance IEC would absolve me of my debt?"

"Is there a case in which the Institute has absolved any employee's debts in the past?" Vasil countered.

Rika thought for a moment. "No. Never. The thing is that as a DeeJee, I'll pay off all my debts in three years. I can't do that if I'm not a DeeJee."

"It's true," said Vasil. "DeeJees receive some of the highest salaries here. You make almost as much as I do."

"I'm not qualified for much else."

"True," he agreed. "Once you're well, the Institute will find a job for you."

"Understood, but after I fulfill my three-year obligation to IEC, I want to be a free agent."

"You've forgotten what it is to be you, but you still remember the desire to work for yourself … intriguing." He closed his eyes for a moment, and she knew he was making a special note of that in Novus Orbis.

"I remember everything," she corrected him. *It's myself I've secreted away in Novus Orbis. If I were naïve enough to access Jaa City in front of you, I'd pass all your idiotic tests. Knowing your type, you'd trace where I've hidden myself and take that away from me, too. Jaa certainly violates your protocols.* "I want to DeeJee."

"Rules are rules. If you fail the psych tests, you can't remain a DeeJee."

"I've got to," Rika insisted. She knew she was in trouble, but hoped that Senator Ortega's interest in her would lead to strings being pulled in Rika's favor so that she could bypass the IEC's policies and wonks like Vasil who enforced them. If she failed as a DeeJee after only one year of earning a high salary, she would drop back into the ranks of low-level employees. It would take umpteen years before her debts were paid off.

Vasil did not answer or even nod, but maintained a *face up to the facts kid* expression on his face.

"I'm going to transfer you from your division into my care so that you can begin therapy. You'll have your own room on campus with a view of the ocean and no stress, no work and nothing to make you worry. Luckily, we've caught this early. If we let this go, you could become permanently impaired. Think of this as a free vacation."

"Hang on, I have project deliverables. Besides, you can't make a decision based on today's tests alone."

"I've seen these symptoms before. It would be negligent to let you go untreated."

"From my perspective, this is bleak," she said. She swallowed hard to keep the bile from rising into her mouth. In her lap, her hands were damp and trembling.

Shifting her concentration to the conference room, the DeeJee shut her eyes and summoned the living components of the IEC building. She accessed the conference room sensors. He had to make an exception for her, something he'd never done. Rika called up Conference Room 310 interfaces and by-passed authorization protocols the way she might flip through her own user preferences. No security warnings went off and the system didn't shut down from the invasion. She issued her commands and let the room suss out and deliver to his specific proclivities.

The color of the walls altered slightly, and then the wall images changed. She smelled mint and perhaps, human female pheromones.

Is that the scent of goat? Her nose wrinkled at the unpleasant scents while Vasil breathed in deeply. They sat there across from each other for what felt to her like an eternity. He smiled.

"You've failed at everything in your life, haven't you?" he asked sympathetically. She sat back.

"No, I'm just different," Rika said. Although potentially satisfying, punching him in the face would be a very bad idea. "Since my enhancements, I've outperformed all the other DeeJees. I correct MAM imbalances no one else can repair, stuff that even baffles those genetically-enhanced, uber-IQ'd scientists — whom the Institute advertises as their big thinkers."

"You were born slow. And now, even the mind enhancements can't save you," he said, still smiling, but his eyes were unfocused as though he'd incorporated her into a daydream.

"What's your point?" Rika asked.

"Tell you what. For the first time, I'm going to ignore protocol. You'll be my pet project," Vasil offered. "I'll keep my eye on you until your next scheduled exams. After you fail those, you and I will begin working together in earnest."

"I'm grateful," Rika said.

"We do risk doing damage by not getting you into treatment right away."

"I'll take the risk," she said.

"You'll thank me once you're better and can work in Collections or Reception. You might even make a good Recruiter," Vasil droned on in his new dreamy way. "You're pretty enough as long as you change your hair."

"Why? It's natural," Rika said, raising her hand to touch her cotton-candy blue hair.

"Precisely, genetically modified blue hair — it's disturbingly natural. No one wants to be reminded of our recent Dark Age before proper regulations, when parents decided willy-nilly on genetic enhancements for their children as though they were buying furniture or new clothes," Vasil said, waving his hand about to emphasize the willy-nilly nature of Rika's existence.

"What does my hair have to do with me becoming a Recruiter?" Rika insisted. She couldn't help herself, with so much frustration bubbling toward the surface. Besides, distracting him from protocol violations and her test results was critical.

"A successful Recruiter can't bring in new DeeJee recruits if she makes people feel uncomfortable from the get-go. That's all. Having nice legs never hurts though, and you do try to be funny."

"I see," Rika said, deciding that before she ever became a Recruiter, she'd swim out into the ocean and keep swimming until her arms were too tired to turn back.

During this session with Vasil, "Recruiter" had taken on a whole new meaning. These shills conned debt-laden graduates like herself into DeeJee-dom. If their mind enhancements failed, they'd be stuck in the same horrible situation that she faced.

While Vasil went into specifics and ticked off how Rika's failure of each test demonstrated that she had an insufficient sense of "id" in the DeeJee mind she shared with the MAM, Rika envisioned herself as the anti-Recruiter who would save hundreds of Undergrounders like her from the Institute netherworld. She imagined Vasil attached to the ceiling, hanging upside down for a very, very long time.

"Rika?" Vasil brought her abruptly out of her fantasy. He'd been detailing all the Novus Orbis formalities he'd have to go through to avoid submitting her failed test to the system. "Rika?"

"I'm so grateful to you for giving me more time," Rika repeated. "So grateful."

"I hope this isn't a mistake," Vasil said. "You're dismissed."

After a polite bow called for by protocol, Rika escaped outside. A warm breeze and the early afternoon sunshine had burned away the fog. She closed her eyes and faced the sun. It warmed her.

Before the enhancements, Rika could strum a decent rendition of any song she heard on guitar and had a natural knack for math. Back then, she processed information too slowly, didn't know the half of what she needed to, and got turned down for every job. Now she had ample funds and was paying down her debt, but had a tin ear — and lately, growing confusion over other people's memory events invading her own memories.

Yori's voice intruded on her thoughts. His face popped up on her MAM interface. His shadow of a new beard and the dark rings under his eyes made him look terrible.

"Rika, if management is done wasting your time, I need you at the lab," Yori said. "You're not going to believe this."

CHAPTER 5

On Monday afternoon a day after the attack, the indie news-hound Lydia DeLydia of the media stream program, *Goodbye Los Angeles Hello*, summed it up succinctly for Noah, "Half the world will suspect you're guilty and the other half won't care. Worse, a good number will want you dead."

"Why?" Noah asked, pausing briefly, but ready to brush past her. Lydia fed the media streams with celebrity scoops. The woman had a knack for locating people when they least wanted to be found. Noah had just gotten out of a heliotaxi in Pasadena to meet his brother Jeremiah at the Sanctuary entrance when she tapped him on the shoulder. She'd startled him.

"Don't play dumb with me. In the next hour, Our World Emissary Falkenrath will announce that Senator Ortega has been assassinated and that the two chief suspects are Bartholomew Soba and you. From that moment on, both of you become walking dead men."

"Ortega assassinated?" Noah repeated what she'd said and stared past her. His eyes focused inward while his feet cemented to the ground where he stood. In his mind's eye, he re-enacted the attack.

I left the senator there defenseless, and she died? The Ghost must be this Bartholomew Soba.

She was waiting for a response.

"I'm no assassin," he said.

"Soba is. I understand he's a violent, political zealot who has been tracking the senator for some time."

This changes everything, Noah thought. After failing to access the datasphere in Novus Orbis, he had asked his brother Jeremiah, a novice training to be a Magi monk, for help in a last attempt to fulfill his promise to Ortega and deliver the datasphere. Now it looked as if his options were quickly narrowing to one: to turn himself in to the Order.

His leftover crawlies gave everything around him an edge. With the constant streams of Magi, Buddhists monks, Catholic priests and the devout flowing in and out of the city's Sanctuary Center for Ecumenical Convergence, he ought to have felt at least some of the harmony and peace that surrounded him. Instead, it was all he could do not to swear at the reporter.

"If I'm walking dead, it's thanks to you and your colleagues," he said. "You'll convict me on hearsay." He glanced around them to see if Order regulars were standing by to take him in. "How did you find me?"

"Everyone always wants to know that," Lydia said. She smiled a white, big-toothed smile, which reminded him of a reptilian predator. "You should grant me an exclusive. Clear yourself publicly. Increase the signal-to-noise ratio. Otherwise, you're finished."

"Figuratively and literally, yes, I realize that," Noah said with a nod. "Instead of wasting airtime on me, you should ask the Order why there was no security in the tower that night. Or how it's possible the best medics in the world couldn't save her?"

"You were a witness, you can't deny that."

"I don't deny being a witness," Noah said.

"Senator Mari Ortega had a fatal chest wound. No medic could have saved her."

"A chest wound?" Noah felt his whole body go cold.

"How could you miss that?"

"She was wounded when I left her," Noah said and stumbled over his own words. "But not in the chest. In your fact-finding, did you discover that the Order picked me up, beat me and let me go Sunday night without ever asking me about what I witnessed? You get answers to my questions, and I promise I'll give you the exclusive interview."

"If I asked those questions, I'd be responsible for instigating Heartlander riots over your bogus conspiracy theory," Lydia said. "The Council and the Order hope to avoid violence by giving the Heartlanders the chance to search and destroy the assassin hiding in their Underground. Once that's done, the Heartlanders will come for you. They'll be out for blood."

An enormous group of argumentative Magi novices, debating the complexities of a living prophet and the finer points of the crane fighting stance, kept Noah from giving Lydia a testy response. The crowd swept the fly gamer with them through the front doors of the Sanctuary leaving Lydia standing there shaking her head. He'd given her a scoop, but she'd have to pay a heavy price for it.

Goodbye Los Angeles Hello would have to splice up the impromptu interview for airtime and risk having Noah republish the uncut version in self-defense, or she'd have to bury the story, at least for now. Otherwise, Lydia risked becoming a victim of the old "kill the messenger" syndrome. *A celebrity chaser risking her personal safety*, thought Noah. *That's unlikely.*

Inside the great hall, the wave of young Magi monks fanned out in different directions. The huge room was circular and grand, each of Earth's religions represented under its high, domed roof. In the hall, world religions were each given equal symbolic representation in a circle around the center flame, but space in the rest of the building was not equally apportioned. As the newest recognized religion, only a century old, the Magi were relegated to a warren of rooms just above the catacombs.

A Magi novice with a hood over his face and no belt, demonstrating that he still lived the life of a novitiate, took Noah by the elbow and discretely led him behind the giant columns toward a metal door inlaid with the golden ratio and the profile of the Prophet Thesni, the Magi faith's only living prophet. For Noah to go any further than the Sanctuary columns in the Great Hall required a religious guide. The fly gamer easily guessed who had him tightly by the arm. He peeked under the monk's hood and was greeted by his younger brother Jeremiah's mischievous grin.

"I never seem to escape my family," Jeremiah said. "You owe me one. I just saved you from the crocodile."

"Next you'll take credit for saving my soul."

"Only you can do that," Jeremiah said with such intensity that Noah pretended not to have heard him. "I have someone I want you to meet."

CHAPTER 6

Bolsa Lab's living offices terminated at the first airtight door to Bolsa, the Institute's only BioSafety Level 4 (BSL-4) laboratory, a building within a building specifically designed to contain unidentified biohazards. MAM security scanned and authorized Rika's access.

She stepped through the narrow airlock and entered a changing room where Angela and one of Yori's colleagues, Huifeng, were changing into street clothes. Huifeng winked at Rika as she slipped passed her out the door.

Angela's pleasant smile vanished as she turned on Rika. "I didn't expect you to burn the day in therapy. It always takes you twice as long to do everything!"

Rika bowed from the waist, but kept her eyes locked on Angela. "I will never go see Vasil again, as you prefer."

"That's not what I prefer," her boss said as she pushed past Rika, adding as she left, "And you know it!"

Rika dumped her clothes into a locker and slammed it shut. She opened the door again and slammed it shut again, and again. The sound of the slamming door echoed in the empty room.

Yori stood in the Cell, an elevated platform in the center of the lab, isolated from the room by thick transparent walls and airlock. He looked more like an acrobat than anything else, as he deftly maneuvered the Cell's robotic arms amongst the sensitive test beds.

Yori gestured for Rika to join him, authorized her entry, and waited as she was dry showered and scanned to ensure she was free of any contaminants.

"Tell me what you've discovered," she said.

Beneath the hazmat anzugs, neither could read the other's facial expressions. "This fungus is not from around here," said Yori.

"It's some kind of rare tropical variety?" Rika guessed.

"No, I've never seen anything quite like it." He refocused the microscope and projected a 3-D image of the fungus to the workspace between them.

"Our sample appears to have a symbiotic relationship with these bacteria," Yori said, pointing to the image.

Rika illuminated several images in the workspace between them. "See the left image; that's the oily, globular fungus from our samples. The right image has matted, scaly fungus."

Yori nodded.

"Look at these in cross section," Rika said and switched images.

Yori stared at one image and then the other.

Rika magnified the image until both clearly showed that there were root-like extensions, which led to a series of cups with tiny sack-like structures inside them.

"Here is a much higher magnification of their fruiting bodies," Rika said and watched Yori study the similarities. "Notice the spores from both."

They had nearly identical stacked cubes lined in rows inside linked rings. Then, she showed him the fungus DNA. Yori nodded again. She'd made a match.

"Our fungus is found in one place in the solar system — the Tharsis Montes caves on Mars," Rika said.

"My intuition is that there's also a gardener. Perhaps, it's one of our native isopods," Yori said.

"How disgusting. I can't think of those creepy crawlers as gardeners," said Rika. It came out harsh and she bit her lip. She had to keep her resentment under control.

"They're adorable," Yori said. "You'd have to be pea-brained not to see that."

"Pea-brained?" Rika said and blinked.

Yori laughed. The laugh triggered something deep inside him. Bending forward against the cabinet, he gasped for air. His chest heaved. Beneath the anzug that blurred his features, Yori made small choking noises.

"Yori!" Rika said, reaching out to help him.

"I'm ... fine. It's just my chest ... tight," Yori said.

He labored to breath normally. "Some isopod is cultivating this symbiotic bacterial-fungi." His voice sounded raspy.

"Yori," Rika said. "Your hazmat anzug was compromised during the 'elevator' mission."

"Don't be alarmist. I may have torn it while I was down in that damnable elevator shaft, but anzugs self-repair. This is simply an allergic reaction." Yori turned back to the cabinet. "I'm fine as long as you don't make me laugh."

"I'm surprised Angela or Huifeng didn't insist that you see a medic," Rika said.

"I've been working alone in this Cell," Yori admitted. "They were both in the outer lab checking on another priority project. Apparently, we get to moonlight on the senator's project for a couple days, but after that we're supposed to 'meet and exceed' our scheduled deadlines."

"Well then, it's up to me to get you to a medic. Either voluntarily come with me to get your chest examined or I'll call Emergency."

"Forget it. The senator needs our results. Pronto. I've barely finished the preliminary DNA studies and comparisons of fatty acid and cell wall composition. It'll take more time to assess the fungus on morphological criteria..."

"If there's nothing wrong, the medic will send you back," Rika said. "Come on. If you leave with me now, we can call it even."

"Call what even?" Yori asked.

"You reported my behavior on the rooftop to Angela and Vasil, didn't you?"

"That's what you think?" Yori said. He laughed again, which caused him to double over coughing. It took a couple of minutes before he managed to stand up straight. "Maybe ... I should have my chest examined."

Rika reached out to steady him.

"Just so you know, I never told anyone about anything. That Order captain reported your behavior."

"Oh," she said. *Yori had kept his mouth shut.*

Without another word, Yori closed down the cabinet interfaces and moved toward the dry shower airlock. Rika closed her eyes and checked if the MAM subsystem had a record of the Order having treated any evacuees from the building where they'd taken the samples.

Careful not to directly access confidential information, Rika let the MAM initiate an internal query. As usual, the MAM returned precise and voluminous data. Twelve evacuees — their names and faces momentarily flooding her mind — had been treated with a fungicide cocktail of ingredients so long and complex that Rika realized the Order must have been involved. No Institute medic would have known where to begin.

Suddenly the Cell lit up and the air was filled with an ear-piercing alarm that indicated a breach. Yori panicked and slammed himself against the outer door. It held firm as the inner door opened and Yori stumbled back into the Cell.

Against protocol, he deactivated his anzug hood and vomited green-black clumps and blood all over the floor between them. Rika stepped around the mess and wrapped her arm midway around his back to steady him.

That's when Angela contacted Rika.

<*I leave for fifteen minutes, and Bolsa goes into lockdown. Yori doesn't answer. What's going on?*>

<*Yori's contaminated. He needs the Order's fungicide therapy.*> Without answering, Angela disconnected.

Yori and Rika watched the floor activate. It surrounded and diminished the slimy globules until they completely disappeared.

"Yori, do you want to sit down?"

"My head is spinning. Sorry I panicked," Yori said.

"I understand. Order medics will be here soon." Rika had both arms wrapped tight around him to keep him upright.

He smiled slightly, then collapsed, pulling Rika down to the floor with him.

Angela and two Order medics rushed into the Cell. All three wore hazmat anzugs.

"Yori?" Angela said.

"Yori's passed out," Rika replied, disentangling herself from his motionless body.

The shorter of the two medics looked directly at Rika and said, "Do you have a headache?"

"No," she replied.

"Did you at any time come in direct contact with the fungi?"

"No." Rika glared at him.

"Did Yori complain of a headache?"

"No, he coughed and had trouble breathing." said Rika.

Angela stepped around the medic. "Look, I've got IEC's best scientist suffering here. He needs medical attention. What's your plan?"

The two medics looked at each other. The taller one addressed Angela. "It's difficult to make a judgment call about how the fungi spread. Besides, we're not allowed to discuss it unless you have top-level clearance."

"Look, Yori has come in direct contact with Rika and me and a bunch of other people without any protective gear. None of us show any signs of infection."

Rika spoke up, "Twelve evacuees are receiving fungicide therapy."

"That's classified information," the medic said. "How did you—?"

"Based on your *dozen* patients then," Angela interrupted, her voice remaining low and even, "the Order must be fairly certain that close personal contact with the fungi or with an infected human is necessary for the fungi to spread. Right?"

The medic hesitated for a moment and then grudgingly nodded. "Given his symptoms and lack of a headache, we should be safe to move him to the hospital."

Taking his cue from the senior medic, the shorter medic undid his briefcase and let it unfold into a stretcher. They moved Yori onto it and activated a bio-containment cocoon.

As they maneuvered him into the airlock, Angela patted Rika on the back and then left the lab.

Her boss hadn't criticized her or demanded that she immediately move to another project. Rika used the time to process Yori's test results and prepare a report for the senator.

Two hours later, Rika initiated contact with Yori by exploiting a Novus Orbis nurse-in-training interface. Periodically, the nurse Smart Intelligence asserted itself with idiotic wellness questions that annoyed both of them. Otherwise, they talked in private.

<I can't believe you got through to me. The medics isolated each of us. I feel like I'm locked in a vault.>

<You sound less hoarse.>

<I'm already breathing easier.>

<Good.>

<Have you taken our results to the senator?>

<Not yet, I wanted to talk to you first.>

<Ack! You have to hurry.>

<Hear me out. Our results may alarm her. The sample appears to be nearly identical to the fungus that was once used to make blackbase: M. somnis. Remember how the fungi reacted strongly to the Pedralbes stained-glass chips? Those chips have fungal growth inhibitors designed to cut blackbase. That reaction can't be a coincidence.>

<Blackbase is illegal. It would be detected and destroyed by the MAM as soon as it reached Earth.>

<Right, it isn't a 100 percent DNA match, but you saw how similar they were to each other back at the lab.>

<Even if the sample's DNA is much closer to the Tharsis Montes M. somnis in the Mars caves than to any Earth fungus,> Yori coughed so long that Rika worried she'd contacted him too soon. Finally, he managed to continue. *<Our sample clearly thrives in another form and a different ecosystem. To grow on Earth would have required someone to intentionally modify this fungus — someone with unusual scientific knowhow and access to high-end technologies.>*

<This is why I had to talk to you before going to the senator.>

<She's going to hate it. The implications are huge,> Yori said. Rika could hear the same apprehension she felt creep into his raspy voice. *<Still ... include everything in the report, even our speculations.>*

<The most logical guess is that someone illegally modified and shipped the fungus, and then smuggled it past the Office of Planetary Protection. That's a great way to get multiple life sentences in some offworld work camp. Why would anyone risk it?>

<Good question. The senator will ask you to find out and also how this modified fungus ended up in a residential building—> Another fit of coughing overtook Yori. Rika waited quietly until he could speak again. *<MAM systems should have automatically reacted to this threat or at least issued an alert. Since that didn't happen, we can only assume this fungus might show up someplace else…. Rika?>*

At the sound of the lab door sliding open in Vetus Orbis, Rika broke off communications. Huifeng entered the lab and hurried over to Rika.

"I heard about Yori," she said. "I hope he's going to be okay."

"Me, too," said Rika.

"Angela has an Order captain in tow and is headed here. Apparently the captain has been making a fuss about some samples you and Yori were supposed to hand over. She says you're withholding evidence."

"Thanks," Rika said. "Would you stall Angela so I can slip out?"

"Sure."

Against protocol, Rika accessed Novus Orbis and made a copy of the test results. After a moment's hesitation, she also included the senator's decryption key and then forwarded it all to Jaa City, her secret repository, so she could surreptitiously access it beyond Institute or Order firewalls.

Rika and Huifeng left the lab, the airlock hissing closed behind them, and entered the changing room. Rika dressed in a bathroom stall while Huifeng greeted Angela, the Order captain and two regulars.

"I hate to worry you, Angela," Huifeng said. "But before the captain meets with Rika, I wanted you to be aware that Rika mentioned to me in private that she'd been feeling ill since Yori collapsed. It's probably unrelated, but she could have been exposed. Maybe the captain would like to examine her?"

The captain threw up her arms. "I'm no medic!"

Rika slipped unnoticed behind the lockers and bolted through the Bolsa complex, dodging any IEC personnel who got in the way. She was determined to help Yori keep his promise to Ortega.

When Rika arrived at the Council Tower in downtown Los Angeles and saw the crowd surrounding the grand entrance, she sighed. Everything was turning out to be more difficult than she expected. She wove her way to the front of the crowd, despite protestations and a few aggressive elbows. Seeing no way to sneak in, she decided to address one of the guards stationed at the front to whom she would insist that she had a personal meeting with Senator Ortega. A commotion stopped her. Rika turned in time to see a guard — twice Rika's size — knock a kid flat on the ground.

The youngster screamed, "Goro promised if I went and got these that he'd let me back in!"

Hearing the high-pitched voice, Rika decided that the indignant young one must be a girl. The kid had one arm full of pink and white peonies. A few had fallen and lay on the ground as the girl bounded to her feet. Rika made her way closer to the confrontation.

The slight girl, dressed in roof gardener browns, attempted to mount the steps again. The same guard grabbed her by the collar and shook her until she dropped the bouquet. He pushed her off the steps, and the crowd began to murmur.

"That's some way to treat a kid," one man grumbled.

Someone else threw a rock, and it glanced off a guard standing beside the bully. Another guard came hurrying out of the front entrance.

"Goro, there you are," the girl said and glared up at him.

"Cricket, are these them?" Goro asked. He scooped up the damaged flowers and added, "I'll put them by her side, but you need to go."

Cricket wiped her eyes with the back of her fist and started toward the door again. Rika couldn't stand it any longer. She ran forward, reached out and grabbed the girl by the back of her gardener's uniform.

"It's not worth it," Rika whispered in her ear. The DeeJee kept an iron grip on Cricket's uniform. "They won't let you in."

One of the regulars spoke to them, barely moving his lips and without once glancing their way. "Look, an announcement is about to be made by Our World Emissary Falkenrath. No one can enter or exit the tower at this time. Step away from the entrance."

"Let's leave," Rika said, not letting go of the girl's tunic until she got a nod of agreement. The girl glared at the guard who'd destroyed her bouquet, but let Rika lead her away from the entrance and into the crowd.

"Are you with the Institute?" she asked Rika when they could no longer see the guards or the entrance because of all the people.

"Yes, can't you tell by this hideous gray IEC uniform?" Rika asked and smiled. "If you don't believe me, check my biostats."

"Peonies were her favorite," Cricket said. She sniffed. "She always had a fresh bouquet in her office. Goro promised to let me back in if I went to get her some. How else could I honor her passing?"

They made their way to the edge of the crowd and then down a less busy side street. Rika studied the person walking beside her and decided Cricket was much older than she looked at first glance — not a girl, but a woman — rail thin, flat-chested and slightly taller than Rika. The woman's black hair jutted out at different angles as though she'd chopped it off herself without consulting a mirror. Cricket had no biostats, public or private. Instead, an old interface tag usually assigned to pets wavered above her head when Rika made a query. The card read simply: *Cricket, Roof Gardener, Council Tower.*

Rika scrolled through a long list of additional rooftop garden addresses Cricket had been approved to tend. To Rika's surprise, her own residence was on the list.

With her newfound companion now in the lead, they headed down an empty, dead-end alleyway with several side entrances. Stopping abruptly at one of these nondescript doorways, Cricket counted out several steps heel-to-toe and then abruptly turned left and motioned for Rika to stand close to her. People passed by the alleyway at a steady rate, but no one ventured down it.

"This is an Order blind zone," Cricket said. "Order regulars and politicians come here to talk. In this spot, no one can eavesdrop or see us via the MAM."

"Right," Rika said. She studied Cricket. "The peonies were meant for someone very important to you, weren't they?"

"Are you working with Noah of Domus Aqua?" Cricket countered.

"No," Rika said. Of course, she'd heard of Noah the famous fly gamer, but she knew he'd become a bit of a recluse over the past year, and she'd never actually seen him. Even in Novus Orbis, the man never used avatars that had his own likeness. "Why?"

Cricket glanced over her shoulder and surveyed the windows above them.

"Allow me to introduce myself," Rika said. She bowed. "I'm Rika."

"My nickname is Cricket, but you knew that from reading my dog tag," Cricket said and then looked her up and down as though she already knew Rika. "You're the DeeJee Mari hired?"

"You mean Senator Mari Ortega? That's right. I'm here to see her today."

"That's impossible," Cricket said.

"Why?" Rika asked, thinking that this Cricket was a character. Like Rika, the roof gardener had lost her ashen skin tone from years spent above ground, but she still had the signature wariness of a Heartlander. Oddly, Cricket couldn't read Rika's biostats. By the look of it, Cricket never entered Novus Orbis. "Is the senator too busy to see anyone?"

Cricket stepped backwards out of arms length from Rika.

"How did you know I'm a DeeJee without accessing the MAM and reading my biostats?" Rika asked. "Or that Senator Ortega hired me?"

Cricket shrugged.

"Sorry, I shouldn't ask so many questions. I need to give something to the senator."

"The datasphere?" Cricket asked. She stared at Rika.

"What datasphere? No, I don't have a datasphere. Why?"

"It's been missing since her murder."

The news hit Rika like a physical blow. The buildings, the pavement and Cricket listed one way and then the other.

"Murder?" she said, and her knees folded.

The next moment, Cricket caught Rika and gently lowered her to the pavement. The DeeJee was astonished by the thin woman's strength.

Cricket gave her the once-over, said, "You'll be okay," and took off toward the high wall at the end of the alleyway.

"Wait!" Rika said, but Cricket ignored her. The gardener upended a manhole cover and replaced it over her head as she climbed down into the Underground.

Once Cricket was no longer in sight, Rika stood, walked out of the MAM-free zone and then closed her eyes to contact Yori. She could no longer find the nurse-in-training interface. When she searched for Yori, he showed up nowhere. Her most urgent communiqués bounced back. Rika hightailed it back to IEC.

After maximizing her organo-pumps in a dash from the URT station to the Institute, Rika arrived breathless and exhausted. She burst into the Bolsa outer lab to catch up with Huifeng and found Captain Lynnfield waiting for her as well. At least, her Order regulars were absent.

"What have you done with Yori?" Rika asked the captain.

"You tell me," the captain said. "When it comes to getting around security features, you're quite resourceful."

"I can't connect with him," Rika admitted.

"He's on a fungicide cocktail that makes him weak and most likely sleepy. Angela has asked me to allow Yori to stay on the IEC campus and restrict his activities to this lab, once his lungs are clear. I hesitate to approve that when Huifeng says you feel sick. We need to take precautions. It's spreading."

"I did feel sick, but I'm fine now," said Rika. Huifeng bowed to them both and left in a hurry. Rika bowed in return and watched her leave. Silently, Rika thanked Huifeng.

Lynnfield ignored the scientist's departure and concentrated on Rika. "Senator Mari Ortega has been assassinated. It's a sad day for the Order. For thirty years, we've successfully stopped every political assassination attempt." If any of what the captain said caused her personal sadness or regret, Rika couldn't detect it in the woman's voice. If anything, the officer's tone had a cheerful lilt to it.

For her part, Rika was well aware of her own pettiness and self-interest: her first response to hearing of the senator's murder was regret that she no longer had a patron to offset Vasil's power over *her* future.

Digging her nails into the palm of her hand to remain focused, Rika said, "Will you allow Yori to return here?"

"That's up to you," the captain said. She smiled, but the smile never reached her eyes, which remained as cold as stones. "I need you to answer a few questions — like why you two kept samples for your own testing when I ordered you to hand them over."

For a moment, Rika hesitated. Although with the senator gone, she couldn't think of a good reason to hide anything from the captain. Besides, she didn't need another person of authority working against her. Rika told the officer about the senator's request for an independent investigation of the building and that the IEC report be delivered directly to her without sharing the results with anyone else. "We wanted to come through for her as we had in the past. How could we provide an independent analysis if we'd given you all our samples?"

"You had no other motivations for helping the senator?"

Rika bit her lip and remained silent.

"Senator Ortega believed that Heartlanders should have the opportunity to move groundside. You're a Heartlander, how do you feel about that?"

"I live groundside. People should have the right to live wherever they want to live," Rika said. She shrugged. "Honestly, I don't care much for politics."

"The man accused of Ortega's murder is a Heartland extremist who believes the senator betrayed her people and that no Heartlanders should be relocated groundside. Between you and me, we think Noah of Domus Aqua may have helped the assassin gain access to her office. He did an internship with the senator. He had authorization to enter the building, and we know he was present during the assassination."

"Why are you sharing this with me?" Rika asked.

"I want to gauge your reaction," the captain said. "Are you in contact with Noah?"

"Never. I've never met the man," Rika said.

"Tell me everything you know about what the senator was investigating," ordered Lynnfield.

"I don't know anything about it, and incidentally, neither does Yori," Rika said. She did nothing to hide the exasperation in her voice. "Senator Ortega told Yori she planned to make public some important investigation, but she wouldn't even tell us her suspicions because she didn't want to falsely affect our findings."

"Does the name Sakoda mean anything to you?"

Rika shook her head. "Nothing."

"Ortega didn't give you any data, any clues, nothing?" the captain bent forward her face so close to Rika's that their noses nearly touched. Her breath smelled like rotten eggs. Rika sat back.

"The senator gave us nothing!" Rika exclaimed, and then she remembered the decryption key, but she kept quiet about that. Now was not the time to start changing her story. Besides, she had no idea what the senator had planned in sending the key to Yori.

"The two of you are so very altruistic," the captain said.

"Yori is," Rika replied. Not only was he like a big brother to her, he also insisted on honesty and doing the right thing. "But I'm not. I helped the senator for my own reasons."

The captain raised an eyebrow and strummed her fingers across her crossed arm. "We're finally getting somewhere."

"I'm not saying anything more."

"Like I said, whether Yori returns here depends upon you."

"But he's done nothing wrong!"

The captain waited expectantly. After a long pause, Rika sighed and said, "I hoped if we provided important findings, the senator might use her influence to help me bypass all the DeeJee exams so that I'd become a full-fledged DeeJee without jumping through all the usual hoops. To be fair, Ortega never actually promised me anything."

"I'll tell you what," the captain said. "I'll bring Yori back here to work on this project and make you that promise of DeeJee-dom if you succeed on our project. The fungus has shown up in three more buildings in downtown L.A. We must discover how and why this stuff is spreading. Even though we have a fairly effective fungicide to kill it once it's found, it's disrupting the city with so many evacuations."

"Thank you," Rika said, and for the first time in the conversation, she felt her tensed shoulders relax.

"Don't thank me. I won't help you unless you help us." The captain pointed to the corner of the lab, which was stacked floor to ceiling with boxes behind protective, controlled-environment glass. "You're working for the Order now. We've provided a set of samples for IEC to analyze."

"You got all those from the sick buildings?" Rika said. Her eyes widened. "I guess I'd better get to work."

Later, on her own time, Rika planned to do some detective work. The timing of the senator's murder, the captain's odd line of questioning and suspiciously generous offer of help, the famous fly gamer Noah of Domus Aqua's involvement in the assassination and a mysterious datasphere on everyone's mind — all these pieces had to interconnect somehow. In the end, the DeeJee would be much more likely to convince the sly-acting captain to keep her promise once Rika had put together the entire puzzle. This was just the sort of work a data gatherer was meant to do.

CHAPTER 7

Through cobwebs, along dusty tunnels, down rough-hewn stairs cut into the rock, all dimly lit, Jeremiah led Noah far below the Sanctuary to a narrow door cast in shadow.

Noah's brother drew back his cowl and looked up at him, "The man you're about to meet is a legend in the Open MAM Movement. Ochbo has been with the OMM since the beginning. He provides technical support to the Sanctuary. Since I entered my novitiate, he has also become a close friend."

Noah felt a twinge of jealousy over his brother's friendship. The two brothers had been close when they were growing up, but the fly gamer hadn't seen Jeremiah in a long time. He asked, "You're sure Ochbo can help me?"

"If anyone can help you, it's him. Honestly though, I don't know if he'll agree to do anything. He's funny sometimes and insisted he see you on your own without me. My best advice is to be honest with him."

"Okay," Noah said. He squeezed Jeremiah's shoulder and added, "I appreciate this."

"Family," Jeremiah said and shook his head. "All this time, I worried I'd end up risking monkhood to help Daniel out of a mess. Instead, it's you."

"He's why I returned to L.A. in the first place," Noah admitted. "I thought I was going to have to explain away Daniel's iffy business dealings to Senator Ortega."

"How did that work out?" Jeremiah asked. Noah heard the tightness in his brother's voice.

"Not how I planned," Noah said. His voice broke, thinking of the senator.

"When you're done here, we'll get something to eat," Jeremiah said, pulling the cowl back over his head. "We'll talk."

Noah watched his brother in his chameleon Magi robes quickly blend with the dim walls, disappearing from sight. He realized how much he missed Jeremiah. His brother's becoming a monk had wedged the ideology of a religion between them, a wall bigger than Noah knew how to scale. Daily urban life proved less tolerable without his brother in it. Jeremiah's religious conversion had been the final push for Noah to escape into Earth's wildernesses.

With a sigh, the youngest son of Domus Aqua turned to formally announce himself and found the narrow door already ajar. Inside, a wooden step led up into the room and demarcated where he must leave his shoes. He put on a pair of slippers that were a little tight for his big feet. Once Noah stepped up, he found himself in a large room filled with warm light emitting from the walls and ceiling. An old man sat cross-legged on the floor in a corner that was not visible from the entrance. Long, scraggily gray hair hung over his face. The burly, disheveled man was dressed in baggy, frayed clothes.

After bowing deeply, Noah approached him. The man made no motion of acknowledgement. Checking the other's biostats, Noah confirmed that the person before him was Ochbo. Not sure how to introduce himself, Noah began formally, "Ochbo of the OMM, allow me to express my deepest gratitude to you for meeting with me—"

A deep honk-shu issued from beneath Ochbo's head of hair. Taken aback by the loudness of the snore, Noah couldn't help but laugh. His laughter jolted the OMM guru from his nap.

"Jeremiah's brother, you are here," Ochbo said. He pulled his hair back and wound it into a tangled knot at the back of his neck while he looked Noah over. "I'm a new man. Have you tried this?"

Ochbo dug a vial from his pocket and tossed it to Noah.

"What is it?" Noah asked. He turned the vial of tiny gold-flecked cubes over in his palm.

"Complete. It just came out on a trial basis for centenarians."

"Wow, you're over a hundred," Noah said, checking Ochbo's biostats, which read "Age: 65." "Did you hack your biostats?"

"Of course not, you punk," Ochbo said.

Noah stifled a retort.

"Among the Magi, I'm occasionally known as Pharmo —
that's for 'Pharmaceutical Ochbo' — because I experiment with
every new drug I can get my hands on, whether it's contrain-
dicated or not. Just look at the positive results," Ochbo said. Noah
had absolutely no comment to make on that score. "I may not be
over a hundred, but I've just experienced the ultimate clarity of
thought of a centenarian-on-Complete."

"While you were sleeping?"

"While I dreamed and consolidated my memories, I solved
several problems..." Ochbo said and yawned. "Complete
promotes clearness of mind and instant brain re-mapping for
learning new skills. This stuff is something else. What they
don't say about it is what's most worth talking about and that is,
the gift of wonder about the world that it endows, the sense of
wonderment we only have when we're kids."

From his crossed-legged position, Ochbo stood in one fluid
motion. He laughed an infectious laugh that reminded Noah of
a child's reaction upon seeing his first snow. In spite of himself,
Noah smiled.

"You're skin isn't purple, is it?"

In alarm, Noah examined his hands. "No, I don't think so."

"Must be an undocumented side effect," Ochbo said and
winked. "Hey, give me back that Complete."

Ochbo grabbed the vial from Noah's outstretched palm,
tucked it away in one of his many pockets and then suddenly
pulled out a knife.

"Let's begin," Ochbo said.

"Pardon?" Noah said and stared at the knife in the elderly
man's hand.

"You used to be one of the top fly gamers, right?" Ochbo
asked. "Fight me."

"There must be some mistake. I came here to ask for your
help."

"And you're getting it," Ochbo said and laughed again, but
this time Noah wasn't amused. The guru skillfully flipped the
small knife back and forth between his hands and approached.
Noah retreated slowly.

"Look, I don't want to fight you," the fly gamer said. "I haven't
recovered from a nasty fight and a triple hijacking two days ago.
Besides, my training is for Novus Orbis. The rules of alternate
reality are different."

"Precisely," said Ochbo. "In the Underground, it comes down
to survival."

He dove at Noah with his knife, and Noah jumped backwards.

"Nice reflexes. What's the first rule to remember in fighting Heartlanders?" asked Ochbo.

"Maestro, if I didn't need your help, I'd leave," Noah said. This was not what he'd expected. He kept a close eye on the knife. For such an aged man, Ochbo moved incredibly fast. Strands of loose gray hair floated around his face as the man moved smoothly from side to side in seemingly random motion, the knife constantly changing hands. Noah kept as much distance as he could, careful not to get backed into a corner.

"That's correct. Always try to escape first," Ochbo said. "Unless you're cornered, then you have to rely on your reflexes and speed. Always expect a knife. It's the most popular weapon of choice these days."

"You're serious about this?" Noah asked. "I have to fight you, before you'll help me?"

He checked the distance to the entrance and calculated how long he'd have his back to Ochbo before he could make it to the door.

"The door and wall panels are temporarily locked. So, the more accurate question to ask yourself is: if you don't fight back, will you survive?"

Ochbo made a fist around the knife and jabbed it upward at Noah's gut. Noah barely escaped the jab. He caught hold of the OMM guru's arm and twisted the elbow toward him to gain control of the knife, but the larger man proved too strong. Ochbo pulled out from Noah's grip and slashed him across his chest.

The knife ripped his tunic as Noah danced away. The tip of the blade grazed his skin. Blood beaded his chest. Noah cursed. They circled each other. Noah saw no way out, and with an empty room, no makeshift weapons.

Relentless, Ochbo came at him again aiming high with a downward thrust toward his neck. Noah closed the distance between them. With one hand, he grabbed Ochbo's thick wrist, wound his other arm up and around so that his opponent couldn't easily maneuver the blade to stab at him. Noah swung one leg behind Ochbo's and slammed a heel into the back of his knee. That threw Ochbo off balance, and he dropped the knife. Instead of picking it up, Noah kicked it across the floor and stood back.

In a flurry of movement, Ochbo produced a metal bat in his right hand and a glock-goku in his left.

"How is this fair?" Noah asked. His mouth dropped open. Disgusted, he rubbed his stinging chest and his hand came away bloody.

"Do you think surviving in the Underground as a fugitive is a civilized gentlemen's game?" Ochbo asked. "That's the second rule of engagement. If your attacker draws a knife on you, it's likely she's packing more than one weapon. If she acts extra cocky, she has backup on the way."

To Noah's surprise, Ochbo laid both his weapons at his feet and bowed to Noah. "That's all for today. You're not bad, but not nearly quick enough for the Underground. Jeremiah is faster."

Turning his back on Noah, Ochbo slid open a panel in the wall. Beyond the panel, Noah saw an unbelievably cluttered space. The OMM guru stepped gingerly around a couple piles of equipment and bellowed, "J-yo! Hrafn!"

From underneath what looked like a precarious heap of pipes, rolls of red, yellow and green wire mixed with indeterminate equipment parts, a small long-nosed kid emerged. He dusted a cobweb from his shoulder and said, "No need to yell, Ochbo. J-yo went home already, but I'm right here—"

Seeing Noah, he dodged back beneath the pipes. Almost immediately, Noah received notification that his biostats had been checked.

"Hrafn?" Ochbo said. He bent down and disappeared beneath the pile. Noah could hear his muffled words. "What's wrong with you? We need to discuss a couple of system optimizations that I just dreamed up thanks to Complete."

A few steps behind Ochbo, Noah considered following him beneath the pipes. A fan blade broke loose from the pile to the left of him and fell, landing so close it sliced a chunk out of one slipper as it hit the floor. Noah retreated to the empty entrance room, sat down and leaned against the wall to wait.

Hrafn, now that's a familiar-sounding name.... And then the memory came: *the bug!*

Moments later, Ochbo re-entered the room through another panel. This time, he had young Hrafn by the ear.

"Hrafn tells me you've come for him. Now why would he think that?" Ochbo said. He sat down in front of Noah and forced the youth to join him.

"I met a Hrafn in Seven Walls," Noah said. "For a fee, he offered to hack into spookdom to take back a datasphere for me, but he got zapped trying."

Rubbing his eyes with his hand as though he might still need waking up, Ochbo said, "You better start from the beginning."

"Considering that you just attacked me with a knife, and he's a hacker, are either of you trustworthy?" Noah asked.

"Personally, I don't trust anyone I haven't known for years," Ochbo said with a shrug.

"Boss!" Hrafn protested, but kept his head bowed.

It took Noah a moment to collect his thoughts. Prior to the knife attack, Noah had planned to be frank with Ochbo, as his brother had advised. Lydia DeLydia had made it clear to Noah that the senator's assassination was going to be made public, and that he would be named as a fugitive suspect. Noah needed to get the datasphere to Gothardi Lotte, the Minister of Internal Affairs. And then, he would turn himself in to the Order to clear his name. This ancient OMM guru might be his last hope of retrieving the senator's data so that Noah could fulfill Ortega's final wish.

After steadying his emotions, Noah outlined in broad strokes what had happened since he arrived in Los Angeles. As he spoke, he noticed Ochbo massage his wrist and felt gratified that he wasn't the only one who suffered from their fight. When the fly gamer's account reached the incident of his failed attempt to access the senator's datasphere, he recounted the full details to Ochbo.

As soon as Noah finished, the guru surprised him by clapping Hrafn's ears. Once Hrafn finished howling, Ochbo asked the kid, "Don't I pay you enough? The Order could have traced you back to me and shut us down. Our work is too important for that. Besides, you were on a cushy assignment. All you had to do was watch out for Jaa City."

"I got bored," Hrafn mumbled. "Everyone was curious about why the spooks showed up. It's rare for the Order to take over any part of Seven Walls. That must have been what attracted Jaa City, too."

"What?! So you saw Jaa with your own eyes?" Ochbo asked.

"Yes, I saw it before I got killed for the third time trying to access spookdom. Noah had given up and left, but I knew whatever was in there had to be important so I tried once more—"

"You went at it three times with simple hacks?" Ochbo made a face.

"It looked so easy to slip past their security. Something went wrong. I'm still not sure what," Hrafn admitted. "I only caught a glimpse of Jaa before the Order zapped me."

"What did you see?"

"It looked like a giant cloud with spires and towers, moving toward me from the horizon. At the top, the towers poked through white puffy clouds and caught the sunlight. From beneath, the clouds rolled black and cast a long shadow over everything."

"Maybe you saw Jaa City or maybe just a storm rolling in," Ochbo said. "Next time, tell me right away. Still, we should check it out. If we're lucky, maybe Jaa is still in Seven Walls."

Listening to them blather on about the mythic city, Noah's patience grew short. He loudly cleared his throat and then said, "I'm in a bad situation here. I committed to the senator to deliver her datasphere to the minister. Will you help me retrieve it from my estate in Seven Walls? I'd be in your debt."

"Yes, you *would* be in my debt." Ochbo scratched the stubble on his chin. "Unlike Hrafn here, I don't care for large sums."

"Boss?" Hrafn said. "He's a son of Domus Aqua. That means loads of credit!"

"We'd have to do a trade," Ochbo continued, sending a sidelong glance in Hrafn's direction that immediately silenced the hacker. "You'll have to promise to do me a favor, Noah, when the time comes, and I ask for it."

"What favor?" Noah asked.

"I'm not ready to ask it yet," Ochbo said. "At the moment I've only the barest inkling of what it might be."

"How can I agree to something when I don't know the cost?" Noah asked. It occurred to him Ochbo might be experiencing some kind of post-high delirium from the Complete, despite the old man's apparent lucidity. That might explain the knife attack. Noah felt tired down to his bones. Everything ached, especially the gash across his chest. The headache that had mostly disappeared came back, pounding over his eyes. "For all I know, you could ask me to do something that might hurt my family or friends or go against my morals."

"I don't know your beliefs, but I won't ask you to hurt anyone."

Noah chose his next words carefully. His sworn promise to deliver the datasphere for the senator had led him to this rather desperate situation. He'd already dug himself a big enough hole. "Considering my options, I'll agree to return the favor as long as it doesn't violate what I believe in or hurt anyone. If you're going to help me, we should act quickly."

"On that, I agree. If we succeed in getting your senator's datasphere, I'd prefer to avoid an Order raid on our offices."

Since Ochbo had agreed to help him, Noah resisted pointing out that a few good blasts from an Order raid might be just what Ochbo's cluttered offices needed to clear out the dangerous piles of junk.

"Before we get started, answer me this. What are your plans once you have the datasphere?" Ochbo asked.

"After I give the datasphere to the Minister of Internal Affairs, I'll turn myself in."

Pulling on his stubbly chin, Ochbo frowned in response, and his face visibly blanched. Although he had attacked Noah with a knife, the OMM guru acted genuinely worried for the gamer's welfare. Noah looked in puzzlement from Ochbo to Hrafn and back again, but neither spoke their minds.

Instead, Ochbo rose and said, "Enough of this. It's time to steal a datasphere. Follow me." Ochbo ushered Noah with Hrafn close behind into the sacred clutter of the OMM back rooms.

CHAPTER 8

Once it became clear to Rika that Yori couldn't immediately move from the hospital to the Institute of Extended Cognition's sick ward, she pestered Angela until her boss finagled approval for the DeeJee to visit him. After that, Rika fretted at work until Angela practically ordered her to go see him. It took only minutes via the URT to reach the Ecumenical Union Center Hospital in Santa Monica. Normally reserved for Order personnel and their families, the hospital had opened its doors to the sick evacuees. Definitely good PR, Rika supposed, but the Order had a practical reason as well. The hospital had the most extensive isolation facilities in the area. Rika followed an attendee through a maze of sterile hallways to a wall of capsule rooms with visitor-monitoring booths attached. Yori resided in capsule 8-12. Since he happened to be awake, the attendee left Rika to visit with him inside the adjoining booth.

"I'm not a good patient. I haven't slept, and I rejected their sedatives," Yori said. His voice still sounded hoarse. He had dark rings under his eyes. An electronic arm constantly scanned him with a low, barely audible buzz that Rika thought would drive her crazy. The booth remained in darkness, though Yori's capsule was as brightly lit as a specimen tray.

"Angela wants you moved to the IEC ward. It's luxurious compared to this," Rika said through the glass. She wanted to give him a hug. "I'm sorry you're here. I didn't know they'd do this."

"It won't be for long," Yori said with a shrug. When he cleared his throat, Rika winced. "Although they're isolating us for now, the medic told me no one has contracted a fungal infection from interpersonal contact."

This meant that before becoming ill, everyone in isolation must have been directly exposed to the fungi. "Is prolonged contact necessary to contract the fungal infection?"

"Exactly, at least for immunocompetent people. So far, everyone has responded positively to the treatments. Well, except a man admitted last night...."

"What about him?" Rika asked. She gulped back the lump of fear forming in her throat.

"He's a strange case. The medic told me Order regulars brought him in and were certain he had been heavily exposed to the fungi, but his symptoms were very different and more severe."

"You were sick enough to pass out," Rika reminded him.

"Yes, everyone here is suffering respiratory problems. That's how the fungus enters its host. And yet, this patient kept saying that his head hurt," Yori said. "Now he's in a coma and not responding to the fungicide therapy. Maybe you could find out more about his case. We might learn something important."

"That's not a bad idea," Rika said.

"His story has weighed on my mind," Yori said. He yawned. "You know having you here it's funny, I suddenly feel less anxious — like it's safe to sleep. Would you mind if I dozed off while you're visiting?"

"Not at all, big brother," Rika said and grinned. She pressed her hand up against the glass. He placed a finger where the glass met her palm and then closed his eyes.

As though she'd transferred all his worry onto herself, Rika felt helpless and anxiety-ridden. The knot, which her stomach had become, tightened. Still, she waited until she heard his snores before leaving the booth in search of the medic who'd been so candid with Yori.

Outside the isolation ward, an attendant immediately joined her. "Allow me to escort you out," he insisted.

"Actually, I'm here to see..." Rika paused to see if the medic's name would come to mind if she asked for it. Sure enough, a name popped up. As a group of medics passed them in the hallway, she added. "Medic Lado Ng of the Ecumenical Union Center Hospital."

Without even the pretense of checking Medic Ng's availability, the attendant said, "I'm afraid that's not possible—"

"Did I hear my name?" asked a large woman with dark eyes. She stopped abruptly in front of Rika and the attendant. Her group of doctors continued on.

"As you can see, I'm with IEC and on Yori's team," Rika said, raising her voice as the attendant tried to step between them. "I had a few questions to ask you if I might."

The attendant glared at Rika and said, "I told you Medic Ng is indisposed—"

"For goodness sake," Lado said. "We're supposed to be working with IEC on Circle Tide."

Circle Tide, Rika repeated silently. *That's what they're calling it.*

"It's against regulations," the attendant said. He lowered his head and refused to look Lado in the eye. "The DeeJee must leave."

Ng said, "Honestly, you're worried about following regs at a time like this? Sure almost everyone is recovering, but let's not forget the poor patient whose brains were inexplicably eaten away by Circle Tide." The woman turned on her heel and hurried to rejoin the other medics. In the guise of reprimanding the attendant, she'd given Rika two clues to follow up on.

With his hand at her elbow, Rika's unwanted escort led her to the hospital exit without another word. Rika saw the crowd of visitors waiting to see their loved ones in isolation and shook her head. At least, the patients — Yori included — were mostly recovering. That is, all but one.

Back at IEC, Rika reassured everyone that Yori was in capable hands. The Bolsa lab had grown crowded. Angela, Huifeng and the lab technician Kanda worked in close quarters to uncover details about the fungus. Rika retreated to the materials collections room. It was a quiet place to access the MAM. More like a high security walk-in closet than an actual room, it perfectly suited the DeeJee. She sat on a discarded stool cushion and leaned against the one empty shelf. Her eyes moved back and forth beneath her closed eyelids as though she were dreaming.

In Novus Orbis, she filled her work grid with hundreds of interfaces and access points. To date, Rika had never hallucinated or confused her identity in Novus Orbis, which made it feel much safer than Vetus Orbis, the old "real" world. Engaging all her senses within Novus Orbis' insular universe, she found herself most intimately connected to the MAM. While she worked, she maintained a state of clarity that she rarely achieved anywhere else. Rika ripped through interfaces and data looking for clues about Circle Tide, Noah and what happened the night of the senator's assassination. She'd even accessed files from the hospital that the Order had not yet released to IEC. Cubed 3D trailers of raw MAM surveillance, sample images and confidential Order data littered her workspace.

Amid these cubes stood a Smart Intelligence cataloguer that Rika had dug up from the private archives of Mencius Wu, the IEC's director and founder. She had activated the S.I. to run fungus-related queries so that Rika could continue to focus on areas of the investigation to which she had never been assigned.

Attired in a gold lamé IEC jumpsuit, instead of the standard-issue gray, the cataloguer could have passed for a voluptuous woman except that yellow fur grew out of its ears and its eyes protruded into cone-shapes with the pupils on the very tips. When the cataloger wanted Rika's attention, it folded its arms under its ample breasts, tapped its shiny spiked-heel on the corner of the nearest data cube and directed one of its cone eyes toward her. Eventually the staring and tapping grew so annoying Rika paused to acknowledge it.

"You've discovered something important," Rika said.

"Ten minutes ago," the cataloguer said. "Don't think I mind working alone. Humans have slow processers and are burdensome, excluding my Mencius Wu, of course."

Rika rolled her eyes at the Smart Intelligence's built-in adulation of the IEC director. She'd learned more about him from this simple S.I. than she liked.

"However," it added, "I do object to what you're doing."

"What's that?" Rika asked.

"You've accessed data outside the Institute firewall that is well beyond our security clearance. Unless you desist, I must report you to the director as a malfunctioning member of this team."

"If I'm doing something I shouldn't, where are the security daemons?" Rika asked. She raised her palms in supplication. It hadn't occurred to her that this flouncy cataloguer would have an ethics module that extended beyond its own actions.

"The way you initiate your queries, the MAM subsystems recognize you as an internal native process," the S.I. clarified. It put its hands on its hips. "You have circumvented major security modules. This violates the Institute for Extended Cognition Ethics protocol 98750.4 and, marginally, 98750.7."

"Only two?" Rika said. She grinned. "Well, that's two too many. I guess. Show me what you've found."

The cataloguer showed her new images of a fungus captured in MAM surveillance. Rika realized they had a second fungus to deal with that looked nothing like what Yori and she had encountered at the sick building. That might explain the one patient's unique symptoms.

"It has the look of orangey-red fur like a fox pelt." Examining it at a higher magnification, Rika silently amended her description. Magnified, she saw many thousands of red needles. "Wow. That's less like a fungus than something man-made. With all those miniscule needle structures, that's one heck of a transmission vehicle."

While the cataloguer organized and reorganized information across the grid, Rika studied each data collection. She discovered a few key details about the two fungi. The red fur fungus never occurred without the presence of modified *M. somnis*.

In all four buildings, MAM surveillance captured the growth cycles of the fungi. In each case, the fungi appeared as red furry patches with a wide *M. somnis* gray outer ring. Speeding up the subsequent twelve hours of observation to minutes, Rika watched the red fur patches grow to engulf the gray fungus border. For a little over a quarter hour, the red fur fungus remained in this state, and then, a narrow ring of modified *M. somnis* reappeared at the periphery of the red fur and took over. Suddenly, the Order name for this shrinkage and expansion "Circle Tide" made sense. "It's actually fascinating to watch," Rika said, more to herself than to the cataloguer.

It replied, "According to the confidential files you stole from the Order, your 'red fur' fungus has a predilection for human brain tissue as a nutritional niche."

"This fungus must be much more dangerous in its early phase before it combines with the second one," Rika said and shivered. "Luckily, so far only one person has been exposed during the Circle Tide's initial phase. I should go onsite and see if I notice anything not picked up by MAM sensors."

The cataloguer nodded. Rika watched the cataloguer and wondered why the director had bothered to archive such a slow Smart Intelligence. How Rika wished she could access Jaa City! That was just too risky from inside the Institute. If her floating city were detected, the Institute would destroy it. The city violated so many protocols, but it held her memories, what was left of her original identity and all of who she had become. Also importantly, Jaa held Prometheus.

Prometheus was an ancient Smart Intelligence whom she had resurrected for Jaa after she found him in a trove of deleted Order projects that were ghosted on an old subsystem. He would be a lot more help right now than the director's antiquated cataloguer. Prometheus ran on his own brand of ethics, and the two of them, DeeJee and S.I., worked brilliantly together. Prometheus reacted to brain-twisters as eagerly as she did, and this investigation had turned into the ultimate puzzle.

After the cataloguer flagged every file that Rika had accessed without permission, Rika decided she needed a break.

"It is time for me to say good-bye," Rika said. "I'm sending a summary of our findings to Angela and then heading home."

"According to protocol 98751, I'm required to inform you that at the termination of this session, I will report your malfunctions to Director Wu," said Cataloguer. It bowed deeply.

"You've just committed to making the report after your session ends," Rika said.

"That's correct."

"Well then," Rika said and blinked. She opened a new interface and created a miniature workspace for the cataloguer the size of a housefly so it wouldn't get in her way. "We won't terminate this session. You'll need to repeat your results again and again."

"Wait," the S.I. said, holding up its hands, but Rika minimized it and its workspace. After setting the session to loop, she exited Novus Orbis. Huifeng and Kanda were so busy with the samples that neither looked up when Rika passed by them to exit the lab.

Outside the Bolsa complex, she smelled the fresh salty air of the ocean and heard the waves on the other side of the Institute's high wall of shrubbery. Everything sounded, smelled and looked normal, but the threat of the fatal, virulent fungus somehow changed everything. The blooming fuchsia lining the path took on a deeper crimson hue. It appeared as profoundly fragile and transient as their lives. The urge to immediately visit a sick building and examine the Circle Tide firsthand almost overwhelmed her.

Up ahead, she heard her boss' high-pitched laugh and saw Angela and Sebastian of Domus Restitio bow to each other at the Institute entrance. Rika walked straight up to Angela and bowed.

"Why aren't you in the lab?" Angela asked. "You're part of the emergency response team serving the Order."

"I just sent you a summary of our, I mean, my findings," Rika said. "It's late, and I haven't eaten all day. I'll be back later."

Without giving Angela time to make any follow-up commentary, Rika politely inclined her head. The DeeJee then bounded out of the gates toward home. She rounded the corner to find Sebastian directly in front of her. Sebastian heard her organo-pumps squealing to a standstill and turned back. The light of the moon and the sidewalk's glow highlighted his broad, easy smile.

"It's a nice habit," Sebastian said.

"What?"

"You running into me."

Rika felt her cheeks go hot.

"Are you just now getting off work?" Sebastian asked.

"I'm headed home for dinner, but actually I need to return tonight. We're on an emergency response project."

"It's terrifying. Isn't it?" Sebastian said. His radiant smile abruptly eclipsed, but he didn't seem at all scared. "The idea there's a fungus right in Los Angeles that kills humans. It makes me want to escape … very far from here."

"Really? It makes me want to go see it. Better yet, I'd like to treat this night as though it's my last. If I weren't needed at the lab, I'd stay up until dawn having fun," Rika said.

"May I take you to dinner?" Sebastian asked. He looked her up and down.

Her eyes widened, and she hesitated.

"Um, maybe another time," she said. "I kind of need to go home."

"I apologize," he said. "Someone as pretty as you must have a boyfriend waiting for you."

That's a corny line, she thought. *He has a nice smile though, and he smells good.*

"I don't have a boyfriend," Rika said. "But I've got things to do at my place."

"You have to eat sometime," he insisted. "To be honest, I've wanted to chat with you ever since we met. I understand from Angela that you're an unusually gifted DeeJee."

"Angela said that?" said Rika. She grinned despite the fact he'd glanced away when he said it as though he'd made it up. She didn't bother checking his biostats. He'd be notified if she did. "Okay, let's eat, but it needs to be someplace quick."

"Got it." Sebastian turned back toward the ocean with Rika beside him. They approached one of the five-star hotels along the beachfront. Rika reluctantly followed him as he headed through the front doors. To her relief, he kept going and walked straight through the lobby and out the back. When she caught up with him, he was turning into an Underground entrance marked for the URT.

Just inside the doorway, Rika smelled fried plantain and heard boisterous laughter. People stood pressed together in the crowded little nook with a bar and five tables. Sebastian approached a lanky man sitting at the bar. He cupped his hand over the man's ear. The fellow nodded. Sebastian passed him something, fist to fist, that the man pocketed before jumping up and yanking his friend off the stool beside him and out of the bar. Sebastian gestured for Rika to sit. He ordered drinks and the night's special. Only then, did he sit down beside her.

Over the noise of the crowd, Rika found it impossible to hear what he said. She enjoyed sitting next to him though. He had to be wearing one-of-a-kind cologne because her MAM queries failed to identify the designer. Still, she detected an amber musk, pepper and vanilla scents.

The bartender served them an assortment of crispy fried treats and two large lime drinks that made Rika's head swim. As more people arrived, they had to squeeze close. He kept brushing against her. New arrivals recognized Sebastian and made a point to bully their way over to him and say hello. Several times, he wrapped his arm around her waist to keep her from getting edged off her stool in the ruckus. At every touch, she found herself deeply distracted, as though he had a special electric pulse in his fingertips calibrated precisely for her.

When they'd finished, they waded through the crowd and emerged from the Underground entrance into the night.

"Fancy enough for you?" Sebastian asked.

"Perfect," she replied. A common Heartlander, she might have taken his question as a slight if it had come from anyone else.

"Would you mind an escort home?"

"No, it isn't necessary," Rika said. "Really, I'm close by."

Sebastian nodded. Facing her, he put both hands on her shoulders. He bent down and kissed her right cheek and then her left. "Like the French."

She didn't correct him. She didn't say, *you're a flirt. The French don't linger in their kisses. It's a light peck to each cheek.* Instead, Rika stood on her toes and kissed him squarely on the lips. When she stood back, she saw his brow furrow above his intense stare. Her cheeks went hot, and she bolted past the back entrance of the hotel toward the main walkway, the ocean and home.

"Let's do that again," he yelled after her.

"Yes," she yelled back over her shoulder without slowing. "Yes!"

Blocks away, much farther from the shore, she reached a modest building without corners or edges. Its bulbous exterior reminded her of a turnip turned upside down with oval purple windows. She'd fallen for the funky architecture the first time she'd visited it. Huifeng, who lived above her, had said the same. Three stories up, she entered her tiny one-window studio, kicked off her shoes and stretched out on the floor. The room read her fatigue from her biostats. The harmonizing floor curled around her in a protective, bedlike cocoon.

"Life is good," she told her studio. She'd spent almost an hour with Sebastian, and it had passed so quickly. She touched her cheeks where he'd kissed her. "Even if there is a deadly fungus next door."

Patting the floor, she told her studio, "Help me focus. I have to work."

A strong peppermint aroma filled the room. With a sigh, she sat up in the lotus position and closed her eyes to access the MAM and enter Novus Orbis. Blood pounded hard in her temples. Full contact with the MAM, which engaged all her senses, gave her momentary vertigo.

To reduce the jarring effects of Novus Orbis, everyone chose a consistent setting for full sensory contact with the MAM. According to her user preferences, she always entered Novus Orbis on a lunar landing pad overlooking Earth. It was a silent homage to her grandfather whom she had never met, a fearless pilot who'd died manning a cargo ship from Mars to Earth. He'd made it almost all the way home, as close as Earth's moon when his ship exploded in a freak accident. Of course, before he died, he managed to heroically save his Martian passenger, the Magi prophet Thesni.

At least, that's the way his daughter, Rika's mother had often told it. Her mother liked to tell stories. Rika had stowed the few she still remembered in Jaa after the mind enhancements. Unfortunately, the enhancements left her emotionally detached from her mother and her storied past, as though they were no more than the shared memories of a stranger. Thanks to her neural-knitting, Rika also had access to strangers' memories, like those of the Order regular who'd actually found her grandfather, Captain Grant, with his throat slit in the Underground — the outcome of his final, risky quest for another blackbase fix. Rika much preferred her mother's truth.

After clearing her thoughts, Rika located Jaa City in her mind's eye. She stepped off the lunar setting into her city, which currently floated through the Seven Walls gaming paradise, as a cloud formation like no other in Novus Orbis. Prometheus waited for her, perched atop the great gate to the high-walled, floating city of steeples and spires. At this altitude, the winds whipped his long, dark hair and robes. Rika joined him and looked out over the wild lands of Seven Walls.

Determined to avoid attracting the Order's notice, Rika and Prometheus floated the city mostly through gaming worlds like this one, where the security was notoriously lax. The MAM treated Jaa as a MAM subsystem, one of its traveling neurons. Other than that, MAM security completely ignored the city's existence. However, humans acted differently. A vigilant Order operator or IEC personnel might notice her cloud city and shut it down. Luckily, Order operators more loosely monitored the gaming worlds, which gave Rika and Prometheus safer places to float Jaa.

Recently, Prometheus had heard legitimate fly gamers talk about sightings of the floating city across Novus Orbis. Since its first sighting, Jaa had become a challenge for hackers to identify and capture. Rika's Jaa was infamous — the ultimate hack. To date, many had attempted and failed to enter her city or identify its true owner and trace it back to her. Thanks to Prometheus' vigilance, Jaa remained free. Prometheus put his arm around Rika, and she leaned her head against his thickly robed chest.

"You sent me all your memories from Vetus Orbis," Prometheus said. "You shared everything, even Sebastian's kisses."

"Yes," Rika said and ran her fingertips over her lips.

"Don't trust him," Prometheus said.

She pulled away to look up at him. "You're jealous. What an extraordinary Smart Intelligence you are!"

"Humph," Prometheus said. "Jealousy is an irrelevant emotion. He lies. Check his biostats when he speaks. Also, you must be careful. If you keep rerouting such large blocks of memories here, instead of automatically passing them to the Institute, someone at IEC is bound to notice. You'll need to account for those missing blocks of time."

"I know," Rika said. She sighed. "If I allowed my memories to go into the Institute repository, they'd find out I kissed an

IEC client. But all this is beside the point, I directed Jaa to Seven Walls because this is the place Noah of Domus Aqua accessed Sunday night. He updated his entire data keep."

"I guessed that's what you were up to," Prometheus said. "Noah entered Seven Walls yesterday, too. He wanted to retrieve something, but the Order had placed his estate in spookdom."

"That complicates things, but Jaa City floats wherever it wants," Rika said. She stood up and looked down at the merging rivers. She pointed. "Jaa could slip past the temporary borders of spookdom right there; they've left a sloppy seam."

"Perhaps, but Order operators will notice and come after us. I'm not sure that I'm good enough to hide from them once they start looking for me."

"Aren't mirrored sites and obfuscation your specialty?" Rika said. She winked at him.

"Pattern recognition is my primary specialty. Other talents are self-taught."

"Impressive. So are you up for this?" Rika asked.

"Absolutely. What do we want from his data keep?"

"If only he hadn't updated *everything*," Rika said, staring down at the fast-moving river. Beneath those clumsy spook-dom seams lay Noah's estate and his data keep. Cricket the roof gardener had mentioned Noah and something he'd stolen.

Rika accessed her memory stores so neatly categorized and memorialized by Prometheus. She located her specific conversation with Cricket and turned back to Prometheus. "We're looking for a datasphere. Why don't I slip in there alone? Never mind bringing the entire city since it's so risky."

Rika sprouted huge black wings to fly down from Jaa into spookdom.

"Hold on," Prometheus said. He took hold of her arm. "This isn't just another one of our adventures. If you succeed in slipping through there, they will come after us. We must develop an escape strategy, or you'll end up in a place far worse than Vasil's ward. Jaa could be destroyed and with it all your memories."

Her enormous Seven Wall raven wings drooped down over her backside. She studied the rivers and weighed multiple scenarios to retrieve the datasphere.

"I have an idea," she said after a very long silence. "But we don't have much time."

CHAPTER 9

Mostly cloudy, thunderstorms and heavy rain — the new forecast from Seven Walls had Noah worried because of Ochbo's change in mode. Since he'd told the man about the datasphere, the OMM guru had been barking contradictory orders at his two underlings. They scrambled in and out of the front room carrying out his demands. Finally, Ochbo ordered them both to sit with him and then explained the plan to secure Ortega's datasphere. The Complete had worn off. That much was obvious. Delight no longer animated his movements. Instead, determination made every action jarring and his tone caustic.

He'd make a terrible poker player and a worse politician, Noah thought.

Since childhood, as the son of a domus master, Noah had learned to mask all emotions behind an implacable façade. The same was true of Jeremiah who sat beside him practically inhaling a bowl of hot noodles — apparently, Magi novices were not expected to practice asceticism when it came to food. Through harsh punishment, their father had taught them it never mattered how his sons felt, only how they acted. During everything they did, they represented the domus. For his father, Noah always failed to measure up, a failure that the gamer demonstrated when he ran off to the wilderness to resurrect giant sea turtles and extinct butterflies from the genetic archives instead of taking up his responsibilities and pursuing the political career that would serve his domus. The latest media reports must have proven what his father always said in private: his youngest son was a good-for-nothing.

The sight of the knife-cut across Noah's chest elicited brief consternation from Jeremiah, followed by one of his classic vexing grins, before he returned to slurping his meal. Despite his growling stomach, Noah had yet to take a bite. First, he'd been preoccupied with Ochbo and his young hackers. Now Jeremiah insisted he recount what had happened. Noah told his brother everything. Periodically, Hrafn stole glances at Noah and his brother. Both Hrafn and J-yo demonstrated an unusual reverence for Jeremiah that the novice ignored. That kind of esteem wasn't easily earned. Noah had a hunch it had less to do with Jeremiah's pending monkhood than with his skills at fighting.

"Jeremiah," Noah said, off topic after he recounted the attack on the senator and seeing Beatrice. "I always pictured your monastic life as meditation and prayer, but I'm beginning to think your days are much more exciting. Ochbo intimated you're fast and adept in combat."

"We pray and meditate more than you could stomach," Jeremiah said. "Tell me what happened once you left Beatrice's place. I still can't believe you went to see her. That woman still has a hold on you."

To keep from saying anything he'd regret, Noah stuffed his mouth with warm noodles. After a few mouthfuls, he swallowed and continued his tale. The only thing that betrayed Jeremiah's concern was an occasional tick that pulled at the corner of one eye. When Noah concluded his story with his plan to turn himself in to the Order, Jeremiah's twitch intensified. Otherwise, the stoic future monk had no reaction, except to call out to Ochbo after a delay, as though he'd been mulling it over in the back of his mind, "What's so important about the sudden weather change in Seven Walls?"

Apparently, while Jeremiah listened to Noah's account, he'd also been tracking the conversation between the other three. Ochbo motioned for Jeremiah and Noah to join them.

"It might be nothing, but unscheduled changes in the world we're about to hack make me nervous," Ochbo admitted. "Bad weather could be code for interrupted service or poor communications. We'll have to coordinate our tactical maneuvers to successfully take the datasphere and get out fast."

Hrafn said, "Pharmo, I understand you want me to head the blitzkrieg on Noah's properties in the Sacred Mountain-Hidden Falls gaming world as a distraction. J-yo will take care of the assault in Valleys of the Future, the second distraction, while you focus on the real attack in Seven Walls. What I don't understand is if we actually gain entrance to spookdom and its properties, what do we do?"

"Destroy everything," Ochbo said.

Hearing him, Noah struggled to maintain his composure. It had taken years for him to amass his holdings in Novus Orbis, and he'd done it all on his own without his family's help. More importantly, a lifetime of keepsakes would be lost along with his favorite fly-gaming weapons.

"All of Noah's holdings are frozen under spookdom," Ochbo explained. "We must mount a full-scale viral attack on Noah's properties for his role in the senator's death. Her assassination has just been made public. A government 'leak' stated that Noah had observed, and possibly assisted, in the assassination. Noah is now officially a fugitive from the Order. Heartlanders' retaliation against him is expected."

"Fair enough, but does it make sense to destroy such valuable items? He has one-of-a-kind weapons, priceless custom-made swords—," Hrafn began.

"Destroy everything," Ochbo repeated and glared at Hrafn until the kid looked away. "You start accepting credit, trades, any kind of funds for Noah's stuff, and the Order will trace it to you and ultimately to us."

"Won't the Order figure out it's us behind the initial attacks anyway?" J-yo asked. He might be soft spoken, but looked just as squirrely as Hrafn.

"Between our own strategic attacks, our Smart Intelligence hits and inciting others across the gaming worlds, we'll cause enough noise that our theft of the datasphere should go untraced — as long as we're careful," said Ochbo.

"So you learned enough from going over the kill methods used against Hrafn to bypass Order security and enter spookdom?" asked Jeremiah.

"We'll see," Ochbo replied. His dark expression did nothing to reassure Noah. "Hrafn, J-yo and I have gone over those three kills of Hrafn's avatars so many times that I think we've successfully reverse engineered their methods and developed work-arounds. It's impossible to be certain until we attempt entry to spookdom."

"Your plan is to have everyone gain access at once?" Jeremiah asked.

"Well, only a few of us will attempt a real workaround that gets us past Order security. The rest will simply bombard spookdom with no possibility of gaining access. They'll distract Order operators and their Smart Intelligence."

"I want to be part of the actual attack on spookdom in Seven Walls," Jeremiah said.

"Me, too," Noah said.

In response, Ochbo stroked the stubble on his chin with the palm of his hand and studied the brothers. When he finally spoke, he sounded tired. "Look, no one will be convinced this is a viral attack against Noah if either of you participate."

"We'll use aliases and new avatars," Noah suggested.

"Noah has an ulterior motive," Hrafn piped in. "He wants to learn how to become a microscopic parasite in the gaming worlds."

Holding up his hand to quiet the hacker, Ochbo silently weighed the dangers of the brothers' participation.

"You made the commitment to the senator," Ochbo said. "This is your datasphere to lose. Having you both along increases the risks, but if you wear MAM embraces and use unknown avatars, you're welcome to join us."

In deference, Jeremiah and Noah saluted him palm to fist. The other two followed suit. For the first time since landing in Los Angeles, Noah forgot to regret being there. Hanging out with the OMM and his brother, the Magi monk-wannabe, gave everything an exciting edge. It was certainly more dangerous than working with the crew of scientists. Later, once Noah had finished the meal of cold noodles and was experiencing a MAM embrace for the first time, he had second thoughts.

"Beatrice always wears MAM embraces to give herself a different look," Noah told Jeremiah. "Can you believe that? They're so uncomfortable. This is worse than body armor."

"Beatrice wears top-of-the-line MAM embraces registered with the Order, not an illegal hack." The novice stretched and added, "At least Ochbo didn't make you a composite MAM embrace of an old white-guy-monk known for his strange habits. I never thought of myself as an 'Emmett.'"

"Get over it," Ochbo said. "You'll survive it for a few hours. Noah must wear his until he's no longer a fugitive."

When Noah had asked about the MAM embrace, Hrafn had described it as "more dense than air, but moving with you so that you sense a light breeze." As soon as he'd been embraced, Noah realized the OMMer must have been relying on some technical description, rather than personal experience. It felt nothing like a pleasant "breeze." Noah had the distinctly creepy sensation of someone standing too close and breathing down his neck or constantly brushing up against him.

"Ochbo, this isn't going to work," Noah said. He tore at himself, trying to remove the MAM embrace, but it simply self-repaired.

"Is it hurting you?" Ochbo asked in alarm.

"No, it's..." said Noah, searching for the right word, "It's claustrophobic. I might as well be feeling my own shadow."

"Noah," Jeremiah said, rolling his eyes. "The MAM embrace isn't a constrictive material, like clothing that's too tight. You're embedded in latticed Smart Intelligence. Don't panic, this is simply a molecular layer over your skin. It moves with you."

Noah barely resisted the urge to tear it away from his face and throat.

"Think of it as body armor that surrounds you instead of weighing you down," Jeremiah went on with a smile meant to be encouraging, but it only further agitated Noah. "It gives you a different appearance—"

"What do I look like?"

"—And your moniker is better than mine," Jeremiah continued, glancing at Ochbo. "Spider Zynx is so much more interesting than Emmett."

Ochbo groaned.

"I asked you what I look like."

"You're a lot like yourself with the added bonus of new moving spider tattoos," Jeremiah said. "If you want the honest truth, the tattoos crawling across your face make it even uglier than usual."

"Now you've spooked him," Ochbo said, chuckling when Noah made a face. The chuckle transformed the guru.

Surrounded by the heavy clouds above the lightning and pounding rain, Jaa City remained invisible. Prometheus and Rika stood atop the city gates, looking down at Seven Walls through the bottom of a thunderhead. The Smart Intelligence had successfully entered a system-level adjustment to the gaming world, altering clear skies to torrential thunderstorms. Rika counted the storm as a good omen. She needed one to counter the strange events on the ground.

Below them, hundreds had gathered in a clumsy onslaught to enter spookdom and vandalize the Order-sequestered properties of the man accused of helping murder the senator, Noah of Domus Aqua. Since the Order quickly zapped out of Seven

Walls' existence anyone crossing its borders, the targeted strikes
only added to the massive lightning storm.

"It appears as though they're all getting royally zapped,"
Prometheus told her. He always adapted his diction to match her
own. "But some special avatars have already made it past Order
security and are busy destroying property. At this rate, others
will get their hands on the datasphere before you."

Grimacing in response, Rika focused on tracing the elements
of spookdom outside Seven Walls, as Prometheus and she had
planned. Since the Order didn't need permission to impose sanc-
tions on any gaming world, it had simply expropriated Noah's
island. Spookdom had never been integrated as part of Seven
Walls or any other gaming world. That lack of integration with
Seven Walls meant a potential vulnerability for Rika to exploit.

Like freed electrons, surfing an electromagnetic wave, Rika
let her mind be drawn toward the structural determinants of this
instance of spookdom. When she mentally arrived, she created
an inversion. Spookdom's borders changed in a femtosecond.
Suddenly, spookdom blanketed all Seven Walls' lands, leaving
the small, unnamed island the only place outside spookdom.
Noah's island felt the eye of the storm and the rest of Seven Walls
became suddenly still. Every hack, every unauthorized trans-
action and unnamed avatar was instantly under the umbrella
of the Order's realm, and each immediately suffered elimina-
tion. The nuanced gray areas of legitimacy allowed within Seven
Walls were destroyed by the Order. It provided its answers in
black and white.

With Jaa City poised directly above Noah's island, Rika
took her chance. She had cloaked herself in her favorite Novus
Orbis avatar: a mysterious dark female figure from whose back
sprouted the glossy-feathered wings of a giant crow. Her load-
bearing scapula made a satisfying crack-crack-crack sound as
she stretched her ebony wings. Prometheus perched on the city
wall ready to help if she needed it although he'd warned her
that his direct involvement might bring her more trouble than
his worth. With a wink at Prometheus that showed more confidence than she actually felt, Rika dove through the clouds down
into the slashing rain toward a large walled courtyard and the
entrance to Noah's mansion.

She landed on the terra cótta tiles and then had to pick her
way through the debris of smashed sculptures and slosh through
large puddles. The front door swung precariously from a single
hinge. She folded her wings back behind her and slipped around

it. Anything that could be broken or torn apart had been. All but the outer structure and a few internal walls had been reduced to rubble.

In her mind's eye, she asked the MAM for the looted goods, anything that had actually gone missing and had not been destroyed. Expecting a long list, she returned one sole item. It just so happened to be a datasphere. While she focused on tracing its whereabouts, she caught movement in the far corner of the room.

A man moved from the shadows to stand in front of her. He had spiders running up his arms and down his neck. Tiny yellow ones wove webs in his hair. Rika froze. She feared she'd begun hallucinating spiders in Novus Orbis. Only when she checked his biostats and found out he identified himself as Spider Zynx did her panic subside. Even if she ignored the spiders, he had a sinister look to him. Around his neck he wore a locket in which she immediately identified the datasphere. Rika's eyes narrowed.

"Hi there," Noah said. He sounded friendly despite the off-putting spiders attached to his avatar. "You wouldn't happen to know how to get off this island, would you?"

"I'll show you if you give me that," Rika said and pointed to the locket.

"I can't do that," Noah said and placed his hand protectively over it. Rika received notification that Spider Zynx had checked her biostats and learned her moniker *Crow.* "How did you get in here after the borders closed?"

"Did you cause all this damage?" Rika asked.

"I had help," Noah admitted. "My friends have all slipped through to the other side, but I ran back to look for something—"

"Lucky move for you," Rika said without thinking. "If your friends are hackers like you, they got zapped on the other side. You're not in spookdom anymore, but they are."

"When I couldn't slip across the border after them, I assumed I was trapped. But wait, if you and I are free of spookdom, I can download the datasphere and exit from here without leaving the island," Noah said.

She didn't answer, but her expression must have given her away. For a brief moment he hesitated and then dashed into the shadows.

"Come back here," Rika yelled and ran after him. Her focus on the datasphere returned encrypted gobbledygook but two datasphere modifiers flashed off its surfaces: Noah of Domus Aqua and Senator Mari Ortega of the Heartland. Rika knew she'd located the stolen datasphere. In the semi-darkness she failed to make him out, but he registered as close by.

"What were you looking for, Spider Zynx?" she asked.

Silence.

Worried he was downloading the datasphere and deleting it from Seven Walls, she felt powerless to stop him. And then, the key that the senator had sent Yori came to mind. On a hunch that he had noticed the encryption and that he'd turned back to find the missing key, Rika said, "If you want to read that datasphere, you're going to need the decrypter. I've already got that."

Quite abruptly, she heard him laugh. "I don't know who you are, but you're clever. I'll give you that."

"What do you mean?" Rika asked.

"You had me second-guessing myself for an instant there," he said. "I thought in all my hurry that I'd separated the decrypter from the encrypted datasphere somehow. If you had the key though, you'd be the person to whom I'm supposed to give this, and you certainly aren't him. That means he must already have it."

While he spoke, she searched for him in the shadows. When she located him, she moved in to yank the locket from his neck. As she dove for it, he disappeared and the datasphere flashed out of existence.

"Aish!" she said. Her hands met air.

Unable to follow him out of Novus Orbis, she stomped through the mansion to the flooded courtyard. Flying up to Jaa City took time in all that rain. She had to fight against strong gusts of wind that tore painfully at her wings. As soon as she stood inside the Jaa, insulated from the storm, her mind reached out to spookdom's origins. Her probe rebounded, returning spookdom to its original boundaries. The DeeJee let her wings disappear and her scapula diminish. Exhaustion sank through her, down to the very marrow of her bones. Still, she couldn't rest.

With Noah's island back under spookdom, Rika directed Jaa to safety. It rolled out of Seven Walls along with the rain clouds. Once her city floated unnoticed in a yet-to-be-explored corner of Valleys of the Future, she went looking for Prometheus.

At the city's only sidewalk café, Rika found him sipping absinthe. He handed her his handkerchief to dry her face and said, "It's about time you made it safely back here. With all these malfunctions, Seven Walls is about to be shut down."

"I failed to get the datasphere."

"I know."

"This creep named Spider stole it from Noah who stole it from the senator, I think."

"Hmm. I appreciate you detaining him there through that little chat of yours."

"Prometheus, you found something out!"

"Perhaps," Prometheus said and looked away to study crows flying overhead.

"Spit it out," she said.

"I'm not sure I should tell you," Prometheus replied.

"Why not?"

"I don't want to put you further at risk."

"Prometheus! I order you to tell me."

He laughed.

"Please? Pretty please?"

"I find it so difficult to say 'no' to you, but you must be cautious here. Jaa City is intact for now, but there'll be an investigation on the Seven Walls incident. We may be discovered. This line of action that you're following results in a set that includes very few favorable, possible outcomes."

"Right, okay, I'll be careful and all that."

"I sense sarcasm," Prometheus said and shook his head. "The unsavory character named Spider is located not too far from you in Vetus Orbis. His signature crossed the ocean and back several times to hide his physical location, but I guarantee I know where he signed off. Besides, his stunt had OMM written all over it."

"Where?" Rika asked and sucked in her breath.

"The Sanctuary in Pasadena — specifically the OMM offices located in its catacombs."

"I've never been there," she said and thought for a moment to find the precise address. "That is close by."

"Don't go."

With a laugh, Rika gave Prometheus' arm a reassuring squeeze that only made him scowl and sink a little lower in his chair beside her.

CHAPTER 10

When Rika returned to the Institute at nearly midnight, she expected everyone to have left the lab except Angela, who survived on three hours or less of sleep a night. The blackout blinds prevented light pollution. From outside it appeared as though everyone had gone home. Once she entered the Bolsa complex, she found the place lit up and bustling with IEC personnel. The first person who stepped into her path happened to be Sebastian.

"Hello," Rika said and hurried to sidestep him. He moved in the same direction.

"It's my turn to run into you," Sebastian said. He caught her by the elbows to keep from stepping on her. "I'm not generally allowed in here, but your boss kindly made an exception tonight."

"Oh?" Rika said. Her heart raced.

"Several of the properties that Domus Restitio manages have become sick — not only here — but in other cities, so I shared what information I had with your team." Giving her a sly glance, he bent down close to her ear and added, "Secretly, I hoped to run into you."

"Rika, must you always be underfoot?" Angela said, walking up beside them. "I'm so sorry the lab called me away for a moment, Sebastian. This night has been crazy. Please allow me to escort you out."

"Oh, it's no problem at all," the domus master said and beamed at her. "I know how busy you are, and I wouldn't dream of taking any more of your time. Rika will escort me to the entrance. Thank you."

With a tight hold on Rika's elbow, he marched them both out of the building leaving Angela standing open-mouthed behind them.

As they walked toward the entrance, he slowed down considerably and took his time. In the semi-darkness, he quickly found her hand and clasped it. He steered her off the path and behind the trees. "I haven't been able to get you out of my mind since our dinner. Would you meet me tomorrow?"

"I expect this project will take up all my time," Rika said. She slipped her hand out of his grip and adjusted her jumpsuit to steady herself. The breeze from the ocean, the scent of freshly turned earth in the flowerbeds and Sebastian's own scent underlying his cologne made her feel as though she'd made it to the calm center of a cyclone. Everything whirled violently around her.

"Everyone must eat," he said. She'd heard that before. "Let's have dinner together tomorrow."

"I'd like that," she admitted and bit her lip.

Sebastian wrapped his arm around her waist and pulled her close. His free hand drew her chin toward him, and he kissed her with more intensity than she'd expected.

This stranger was twice her age and had many times her experience, yet he'd stolen her heart. Rika caught herself. *Maybe he's affecting another organ, and it's a case of overactive hormones.*

Leading him back to the path, she walked silently, if slightly breathlessly beside him, but at a respectable distance. At the gates, she formally bowed to Sebastian in front of the guards. He gave her a wink and another brilliant smile as he left.

All the way back to the Bolsa complex, she ran her thumb across her lips and remembered. She had yet another memory to secret away to Jaa so that no one at IEC found out. Once she'd packed off the memory, she felt empty inside and a little nervous.

Inside the lab dressing room, the day team was changing to go home for the night and the night crew were just pulling on their lab coats. Almost as soon as Rika entered, Angela had her by the arm and was leading her down the corridor away from the others.

"You've come back too late," Angela said. "Go home. We need everyone in here early tomorrow, and I'll need you focused."

Angela released her grip on Rika's arm, and she added, "Director Wu and Vasil came by to speak to me about you. Vasil has recommended that we check you into his ward for observation."

"I don't want to go to the sick ward," Rika said, rubbing her arm.

"Vasil thinks you've had blackouts. He theorizes that these long periods of missing data from your IEC experience bank are due to either blackouts or hallucinations."

In answer, Rika simply shook her head in an emphatic "no," as in no she wasn't having blackouts, no she didn't want to go to the IEC ward or deal with Vasil — even if he had correctly diagnosed her, which he hadn't. *Blackouts?* She thought. *What an idiot!*

"Rika, I'd like you on this team until the end of the project, but I don't want your condition to deteriorate. I support your choice."

"I'm fine," Rika said, but she felt the blood drain from her face. Vasil had acted much more quickly than she expected. "Was my report helpful?"

"Yes. On another delicate topic, may I ask how you've come to know Master Sebastian of Domus Restitio?" Angela asked. The sudden tension in her stance and her furrowed brow made Rika wonder if Angela was jealous.

"You introduced us," Rika said, stepping back.

"Between you and me, I'd prefer that you avoid him," Angela said and closed the distance between them. The undertones in her voice struck Rika as something other than jealousy. Fear. Angela spoke in a low voice. "It'd be safer for both you and me."

"Safer?" Rika said. She'd come to expect Angela ordering her about at work, but never in her personal life. "I know it's preferred that we avoid dating clients, but I'm not on his project. Is that what worries you?"

"You heard me. Thinking about it, maybe it is better for you to go to the sick ward," Angela said and glanced away. Huifeng and a bunch of other exhausted team members streamed out of the lab's outer door. Huifeng glanced over at them and smiled. Angela smiled back. When she turned back to Rika, her smile vanished. "The director expects a lot from you, don't disappoint him more than you already have. I'll leave first."

Rika watched the tension apparent in Angela's stiff walk melt away as the boss met up with Huifeng, who immediately said something to make her laugh. Rika shook her head. Everyone who worked with Angela liked her. For Rika, Angela was ice and bitter cold, an endless winter the other Los Angelinos never experienced.

Her boss irritated her so much, Rika remained where she stood, closed her eyes and accessed Angela's private memories. She searched for discussions between Angela and Director Wu about her. The woman had been dismissive of Rika from day one because of her DeeJee status. Yet in a few generations, her boss would still be alive to see her own intellect lag far behind the newly modified embryos of 2150. If Angela was so smart, how could she not see that? Pursing her lips in disgust, Rika zeroed in on her boss's memories of meeting with the director from the point where they first mentioned Rika's name.

"Lost ones like Rika are youngsters from an era before proper genetic engineering controls were in place. Those were strange times," Mencius said. "One day we weren't allowed the slightest genetic modification of human DNA except for disease prevention, and the next it became a free-for-all."

Angela nodded. "Well, at least she's no chimera. Those human-animal hybrids were some of the most freakish results to come out of deregulation."

Rika winced at the comparison. Exploratory genetic modification of human embryos had brought mythological creatures to life with terrible consequences for the modified. They'd been treated as monsters. Even worse in the aftermath of these bizarre hybrids, animal diseases that no one had ever expected to jump to humans had caused terrible epidemics.

"Luckily, Rika represents a tiny percentage of those who fell through the cracks in her generation," her boss said.

"Let's be clear now," Mencius cautioned. "The Institute has increased her cognitive capacity and established a new relationship between the MAM and her mind, as we do with all our DeeJees who've successfully integrated into society for decades."

"My select team of scientists is the most productive at IEC," Angela said. "I'd like to keep it that way."

"Understood," Mencius said. "Rika and her two colleagues are the only Eye-47s anywhere in the universe. Because of their unique and unbounded MAM-human relationship, you may be pleasantly surprised by what Rika will achieve."

"Prior to the neural-knitting, all three Eye-47s proved too slow to compete with their peers in any field. They failed at everything they did," Angela said. "Is that correct?"

"Yes."

"These lost ones couldn't keep up with either their mended elders or their contemporaries," Angela said. "IEC isn't a charity. Wouldn't it be better to assign them to roof gardening, reception or other suitable areas instead of giving them false hope?"

"Absolutely not. That's why I developed the mind enhancements. I'm mended remember?" Mencius said. He enunciated clearly and slowed his speech.

"You qualified for mending because of your high IQ and your numerous contributions to society. These young people can't boast either."

Wu shrugged. "With cognitive boosting and the neural-knits, DeeJees find common ground with all quantum thinkers."

"Don't you find it tragic that quantums and the lost live side-by-side in the same era? We'll be paying for the dark age of genetic engineering until long after I die. Frankly, the Institute can't afford to take on these lost ones."

"You're wrong," he replied. "We have something to learn from everyone we meet. You have a lot to learn from Rika. She thinks differently from either of us. I find it refreshing."

Angela's grimace demonstrated she did not share the director's view. "We'll see about that. Since it's so important to you, I'll take this DeeJee onto my team," she said. "But don't expect me to agree to all your social experiments."

"I most certainly do expect just that," Wu said.

When Angela cursed him, Wu laughed. Rika shuddered. Unless scientists included empathy in their intelligent design of the human genome, no one alive today would stand a chance in their own futures — including Angela.

Jolted back to the corridor by hands on her shoulders and a rough shake, Rika opened her eyes to see Huifeng looking at her with concern. She realized that the scientist had been shaking her.

"Rika, are you all right?" her friend asked. Rika staggered forward from the force of Huifeng's shake. The other woman kept her from falling. "I thought we might walk home together so I waited for you outside, but you never left the building."

Using the sleeve of her jumpsuit, Huifeng wiped Rika's cheeks. Rika noticed she had tears running down her face. She groaned. Huifeng lived in Rika's building, and Rika welcomed her company. "Thanks for coming back to get me. I'm exhausted."

"Me, too," Huifeng said. "Let's go home."

It didn't take long for them to reach their turnip-shaped building, especially since Huifeng passed the time making Rika laugh by mimicking Lydia DeLydia's over-the-top attacks against the stars interviewed on *Goodbye Los Angeles Hello*, a show Huifeng secretly adored.

As soon as Rika had stretched out in her studio and let the room curl around her, she fell into a nightmare where a stranger kept shedding masks, each visage more terrifying than the last. He approached her with a knife. Medic Ng intruded into her dream.

<Rika Musashi Grant of the Institute of Extended Cognition? This is Medic Ng.>

Rika woke with a start. The medic had accessed Rika on a secure, family-emergency *For-Your-Eyes-Only* used in notifying next of kin.

<Yes?> Damp with sweat, Rika's nightshirt clung to her back as she sat up.

<I apologize for waking you at this early hour in the morning, but Yori desperately wants to speak with you. Naturally, that's impossible since he's in isolation.>

Rika switched to visuals and noticed that the circles under Ng's eyes had only gotten darker.

<I told Yori I'd contact you right away.>

<He's still recovering?>

<He was.>

Rika felt her heart skip a beat. After a long pause during which Rika waited impatiently for the medic to continue, Rika finally prompted Ng.

<You wanted to pass along a message from Yori.>

<He needs you to get a datasphere for him. He's been beaten and badly hurt. Someone interrogated him. We don't know who did it, because our usual MAM surveillance was disabled during the incident. I've issued a formal complaint demanding a hospital inquiry, but that

won't save Yori if he has as little time as he says to come up with this datasphere. These people got to him in a highly secured facility.>

<*What datasphere?*> Rika played dumb while she slipped on shorts and a shirt. She yanked on and laced up her organo-pumps.

<*I don't think he even knows, to be honest.*>

Rika watched Ng rub her eyes. <*How much time do we have, Medic Ng?*>

<*A couple of hours. It doesn't seem right to mix you up in this.*>

<*Tell Yori not to worry. Get him caramels. He loves those awful candies.*>

Ng grinned for the first time during their conversation before signing off.

After querying Prometheus in Jaa, the S.I. assured her he would notify her if the datasphere showed up for sale or in someone's mailbox. With Novus Orbis covered, she took a heliotaxi to Pasadena. During the ride, the only physical layouts Rika called up of the Sanctuary's OMM were sketchy at best and dated. Instead of accessing the Sanctuary via its main entrance, she used a URT entrance and went down to the Sanctuary's public library. It had a private, high security entrance to the OMM suites. The door was at the far end of the hall near the restrooms and furthest from the access points where library patrons sat or stood to enter Novus Orbis.

MAM security scanned her and gave her immediate access. Her plan to steal the datasphere out from under the thief Spider Zynx's nose went as far as gaining access to the OMM suites. She stifled a nervous giggle as she slipped inside. Here Rika had expected topnotch security, and it was so easy to enter.

Looking around, she found the OMM suites puzzling. Debris filled the room in precarious columns and large piles, with dubious caves leading into the darkness. A fine coat of dust covered every surface, and the odor of the stuffy, poorly ventilated room overwhelmed her. The pathways between the walls of sharp-edged, wiry junk might be dangerous to navigate unless she knew where she was headed. Every type of metal, wire, screw, pipe and blade jutted out from these bizarre collections of stuff.

Determined to avoid the caves, she took one step down the widest of the narrow pathways and then took another. The room and whatever lay beyond remained completely silent. She took another cautious step and inadvertently touched the thinnest of wires. The pile to the left of her made an ominous creaking sound and several pieces of old equipment slipped toward her.

She jumped back into the column on the right. It wavered above her for a moment and collapsed.

Everything fell on her at once. She screamed and covered her head with her arms hoping to avoid the blades so clearly visible on both sides. Bolts and pipes pummeled her arms and head. When the dust and debris settled, she had bruises everywhere and a bloody nose. Rika wiped away the blood with the back of her hand and looked around.

The debris had formed a cage of sorts around her, a cage with legs that lurched into motion following the same path she'd been on. It took her into the next room. Working to break through the sides while her prison moved won her only scratches and cuts to her hands. When the cage jolted to a halt, a Magi monk and four other men filed out from yet another cave beneath more junk.

Immediately, her gaze zeroed in on the last man out of the cave. He was very tall and had white spider tattoos that moved over his dark skin. She shivered. The datasphere pulsed red in the breast pocket of his tunic. Under the circumstances, it appeared unlikely that she'd sneak away with it. So, she did the next best thing.

"Spider Zynx!" she cried, holding her nose to slow the blood that ran down over her chin and dripped down her front.

Squeezing her nostrils gave her speech a nasal tone. "Helpz-me! I-beg-zyou-not-to-hawk-thatz-datasphere. I-payz-your-fee, whatever-itz-iz. My-friendz-life-dependz-upon-itz."

"What did she say?" the old man asked the others.

"Ochbo!" the spider-tattooed man said. "You've nearly killed this girl. She's bleeding everywhere and completely incoherent. What if she's suffered brain damage from all this junk falling on her? That's no security system."

"It most certainly is. The best available," the one addressed as Ochbo replied. "That bloody fox could slip by, in or through any MAM system. Not even an Order regular can open the library emergency door without setting off warnings. She just did. The woman before you is a true master, but even she can't get through arcane robotic byproduct. No one can."

Ochbo bowed low to her without making the slightest movement to help her out of her predicament. "This evening I saw Jaa in Seven Walls with my own eyes. Magnificent."

"Let her go." After cautiously searching for something around the room and not finding it, Spider approached the cage. He pulled his tunic over his head and stuffed it through the bars.

"Please use this to wipe off your face. My humble apologies that we have nothing better to offer you in this hellhole."

"I'm offended," Ochbo said.

Rika took the tunic and wiped her face and hands. Pressing it against her nose slowed the bleeding. She stared at Spider's front. *Is it just that he's so thin or does this weirdo have six-pack abs?*

Clearing her throat, Rika repeated herself, "Spider Zynx, I beg you not to hawk that datasphere. I'll pay your fee, whatever it is. My friend's life depends upon it."

This time they all looked at each other with puzzled faces. After checking her biostats, Spider spoke up first. "Rika of IEC, how is it possible that your friend's life depends upon this datasphere?"

"If I tell you, will you give it to me?"

"No. I've already promised it to someone else."

"What if I give you the decrypter you were searching for," Rika bartered. She didn't bother to hide her desperation, not because they had caught her in this odd contraption, but because she had to hurry back to the hospital. "That way, my friend's life will be saved in exchange for the datasphere, and you'll have the decrypter."

Spider turned to Ochbo. "Will you show me how to get her out of this thing? Even if she's a whiz at getting past security, it'd be hard for her to escape the five of us, don't you think?"

"I'm not so sure," Ochbo replied and pulled on his chin. "You know, Noah — I mean Spider — you assume the minister who you're giving the datasphere to has the decrypter. What if Ortega never got around to sending the decrypter to him? It might be a fair trade. We could give her a copy of the datasphere."

"Absolutely not. Remember, I've no idea what's on it." Spider turned to Rika, "If Ochbo frees you, do you promise on the honor of your Institute not to cut and run or steal the datasphere?"

Rika glared at him and then nodded. Ochbo snorted. "That's naïve. Do you think everyone has an allegiance to their work like you do to your domus? Just because we're identified by our jobs doesn't mean we align with them the way you domus people do."

Still, the OMM guru started clicking with his tongue in rapid succession. The DeeJee mapped the speed, volume and tone just in case she needed to free herself again anytime soon. The bars of the cage collapsed into rubble. She crawled out and away from it. When she stood, her back hurt so badly she realized how much damage she had suffered. Rika handed back the bloody shirt. Spider slipped it over his head. The bloodstains were already fading from the designer nanobreeze tunic.

"Okay," he said to Rika. "Say I did agree to giving you a copy, who is threatening your friend's life for it?"

"The Order," Rika admitted. "Or, at least someone in the Order."

"The Order?" said the one in a novice habit. He turned to Spider.

Before the other man could answer, the room shook from a heavy concussion that sent debris clattering to the floor and brought them to their knees.

CHAPTER 11

Noah struggled to his feet. His ears were ringing so loudly he could hear nothing else. Miraculously, the debris around them remained in place, as though only the vibration of a human foot against the floor would dislodge them. He helped Rika and Ochbo up while Jeremiah pulled Hrafn and J-yo to their feet. Once they were all standing, Ochbo gestured for them to follow him. Since neither Noah nor Rika had any idea how to avoid triggering his room traps, Ochbo mimed what they should do to avoid stepping on the pinhead-sized triggers. Noah nodded his understanding, and Rika followed suit.

Crouching down and entering the cave with the lowest clearance, Ochbo assumed the lead with Jeremiah, J-yo, Noah, and Rika following him. Hrafn took the rear. Noah had to bend low to keep from hitting his head against the false roofs of junk above him. They moved quickly through one cave and then another. Each cave re-organized after they passed through it. Caves became pathways leading to hidden doors that appeared for Ochbo and disappeared after Hrafn stepped through them.

Within minutes, they'd reached a stairwell and left the OMM suites. The rumblings of distant explosions shook the floor. At the stairwell, Ochbo barely paused before leading them downwards into Level Four, the deepest part of the Underground. Noah knew their pursuers couldn't tag them while they were down in an area that didn't have MAM coverage, but L-4 might as well have been the crawlspace between humanity and hell. Only addicts and hunted murderers were desperate enough to spend time there. The tunnels were often flooded with poisonous, bad air. He glanced back at Rika and saw her grim expression.

After jogging down three long tunnels, they passed one half-seen lurker and a snuffer snorting deep-glow wrigglies. Both ignored them. Ochbo brought them to a wall of ladders and chose one covered in a thick veil of cobwebs. They climbed rapidly, ascending past L-3 to L-2. When they cleared the tunnel edge near a URT entrance, Ochbo stopped, and they gathered around him. Noah wiped his face with his shirt and came away with a fistful of minute baby spiders that made him curse. Rika looked at him in surprise. He heard her voice as though she spoke through a blanket, "I thought you liked spiders."

"Hate them," he mouthed more than said, remembering too late that his MAM embrace showed white spider tattoos running up his arms. Ochbo tapped him on the shoulder to get his attention.

"My hearing is shot," Ochbo admitted. "I'll speak slowly so what you can't hear, you'll lip read. The Order has finally visited the OMM premises. I've waited all these years for a visit, and it's one I'll remember."

Addressing J-yo and Hrafn, Ochbo said, "We've practiced this drill plenty of times. Do *not* go say good-bye, even to a girl-friend. No stopping at your place to pick up things. Go directly to your safe houses. I'll be in touch."

When J-yo and Hrafn hesitated, Ochbo waved them off. Hrafn chose the opposite direction from J-yo, but they both left at a fast clip. Ochbo focused on Rika and Noah. "Rika, my gut says you're walking into a trap."

"I know," Rika said. "The Order must have followed me to the OMM figuring I'd lead them to the datasphere. Honestly, I didn't mean to hurt you. All I was thinking about was Yori."

"How could I entrust the datasphere to such a clueless woman?" Noah asked Ochbo and Jeremiah. "She brought the Order directly to us."

Rika's hands curled into fists, as she stared, not a Noah pre-cisely, but at his breast pocket where he'd placed the datasphere.

"With their over-the-top response to my security system, it will take the regulars a long time to clear out the rubble and figure out they didn't kill anyone. Besides, now the Order has gone up against the Sanctuary. No one should do that lightly," Ochbo said. "Rika, I suggest we part company unless you—"

Rika surprised Ochbo into speechlessness with a sudden hug. Next she threw her arms around Jeremiah. Noah felt a tinge of jealousy — absurd under the circumstances, he knew — that she chose his brother first. Finally, she reached her arms up and Noah bent down to give her a hug.

Instead, before Noah understood what Rika was up to, she was sprinting past him toward the URT entrance without looking back.

"She must try to save her friend," Ochbo said. "My fear is they'll both end up dead."

For being so small, she had speed. Noah gave her that. He could no longer see her in the tunnel. He glanced down and grabbed his pocket.

"The datasphere! It's gone!" Noah said. He dashed after her. If the senator's data fell into the wrong hands, Noah had no idea what would happen.

"She's headed for the Ecumenical Union Center Hospital in Santa Monica," Ochbo yelled after him.

During her URT ride to the EUC hospital, Rika saved a copy of the datasphere to Jaa City. She also researched the unregistered MAM embraces of Emmett and Spider Zynx. Although she failed to find out who they really were, she learned how to create her own unregistered MAM embrace. Rika wondered how they'd discovered such complex, clever workarounds.

Several times she startled a nearby passenger when she became first an unregistered centaur, then a tall blonde and finally settled into a MAM embrace that disguised her as a fifteen-year-old boy named Simic. The passenger rubbed his eyes, checked and rechecked his temperature. Rika wanted to assume the identity of Yori's younger brother, but unregistered MAM embraces for existing people failed her every time so she settled on a composite. Unfortunately, it chafed against her skin. By the time she arrived at the hospital, she could barely wait to remove it.

Inside the hospital entrance, attendants escorted family members to visit with those stricken by Circle Tide and confined to the isolation wards. Rika marched straight up to the front desk. The burly receptionist deliberately cleaned his fingernails and ignored her until she coughed hard. The receptionist stood so fast his chair slammed up against the back of his cube.

"Are you sick, young man?" the receptionist asked Rika.

"No, I just got something caught in the back of my throat. Thanks for asking," Rika said. "I'm here to see a patient in Isolation, Yori of the Institute of Extended Cognition."

"Are you his next of kin?" the receptionist asked. He sat back down with an exaggerated yawn.

"No," Rika said. "I'm with the IEC and here to check on his progress. Yori is supposed to transfer to the IEC sick ward."

Barely stirring, the functionary blinked through several interfaces before he reached Yori's file. It was as though the slower he dealt with one person's request, the more likely it was that another receptionist would magically appear and deal with everyone else's demands in the crowded reception area. Rika bit her lip to keep from saying something she'd regret.

"Are you a close friend of this patient?" the receptionist asked. He cleared his throat uneasily and pulled on his collar as though it'd suddenly become too tight. When Rika received notification that the awkward man had checked "Simic's" bio-stats, she tensed.

"Yes, I'm a friend," Rika said. "Why?"

"Simic, I'm terribly sorry to be the one to tell you this," the receptionist said. "Yori passed away earlier today."

"There must be some mistake," said Rika and slumped against the counter. "I still have a quarter hour before I need to be here."

"Excuse me?" the receptionist said. "We have grief counselors if you'd like to speak with one."

"I must see Yori," Rika said. She stood up straight and stared him in the eye until he looked away.

"Only next of kin are allowed—" the receptionist began.

"I declare work-of-origin," Rika said, cutting him off. She closed one eye and scrolled through hospital regs, which clearly stated that as long as no family member identified the deceased, a representative from his/her workplace could do so.

"Look, his family hasn't been notified yet," the receptionist said. "You'll have to wait twenty-four hours."

"All right then," Rika said. "I'd like to speak to Medic Ng."

The receptionist stared at her for a moment and then contacted the medic. Rika fought back tears. The man's movements had sped up, making it clear he wanted to be done with this awkward situation.

"My apologies, Simic. Medic Ng has taken a sabbatical. She won't return to the hospital for at least a month."

"Since when?" Rika asked.

"Since ... Since today in fact," the receptionist said. He raised his eyebrows.

"Medic Ng is taking an unscheduled sabbatical in the midst of a citywide emergency?" Rika said, her voice rising.

"It appears so," replied the receptionist. He looked past Rika. "Would you mind stepping aside? People are waiting."

Inclining her head in courtesy to the people behind her, she left. Outside, she climbed up onto the granite wall that formed the garden entrance to the hospital. On the opposite side of the wall, the ground rose in a small hill with bushes. Beyond that, the hospital campus sprawled. She shifted over a little so she had a clear view of the reception area and contacted Medic Ng in Novus Orbis.

<Medic Ng, I have the datasphere.> Rika checked her time and had a few minutes to spare before Ng's deadline. *<I'm not too late, am I?>*

<Rika, nonsense, are you at the hospital?>

<Yes, I'm in reception.>

<Terrific, I'll come meet you. Stay where you are, Rika.>

A minute later, Rika saw an Order regular sitting unnoticed among the families abruptly stand up and walk around the reception area. He clearly searched for someone, and he paused to ask the receptionist a question. The receptionist shook his head.

So it was a trap! Rika thought. Someone had gotten to the woman.

<Rika?> Ng's voice trembled, but she didn't provide Rika a visual of herself.

<Yes?> Rika answered.

<I'm at the main entrance, but I don't see you. Are you sure you're at the main entrance to the hospital?>

<I think so, but I don't see you, either.> Rika said. She queried the names of everyone in reception and Medic Ng was not among them. And then, Rika pushed the medic a little further to find out what she'd say. *<I'm confused. I just asked the receptionist about Yori, and she told me Yori had died.>*

<We have one female receptionist in the West Wing entrance. You're not at the main entrance. That's an odd logistical mistake for a DeeJee to make.>

The Order regular turned around slowly scanning the room. Finally, he glanced through the glass doors and noticed Rika perched on the wall outside. Leaping through the doors, he checked *Simic's* biostats, cursed and went back inside. A moment later, Rika slipped over the other side of the wall and jumped down behind the bushes. Hidden in the foliage, Rika deactivated the MAM embrace.

<*Rika, you're not at the West Wing entrance. Is it the East Wing? How is it possible no one can locate you?*> Ng's voice had risen to a shrill, desperate pitch.

<*Tell me what happened to Yori.*> Rika's demand met only silence, but she had managed to trigger Ng's memories, which is what she wanted. Leaning against the cool wall under cover of the bushes, Rika let the MAM engage all her senses as she entered Ng's memory event.

Hands clenched in her lap, Ng sat in the darkness of the visitor's booth, which contrasted the harsh light from Yori's isolation capsule room. A woman sat beside her, but Rika could not see her face.

"Your job is to revive him," the woman beside Ng said. "He's gone into shock."

"You set the Life Sustainer to flay my patient. That's his skin on the edge of the bed. Understandably, he's in shock," Ng said. Her monotone made it sound like she herself had gone into shock. "Stuffing the bed sheet into his mouth so he couldn't scream may suffocate him."

"Make no mistake. This is a dangerous man. We need to find out what classified information he laid his hands on and what he did with it. Revive him," the woman replied. The torturer had a gravelly, familiar voice. "You realize I don't have to explain myself to you."

"No," Ng said. "Just to your gods if you have any. I revived him once following your first session. After this, I'm not certain I can do anything to save him."

"Just get him conscious. I don't care about saving him."

Rika tried to discover the torturer's identity, but Ng never checked the woman's biostats or looked her in the eye. Ng stared at Yori. Through Ng's lens, Rika stared at Yori, too. He convulsed violently in front of them and then lay still.

After checking his biostats, Ng closed her eyes and told the woman beside her, "You've killed him."

The palms of her hands — when the torturer grabbed and slapped Ng with enough force that Ng fell from her stool into the booth wall — were as soft as velvet. Even then, Rika never got a real glimpse of the torturer, but she'd never forget those hands.

"Contact the DeeJee who visited Yori," the woman ordered Ng. "Maybe she's in on it with him."

After searching for Rika, Noah became suspicious of the young guy's antics. At first, the teenager appeared to be playing some sort of trick on a hospital receptionist and an Order regular. When he jumped off the wall and disappeared from view, his small, lithe build reminded Noah so much of Rika that he took a closer look. While the Order regular was busy talking to the receptionist and two more Order regulars arrived, Noah climbed over the wall and jumped down into the bushes. He nearly landed on Rika who sat huddled against the wall.

Startled, she cried out. Noah put his hand over her mouth. "Careful, they're looking for you."

"Figures ... what are you doing here?" Rika asked.

"I'm protecting the senator's data."

"You'll be happy to know I didn't give it to them," Rika said. Her face contorted for a moment. "It was no use. They'd already killed Yori."

He bent down beside her, but her spine-chilling glance kept him from saying how sorry he was about her friend. Her wild blue hair had fallen over her eyes. Noah resisted smoothing it back.

"We need to leave," Noah said. He could hear the Order regulars on the other side of the wall.

Noah offered Rika his hand, which she ignored. She got up rather shakily and dusted the twigs and dead leaves from her backside. As they left the bushes and headed toward a hospital path that would lead to the closest URT entrance, two Order regulars climbed over the wall and jumped down into the bushes where Rika had just been. The two fugitives bolted for the entrance.

"That's her! Over there!" yelled a third regular, struggling to climb over the wall. He shouted at his two colleagues below, "They're headed for the URT."

As fast as Rika and Noah sprinted for the entrance, the regulars gained on them. In the shadow of the Underground, Rika tugged on the fly gamer's arm. "Distract them. I'll close down the entrance, but you'll have to hold them off until the last moment."

Noah nodded. Rika pointed to the teeth of the enormous gate high above them. "When that comes down, you'll have only seconds to get to this side."

"I'll do what I can," Noah said and turned to face the Order regulars. He felt an adrenaline rush from his feet up. Once they'd drawn their glock-gokus, he wouldn't stand a chance.

Before the nearest one could pull a weapon, Noah launched himself at him. They grappled. The third Order regular showed up with his glock-goku drawn and knocked the second one out of his line of fire, yelling, "Follow the girl. She's getting away." The man immediately fired on Noah, but the gamer was already swinging the first regular around. Noah felt the edges of the glock-goku's force, but the regular absorbed it. As the spasming man hit the ground, his hold on Noah relaxed, and Noah bounded up and out of the other regulars' path. Both bent over their colleague as he convulsed. At that moment, Noah heard a mechanical grinding noise from overhead. The gate gears were turning, and the great barrier was rapidly descending. Noah cursed and flung himself to the ground, rolling over twice to pass through the narrowing gap just before the teeth locked into place between him and the Order.

Springing to his feet, Noah sprinted after Rika down the tunnel to the nearest URT platform. Once there, they waded into the crowd. Rika clung to his side. This time, he felt her return the datasphere to his pocket. As the crowd grew, Noah heard complaints among the commuters that they had to wait for the next train because this URT exit had closed without warning.

"I have no idea how you activated that gate," Noah whispered to her. "Honestly, I could use your help at the Ministry of Internal Affairs."

"Just who are you beneath that MAM embrace?"

"It's so obvious I'm wearing one?"

"Yes. Who are you?"

"Do you really want to know?" He weighed being honest and revealing his identity to her against his own safety.

"Yes."

"I'm Noah of Domus Aqua."

Her eyes widened. She stepped back. The way Rika looked at him she might as well have said, "You murderer!"

Before he could say anything in his defense, Rika leapt off the URT platform and ran down the tunnel in the same direction from which the train would soon arrive. Internally, he cringed. Outwardly, he smiled so that the people pointing at her and looking in shock from her to him might assume she knew what the heck she was doing. He hoped she did. She had just risked a head-on with an oncoming train to avoid him.

Once he'd delivered the datasphere to the Minister of Internal
Affairs, he told himself, he'd find Rika and make sure she was
all right.

CHAPTER 12

With only seconds to spare and the roar of the oncoming train growing louder, Rika sprinted down the tunnel toward the next platform. The vibrations from the floor of the tunnel reverberated through her. She spied the ladders that were set into the wall at regular intervals, and scrambled up and into the service tunnel above the URT.

As soon as she poked her head up into the service tunnel, hands clutched her hair and arms. Two men hauled her off the ladder and onto the tunnel floor. One of them wrapped her hair around his fist and yanked hard.

"You'll pull my hair out!" Rika yelled, but the train drowned her out. Held down on her back in the tunnel, Rika recognized the two Order regulars from whom she'd just escaped. Cursing, she kicked furiously.

Landing several blows to their legs and arms resulted in the bigger regular sitting on her. He slapped her hard across the face, wrenching her neck to the side. Rika moaned.

"Shut up," he said and slapped her a second time. Her cheeks stung, but her neck hurt worse. Unable to stop herself, Rika moaned again. His weight on her stomach and diaphragm made breathing difficult.

"Although I'd prefer you unconscious, I refuse to lug you out of here," the regular said. "So, we can keep this up until we break a few bones and every step you take causes you pain. Or, you can stop fighting us and cooperate."

In response, Rika let her body go slack.

"That's a good girl," the regular said. He stood with her beneath him. Unable to resist, Rika brought both legs up to her chest and whipped them back out and up with as much force as she could muster. With a groan, the man toppled forward on top of her. She rolled out from under him. The other regular came at her. The larger-than-life shadow of his fist flying across the tunnel wall toward her head was the last thing she saw.

When Rika regained consciousness, she found she could do little more than move her head. Blood pounded in her temples. Her face and neck ached. Her eyes wide open, she made out a table in the darkness. She sat slumped in a chair with her hands in her lap. For some reason, she couldn't move her hands or legs. Everything below the neck had been immobilized. Querying the MAM for answers began and ended in one word: lockdown. The letters scrawled across her vision in fanciful font as though someone found her query funny.

Otherwise, the DeeJee had no access to the MAM — not to her stored memories or anyone else's — nor any data or communications. The most active part of her brain had been walled off. Rika lifted her head up and cracked her neck to ease the pain.

Harsh lights flashed on. Rika blinked, adjusting to the brightness. She sat at a metal table at the center of a small windowless room with one door. An empty chair sat across the table from her. The room felt dead, more like a laboratory than a living building. No scents beckoned to her. No images played across the stark white walls.

The door slid back, and an officer entered. The pose of the crane on the insignia on the woman's lapel told Rika that the officer ranked as a captain in the Order. Tall and slim, the woman had white-blonde hair, gray eyes as cold as steel and a smile that never reached beyond the curl of her lips. Rika experienced a strong physiological response to her entrance; damp palms and a sudden dry mouth. *How do I know her?* Rika thought. Without access to the MAM, she could not call up her conscious memory, but some part of her psyche knew the Order captain and responded with animal fear.

The captain sat down opposite her. Rika's mouth felt parched while sweat trickled down between her breasts and down her sides. Her heart beat fast. If only she could move more than her neck and head, she might overpower this officer and find an escape route. Also, she needed more to work with than the buffered memories of the previous eight hours, recorded in such fine and useless detail that she could give the precise intervals of the tattoos moving across Noah the Spider's arms. Rika queried the biostats of the ice queen sitting silently across from her and received the same message: lockdown. This time it appeared to Rika in red bold font. Someone was toying with her.

The captain bared her teeth in a simulated grin and said, "It's no use. You have zero access to the MAM here. Novus Orbis might as well be as far away from you as Mars."

She received notification that I checked her biostats. MAM access exists here. Only I'm blocked.

"This is the first time you've been restrained," the ice queen said, studying her, as though Rika had the traits of some interesting bug about to be squashed. "You suffer high levels of anxiety."

Yes, you evil witch! I can't move my arms and legs. Paralysis tends to scare people. Nothing's visibly restraining me. That means something, some MAM subsystem must be in operation to block my motor skills. Rika stared silently at the captain and willed her to keep talking. She might just learn enough from this blonde freak to escape.

"Since your DeeJee enhancements, every action you take, everything you see is recorded and sent to IEC archives. Are you too stupid to realize that we have direct access to your experiences?" asked the officer.

The captain reached over the table with both hands and cupped Rika's face. It looked like such a gentle gesture, but the woman pressed her velvety soft palms hard against Rika's swollen battered cheeks. Tears streamed down Rika's face. Helpless to pull away from her, Rika bit her tongue to keep from crying out under the officer's vice grip.

Satisfied with the tears, the captain released Rika and sat back slowly. The pure enjoyment that flitted across the ice queen's face made Rika wince. More than was normal for any law enforcer or military officer, this person delighted in her job. Rika had to respond warily, or she might just end up dead.

"You have neither the datasphere nor its decrypter. Why did you pretend to Medic Ng that you did?" the captain asked. The cat had cornered its mouse.

Rika's mind raced. The Order had no clue about her copy of the datasphere and decrypter. That meant Jaa City remained safe. Also, it implied she'd successfully rerouted her memories without causing suspicion. This woman gave out good information. Rika bit her lip to hide her satisfaction.

"I asked you a question," the captain said.

"I wanted to save Yori," Rika croaked and tried to swallow. "Medic Ng told me Yori's life would be saved if I came up with a datasphere."

"So you know its location," the captain said and leaned forward. "You went to the OMM headquarters because Yori and the OMM were collaborating. Right?"

"No, Yori had nothing to do with the OMM or any datasphere," Rika said, careful not to mention Noah. After all, the connection between Noah the Spider and the OMM remained a puzzle. Rika wanted to avoid any association with the senator's murderer or the stolen datasphere. That would only make more trouble for her.

"I wanted the OMM to locate the datasphere for me," Rika explained. "In the Heartland, OMMers have always been known for retrieving lost data."

A loud commotion outside the door brought the captain to her feet. The door shuddered, as though someone had been slammed against its other side. Multiple shouts were followed by a prolonged hush. The captain approached the door. While the officer was distracted, Rika focused on whatever restraint held her arms and legs immobilized. Her mind drifted over her captor who maintained MAM access and remained unfettered. She focused on the subtle differences between her person and her interrogator. An access point had to exist. Momentarily forgotten by the captain, Rika relaxed a little so that her enhanced neural-knits were open to the MAM's omnipresence. Almost immediately, she felt its first minute tug. Like a magnet, the MAM drew her toward it.

Help me! Rika invoked the MAM. She envisioned the block on her motor skills as tendrils disentangling themselves from her cerebellum and floating away. Her fingers twitched. Rika shifted slightly in her chair, and her eyes lit up.

Oblivious, the blonde put her ear against the door. She jumped back, drew her glock-goku and positioned herself to one side. Instead of sliding back, the door abruptly buckled inward, and three men fell into the room. Having regained her MAM access, Rika immediately recognized the man who stepped in coolly after them.

"Master Sebastian?" the captain said. She lowered her weapon.

Sebastian ignored the officer. He rushed to Rika, pushing aside the table. The DeeJee, now free of the MAM blockage, stood up. The ice queen gasped and said to him in an accusing tone, "You let her go. What's wrong with you?"

To Rika, Sebastian said, "Let's get out of here."

He took her hand. The three men stationed themselves around Sebastian and her. They had weathered, grim faces and surprised Rika by how much space they filled. She wondered where Sebastian had found this team of thugs.

The captain had eyes only for Sebastian. "I don't know what you think you're up to, but that DeeJee is a suspect."

"Then formally arrest her," Sebastian said. The woman's steely eyes narrowed in response. "Otherwise, I'm taking her with me. What you're doing here is inhuman."

"Really?" the captain sputtered, but before she could continue Sebastian rushed on.

"Rika is essential to solving the Circle Tide case. Her team lead thinks so. Director Wu agrees. Good day, Captain Lynnfield."

The captain blocked the broken doorway. "Your antics end here. Consider this your only warning. If any of my men are seriously injured, I'll see to it that you suffer tenfold."

In response, Sebastian beamed his megawatt smile and strode forward so that the woman had to jump out of the way to keep him and his men from mowing her down. As they left, the blonde's eyes shifted to Rika. The officer mouthed, "You're dead," as the DeeJee passed.

Sebastian held tightly to Rika's hand as they stepped over the mangled door and into the hallway. The two Order regulars who'd attacked her in the tunnel were lying on the floor. One raised a hand above his head in weak self-defense when he saw Sebastian, but the other lay still. Sebastian kept moving. Glad to be free of the captain and her men, Rika let him guide her down the hallway and up several flights of stairs to the first floor.

When Rika recognized they were on the main level of the silver-bullet building on the IEC campus, she pulled her hand away. "I had no idea a place like that existed at the Institute."

"It doesn't, not formally. This used to be a military establishment," Sebastian said. "Knowing Lynnfield, I guessed where you'd be."

"Captain Lynnfield," Rika said. With access to the MAM, she had regained access to her memory events. Lynnfield had demanded the samples from Yori. She'd also enlisted Rika's help on the sample analysis in return for promising to have Yori transferred to the Institute sick ward and helping Rika retain her

DeeJee position. Two lies. Rika knew for certain never to trust the officer.

Accessing the MAM, Rika queried the secret room in which she'd woken up. No Institute schematics gave any hint of its existence. The domus, the government and the military were notorious for their secret rooms. Love trysts, backroom deal-making and interrogations went on without any record that they'd occurred, and usually ended badly for someone. This time, that someone had almost been her.

"I thought Angela was scary, but she doesn't have anything on that ice queen," Rika said. Sebastian glanced down at her with a puzzled look as they headed out into the fresh air. "Er, I mean the captain."

"Are you involved in this datasphere business?" Sebastian asked. When Rika hesitated, Sebastian held up his hand. "Never mind. Tell me later. I'd like to borrow you for a while if you don't mind going off campus."

"Angela needs me on the case."

"Yes, but not necessarily in the lab," Sebastian said. His assuredness demonstrated he'd already cleared it with her boss. "I'd like to show you several sites contaminated with Circle Tide and see if you discover anything others have missed."

"Honestly, I'd prefer be out in the field," Rika said. "Working in the Bolsa complex right now would be almost impossible for me. I always thought of it as Yori's lab."

"I was sorry to hear that he passed away. At least he received the best care possible at the hospital," Sebastian said. An odd, intense expression crossed his face.

Ng's memory event of Yori's torture sprang to mind. Rika tripped over her own feet and sprawled flat on the pathway, skinning her knees and elbow. Sebastian lifted her up and carried her. Somehow his concern allowed all the anxiety and loss she'd held back to claim her. Hiding her face in his tunic, she sobbed. At the Domus Restitio heliovan, one of Sebastian's men hopped into the driver's seat. Another sat upfront while she slid in back. The biggest among them nudged in beside her while Sebastian took the other side. Rika felt comforted by their presence.

Still, her mental replay of Yori's convulsions, of his skin hanging off the bed rendered her speechless. By the time the heliovan lifted into the air, Rika sent Ng's deliberately recorded memory event to Jaa City so that it wouldn't be erased. The passenger in front handed Sebastian a medical bag. He opened it and scanned her face and head. After several painful pricks across her swollen face, she felt the pressure on the left side of her face ease.

"Thank you, Sebastian, for everything," she said and smiled up at him.

Fatigue caught up with her, and she rested her head against his arm. As soon as she closed her eyes, Noah the Spider popped into her mind. The irritating, bizarrely tattooed man preoccupied her. She couldn't shake the sense that he might be in danger. No one should ever suffer Yori's fate, even Noah the Spider. Rika shuddered.

"Why do I care?" Rika realized she had spoken the thought out loud. The man beside her glanced over at his boss.

"Pardon me?" Sebastian said. He touched the back of his hand to her forehead and checked her biostats. His breath smelled of cinnamon, her favorite spice. Kissable. "Your temperature is above normal. Why don't we drop you off at home and begin work tomorrow?"

Rika nodded.

Disguised as Spider Zynx, Noah walked past Order regulars on the street and they never noticed. However, to gain access to the ministry in an unregistered MAM embrace would be impossible. The Order would arrest him. Ordinary citizens only entered the Ministry of Internal Affairs on official business. He had to find another way.

In a café around the corner from the Ministry of Internal Affairs, the fly gamer settled into a private booth. Noah accessed the directory of ministry employees working for Gothardi Lotte and researched their backgrounds. He hit on a useful tidbit. Lotte had a newly hired, young aide on his staff. Interestingly, she happened to be a second cousin of his brother Daniel's wife. Her name was Gigi of Domus Superna.

After some strategizing, Noah contacted the young aide and was surprised when she immediately responded. Her dark short hair and smoky eyes were striking.

"Spider Zynx? Did somebody put you up to this?" she asked. Her high, chirpy voice clashed with her sultry looks. "I already told him that I'm not available for any more blind dates."

"Sorry, this isn't about a blind date. I'm the new alternate driver for Minister Gothardi Lotte."

"Who says?" she asked.

"I'm self-appointed," Noah said. He worried he'd overdone the sarcastic tone, and she'd check his biostats. If she did, she'd discover he'd told the truth and had appointed himself a driver unbeknownst to anyone else, but Gigi simply laughed.

"You're a funny guy."

"Hey look, I'm supposed to pick the minister up to take him across town. He hasn't shown up," Noah said.

"You've got the wrong day, Spider. You won't last long with Goth if you mess up his appointments. That's one thing that makes him go nuts," Gigi said. It sounded as though she spoke from experience.

"What makes you so sure I have the wrong day?"

"Because, silly," she said and winked. "Everybody on staff knows that Tuesday and Thursday noon 'til 14:00 are reserved for Lady Whisk-Away."

"Lady Whisk-Away?" Noah said. "You mean the courtesan?"

"Around here," Gigi said, "we call her the spank diva, but not in front of the Minister. He must be one of her most frequent patrons. Between you and me though, I think he goes there less for the spanks than for confidential intel on her other clients."

"Do you have the address?" Noah asked. "He'll want me to pick him up."

"Forget it. He takes the URT, and it's only one stop from here. No driver necessary."

"I'd like the address."

"Can't you see the other drivers are setting you up? You'll get fired if you show up there."

"I might get fired if I don't," Noah pressed.

"Fine. Here," she said, giving in and sending him the address. "But don't say I didn't warn you."

"Much appreciated," Noah said. "Sounds like I should have a heart-to-heart with my colleagues."

"They're messing with you just like the staff did with me. Let me know if you want to go out sometime," she said and ended the contact.

Finding Lady Whisk-Away should have been easy. Noah had an address. But with a half hour left before 14:00, the gamer still hadn't found the place. His last chance to hand over the data-sphere to Minister Lotte, before the Order closed in on him, was fast disappearing. For the umpteenth time, the MAM brought him to the same narrow archway above an alley that led to the trash epicures and grease refinery, fed by the two cafes on either side. Unless Gigi had confused the address, this was Lady

Whisk-Away's exact location. It didn't look much like the premises of a high-class courtesan.

Perhaps a discreet, hidden entrance existed. Noah walked down to the far end of the alleyway. He edged behind the silver-encased epicures inside which optimizing microbes silently gobbled trash. The epicures stank so badly Noah gagged and retreated to the archway. The high buildings cast the alley in shadow. He deactivated his MAM embrace in preparation for meeting the minister and waited, hoping Lotte would appear somewhere along this stretch of street so that he could intercept him.

To his left, Café V sported a multi-tiered veranda of bulbous living architecture — part thriving bark, part stone — where the staff served people milky drinks. Upon the clients' first sips, Noah observed their drinks turn the hue of their clothing: swirling green, rich mahogany, tangerines and purple-blues. Their eyes shone gold when they noticed him watching them. *This is just the sort of trendy place Beatrice would frequent*, Noah thought.

To his right, Café X's outdoor patio served gastronomical delights, narrow, wavering and delicately stacked on glass plates. The closest dish to him looked like blue mushrooms with the thinnest slices of steaming, succulent meat. Rika's wild hair and tiny figure suddenly supplanted his image of Beatrice.

What's happening to me? Noah thought. The garbage odors had left him queasy and light-headed. A feminine voice whispered nearby, "Kee-kee, kee-kee," like nails on glass. She asked him, "You want your whisk-away?"

He glanced around and turned back toward the alleyway. No one. The whispers sent icy chills up his spine. Somebody tapped him on the arm. He spun around.

"Whoa. You stink," Rika said, moving away from him. She wrinkled her nose. His mouth fell open. Noah reached out and touched her shoulder. Staring up at him with a vexed expression, Rika asked, "What's wrong with you?"

"I was worried I'd imagined you," Noah said. His heart pounded in his throat.

"You're better looking without those spider tattoos," Rika said, squeezing her nose shut.

"How did you find me?" he asked.

"I searched for the minister," Rika said. "I'd get flagged if I searched for you. Besides, Order regulars would show up as soon as I found you."

"That damnable, elusive minister," Noah said with a grin.

"Right now, you're the only one who is interested in the minister's location. If I found Gothardi Lotte, I knew I'd find you."

"So he *is* here, somewhere," Noah said. Relief washed over him.

"He was," she corrected him. "He entered Café V a couple hours ago, but just left via Café X's side entrance and is headed back toward the URT—"

Without waiting for Rika to finish her sentence, Noah sprinted out of the archway. He raced around the side of Café X. Up ahead of him, Noah glimpsed the minister who was headed toward the URT entrance. Winding his way through the crowd, Noah almost caught up with Goth. But then, Lotte disappeared into the URT entrance, oblivious of the gamer's pursuit.

At the edge of Noah's peripheral vision, a blur of blue sailed by him. Rika's cotton-candy hair bobbed up and down in the crowds while she leveraged her organo-pumps off anything that quickened her pace, which included pedestrians. The DeeJee left a string of cursing people in her wake. Noah bolted into the URT entrance, down the escalator and into the tunnel. Moments later, he caught up to Rika standing over the Minister of Internal Affairs. Lotte sat sprawled out on the tunnel floor dabbing at a bloody nose. Noah gathered that Rika had barreled into the man on purpose. Noticing Noah, the DeeJee took him by the arm and pulled him down beside the minister. She quickly stepped aside and kept an eye on the crowd. Noah took his chance before the Order arrived. With this spectacle of a mowed-down minister, Noah's time had definitely run out.

"I — I'm sorry to approach you like this, Minister Lotte, but Senator Ortega's dying wish was that I give you this datasphere," Noah said. He was fumbling in his breast pocket for the locket that held the datasphere.

"No, no, no," Lotte said. The man curled up in a ball and refused to make eye contact. One leg twitched nervously. "I won't take that. The datasphere belongs in the hands of the Order and so do you, Noah of Domus Aqua."

"Okay," Noah said and glanced up at Rika who stared at the minister in astonishment. "The Order is welcome to the data-sphere, if that's what you want, but the senator wanted you to review it. I assume the datasphere has information that is relevant to Internal Affairs."

"Are you trying to get me killed? Or do you just want to ruin my career?" Lotte asked so softly it sounded more like a series of hisses.

"Minister," Noah said, taking Lotte by the shoulders and forcing the man to look him in the eyes. "I have no idea what's on it, but Mari Ortega was my friend, and it was her dying wish that I deliver this to *you*. She made me promise on the honor of my domus, so like it or not, Minister, I'm leaving this datasphere in your hands."

"I won't take it," Lotte said. Perspiration dripped down the sides of his face. The man was clearly terrified, and at any other time, Noah might have taken pity on him. Instead, the fly gamer felt a surge of anger.

"If you don't take it, I'll make you swallow it," Noah said. He gripped the man's jaw in one hand, but Rika caught and held his other fist.

"It's over," Rika said. She yanked his tunic hard enough that it ripped in her hands, but Noah remained determined. Implacable as stone, Noah's grip tightened around the man's jaw.

"You've honored your promise, Noah," Rika pleaded. "Let's get out of here."

Instead of stuffing the locket down Lotte's throat, Noah released the man's jaw and shoved the datasphere into the bureaucrat's pocket. In response, the man dug it out with a shaky hand and tossed it onto the tracks. Seconds later, the train arrived. Roaring a curse, Noah punched the man in the gut.

"Is this what Senator Ortega wanted?" Rika asked.

Noah rounded on her, and the world went crimson for a moment. Then, her words sank in, and he staggered backwards. "No, no, never."

CHAPTER 13

Synchronized footsteps of boots slapping stone echoed across the cavernous URT tunnel. Noah had lingered too long, despite Rika's pleas. With their glock-gokus drawn, Order regulars surrounded the two fugitives. Minister Lotte remained slumped against the wall between them.

"The two of you: down on the ground, hands on your heads!"

Rika complied. An Order regular kicked Noah in the back of the knees and he landed on the ground beside her. Minutes passed. No one in the tense semicircle of uniforms and weapons moved. Noah remained frozen, too, resisting the temptation to scratch the ferocious itch that had developed in his nose. His foot, pinned underneath his opposite leg, fell asleep. Needling pains shot up his leg. Still, Noah refused to shift his weight and give them an excuse to hijack him. Staring from the tunnel floor past the hyper-muscular regulars, he saw the panicked crowd of commuters quickly dwindling. The dusty boots and wrinkled leggings of these sorry representations of authority put him in mind of an old-fashioned firing squad. He glanced over at Rika without moving his head, blaming himself for getting the pipsqueak cornered in the Underground without witnesses and limited MAM surveillance. This could turn very ugly — permanently ugly — for both of them.

From down the platform, an officer marched toward them. The regulars deferred to him, making way for the officer to assess the captives. The man's lapel glinted with multiple medals of honor; Noah took hope from that. His rank insignia was a crane poised on one foot beside a crescent of three more cranes in flight that signified a major.

The officer ignored Rika and Noah, but knelt beside the minister. Noah queried his biostats: Major Fingrif, with twenty-five years of service and five honorable citations. While the major had a wiry medium build, his hard-set jaw and calm assuredness gave him a larger-than-life aspect.

"Are you able to stand, Minister Lotte?" Major Fingrif asked. When the bureaucrat nodded, the officer lifted him to his feet. "I'd like a formal statement from you if you're up for it."

"That's Noah of Domus Aqua," the minister said, needlessly pointing. He adjusted his collar and then patted his wisps of hair back into place. "As I understand it, he's wanted for murder. However, I have no intention of giving a statement."

In response, Fingrif tilted his head and scratched his temple for a while as though he'd been working out a puzzling math problem and arrived at the wrong answer.

"I'd be more than happy to give a statement about what brought me here and what happened last Sunday night," Noah said. He kept his voice quiet and low.

In one rapid step, Fingrif reached him. "Let's get something straight. I don't care what domus you belong to, how rich you are, or whose son you happen to be, you'll only speak when I ask a question. Is that clear?"

"Yes, sir," Noah said. He stole a glance at Rika, but her eyes were closed.

Next the major bent down in front of Rika and rested his hand on her shoulder. Startled by his touch, her eyes opened wide.

"Whatever you're doing in Novus Orbis, young lady, I suggest you stop," Fingrif advised.

She nodded and bit her lip. When her gaze shifted beyond the major, she visibly trembled. Noah followed her line of sight. Another Order officer and two regulars had arrived.

"Thank you, major," Captain Lynnfield announced, "I'm taking these three into custody."

Strikingly good-looking and tall, the blonde simply pushed the drawn glock-gokus out of her way to stand beside the major. Her voice had an edge to it that could draw blood.

The major looked unimpressed. "To what do we owe the pleasure of your company, Captain?" he asked. "I believe you're out of your jurisdiction."

"Be that as it may, I'm here to arrest these three," Lynnfield sputtered, clearly shaken by the major's tone. His raised eyebrows in response caused her to continue, "This concerns planetary security. I'm not at liberty to discuss the case."

"Minister Lotte," said Fingrif, turning to the minister who had his arms crossed tightly over his chest. "Do you have time to be questioned by the captain?"

"I'd prefer not," said the minister. "But if planetary security is at stake, I'll do what I can to help."

"Fair enough," the major said. His hand slipped absent-mindedly to his holster and his thumb played with the clasp. "Since you're so often called in on high-level cases, Captain, this should be easy to clear up. All I require is the case number and your superior officer's contact information."

"That may be difficult," said Lynnfield. She shifted from one foot to the other and back again. "It's top secret."

"Surely even top-secret cases are assigned a designation, a few letters from the alphabet, anything?" the major asked. The woman frowned and shook her head. Smacking his lips together as though he'd just tasted something close to satisfaction, Fingrif added, "Well then, let's all go to headquarters and sort this out with my lieutenant colonel."

"Oh no, that shouldn't be necessary," the captain said, speaking quickly. "I'll be satisfied to leave with the murderer and the girl."

"Captain Lynnfield, you misunderstand me. I just issued an order," Major Fingrif said. His Order regulars shifted slightly to focus on the captain and her men who rested their hands on their holsters, but hadn't drawn. The major turned to the captain's men, and ordered, "Stand down."

Major Fingrif outranked the captain and had twice her number of regulars, which meant the captain had little choice, but to acquiesce. Fingrif took Lotte aside. They spoke momentarily before the two bowed to each other. Escorted by one of Fingrif's men in tow to provide protection, Lotte headed off separately toward the URT platform and no doubt the ministry. Home free. Noah scowled.

The major forced the captain to sit in the very back of his heliovan beside Noah and Rika while her people drove alone to headquarters. Noah studied her angular face and gray eyes, but she ignored him and stared straight ahead. Pressed against the window gazing out, Rika spent the time edged as far from Lynnfield as she could get. He wondered what history they had together.

As they passed under the white archway with its crane etched in stone overhead and the axiom, "Justice Best Served By Order," Noah felt the living building's first tugs at his psyche. Here the MAM would ensure that he told the truth, at least as he understood it. Ever since he'd made his promise to the senator, he'd been anxious to clear his name. Here he'd be required to do so.

Yet sitting beside the icy captain and Rika, frozen in fright, he thought twice about spilling his guts to the Order. It might be smarter to say as little as possible and simply walk away, except he'd have to take the DeeJee with him to make sure she stayed safe.

Each interview took time. The major himself sat in on the first interview with Noah. Fingrif said nothing while Noah gave his detailed account of the night Senator Ortega was murdered. He recounted everything he knew about the datasphere, which wasn't much. To protect Ochbo and the OMM, Noah conveniently left out losing access to the datasphere under spookdom and how they got it back. His only cause for anxiety was whether his account would match up with Rika's story. For all he knew she'd given the OMM away. Rubbing his temples as though Noah had given him a headache, Fingrif left with the first interrogator. Two others took their place, asking the same questions as the first interviewer in an attempt to trip Noah up on his witness statement. Noah remained confident. He knew what he'd seen that night.

By the time the fly gamer was brought into another room, crowded with interrogators and the interrogated, everyone had circles under their eyes and looked sweaty, especially Fingrif. The major sat at the head of the long, oval table. The Order interrogators sat to his left. Noah was told to sit at the far end. Rika was seated nearby, next to the blonde captain. Noah was struck by his pipsqueak's posture. The DeeJee had physically drawn in upon herself, knees bent almost to her chin with her arms wrapped tightly around her legs. She visibly leaned away from the captain, who sat stonily beside her.

"Do you mean to tell me, Captain, that all the copies of the datasphere were destroyed?" Fingrif asked.

"Yes," said the blonde. She enumerated the copies on her fingers. "Noah had the last remaining copy. The minister threw it onto the tracks, and an arriving URT train crushed it. The one in Seven Walls was deleted from Noah's data store. One of our own took the original datasphere from Noah the night of the senator's murder. We eliminated it as well."

After studying her, Noah wondered if she'd also eliminated the Order regular, who'd lifted the datasphere off him. Her merciless style certainly gave him the impression she was capable of it.

"Okay, I want to make sure we've all got this straight." The major rubbed his face hard with both palms before continuing. "All this fuss over a datasphere and no one knows what's on it! Not the DeeJee, not Domus Aqua's son, not even the Minister of Internal Affairs for whom it was intended, only you, Captain Lynnfield know of its contents."

"Yes, but—" the captain began.

"I know, you've made it clear that you can't discuss the contents because the data is a matter of 'planetary security.' Would you agree with me that these young people should go free?"

The blonde glanced over at Noah as if he were a bug that had fallen in her soup. She ignored Rika.

Not getting an answer from her, the major continued, "Noah's story is highly plausible, given what we know, and his biostats show he's telling the truth."

"He's a member of The Diversity Club, which may be responsible for the Circle Tide," the captain said.

The tension in the room increased tenfold.

"Hang on," Fingrif said, "My head is swimming. Are you agreeing this young man is innocent of being involved in the senator's murder? Or, are you alleging that he was involved in the murder and that somehow Circle Tide is related to the senator's assassination?"

"Circle Tide has nothing to do with the senator's death," Lynnfield blurted out. Noah checked her biostats. She'd lied! He suspected everyone else had checked too. Her pale face flushed red, as if she'd been slapped several times. Caught in a lie, the captain fumbled around, unable to regain her original poise. "What I mean is that, even if Noah is only a witness and not a murderer, he's suspected of illegal activities related to our city's crisis."

Major Fingrif pushed his chair back from the table. His face was now as red as Lynnfield's. Veins stood out at his temples. As he was about to speak, a loud commotion outside the door distracted him. The major excused himself and left the room, only to reappear backing up to make way for a beleaguered, portly officer and a furious, gesticulating madwoman who Noah recognized as his mother.

Master Lila's mass of ruby-studded black braids had come loose from the intricate swirls atop her head and whipped about her face as she glared at the assembled Order personnel. Her gaze flicked briefly over Rika and locked onto Noah, then she strode around the table and came to an abrupt halt behind her son. Her fine-boned hands clamped onto Noah's shoulders and squeezed so hard he flinched.

For maximum effect, the Domus Aqua Master wore white formal domus robes emblazoned with Aqua's blue-circle emblem. A parade of legal counsel had filed in behind her, causing the Order personnel to scramble to make room. As usual, everyone looked cowed in his mother's presence except, strangely, the blue-haired pipsqueak. Rika uncurled from her self-protective ball and studied Lila with obvious interest. Her change in countenance surprised him until he counted who remained. When the commotion subsided and all the lawyers had been given seats, Noah noticed that Captain Lynnfield and her two regulars were no longer in the room.

Lila had noticed, too. "Colonel Gribbin and Major Fingrif, where did Captain Lynnfield go? Does she have more important matters to attend to?" she asked. Her tone reminded Noah of superheated oil dropped in water. "Colonel, I have the utmost confidence that you will persuade the Director to make a public announcement. Everyone must hear that the Order no longer suspects my son of any involvement in the assassination of our dear friend, Senator Mari Ortega."

Gibbon bowed low. "Domus Master Lila, thank you for coming to us from Denver. Your presence at our headquarters is a great honor," he said. Noah saw that nervousness caused the colonel's neck to expand like a frog's over his tight collar. "It is doubtful, however, that the Order will be compelled to clear your son's name until after the investigation is formally concluded. That is our practice."

Lila's mouth formed a grim line. "In the meantime, I would need an army the size of the Order to protect my son from getting killed. The Heartlanders miss their senator, arguably the most important political figure in this century. I understand there's more than one bounty on his head." Her fingers dug into Noah's shoulders so uncomfortably that he raised his hands to hers. She slapped them away without glancing down. "So I have faith in you that you'll detain Noah until my counselors convince the Order of the necessity of this public statement."

"That will also be difficult," Fingrif said. Gribbin made the finger signal across his neck to shut his major up, but apparently,

Fingrif had been pushed too far by her antics. The major finished with, "We have nothing to keep him on."

"You're welcome to do what you like to him while he's in your custody," Lila continued as though Fingrif had never said a word. "Treat my son like you'd treat your worst criminal. Break his bones. I don't care. He'll heal."

Noah gulped. Rika's jaw dropped open and stayed that way.

"But know this, if my son dies an innocent man because some assassin or misguided Heartlander believes Noah murdered the senator, then you will each suffer. Everyone is this room and in this building here tonight will suffer."

"Mother!" Noah exclaimed.

"Shut up," his mother said quietly. "I haven't come to you yet."

When Fingrif cleared his throat to speak, Noah realized they were in the company of either a very brave or foolish man, willing to openly challenge one of the most powerful women on Earth. The lieutenant colonel quickly interceded. "Major, I need some hot tea. Go see to it."

The major hesitated a moment, bowed and closed the door behind him when he left. Gribbin adjusted his collar again. "We understand the gravity of the accusations against your son," he said. "We will do everything within our power to keep him safe from harm."

"I take you at your word and am deeply grateful," the domus master said. She released Noah and clasped her hands together as she bowed to the officer. He did the same. Addressing the room, she added gently, "Now if you'd allow me a moment with my son and this ... young lady."

"Of course, we have to stop the Circle Tide. It's destroying our city," Gribbin said. Noah thought he spoke more to refocus his people than to inform Lila. He motioned to his third-in-command, and she organized a rapid evacuation of the Order and the legal profession from the room.

When they were alone, Lila chose Gribbin's chair at the table. Sitting, she deftly wound her loose braids up into their usual elaborate swirls atop her head. Mended, Lila looked only a few years older than Noah's twenty-five years. The media streams regularly touted her, at sixty-six, as a rare beauty. Noah was used to his mother getting a lot of attention. She ranked among the richest, most powerful women on Earth. All he wanted to do was give her a hug and explain everything that had happened, but his mother was still on the warpath.

Glancing over at Rika, he saw that the DeeJee had returned to her defensive position, chin on knees and arms wrapped tightly around them. Wedged between chair and table, she looked to Noah like the living definition of a pipsqueak. Just looking at her made his heart beat inexplicably fast.

"Now you've really succeeded," his mother said, her words slow and acidic. "Your father has always said you're a worthless good-for-nothing who loves wild animals more than his own family. As of today, I agree with him."

"At least you two agree on something," Noah said.

"I'll clear your name for the sake of Domus Aqua, and you will stop your errant ways. You'll become a politician and marry the bride I pick for you," said Lila. She gave Rika a scathing once-over that the DeeJee ignored, but Noah saw red.

"No, Mother," Noah said. Too angry to respond coherently, he simply repeated, "No."

"Is it because of this commoner?" Lila asked, her voice rising, which gave Rika a start. "After that horrid Beatrice, you choose someone who doesn't even have a domus to her name? This girl? A DeeJee so mentally slow she had to have neural-knits to relate to the rest of us?"

"Noah and I aren't together," Rika asserted. She unfolded from her position and sat up straight, speaking with quiet intensity. "In fact until you arrived, I believed he was the biggest idiot I'd ever met. He's the type to follow through with whatever he wants to do, no matter what the consequences to anyone else, because he's been spoiled rotten all his life."

"You got that right," his mother said and broke into an unexpected grin. "Maybe this DeeJee is good for you."

"But now I realize, after meeting you, that it's genetic," Rika concluded, sitting back in her chair and returning the smile.

"Take care what you say about my son," his mother replied. Her smile faded.

Noah realized it was up to him to do something before his mother said things to hurt Rika that Noah wouldn't be able to forgive. He also found that he did not want to hear any more nasty impressions of him that Rika might have formed, so he got up from his chair and went over to his mother. Without waiting for her rejection, he bent over and gave her a big bear hug. Despite Lila's strength, she was no match for her son. He held her in his arms until she finally returned the hug.

When he let go, his mother wiped her eyes and left the room without a word. Noah watched her leave. When the door closed, he turned back to Rika. Her head rested on her crossed arms against the table. She faced away from him. Clearing his throat, he said, "I'm sorry. I care about you. Hey, I said I'm sorry."

Rika didn't move or bother to respond. He crossed over to her and saw that her eyes were closed and her mouth was open. There was a little drool on her chin. For the first time all night, he shook his head and laughed.

CHAPTER 14

Rika and Noah were left in the locked room. For Rika, the night passed slowly, as though the hour reset itself each time she rested her head on the conference room table and closed her eyes to nap. First she awoke to the sound of Noah banging on the locked door. Next he was yelling for water, which reminded her of her dry lips and throat. Another time, he demanded food. Her stomach responded with loud grumbling noises, which made him laugh.

"You're a jerk," she responded. Rika laid her head back down on the table and closed her eyes.

Mostly, Noah pounded the door hard in short bursts. No one ever opened the locked door, but he woke her up each time. When he took a chair to the door, she raised her head and shouted at him, "Stop!"

Noah set the chair down. The next time Rika woke it was because of his snores. He sat slumped down in the chair beside her. Her neck ached from resting her head in an awkward position. She scooted her chair over a little and tested Noah's shoulder as a pillow. Since he didn't wake up or shift away, Rika settled in and closed her eyes.

In the morning, Rika didn't hear the door open. She sat up and yelped in surprise to see the major standing over them. Her yell jolted Noah awake. Fingrif had brought them two cups of steaming tea. The major placed the cups in front of them and sat down on the other side of the table.

"You two look awful." The officer softened his assessment with a grin. The shadows under Fingrif's eyes and his rumpled uniform reminded Rika that they weren't the only ones who'd had a rough night. "Drink some tea."

Rika hesitantly picked up the cup and cradled it in her hands. The green tea tasted bitter and burned her mouth, but she gulped some down anyway.

"Sadly, you two are the least of my worries," the major admitted. "Rika, you work for IEC and are assigned to the Circle Tide project along with the rest of the Institute. Right?"

Rika nodded.

"By now, you're late for work. You need to leave," the major said. Turning to her companion, he added, "Noah, you're free to stay."

"Does that mean you're giving me a choice to stay or go?" Noah asked.

"Of course. However, your mother didn't exaggerate when she said she'd need an army to protect you from revenge-seekers and bounty-hunters," Fingrif cautioned. "Stay with us until she strong-arms our bosses into clearing you of any involvement in the assassination. We'll set you up in a cell. It shouldn't take more than a couple of months."

The memory event from Medic Ng flashed before Rika's eyes: Yori convulsing after his torture. Her hand shook so badly that she spilled the rest of her tea.

"How is Noah safer in here?" Rika challenged. To the fly gamer, she added, "Don't trust the Order."

"Excuse me, young lady," Fingrif began. He stopped and studied her as though confounded by her facial features. She covered her nose and lips with her hand. "You're so afraid that you're trembling. What makes you distrust us so much?"

"I want to leave," Noah interjected.

"It's a bad idea," the officer answered, while he remained fixated on Rika.

Rika answered the major's question: "Captain Lynnfield, for one."

"She can be intimidating, is that it?" Fingrif said. He stood, placed both palms on the table and leaned toward her. Rika ignored him and kept her eyes lowered. Even though he came off as an honest officer, his ignorance about others like Lynnfield could only mean bad things for Noah if he remained in custody. "What happened to you?"

"Are you holding me on any charges?" Noah demanded.

The major turned to face him. "Absolutely not, you're free to go and welcome to stay. It's almost as nice as a hotel. We promise not to break your bones, as your mother suggested."

Rika cocked her head. "You can't really let Noah walk, can you? You'd be in serious trouble." She had experienced Noah's mother firsthand. Crossing her would be dangerous. "If he leaves now you'll be fired won't you, Major?"

"Frankly, my boss doesn't have time to fire me. We're in a crisis here, with the fungi cropping up everywhere and so many people sick. Lots of things scare me, including Circle Tide, but domus masters never intimidate me." The major folded his arms across his chest. "But I'd prefer not to see something bad happened to you, Noah. To make your girlfriend more comfortable, I will personally vouch for your safety here. That's something I can't do if you're out there on your own."

"She's not my girlfriend," Noah said, "but I'll take my leave with her." He spoke with such finality that when he stood and bowed low, Fingrif simply accepted his statement with a curt nod.

Scrambling to her feet, Rika bowed to the major.

"Here's my contact information," offered the officer, raising his palm to hers to pass his data via the MAM. His harsh expression softened as their palms met. "Don't hesitate, should you or your foolish boyfriend need my help for any reason."

Outside of the gates, Noah re-activated his Spider Zynx MAM embrace. Rika expected him to take a different direction, but he stayed beside her.

"The major is a fool," Noah said.

"Why, because he thought we were dating?"

"What? No. Well, I guess that, too. I was thinking of my mother," Noah answered. "She'll punish him for disobeying her orders."

"I think he's brave," Rika said. The pedestrians and cyclists in the street distracted her. Almost everyone wore decorative facemasks. Some people had on full-body, designer clear-skins resembling industrial hazmat anzugs, although far less effective.

During the time they had spent in the Order headquarters, anxiety about the potential spread of Circle Tide sickness had become rife. Rika let her mind dip into the media streams. Circle Tide dominated the news. Overnight, the Order had evacuated another five buildings in downtown Los Angeles. No wonder Major Fingrif looked haggard.

A woman walking toward them sneezed loudly. People lunged out of her way, bumping into others who ran from them in turn, in a domino effect. People rushed toward their destinations. They kept their shoulders curled toward their chests and their heads down as though they risked collapsing in on themselves.

Since Rika felt famished, she got in line at the first food vendor. Noah stood beside her. An oily-haired commuter ahead of them ordered a noodle bowl and pulled out a mini-microscope to verify the food's safety. Bringing out the microscope had a negative effect. Customers in line behind Rika started murmuring to each other, and the line ahead of her disappeared. When only Rika and Noah were left waiting, the vendor testily told the commuter to put his microscope away. When the man refused, the vendor cursed and poked the man in the chest. The man cried out as if he'd been threatened with a knife.

"For all I know, you're covered in spores!" the commuter yelled. "You could be sick; your noodles deadly!"

Noah wrapped his arm around Rika's shoulders and steered her away from the spot just as two Order regulars showed up.

"We'll get breakfast somewhere else," he said, as they headed into the crowd. He stopped abruptly, stared and nudged her. "Would you look at that?"

Rika followed his line of sight. Not far away, a group of boys were faking coughing fits and then collapsing into helpless laughter. They caused passersby to dash away from them when they coughed. One startled commuter stumbled his way into Rika, knocking her down as he passed. Still oblivious, he barreled into a little girl who lost her balance and fell into cycle street traffic. The child screamed for her mom. Rika dodged out and scooped her up in her arms. Dashing after Rika, Noah yanked them out of the way.

"This is nuts," Noah said. He surveyed the commuters and pointed to a woman frantically looking around, yelling a girl's name. "That's got to be her mother."

Rika wove her way through the crowd and delivered the terrified child to the woman. The mother grabbed her daughter from Rika's arms and hurried away without a word. When the DeeJee returned to Noah's side, he said, "Things have changed considerably during the time we were locked up."

"Yes, I'm glad you came with me," Rika said. "That mother was so scared she didn't even thank me. I'm looking forward to going home."

"About that," Noah said and ran a hand across the night's stubble on his chin and jaw. "I need to hide out where no one expects me."

"I agree," Rika said, expecting him to take his leave. She stole several glances at him as they headed down into the Underground. "Ochbo cautioned his OMMers to avoid their usual places and friends. You should do the same."

"Well, that's a relief," Noah said and slapped her roughly on the back.

"Ow, that hurt!" she said and massaged her back where his hand had been. "What's a relief?"

"Crashing at your place, I'm exhausted and famished."

"Huh?" Rika stopped in her tracks and looked up at him. "That may not be such a good idea. I've got to go to work — oh, oh — oh no!"

"What's wrong?"

"This morning, I was supposed to get picked up and go to the Circle Tide sites," Rika said. "I should have contacted Sebastian."

"Who?"

"The Domus Restitio Master."

"How do you know—" Noah stopped himself. "It doesn't matter. Just tell him you were incarcerated. That's a good excuse. How could you have contacted him from an Order cell?"

"Still..." Rika said and trailed off. She checked her communications, expecting to find numerous messages. Only one message popped up from Sebastian.

<Contact me after you're released. When you're ready, I'll pick you up.>

When she queried the MAM about how he'd known about her arrest, her mind remained silent. *A domus master probably has resources that would surprise even a DeeJee,* Rika thought. "Sebastian is amazing," she exclaimed more to herself than Noah.

"Sure," Noah said. For the rest of the trip home, Rika watched him fidget with everything he had in his pockets. Once inside her apartment building, Rika accessed the front door to her studio and let Noah in first. In a few short steps, Noah stood in the center of the room and did a slow 360-degree rotation.

"Is this it?" Noah said. He found the sliding door to her bathroom and peeked in. "You never use water? Just dry showers?"

"Hey, water is expensive," said Rika. "A son of Domus Aqua should know that. You're welcome to find someplace else."

"No, this is perfect," Noah said and chuckled. "No one would ever suspect I'd stoop to coming here."

"Didn't you just spend a year in Earth's wildernesses tracking animals?"

"Yes, this is just like camping," said Noah. "That's a good analogy."

"Why you rude—" she began, but Noah held up his hand.

"Don't go out of your way on my account," Noah interrupted. "Do you hear my stomach?"

She did. It made loud gurgling sounds.

"What delicious meal will you offer your guest?" he asked, dramatically rubbing his belly.

"Meal? I'm leaving now," Rika said.

He laughed as she backed up and out the door. It slid closed. In the corridor, she was tempted to go back and offer her unwanted guest a few choice phrases. She reminded herself that she was the one who had advised him to leave Order headquarters. For the day, he could hide out at her place. After all, she'd be gone, and he'd be safe. Tonight she'd make certain he went someplace else.

At the entrance to her building, two men holding large boxes stopped her. "Rika of IEC?"

"Yes?"

"Where would you like these delivered?"

"Excuse me?"

"The breakfast you ordered," he replied.

"I ordered?" she asked in astonishment. "Okay, I'll take them."

The two men looked at each other.

"I insist," she added in case it was a trap to get to Noah. They loaded her arms with the two boxes. She hefted the boxes up to her third floor studio nearly dropping them twice on the way.

When she stumbled into her studio unable to see over the heavy boxes, Noah exclaimed, "Breakfast!" He immediately took them from her and laid out their contents on her tiny counter. "Sit down, Pipsqueak. I ordered enough to feed both of us."

The aroma of breakfast reminded her how hungry she was. She sat at the counter. He covered its surface with plates of vegetable omelets, seasoned tofu, radish kimchi, seafood salad, grilled grown pork, cucumber soup, rice and watermelon. They ate across from each other.

"Delicious," admitted Rika with her mouth full of egg.

"The omelet is too salty and the kimchi not spicy enough," Noah said. He helped himself to more of each.

When Rika was finished stuffing herself, she straightened out her arms behind her back and yawned. With such a full stomach, she hoped she wouldn't fall asleep on the job. That wouldn't go over well with Sebastian. Glancing down at the boxes, she noticed that a large portion of one remained packed. "What's in that one, Noah?"

"I ordered you a meat grower so that I'd have protein for dinner," Noah said. "I figured you didn't have one."

"That explains why it was so heavy. Noah, a meat grower is very expensive."

"So?"

"If you access your accounts to have luxury items delivered to my apartment, people will track you here. It's possible someone already figured out we were held at the Order headquarters together."

"Everyone needs protein," he insisted.

Shaking her head, Rika forced a smile. Unless he started acting like a normal person, he wouldn't stand a chance. Aloud, she said, "Thank you for my breakfast."

"I'm bribing you," he said.

"For what?" she asked with a start.

"For tonight," he said.

"What do you think is going to happen tonight?"

"I'm hoping you'll give me access to the last remaining copy of the datasphere. I know you made one. Lotte destroyed mine. According to what Captain Lynnfield told the major, the Order destroyed the original," Noah said. "I need to review what's on it."

"Actually, I'm curious, too, but you'll owe me more than breakfast," Rika said and shivered. The datasphere reminded her of Yori, but then, she thought, so would simply seeing someone eat a caramel. She pulled herself together. Today, she'd tackle the Circle Tide epidemic, tonight the murders of the senator and her best friend, Yori.

The counter folded back into the wall once the leftovers were stored away. Noah tested out the floor for sleep. First, he complained about her antiquated studio technology. One hard pillow rose to meet his neck. Second, he explained to her how inadequately the floor curled around his large frame. As soon as he closed his eyes, she heard an obnoxious snore. Wishing she could sleep, Rika nudged him with her foot as she left.

It was already midmorning, so Rika gave up her plan to visit the Institute before her offsite work. Instead she contacted

Sebastian and climbed the stairs to the rooftop to wait for a personal pickup by the Domus Restitio heliovan. She took the pebbled path that wound through multi-tiered rows of vegetables. Enhanced crows sat on their lookout perches above her, jealously guarding the fresh produce for the roof gardener.

When a plump red tomato caught her eye, she reached out to examine it. The closest crow lifted off its perch, flapped its wings and cawed at her. Waving at the indignant bird, Rika walked on, headed for the far end of the roof with its circle of trees for the crows to roost, its heliopad, a bench and a few chairs. She rounded the corner of tiered rows into the open space and noticed a new much younger roof gardener sitting with his back to her. Crows perched on either shoulder and on the bench beside him. They all faced the ocean and the rooftops in-between, which gave Rika the funny impression that the crows were enjoying the view along with the gardener. As she approached, the crows silently lifted off. Each held a red ribbon dangling from its beak.

Sitting where a crow had been, Rika glanced curiously at the roof gardener beside her and gave a start. "Cricket?"

"Rika of the Institute of Extended Cognition," Cricket said and inclined her head without looking at her. "What brings you up here in the middle of the day?"

"I'm getting picked up to investigate sites afflicted by Circle Tide," Rika said. "What about you?"

"I'm feeding the guardians."

"So that's why the crows like you so much," Rika said and grinned. "When we talked last, you were very anxious."

"Let's just say I'm hiding in plain sight," Cricket said with a shrug.

"I noticed the red ribbons. They allow you to communicate with other gardeners without entering Novus Orbis," Rika said. "There must be important things going on."

"Do you always ask questions by making statements?" Cricket asked, without making eye contact.

"Usually I don't have to, but you're different. You don't access the MAM, and it doesn't access you, which is awkward. I can't judge how you're feeling or thinking without your biostats or memory events," Rika replied. Mulling over the question, Rika realized how rarely she actually needed to ask questions.

"It's okay." Cricket stood and pointed at the sky. "Your ride is almost here."

Rika stood, too. She wanted to find out how Cricket knew the senator. Unfortunately, before she could formulate an inoffensive question-not-statement, Cricket bowed and said, "I'll leave first."

The heliocar was silver and green, Domus Restitio's colors, and had the "well springs" emblem emblazoned on its side. The heliocar's ultra-modern sleek lines and soundless, instant dropdown onto the heliopad reminded Rika that Sebastian, like Noah, came from a world of opulence and wealth far removed from hers. The door slid open. She stuck her head inside and recognized the driver as one of Sebastian's men who'd rescued her from Captain Lynnfield. He gestured for her to climb in back. Since it was only the two of them, she jumped in front.

"Good morning, Frisardi."

"You can call me Fritz. Sebastian wants me to escort you to the Elysian Fields Retreat so that you can speak to some of the evacuees and medics, if you're willing. After that, there is a building that he suggested you investigate," the driver said. "I hope this works for you."

"I don't have my climbing equipment or anything else with me," Rika said.

"Sebastian had me pick up your IEC bag and hazmat anzug from the Institute this morning. It's in back."

Rika nodded and slid back in her seat, focusing on the console in front of her. It showed the optimal path the heliocar locked onto as they headed up into heavy skyway traffic. Glancing over as he deftly maneuvered the heliocar, her hands itched to control this perfect specimen of a machine. It reacted incredibly fast with an accelerated ride so smooth that they might as well have been floating.

Still, she'd hoped to work with Sebastian and a sigh escaped her lips. As though the driver read her thoughts, he added, "Sebastian will meet up with us at the end of the day. He wondered if you might be available for dinner."

"I think so," Rika said. Perking up, Rika grinned and adjusted her seat to view the city passing beneath them.

"Do you enjoy the view?" Fritz asked. Below her the pure density and spiraling heights of the city took her breath away. The multi-colored patches of roof gardens only added to the beauty.

"Oh, yes," she said and noticed him grimace. "You don't like Los Angeles."

"I admire uniformity, order and people who take life seriously. These Los Angelinos invert who they are by showing it all off on the outside of their buildings. There's nothing left inside. It's garish. No dignity."

Rika frowned and wondered what stereotypical, offensive generalizations he made about Heartlanders like herself. Silently, she admitted to herself that only Los Angeles took architectural individuation to the extreme. As long as a living building met safety codes and provided its own energy microharvesters and water/waste reclamation and conservation, the style could be just about anything. What he called garish, she called freedom of expression. Still, it wasn't worth an argument with him.

"What city do you like?" she asked.

"Las Vegas."

"Vegas?" she said and burst out laughing. "It's an adult funhouse. Why the latest media stream reports that they are growing a miniature lunarscape in 4-D so that people can be in two gambling spots to lose and win at the same time, all the while enjoying a view of Earth."

"It's honest, and never pretends to be anything but a place where people lose or gain and don't complain," he spat the words at her.

Without meaning to, the DeeJee allowed the power of his memory event series to overwhelm her senses.

Seeing it from Fritz's viewpoint, Rika found herself standing on a balcony beside a slim, young girl. She had a hunch his preference for Las Vegas had less to do with architecture and more to do with his association with this person.

Fritz was talking animatedly. Gesturing with the hand that held his drink, he dropped it. The girl caught it, flipped it around without spilling a drop and then mischievously took a sip before returning it to him. Judging by the strength of emotion Fritz attached to this memory, Rika thought the girl might as well have come with a halo and a heavenly choir.

The moment did not last. Sebastian walked onto the balcony and slipped his arm around the girl's waist. The girl scowled, and it was only then that Rika focused on her face. Under the make-up and the once-fashionable hairstyle, the gardener who she knew as Cricket stood before her.

Rika needed to jolt herself out of this volatile man's memory event. She slammed her head against the console.

"Hey, kid! What are you doing?" Fritz said. The heliovan dipped slightly as he reached out and seized her arm.

"Just trying to get an image out of my head," Rika said, pulling free of him. Determined to change the subject, she added, "Do you like the Los Angeles' extensions at least?"

"Sure, kid."

Her appreciation of the extensions, those vast tracks of agriculture that started at the city perimeter and eventually gave way to wilderness, was based on little experience. She'd rarely taken advantage of the two days she was allotted monthly to visit planned rural areas or the planetary wildernesses that surrounded each concentrated city. When she had a day off, she preferred to cycle down the coastline near work or travel in Novus Orbis.

"They're okay," he added.

As they wound around the city center away from the ocean, she noticed several buildings that had deformed, blackened rooftops. Strangely, her eyes couldn't bring them into focus. The Order had coated each sick building in a transparent polymer covering to protect the adjacent buildings. The unintentional trompe-l'oeil made the lines of the sick buildings look diffuse, as though they were caught midway between vanishing completely or appearing full and clear. The further they flew, the more sick buildings they saw.

"The Order can't keep up with the number of sick buildings," she said. Her forehead pressed against the cool window had a large bump forming on it where she'd smashed it into the console. Rika stared at the cityscape below.

"By the end of the day, there will be more evacuees than there are retreats. Too few people have family or friends to take them in," Fritz said. "If I had clearance, I'd take you into downtown airspace. It's really bad down there."

"A couple weeks ago, I flew downtown to the first building afflicted with Circle Tide," Rika said. "We didn't even know what to call the fungus then."

"The first sick building," he murmured.

Frisardi's memory events burst into her consciousness so fast and strong that they might as well have been her own. He flipped through snippets. A man in a lab coat held his head between his hands. He staggered around a lab, screaming. In a hazmat anzug, Fritz struggled to free himself from a wall of fungi in a lab much like the Bolsa Complex.

Rika pounded her fists into her legs until the pain forced out his memories.

"Frisardi," she said.

"What's this about? I wish you'd stop beating yourself," he said. "It'll be hard to explain your bruises to Sebastian."

His private memories made her head ache. The heliocar interior and the driver moved in and out of focus. Still, he'd shown her glimpses of Circle Tide's true origins.

"Frisardi," she said.

"Yes?" he asked.

"Show me the lab, the place where Circle Tide first started."

CHAPTER 15

A persistent tapping nearby made Noah aware that his face felt slightly numb against the rock hard pillow. Camping had definite drawbacks.

"Leave me alone, guys," he yelled out to his crew of scientists. Something felt wrong. The forest had gone silent, no birdcalls or acoustic insect rhythms. "Go on without me. I'll catch up. I always do."

Tap-tap-tap.

With his face pressed against the unforgiving surface of the pillow, he smelled tantalizing mint, green apple, sea-salt sweat. *What smells so tantalizing?* He thought, *Rika!* Noah sat up and the floor curled away from him. He emerged from his drowsy haze enough to recognize the tiny studio in Seal Beach.

Tap-tap-tap.

"It's your place. Don't be so shy. I'm dressed," he yelled at the door. *That pipsqueak is determined not to let me sleep when she has to go to work.*

Tap-tap-tap.

He rubbed his sleepy eyes with his palms and stumbled to the door. It slid open, but no one was there. As he stepped forward into the hallway, he saw the blur of a boy rotating his back to him with a swift rear kick. The steel-heeled boot landed squarely in his solar plexus. Noah doubled over holding his stomach and staggered backwards into the studio. With the wind knocked out of him, Noah managed only a weak "h-e-e-y." His foot caught on the uneven floor where he'd slept. He lost his balance and landed on his back. The tall kid jumped on top of his chest

and straddled him. In his left hand, the boy flipped a long shard
of glass and then pressed it against Noah's neck.

"You can toss me off, but I guarantee a deep slice first," his
attacker said. The voice had a feminine edge to it.

Staring up at her, Noah realized the kid was no boy at all, but
a slight woman with a fine jaw line. In the loose brown clothing of a roof gardener, and with her short black hair pointing in
every direction, she could easily be taken for either sex. Noah
imagined several ways he might knock her off him and avoid his
throat getting sliced open. When he queried her biostats, an odd
interface bobbed for a few seconds beside her head that read,
"Cricket."

"Why did you kill Mari?" Cricket asked, pressing the point
of the makeshift weapon into his throat. "Be honest. I smell lies."

"Hey, why don't you put that thing away?" Noah said. She
slid it over to press on his jugular. He thought of the senator's
real killer: Ghost, the Underground extremist with hidden biostats whom the Order identified as Bartholomew Soba. "I didn't
kill Mari. We were friends."

"I saw you there the night she was murdered," she said. Her
hand slipped slightly. A sharp pain jolted through his neck and
warm blood trickled over his throat.

"Careful or you'll do damage! If you saw me, you must have
seen the Ghost, I mean, Soba."

"I saw a lot that night — Soba, you and then that Order
captain and her regulars. The medics, more Order regulars and
the guards came later."

"All I know is that when I left the senator, she'd been wounded
in the abdomen. Soba stabbed her."

"You left her to die?"

"The Order medics were less than five minutes away. I
stopped Soba from killing her, but he escaped."

In her anger, she pressed harder. The shard was cutting into
his skin. He felt more blood drip down his neck. He brought his
hands up in supplication near her left elbow.

"Please, you're hurting me," he said.

"If you're Mari's friend, why did you abandon her when she
was dying and steal the datasphere?"

Noah knew he wasn't convincing her. Another few seconds
and she'd be ready to cut him for real. A surge of adrenaline went
through his limbs. He grabbed her arm above the elbow and
yanked her over his right shoulder, throwing her forward. Her
chest landed on his face — definitely not a boy. Using his legs,

he easily knocked her off him, rolled her over on her back and pinned her arm so she couldn't stab him. She punched him with her free hand and then reached down toward her leg pocket. Noah remembered how Ochbo had lost the knife and drawn a glock-goku, but right now he had to focus on the weapon he could see. Bringing her left wrist forward over his arm, he forced her to drop the glass. She cried out in pain.

At that moment, he suffered a twinge of guilt for being so rough with her. This woman had tiny wrists and couldn't be more than half his weight. Her attack reminded him of the typical Heartlanders' fighting style. Maybe she'd help him get the word out in the Underground about his innocence; that is, if he could convince her without getting stabbed to death in the process.

"If I let you up, will you stop attacking me?" he asked. "I'll answer your questions."

"Fine!" she spat. He hesitated and then sat back on his haunches. She scrambled away from him and scooped up the glass shard. From her leg pocket, she drew a glock-goku with her right hand and pointed it at him. "I was hoping to avoid using this."

"We just made an agreement. Put down your weapons," he said.

"Why did you steal Mari's datasphere?"

"The senator gave me the datasphere to deliver to one of the government ministers. She didn't trust the Order and asked me to escape with it."

"If that's true, why isn't anything from the datasphere public yet?" she asked. A tear dripped down the side of her nose and hung there.

"Does that mean you know what's on it?" Noah asked. She gestured with her glock-goku. He crossed his arms over his chest. "Don't threaten me. People have been doing that a lot lately. You don't know how tempting it is to take one of you down."

She kept her weapon pointed at him. He closed his eyes for a few seconds and breathed slowly to calm himself.

"That weasel bureaucrat — I gave him the datasphere, but he destroyed it." He reflected a moment and then said, "Though I doubt he would have made anything public."

"The weasel?"

"Minister of Internal Affairs Gothardi Lotte. He threw the datasphere under a commuter train after I gave it to him. He didn't want anything to do with it."

"Mari trusted him." Cricket sniffled. She gestured around the room. "How do you know the DeeJee?"

"It's complicated."

"Yeah." Cricket took aim. He held up his hands again. A quick study, she stepped out of arms length from him.

"My short answer is Rika wanted to get the datasphere from me to save her friend's life."

To his astonishment, she nodded as though that made perfect sense and asked, "What are Mari's favorite flowers?"

"If you're testing how well I know Mari, that's too easy," he said. "Peonies."

At that, Cricket lowered the glock-goku in her right hand. With the left, she hurled the glass shard past him into the far wall. It wedged so deep in the surface that only its tip showed.

"Mari would still be alive if I'd stayed by her side that night," Cricket said. Noah noticed she'd sliced her palm while handling the glass shard. Blood dripped from her fingers onto the floor.

On the wall, concentric circles formed around the glass as the room reacted to her violence. A sudden loud pop made them both start. The wall expelled the shard back at them. It clattered across the floor at their feet.

Out of sheer relief that Cricket hadn't seriously wounded him with either weapon, Noah laughed. His neck stung where she'd cut him. He touched his fingers to the wound. They came away covered in blood. He laughed harder. She stepped further away from him toward the studio door.

"Follow me," he said.

In the bathroom, he cleaned and sterilized her hand. Cricket pulled away as soon as he'd finished. Alone in the bathroom, he closed the door, dry showered and sterilized his neck. When he came out, he expected Cricket to be gone. Instead, she'd taken out the breakfast remains and was busy finishing off the remains. Noah tentatively approached the counter and reached for a slice of watermelon. She slapped his hand away.

"Mine," she said.

"You're bold for someone who owes me an apology," Noah said. "My neck hurts."

"What's a neck scratch to a dead man?" she asked between oversized bites. Her cheeks bulged.

"Just because there's a bounty on my head, doesn't mean I want to be cut up piecemeal by a madwoman," Noah said. He snatched a watermelon slice before she could slap away his hand. He bit down and the sweet juice filled his mouth. "How did you know it was me with my MAM embrace on?"

"I've kept tabs on you since that night. You're even wearing the same clothes."

"The MAM embrace must be malfunctioning," Noah said and got up. He examined himself in the bathroom mirror and a stranger's face stared back at him with that obnoxious white spider tattoo perpetually crawling across his skin. This time it perched on the bridge of his nose. He returned to the counter and sat down across from her. "Isn't it odd that I see my own MAM embrace, but you don't?"

"My brain can't recognize MAM embraces. I cannot connect to the MAM," she said.

Noah had to struggle to imagine how isolating that would be. He wondered what other deficiencies she had. He'd never met anyone who couldn't access the MAM.

"Don't look at me like that. I don't need your pity," Cricket said. She tossed down her chopsticks and pushed herself away from the counter even though a large serving of meat and watermelon remained. "Since I'm restricted to Vetus Orbis, I see what's here. Novus Orbis never pollutes my world like it does yours."

A complex series of raps caused Cricket to leap up and dash to open the front door. A short, hunched-over man in brown roof-gardener garb stood in the doorway.

"Cricket, we've got visitors upstairs from Domus Aqua, and they're headed this way." He winked and added, "They're stuck in the elevator between floors at the moment, which buys you a few minutes."

With that, he turned and hobbled down the hallway. Cricket turned to Noah. "Do you want to be kidnapped by your family or to come with me?"

Noah didn't hesitate. Once his family had him, he would have to remain in confinement until the Order cleared him of murder. Despite political pressure, the Order might take far longer than Fingrif's estimate of a couple months. In the meantime, while Noah was tucked away in solitary confinement, his father would blame him for causing the family so much trouble. Allowing his mother's men to take him meant Noah would be safe, but he'd never live it down. Noah planned to clear his own name.

Cricket climbed the stairs, pulling herself up via the railing so that she could skip up two and three steps at a time. Noah didn't have time to ask her why she went up instead of down into the street. He followed. Once they reached the rooftop,

Cricket turned to him and said, "You should board your family's heliovan."

"No. Cricket, help me escape!"

"If you promise to help me," Cricket replied.

Hearing a commotion behind them in the stairwell, Noah said, "Fine!"

In response, Cricket crawled beneath the rooftop's tiered planters, inched her way to the far end, and disappeared from view. Noah quickly followed her through rotting plant detritus and scooted out into a narrow open-air room formed by the three backsides of the tiered walls with a long planter overhead providing a ceiling. The tiny space had a cot and a side table with a tremendous view of the rooftops and ocean.

The rooftop door burst open. Cricket pressed her face against the planters and peered between them. Noah joined her. A man with a woman beside him, both dressed in Domus Aqua attire, dragged the old roof gardener from the stairs onto the roof. Crows squawked and swooped down around the captors. Harassed by the birds and swinging in vain at them, the man's captor had to let him go. Noah recognized the woman, Mae, his mother's hard-nosed assistant since he had been a boy. She had come to Domus Aqua as part of the entourage of a daughter of Domus Superna who was to marry Noah's brother Daniel. When the ceremony concluded, Mae had stayed. The head of the domus had noticed Mae's stern, bullheaded style and appreciated it. Gradually, Mae had become Master Lila's most trusted and ruthless helper.

"Don't deny Noah is staying here," Mae said to the cowering man. She glanced up at the crows flying overhead. "He accessed his funds to pay for the breakfast. Where is he?"

"Roofy roof-roof," the gardener said. He dropped to his knees, ducked and covered his head with his arms. "He's with us here."

"Stop talking nonsense," Mae said. Her long-nailed hands dug into his shoulders. She shook him. He remained where he'd fallen to his knees. A crow dove down and pecked at Mae's head.

Yelping, Mae jumped back. Turning to her underling, she snapped, "This is the most poorly run building I've ever been in. The elevator breaks down. The roof door jams, crows attack, and this gardener is a blathering idiot."

Mae's underling had a receding chin that disappeared into his muscled neck when he nodded, which he apparently did a lot.

"Take me back to Lila. I have to tell her the bad news in person," Mae ordered.

"Bad news?"

"We don't have her son yet, you imbecile," Mae said. "She's got enough to worry about with three of our buildings in Denver sick with Circle Tide and hundreds of evacuees to relocate."

The man nodded.

"Listen, when you return, park somewhere out of view," Mae instructed. "Contact me as soon as either Noah or his girlfriend show up. If he resists, we'll take her. That'll bring him to his senses quickly enough."

The chinless man continued nodding as he opened the door to the heliovan for Mae and then loped around to the driver's side.

After the heliovan lifted off, the roof gardener got up and hobbled over to the planters. He stopped where Cricket and Noah stood on the other side. "Cricket, you rascal, you owe me one." With that, the gardener ambled over to the rooftop stairway and left them alone on the roof.

Massaging her wrist, Cricket sank down on the cot. Noah sat down beside her.

"Here, let me see your wrist," Noah offered.

"No," she said. "Don't touch me. It's time to test if you're a man of your word. You said you'd help me if I helped you escape."

"Yes. What do you want me to do?" Noah said.

"We're going to pay Bartholomew Soba a visit and find out who hired him to attack Mari," she said.

"Assuming we can find him, how do you plan to convince him to talk?" Noah said. "I know I'm good, but you think I can force a trained killer to talk?"

"No," Cricket said. "But your Domus Aqua funds can. He'll do anything for financial gain."

She stood and motioned for him to follow her. Noah groaned and lay back on the cot. It had a lumpy cushiness that gave under his weight. The breeze from the ocean cooled his face. His eyelids felt heavy. Mentally, he swore to himself that he'd make no more promises to the extraordinary women of this cursed city. Otherwise, he'd never find his way out of it. The idea of paying Bartholomew Soba for anything made Noah's blood run cold. Cricket slapped him on the stomach to get him up.

Luckily, he didn't have to crawl beneath the nasty smelling underbelly of the planters again. Cricket showed him a proper door to the garden's secret room. It opened directly in front of the stairwell. The doorway was completely camouflaged. Few would find the room's entrance unless they knew where to look. Even the highly observant Mae had walked right by it.

For the second time that day, Noah found himself following this lanky, sphinx-like woman who gardened the rooftops of Los Angeles and came from the Underground. Without once entering Novus Orbis or accessing MAM data warehouses, she had revealed things no one else knew. Now she made certain no one tracked them, moving quickly down the back alleyway to a manhole. She slid it back and dropped down. Noah climbed in after her and closed the lid overhead. He cautiously descended the metal rungs into darkness. When his feet touched the tunnel floor, he felt the slight tremor of a train passing beneath them. Side-by-side they walked the service tunnel at a rapid clip.

"I see how you stay so fit when you travel everywhere on foot," Noah said. She kept going, so he said what was actually on his mind without peppering her with more compliments. "Even though I agreed to this, I'm confused. We're headed to see Bartholomew Soba, right?"

Cricket gave him a sidelong glance and nodded in the dim light of the tunnel. Noah kept hearing the scuttling of tiny feet and seeing movement on the periphery of his vision. He felt skittish. The disturbed vermin and insects heightened his sense of impending doom. Apparently immune to such minor distractions, the gardener walked on.

"Cricket, we need to talk this out. I saw that sicko brutally attack the senator," Noah said. "If you know where he's hiding out, I'd prefer to contact the Order so they can arrest him."

"He scares you," she stated. Noah bristled. "He scares me, too."

"It's more than that. Say we confront him, the way you did me. My gut tells me he'd kill us."

"No confrontations. We'll make him a financial offer he can't refuse," Cricket said, moving at a steady clip. Her arms sliced the stale tunnel air.

Speeding up, Noah stepped out in front of her and grasped her upper arms forcing her to stop. "That's not going to work with a political extremist. Listen, this man killed the senator because she had relocated some Heartlanders groundside. I don't pretend to understand his belief that Heartlanders should only live in the Underground. Or worse, why he felt Ortega deserved to die because she wanted a better life for her people groundside."

"There're plenty of people in the Underground who believe that," Cricket said with a shrug. "But he isn't one of them."

"What?" Noah said. He flashed back to the political signs the killer had scrawled across the walls of the senator's office, *Heartland=Underground* and *Traitor*. "Are you sure?"

"Positive. He's an independent contractor and does whatever for whomever, as long as the price is right."

Noah's mind raced with the full import of Cricket's statement. The political graffiti had just been a smoke screen. Someone had paid the killer to shut up the senator. Most likely, the same person or persons were behind the destruction of the datasphere. Noah let his hands drop from her arms and stepped aside. They walked on.

After a little while, they came to another ladder and dropped down into a URT tunnel in a well-appointed section of the Underground. Shops and restaurants were interspersed with residences in the wide high-ceiling tunnels. The rush of URT trains sent mild vibrations through his feet every so often. In a low voice so as not to be overheard by passersby, Noah asked, "What makes you think he'll admit who hired him to kill the senator?"

"He's infamous for one rule: never turn down a job for the right price," she said. "Soba is notoriously expensive. It'll cost you."

They took a turn down a side tunnel where the shops were tiny affairs one on top of the next. Cricket opened the door to a place brightly illuminated in red. It sold every type of colorful candy, especially jellybeans in large canisters floating above the customers. A synthetic strawberry smell filled the room. Noah swallowed hard to avoid gagging.

"Skyway technologies at work, boys and girls," a chubby, smiling woman told the group of little kids and their parents surrounding her. She tapped one of the floating canisters. "Ever wonder why a heliocar doesn't fall on our heads in an accident?"

"Accidents don't occur because all vehicles are equipped with automated navigation," one boy said. He looked no more than six. Another added, "Even though the law requires human drivers, flying cars are precision-controlled through the network."

"Yes, well," the woman cleared her throat and a parent came to her rescue.

"I think the candy lady is referring to the clear-bumble strips and tumble guards that would be activated if the network failed.

See the canisters? That's the same technology supporting them. That's why the jellybeans look like they're floating."

One kid yawned. Two others were already starting to squabble about who would get what flavor. The chubby woman reacted fast to save the sale and whipped through a few interfaces at her side.

Jettisoned through a complex series of tubes woven around the room, the jellybeans triggered robot arms and alarms so obnoxious that one parent covered her ears. The kids laughed and clapped. The parents filled their bags with the candy falling from the canisters. Eventually, they paid. Another group of parents and kids squeezed past Noah.

The saleswoman finally acknowledged him and Cricket.

"We're here about the new candy dispenser," Cricket said.

The woman motioned with a chin gesture to Cricket to head on back behind the candy contraptions. The kids had begun selecting and buying what looked to Noah, judging by the size of their sacks, like a year's worth of candy.

Behind the candy store, Cricket announced herself to two antique entertainment robots dressed in schoolgirl uniforms that led the visitors through a series of connecting rooms.

Each room contained candy dispensers of all kinds, beginning with the most modern, and gradually working back to true antiques the farther they traveled from the storefront. Intermixed with the candy machines was an assortment of old-fashioned and oddly disturbing girl robots, each immaculately maintained. Every surface gleamed without a speck of dust. Still, Noah noticed flies and, above the cloying scent of candy syrup, a terrible odor.

"This is creepy," Noah commented. Cricket nudged him hard in the side and he grunted.

"Keep it to yourself," Cricket replied.

"No, we should leave. Whoever set this place up is seriously disturbed," Noah said. Just as he turned to go, an especially ancient model robot approached them. The robot stood no higher than his waist and rolled on wheels. Its realistic face focused on Cricket. Its mouth was covered in red, and dark streaks ran down the front of the pinafore that covered its torso. Instead of hands, it had clamps and it immediately attached these to Cricket, pulling her toward the next room.

Someone was standing in the doorway with her back turned to Noah, but he recognized her even before he checked her biostats. His MAM query returned "Lydia DeLydia." The host of

Goodbye Los Angeles Hello stood immobile, staring into the next room, blocking Cricket's and Noah's view of whatever held DeLydia's attention. The half-sized robot drew Cricket to the doorway, despite the gardener's struggle to free herself. They barged into the newshound, jarring DeLydia from her stasis. She backed up, turned and plowed straight into Noah. He seized her upper arms and held her off. Her face was white. Wide-eyed, she looked up at Noah without really seeing him and screamed.

Noah spoke her name and repeated it. She closed her mouth and stood staring numbly at him until he gently moved her out of the doorway.

Cricket had given up trying to pull free of the small robot. Instead, the gardener swung a leg up high and brought the sole of her foot down hard on the doll face, knocking the machine's head half off its flexible neck. She then jumped with both feet off the floor, delivering a two-footed kick to the thing's pinafore that looked to Noah as solid a blow as any professional could have managed. Robot parts shot in every direction. Cricket landed neatly on the balls of her feet. The robot's clamps were still around her forearms, but she pried them off and tossed them beside the rest of the smashed machine.

She and Noah confronted what had made Lydia DeLydia scream. A man hung upside down from the ceiling. His clothing had been torn off him. So had his skin. His face was battered and swollen to twice normal size. From the odor and the bugs that crawled over the skinless flesh, Noah guessed he'd been dead for a while. He had an impulse to reach out to protect Cricket. When he touched her, she sprang away.

"Let's go," he urged. She turned abruptly and followed him out of the room.

"I've contacted the Order," said Lydia DeLydia, just outside. Although trembling and a peculiar shade of green, she appeared to be regaining her composure. She blocked Noah's way. "I'd like to interview you two about this incident."

Noah paused for a moment. His MAM embrace hid his true self, but she might figure out his real identity if he stayed too long in her presence. He was about to refuse to make a comment when Cricket stepped around him and addressed Lydia.

"Excuse us, Great Lady Lydia, I'm going to be sick." Cricket said and her voice came out as a hoarse croak. She grasped Noah's hand, cupped her other hand over her mouth and rushed them past the newswoman, through the string of rooms and out of the candy shop.

CHAPTER 16

Frisardi rapidly thumbed the controls of the heliovan, taking them in the opposite direction. Rika sat uneasily on the edge of her seat, not certain what the driver planned. The heliovan retraced its wide arc through traffic around the city center. Instead of arriving at Elysian Fields Retreat, they headed up the coast.

"I'll take you to the lab in Goleta," Frisardi announced. "The Retreat and sick building can wait until later in the day."

Not wanting to break the spell she had apparently put the man under with her demand to see the lab with the first Circle Tide outbreak, Rika remained silent. When the sunlit, sparkling ocean came into view, she took a deep breath and relaxed against the seat, reassured they were truly headed for the lab.

"Sebastian believes you'll find clues we've overlooked," Fritz continued. "But you need to have a full understanding of everything to uncover clues we've missed."

Rika gulped and nodded.

"Understand that I only take orders that come from the boss. Did Sebastian order you to visit the lab?" he asked.

The man sat beside her, an intimidating mass of muscle and bone. Waiting for her response, he was tense, his head more like that of a bird of prey than a human. She followed the path of his reasoning. If Sebastian needed her to find clues about Circle Tide, the boss had essentially ordered her to go there in spirit if not in words.

"Yes," Rika said. The notification that he'd checked her bio-stats blinked across the back of her eyelid. She passed. No lie.

Through her rationalization process, her saying "yes" amounted to the truth. It occurred to her that if Fritz shared this conversation with his boss, Sebastian would consider her a first-class liar. Rika felt her cheeks go hot and leaned against the window watching the waves buffet the cliffs.

"Will I need my hazmat anzug?" Rika said.

"That's a good idea," Fritz said. "You can keep it deactivated until we go inside the lab."

"I'll change in back," Rika said. Climbing behind her seat, she squatted down and put the hazmat anzug on under her clothes without activating it. Every time she glanced up, the driver had his attention on the skies, but she had the uneasy, icky feeling that he was watching her when she wasn't looking. When she returned to sit upfront again, Fritz's manner was so proper and reserved that she wondered if his watching had just been in her overactive imagination.

Below, the rocky coastline gave way to sandy flat beaches and later the rolling hills that embraced Montecito and Santa Barbara. The old wealth of several domus glittered, so many ruby-topped pearls nestled in the emerald green slopes above a sapphire sea. The architecture remained faithful to the towns' building codes and their history of red-tiled roofs and white stucco walls, long after living buildings replaced all but the original mission. The roots of these living buildings went so deep, they had become an integral part of the landscape.

With no expense spared, the domus adopted every new advance in design and each MAM enhancement. To Rika, the town practically glowed. Each dweller's dreams became the home's promise. In this place, people lived on an exalted plane.

"It's paradise," Rika said.

"I used to think so," Frisardi said.

Here, when they fell in love, married, raised extraordinary children to be the leaders of tomorrow, they innovated on themselves and their world to create unsurpassed aesthetic perfection. It took Rika's breath away. She had difficulty imagining a nasty word ever being said or that anything bad could ever happen here. The harmonized MAM-human environment made her feel giddy drunk. It reached for her.

"Once you come to work for a domus in Santa Barbara, it's said you never leave," Fritz said, turning the heliovan inland, northeast into Goleta.

She watched his thumbs blitz across the control panels as they left the light traffic for a glen of trees that obscured a row of heliopads that lay hidden until they hovered directly over it. At the far end of the row, several black heliovans were parked. Fritz landed on the heliopad furthest from the group.

"What in Thesni's name are they doing here?" he said and slammed his hand against the console so hard a piece broke off. It jetted past Rika's head into the back. "Sebastian isn't going to believe this."

Without explanation, he jumped out and stomped over to the vehicles at the other end. Uncertain whether she should follow him, she got out and waited. He walked slowly back, every step heavy and deliberate. His bird of prey expression had returned. This time his steady gaze didn't focus on her, but on the unassuming gates of Homenaje Laboratories.

To Rika, the place looked abandoned. Thick vines covered the high walls and stretched unevenly across the entrance. Leaves obscured all but the letters of the Homenaje Labs sign engraved there.

"Get back inside and stay there until I return. I'll find out what's going on," he ordered, gesturing vaguely toward the vehicle. He stared transfixed at the gates as though he could bore a hole through them and didn't once look back as he marched to the entrance.

Rika opened the back of the heliovan, pulled out her bag, and slung it over her shoulder. Keeping a safe distance, she followed the intense birdman. Rika was mesmerized by the way his massive structure displayed energy with his every ponderous step. It was as though he could solve whatever problems waited inside the walls of this compound by pure, brute force.

After the MAM security scan, he pushed through the gates. Rika followed and tried peering through the mat of vegetation. She pushed back some leaves from a tangled vine to see where Fritz was going. The driver entered the center building.

The labs were three nondescript, squat buildings set in a row with a closed bridge linking the top floors. Oddly, between the high-wall fence and the three buildings, no vegetation grew. On this side of the wall, the vine growth ended abruptly in a distinct line along the barrier's upper rim. The ground sparkled white and rose, resembling crushed seashells or broken glass. She leaned against the gate and was surprised when it clicked open.

She stepped inside, and the gate closed behind her. After a few moments, the chill of the white-rose surface touched her. She focused on the ground. The crunching sound of her footsteps had less to do with shells or glass, than the crystallized carcasses of insects and other small living beings that had attempted passage across the moat between compound wall and the buildings. Bending down, she identified spiders, crickets, worms and dragonflies fossilized in mid-motion. The whitened ears and tiny face of a squirrel made her heart ache.

Standing there, her feet became ice cold and then came a sharp, persistent ache. First her toes went numb. Her soles tingled painfully and lost feeling, then her ankles. She clomped across the space and stood in the doorway of the building looking back. Her feet had been reduced to inflexible stumps. Once past the forbidding surface in the shadow of the lab entrance, she stood for a long while until the blood slowly returned to her feet. The burning of the dissolving frostbite-like symptoms made her cry out. Looking around apprehensively, Rika hoped no one heard.

With the impact of the moat wearing off, the full force of the MAM hit her. From her legs to the top of her head, Rika had the sudden sensation of simultaneous tiny stings everywhere. She pulled back her sleeves and then examined her legs, but observed nothing. The DeeJee was familiar with the dead zones of the Bolsa Complex and the Order hospital with their enforced sterility, but nothing had prepared her for this. These could only be microscopic MAM agents that trolled surfaces here to destroy every living thing in their path. They'd found her. Although invisible, the agents overwhelmed her senses.

She stood in the midst of a kill zone. When the stinging ended, a new assault began. Tremendous pressure grew inside her ears. It became difficult to breathe. Shutting her eyes tight and concentrating to turn the MAM agents away before she passed out, she called for the MAM she knew, the internal friend that daily answered her queries. Together, they built a barrier between these relentless Homenaje agents and herself. Mentally, she tore through security features, knocking aside one after another so that she might escape.

When Rika finished, she saw a pigeon crest the compound wall and land on the white-rose mote. She tried to save it by shooing it away, but it ignored her. After a few pecks, it flew off. Relieved that the pigeon escaped and that she'd survived the attack, she burst into tears. She had disarmed potentially critical components of the lab's security to protect herself and sent Sebastian a communiqué: <Homenaje Labs — help!> Then, she stumbled through the front doors.

Inside, she wiped her cheeks with her sleeve and looked around. In front of her, the centenarian Director Mencius Wu sat in an overstuffed chair. Her boss Angela perched on the settee beside him. She seemed composed, but in tight-lipped misery. The birdman stood behind at attention. Every muscle in his body appeared to be straining to leap into action, but he remained on an unseen leash. She frowned at him. Fritz avoided her gaze. The three must have had a perfect view of her struggle across the mote and in the entrance. Only the IEC director looked tremendously pleased with the situation.

"You are an impressive young lady, Rika Musashi Grant," Wu said. "Since you've overcome our security measures, I'll take you on a tour."

"Let's wait for another time," Angela said. "She looks exhausted."

"Nonsense," Wu replied.

"I object," Fritz said. "It isn't safe."

"It is safe," Wu said. He stood. "Come with me, Rika."

Her eyes welled up again. Rika suffered a sudden fit of coughing, a delayed reaction from the attack. She pulled back her sleeves and was relieved to see that her arms weren't covered in welts from the stings she'd taken.

"If you take her anywhere in this facility," Fritz said and stepped between them, "I'll tell Sebastian everything."

"You will never speak of Homenaje events outside these walls," Mencius Wu said and his tone conveyed no room for doubt. "Don't be a fool."

"We shut this lab down for a reason, Mencius."

"Pardon?" Mencius said. His thin frame dwarfed by Fritz's, and still he commanded the man's attention. "Correct me if I'm wrong, but you no longer manage this facility, do you?"

"Don't push me."

"Let's face facts, Fritz. You're just a domus driver now. If you lost that job, too, you'd be hard-pressed to find another. That's not so good for your family, is it?"

Frisardi's fist tightened behind his back and the muscles in his neck flexed, but he stood aside. Rika studied him. The memory events came at her rapid-fire, haphazardly recorded and strung together.

Screaming, panicked lab technicians ran in the opposite direction down the hallway. Fritz grabbed one technician by the arm and asked, "Have you seen Bae?" The man shook his head and pulled his arm away. Fritz walked. His hazmat anzug barely stretched over his muscle mass, but he kept it activated.

He passed more frightened technicians until he came to a locked door. He stood there for a moment and cursed before issuing an override command.

The door opened and Circle Tide oozed past him into the passageway. He trudged through muck toward a wiry man slumped over lab equipment covered in black-green slime. "Bae! Bae!" No response. *Skip.* Through Frisardi, Rika pictured Bae prior to the accident: a bent over, solemn technician with wide brown eyes. *Skip.* Much earlier, Cricket and Bae stood side-by-side, smiling in front of the lab. The eyes of father and daughter matched.

Shaken by the brief memory events, Rika remained focused on Frisardi. He'd done nothing for her while she struggled outside, but the birdman clearly had wanted to help. On the other hand, the cool attitudes of Director Wu and Angela were terrifying. This was no normal test of her skills. The MAM defense agents had been set to kill.

The director took her by the elbow and led her out of the entrance hall. All the while, the tiny Fritz bombs bursting in her head made it impossible to clear her thoughts of his episodic memories.

"Do we need hazmat anzugs?" Rika asked. "I'm wearing a deactivated one under my clothes."

The question stopped the confident Director Wu in his tracks. He peered down at her.

"No," Wu said. His jaw worked silently for a moment before he continued. "What lies did Frisardi tell you?"

"He didn't tell me anything," Rika reassured him. "I've just come from Los Angeles where I'm on the Circle Tide project, and we wear hazmat anzugs."

"Ah. What a waste for Fritz to bring you here, although I never would have guessed the depth of your capabilities if he hadn't," Wu said. He held her tightly by the elbow and steered her through several hallways.

They came to a wall of glass that overlooked an enormous two-story room with long rows of large, domed cases. Robotic arms and other equipment were burping, buzzing and humming beneath and around the opaque domes. Next to the wall of glass was a door to an airlock that opened onto stairs. These descended to the floor. Rika looked from Wu to the door, and he only shook his head.

"You can observe the garden with its sublime ecosystem and manufacturing process behind touch-sensitive glass. No danger. No need to venture into the manufacturing area," he explained.

Before Wu could continue, a thin man with slicked-back hair and wearing a lab coat hurried down the hall toward them. He nearly collided with Rika in an effort to get to the director. "Mencius, we've got a problem. Three security breaches have occurred in the last fifteen minutes."

"Is this a deliberate attack?" the director asked.

"It's hard to ascertain," the man said. Up close, Rika noticed an oily sheen not only to his hair, but also his face. "So far, the breaches are minor, but we must commence a temporary emergency shutdown and evacuate all personnel."

"Shutdown? Is that really necessary? Show me the breaches," Wu ordered. Turning to Rika, he added, "Wait here. I'll send someone to escort you out."

Both men continued talking as they rushed down the hall together and disappeared around the corner. Rika stared out over the manufacturing floor and wondered what they produced. When she ran her hand over the glass, wherever her finger pointed came into abrupt focus. Tapping the glass to view inside a dome, she observed thick gray matter. When she zoomed in to the microscopic level, she observed mutant isopods with zebra-striped, jointed protective plates and seven pairs of legs. Some carried egg sacs on their sides as they climbed over and fed from the gray expanse. Others held flakes in their mandibles that they dropped at regular intervals. It appeared as though they were fertilizing the growth medium because wherever the flakes landed the gray matter formed higher mounds. Rika became so transfixed by these microscopic creatures that it took her several seconds to register the commotion at the far end of the manufacturing floor.

Clearing the glass to see the entire facility again, Rika stared at the lone figure in a hazmat anzug who was frantically yelling and pounding on a piece of equipment. Smoke rose around the woman. She collapsed. A high-pitched alarm sounded overhead. Activating her anzug, Rika went to the manufacturing airlock and dug out her portable Snuffire from the bag slung over her shoulder. As soon as the hood had locked in over her nose and mouth, she attempted to open the outer door.

For a moment, she felt a warning tingling of MAM agents and then they dropped away as though she'd been recognized and accepted as part of the lab. The door swung open for her to pass, but then it locked behind her. She attempted to open the inner door, but first she had to undergo a rapid dry shower. When the second door finally opened, she raced down the stairs and around several domes to reach the fallen technician.

Strong fan-filters pulled plumes of smoke from the area. Rika saw no flames where the woman had fallen, but plainly a nearby box had caught fire. She could feel a wall of tremendous heat around the equipment that the box had held. The apparatus had melted away, revealing a wide pellet of dark material.

To contain the searing heat and reach the technician, Rika sprayed her Snuffire toward the melted equipment. The fire suppressant spanned out across the area and collapsed around the dark pellet, sealing it away from the surrounding air. The scorching heat reduced enough for Rika to reach the technician. Rika took the woman by the arms and hoisted her up onto her back to drag-carry her to safety. She got only as far as the first dome before the Snuffire seal exploded, sending its own material in flames across the floor. Fire ignited in new areas.

The technician coughed and struggled to get to her own feet. Rika directed her up the stairs away from the inferno below. Rika suspected the woman was in shock and badly burned beneath her anzug. Still, the technician managed to climb the steps on her own. Before they reached the door, the fans stopped and hidden interior panels activated. The panels slid down one after another in fast succession over the walls and ceiling, clanging into place. A thick-paneled metal sheath replaced the glass wall above them and covered the airlock.

"We're trapped in here," the technician wailed. "We'll die."

"We've got our respirators," Rika assured her. "And we're above the fires so we can work on opening this door."

"No," the woman shook her head. "They won't risk the rest of the facility getting open exposure. This room is about to be contained, which will definitely kill us."

They sat together on the highest step closest to the sheathed door. Rika closed her eyes and concentrated on any mechanism that might open the airlock long enough for them to escape. Her dizziness kept her from focusing properly. She put her head down between her knees, hoping that might help. She felt the woman sag against her. The world went dark.

The screeching of metal against the door behind her caused her to lift her head. An instant later, two men had hold of the technician. They dragged her through first and then Rika felt their hands beneath her arms, hauling her through a small opening in the door below the metal panel. They'd propped the panel open with a bar that immediately began to buckle from the strain.

Just as they managed to bring Rika through the door, the panel came crashing down. They paused in the airlock for the mandatory dry shower and entered the hallway. The men didn't stop there. The smaller one hoisted Rika on his back and ran through the hallway, ahead of the larger man who carried the technician in his arms. The jostling made her dizziness and nausea even worse. Both men had on hazmat anzugs. With her blurry double vision and inability to process information, she failed to identify these men or the route they took. Ultimately, she gave up, closed her eyes and rested her head against the man's back.

Outside the compound in the parking lot, medics surrounded the technician and Rika. One of them deactivated the DeeJee's anzug and scanned her. She tried to fend him off, but was too weak. Other medics loaded the technician up on a stretcher and took her away. Rika wanted to see her face or at least say a few kind words. The medics kept her pinned down until they were satisfied she'd suffered no serious wounds or contamination. Frisardi threatened to knock the medics down to make way for his boss who held a glass of water to Rika's lips. She looked into Sebastian's face and realized immediately he'd been the one who carried her out of that hideous place to safety.

"Try to take a sip," he said. "You look like you need it."

She held the glass with both hands and drank it down. Sebastian knelt on one side of her and Fritz on the other. They lifted her to her feet and helped her to the Domus Restitio helio-van. The medics moved off to look after other evacuees from Homenaje Labs.

Perhaps it isn't too bad, she thought. She smelled no smoke. Almost everybody who came out through the gates could walk without assistance.

"We should get out of here," Fritz said in a low voice.

"Yes, I just want to make sure she's okay first," Sebastian replied.

Director Wu came out of the gates and made straight for them. Fritz groaned.

"I'm relieved you made it safely," the director said to Rika. He fixated on her as though the two of them were alone. "I'll take you down to the Institute so that Medic Vasil can examine you."

"Director Wu, we've already made plans for tonight," Sebastian said.

"Are you still having hallucinations, my dear?" Wu asked Rika.

"No," Rika said. It was true. She never had hallucinations, but she did tremble at the mention of Vasil.

"Even so, Vasil is worried sick about your mental health deteriorating. This capability you have to interact with MAM security. It's baffling. I need you to check into the sick ward so Vasil can work with you on the blackouts and run further tests. After your possible exposure, we'll also monitor your lungs."

"Pardon me," Sebastian said. He stood between them, forcing the director to acknowledge him. "Rika has been through enough for one day and doesn't appear all that interested in seeing the medic."

Fritz jumped up and held his arm out for Rika. He silently opened the door to the heliovan and practically lifted her into the back. She gratefully accepted his help and sank back against the seat while Sebastian and the director argued outside. They kept their voices low, but Wu signaled several times for Rika to come back out of the heliovan. She closed her eyes and turned her head away.

CHAPTER 17

Noah and Cricket emerged from the candy store into a side tunnel. The gardener's face looked pale and expressionless. Noah had to fight down a surge of nausea every time his mind showed him an image of the flayed, fly-ridden corpse of Bartholomew Soba.

One of the *Goodbye Los Angeles Hello* crew, his head encased in ultra-sensitive sound-and-image recording gear, was interviewing parents of the children. When he noticed Noah and Cricket coming out of the back of the store, he broke away and managed to corner them in a bend of the tunnel before they could escape. Noah's first impulse was to punch him and flee, but that would make the news streams for certain, and media attention was the last thing he needed. Their only option was to present themselves as just another boring couple who'd come to buy candy. He put his arm around Cricket and pulled her close. She elbowed him hard in the ribcage and glared up at him.

"Look here, I just want to ask you a few questions," the crewman said. "My boss is in there interviewing someone you might know."

"We don't know anybody here," Noah said. "We were simply buying chocolates." Suddenly alert, the guy zeroed in on his face. Noah realized his mistake and groaned. A lie to the media only made them more curious and persistent. Cricket jabbed him again, and he grunted. This time he deserved the elbowing, but he hugged her tight.

Hurrying up behind them in her elevator shoes, Lydia DeLydia nearly twisted her ankle. The crewman caught her and kept her from falling on her face while still managing to block Cricket and Noah from escaping.

The crewman must have a lot of practice saving Lydia from her tumbles, Noah thought. The ridiculous platform shoes wove directly into her tights. The reporter also wore a short skirt and a blouse that mimicked a schoolgirl's uniform. *Lydia does her homework*, the gamer thought, remembering the dead man's collection of robots. *That's just the look Bartholomew Soba would have appreciated if she'd gotten to him before his murderers did.*

"Hey! Hey, you two!" Lydia said, having pulled herself up and straightened her clothes with the help of her assistant. "I talked to the salesclerk. You went to see Bartholomew Soba to buy a candy dispenser."

Turning to the crewman, Lydia added, "We have to shoot something truly horrific. Soba is dead."

"Dead?"

"Tortured to death. These two came in after me and saw him there, too. He was hung upside down and skinned."

"Lydia! Are you okay?" the assistant asked.

She nodded, then held her hand to her mouth and abruptly hurried away down the tunnel. Noah made a motion to leave, but that made the crewman focus his headgear on him. Noah remained where he was. Lydia returned, her face blanched. She told the assistant, "I've contacted the Order. Get in there and record the scene if you can stomach it. I tried a first pass, but couldn't bear it."

"I can handle it," the crewman said. Lydia nodded and turned to Noah and Cricket.

The gamer felt Cricket grow still under his arm, practically frozen in Lydia's presence.

"You've both received a shock," Lydia said. "I have, too, but the two of you weren't simply buying a candy dispenser. You know something."

Lydia paused. Noah studied the tunnel floor.

"I'll trade you what you know for what I know," the newswoman said. "Soba contacted me. He told me he had a story to tell — that he was innocent of the Order's charges and that he didn't kill the senator."

"Innocent?" Noah asked. His heart raced. He remembered Soba stabbing his mentor. He'd fought the man using his fly-gaming skills and had chased him off. Noah had left Mari Ortega fatally wounded. The guilt he felt for leaving her side before the medics arrived stayed with him. It colored everything he did. The idea that the hitman had attempted to exonerate himself made him see red.

"Ouch! Ow!" Cricket yelled out and stomped on his foot. Feeling the crunch of her boot, Noah released her. Only then did he realize he'd crushed her shoulders with his arm.

"I'm sorry," he said, wincing from the pain of his bruised foot.

Cricket glared up at him and threatened to stomp his foot again. He stepped away from her.

"Lady DeLydia, every Heartlander knows Bartholomew Soba was a hitman," Cricket said.

"A hitman?" Lydia said and drew in a breath. Noah could imagine the gears in her head grinding on that piece of information. "A hitman, not a political fanatic?"

"Bartholomew Soba the hitman," Cricket repeated, emphasizing each word and then her tone softened, "But that wasn't Bartholomew Soba in there, that was the Candyman."

"Hmm, yes, well, look my dear, you mustn't be so naïve in life," Lydia said and looked up at Noah as though Lydia wanted his support for such a statement. Noah stared blankly at the newswoman. His foot hurt. Cricket might be crazy, but if there was one thing she was not, it was naïve.

Wondering where Cricket planned to take this Candyman business, Noah leaned against the tunnel wall and massaged the top of his foot. Lydia cleared her throat. "I'm quite certain these two men are one and the same. And you and your boyfriend Spider came to see him."

"We just wanted to buy a candy dispenser," Cricket said.

"And why is that?" Lydia asked, putting her hands on her hips.

"My little brother, Bae," Cricket said.

"Your little brother?" Lydia said. Noah watched Cricket's face to see if she might be lying since she had no detailed biostats to check — just the antiquated dog tag interface with her name and workplaces.

"Yes, my brother," Cricket said. "When my dad passed away, my mom and brother had to move down from Santa Barbara to L.A. Now they've been evacuated to Elysian Fields Retreat because of the Circle Tide. To cheer Bae up, we planned to surprise him and his friends. So—"

"You went to the Candyman to buy one of the new candy dispenser models. Is it the kind that floats and tosses candy in the air to anyone who gives the answers to its algebra and calculus problems? I bet it is," Lydia said, clapping her hands. "I always dreamed of one of those, too. Especially the ones that had the peanut butter-flavored jellybeans!"

"Math problems?" Cricket asked and made a face. "Something more fun might be better suited for—"

"We'll do it!" Lydia said. "I knew I'd find the happy ending to this horrible situation."

"Happy ending?" Cricket echoed.

"Go to the Elysian Fields Retreat. My crew and I will meet you both there," Lydia ordered. "Spider, you're her boyfriend, right? You come, too."

"No," Cricket said and blanched. "Spider and I can't be part of any media event. This is a private gift for my brother and his friends."

"Exactly; your brother," Lydia said, "the Circle Tide refugee orphan." She beamed. As usual, her smile brought to Noah's mind a crocodile. "Will you be there for the candy dispenser delivery? I want to make certain we get it to your little Bae. We probably won't need you in the story."

"Gee," Cricket said. She gazed up wide-eyed at the reporter. "Lady Lydia, you'd do that for us?"

"Of course, it's not just for you. With all the bad things happening, everyone needs some uplifting news right now."

Cricket tried to reply, but the reporter had turned away from them and was gesturing "bye-bye" with her hand as she headed back toward the store. "See you there!"

Clutching Noah's arm, Cricket led him away just as several Order regulars arrived and pushed past them.

When they'd traveled out of earshot, Noah yanked his arm free. "Cricket, what was all that about? Do you have a brother?"

"Of course, I set up an appointment to see the Candyman so I could buy a candy dispenser for Bae," Cricket said.

"Are you serious?" Noah said. "That's a true story?"

"Yes," Cricket said. "If I'd approached him directly on the murder, Soba would have killed us. Slice-slice, dead. He'd never have given us the chance to make a financial offer he couldn't refuse."

"Huh?"

"Word in the Underground has been that, once the Order gave out his name, he went crazy paranoid and believed everyone was out to kill him.

"So you planned to buy a candy dispenser?"

"Possibly. When you're dealing with users like Soba or Lydia, always have two or three layers of truth for them to sift through. Otherwise, they figure out what you're really after."

"What are you really after?"

Cricket shrugged and kept walking.

Stepping in front of her, Noah laid his hands on her shoulders. "Talk about users! You knew I was innocent when you came to see me, didn't you? You were manipulating me so I'd pay Soba's fee and he'd admit who hired him to kill the senator!"

With a burst of energy, she shook herself free. "So what if I did use you? You want to know who's behind her murder as much as I do."

Noah hated manipulation. His parents were masters at it. Still, she had a point. He wanted to see the senator's hidden enemies exposed and punished, not simply the hitman.

He hadn't been aware of following any particular route, but they arrived at an URT platform where a train would take them to Elysian Fields. They were alone for the moment.

"You said yourself that Mari had only been stabbed in the stomach when you left her," Cricket began.

"So what?" Noah asked. Still angry, he breathed in deeply to remain steady, and exhaled.

Cricket poked him in the chest. "The fatal wound was here! So who stabbed her?"

"Hey," he said.

"What if Soba was hired to scare her, and he was set up?"

"Set up? I saw him attack her. We fought. He left."

"If you chased Soba off and he managed to escape, who finished the job?"

"Soba returned after I'd left," Noah guessed.

"Really? He hung around after you contacted the Order?" Cricket asked.

"I don't know," Noah admitted.

The platform was filling with commuters. Noah bowed to Cricket.

"I'll take my leave," Noah said.

"No, you'll come with me," Cricket said. "If you don't show up, Lydia might research who you are underneath that MAM embrace. And then, won't she wonder what you were doing at the scene of a second murder?"

"You gangster!" Noah pulled her close and whispered in her ear. "Are you blackmailing me?"

She nodded. He pushed her away. "This is unbelievable. I've got to get out of this town as soon as possible."

When the train arrived, he boarded with her. Cricket motioned with her finger for him to bend down so she could speak in his ear. He ignored her for several stops until he thought of his own question about the assassin. He bent down and whispered, "Maybe Soba wanted Mari to suffer before he finished her off, and I interrupted him. Only the senator knew about me coming for our meeting."

Cricket shook her head. "Think about it. He's a professional. He'd have made the murder look like an accident and never become a suspect. Instead, he scrawls crap on the walls, wounds her and leaves, giving you the time to contact the Order."

"You know, when I considered him a fanatic, I believed he murdered the senator," Noah said. The "Heartland = Underground" and "Traitor" on the walls of her office were seared into his memory. "To kill Ortega like that makes no sense if it wasn't a political hate crime."

"Exactly! My bet is his contract was to scare and wound Mari," Cricket said. "And he got framed for murder instead. Don't get me wrong. Soba deserved to die just like he did. He hurt Mari."

"You really are a gangster. You don't need me here for this," Noah said.

As soon as they got off the train, they headed groundside toward Elysian Fields. Noah lagged behind. Cricket looked back and shook her finger at him. He touched his neck. It still stung from her attack. He wondered how she could pull off such cuteness so soon after her determined attack on him. She seemed to have gotten over witnessing Soba's tortured corpse.

Cricket walked back and wrapped her arm around his, ensuring he wouldn't slip away at the last minute. Moments later, they reached Elysian Fields Retreat gates and requested entrance.

Noah realized he was sweating. His shirt licked away the beads that rolled down his sides as he imagined spending more time in front of Lydia, the media crocodile. She had proven herself resourceful at getting stories, if not the truth. The newswoman had already speculated that Cricket and he had been at Soba's for more than a candy dispenser. Noah dreaded being cornered by that woman again before he'd managed to clear himself as a suspect.

After some discussion with the guards on duty and a MAM scan, Noah entered the retreat with Cricket holding tightly to his arm. He'd seen Elysian Fields in the media, but those brief

glimpses hadn't prepared him for the place. Stark white buildings in tight rows radiated out from a center square. People
waited in lines almost everywhere he looked, for bathroom facilities or supplies. Magi monks and other clergy walked among
the groups providing assistance. Pairs of Order regulars were
planted at every major corner. The refugees gave them a wide
berth.

Where people weren't in lines, they sat in small groups and
spoke in muted voices. When Cricket and Noah crossed one
line to get to the building where Cricket's mother and Bae were
housed, a burly man with a full beard grabbed Noah by his shirt.

"No cutting," he said. "We've been waiting for over two
hours."

Noah squeezed the man's wrist until he yelled out and let
go. Noah walked on. "This is wrong," he told Cricket. "Humans
can't live on top of each other like this with no relief. This is
bound to cause serious problems."

"It's claustrophobic. The wise people here spend most of their
time in Novus Orbis just to keep their sanity," Cricket said quietly. "Wait until nightfall. It gets worse."

Noah wished Lydia DeLydia would hurry up and arrive so
that he could leave.

"It's so crowded," Cricket said. "This is worse than the last
time I visited."

Even growing up as he had, the privileged son of a top
domus, he'd spent plenty of time in crowded places. Every city
center maximized its population density to leave room for the
surrounding agricultural lands and wildlife parks. The wasteful
suburban sprawl of centuries past had been eradicated. However,
more than any high-density place he'd experienced, the retreat
reminded him of hardcore media streams depicting an offworld
work camp for prisoners. Everyone looked miserable. No wonder
Cricket wanted to cheer up her brother.

"This is getting to you, isn't it?" Cricket asked.

"Not at all," Noah lied, as they entered a white building. The
main floor looked to be a giant dining hall and laundry facility.
The sleeping quarters must be up on another level. Cricket and
Noah arrived before dinner, but every seat in the place was taken,
along with every spot against the walls. The room stank of body
odor. Several people had deep, hacking coughs. He shuddered.

Out of the solid block of seated evacuees, a woman with dark
hair and a young boy jumped up.

"Cricket!" the woman yelled and people made way so she could emerge from the crowd. The boy had an easier exit. He simply climbed over everyone to get to the visitors, which earned him grumbles and a few half-hearted swipes at his legs and head. His reckless path reminded Noah of Rika the pipsqueak with her bounding organo-pumps.

"You must be Cricket's mom," Noah said. The woman threw her arms around him after hugging Cricket.

"Oh, no," she said. "I'm Bae's aunt. My sister is still in the infirmary at the north end of the retreat. You'll go see your mom this time, right Cricket?"

At that moment Cricket couldn't answer. Bae had leapt into her arms, and she struggled to remain standing. The boy let her briefly hold him before breaking free, bumping into nearby people and climbing on the table so he could jump at her again. His biostats showed he was eight and small for his age. Each time, Bae bounded at her, Cricket almost lost her footing. Her exasperated laughter only encouraged him. Noah stood back out of his way to avoid becoming another one of Bae's launching pads.

A kid not much bigger than Bae rushed into the building. "Hey everyone, the crew from *Hello Los Angeles Goodbye* is in the square."

Some people perked up at the news and started for the door. Cricket took Bae by the hand and together they joined the crowd headed toward the retreat center square. In the few minutes it took them to walk to the square, Lydia's crew had set up a tall platform with a big draped object in the center. Noah was impressed by their speed. The crew called for kids to come forward and sit in front. All sides of the square had become standing room only. Even the temporary streets that fed into the square were clogged.

Bae let go of Cricket's hand and made his way toward the growing group of children. She followed close behind. Noah marveled at how she moved so easily in such tight groups without disturbing anyone. He kept getting elbowed by people, whichever way he moved.

One unusually wrinkled woman poked him particularly hard in the stomach and clutched his tunic. "You're so tall and young with plenty of time to see the world's wonders. Don't be so greedy. Stand back so your elders can see."

He felt his face go hot and thought about sneaking off, but Cricket turned back and took him by the arm again to bring them both as close to Bae as possible.

The *Hello Los Angeles Goodbye* program alternated between Novus Orbis and the stage. Lydia had several third-tier celebrities she interviewed who agreed to suffer minor humiliations like singing when they couldn't or dancing when they shouldn't or if talented in all areas, receiving pies to the face, though the missiles came from one of the city's top pastry chefs. In one instance presenting a pie to Lydia on stage, the chef complained that he'd had no idea his masterpieces would be showcased on faces rather than delighting people's palates.

The whole program grated on Noah's nerves. He needed sleep and hated this sort of sideshow at the best of times. Yet the kids were so enthralled, their infectious laughter made Cricket grin more than once. Even Noah cracked a smile, but he thought of little else besides leaving. Nothing about this business sat right with him. For one, no one from Lydia's crew had met up with them to ensure that they had the correct Bae. That probably meant the crew had been monitoring them from afar, which didn't strike Noah as upfront or good intentioned. He wondered if Lydia might have another reason for insisting that he and Cricket show up.

At the end of the show, Lydia snapped her fingers and the *Hello Los Angeles Goodbye* theme song played while two girls from the crowd were brought up to remove the tarp covering the candy dispenser. Lydia recounted a schlocky story about a girl who wanted her brother to be happy and how they'd met this wonderful Candyman who'd offered to donate a candy dispenser. The back-story came straight out of some fiction archive as far as Noah could tell. When she mentioned Bae's name and a spotlight shown upon him, both Cricket and her brother were visibly stunned. On cue, the girls standing on stage yanked down the sides of the tarp, and it fell away to reveal an enormous contraption that immediately shot out colorful bubbles containing elaborate math questions that hung in the air waiting to be answered.

"This is a present to Bae and the children of Elysian Fields," Lydia said and beamed that horrid reptilian smile. "Of course, it wouldn't be a real gift unless it had an educational component."

The kids all sat in silence. Noah studied Bae's face and saw the uneasiness there. These weren't genetically enhanced kids who had already mastered calculus. They were Undergrounders with all the genetic flaws of their parents, who'd been moved groundside to enjoy new housing, only to see their homes succumb to Circle Tide. Unlike people of means, once their places were destroyed, these families had no place to live except in the retreat.

No one was answering the questions, and no candy would start to fall until someone did. Quickly Noah crouched down, pulling Cricket down beside him. Noah leaned over and whispered several answers to Bae and his friends. They rocketed to their feet in rapid succession, calling out answers and receiving a blast of jellybeans that delighted everyone around them. When Bae sat down again, he reached over and handed Cricket and Noah some candy.

"Don't worry," Bae told Cricket. "We'll hack it so your friend won't have to be here next time to get us candy."

Cricket ruffled his hair. Bae growled at her and pulled away.

"Now for the adult part of the programming. I warn you there're some gruesome streams you may not want to see. They're accessible via Novus Orbis, if, and only if, you're over eighteen," Lydia said. Her crew was busy luring the kids off to the side with more gifts.

"We should leave," Noah said. The space separating them from Lydia had cleared, which gave them an exit, but also a clear path to the stage.

"Give me a chance to hug Bae goodbye," Cricket said.

Right then, the spotlight fell on Noah and Cricket. She gasped. Suddenly Lydia stood in front of them. The crowd's focus shifted to the couple, along with the crew and their extra headgear. No moment could ever be lost with them around.

"This is Bae's big sister," Lydia said and the crowd clapped politely. "But there's a darker side to this wonderful event. Do you want to know what it is?"

The crowd roared. Noah thought his knees might melt into the pavement. Cricket had her head down so that her hood shadowed her face. No one outside the immediate circle could catch a glimpse of her features. Lydia nodded to one of her crew and suddenly hands were yanking off Cricket's hood and the crew's headgear zoomed in. To Noah's surprise, Cricket did not fight back. Her hands balled into tight fists, but otherwise she remained completely immobile.

"Cricket and her boyfriend went to see the Candyman to buy a candy dispenser for Bae," Lydia said and her voice reverberated off the white buildings facing the square. "Look what they found instead."

Murmurs rose in response to the images of Bartholomew Soba in Novus Orbis. Noah rejected all of them. His personal memory of the upside down hitman was awful enough. And then, Lydia replayed Cricket telling her that Soba was a hitman for hire. Noah listened with fascination, and, although he remembered the conversation word-for-word, it astonished him that Lydia had the nerve to air it. "Hitman" implied someone had hired Soba to kill the senator, and that was not something the Order had ever made public.

"These two told us they went to meet the Candyman, but never knew he was also the traitor and fanatic Bartholomew Soba. Bartholomew the Candyman killed our beloved senator," Lydia said. "The Order found Noah of Domus Aqua's DNA at the place where Soba was killed, along with several others: mine, Cricket's and maybe this man's. Do you have any information to share, Spider?"

When Noah remained silent, she said, "Would you deactivate your MAM embrace? Is there something important you're hiding?"

With the spotlight full on his face, he saw only bright white light and heard Lydia's disembodied questions. He donned the mild expression that Senator Ortega had taught him and simply shook his head, as though the whole event bewildered and saddened him. He knew he wasn't fooling Lydia DeLydia. He hoped he was pulling it off for the media-stream viewers, but the crowd here in the retreat's central square was pressing closer. Someone jabbed him in the back and he fell forward at Lydia's feet.

CHAPTER 18

Inside the parked heliovan, Rika listened to Director Wu and Sebastian arguing outside. She noticed that Wu had moved away from Sebastian, closer to her window, and that he was speaking in a louder voice. He wanted her to hear their heated discussion.

"I know she prefers to go with you, but Rika should return to the Institute for her own sanity and for everyone else's safety," the director said. Rika tapped on the window, but the centenarian had his back to her and was focused on Sebastian. What he was talking about — her uncanny ability to bypass MAM security as she had when she'd overrode the moat to enter the secure lab implied that she had capacities beyond anything she'd expected. If this made her dangerous to others, she wanted to discuss it with Wu. When she couldn't attract his attention, she tried the door. It was locked.

Frisardi sat rigid in the driver's seat with his fists resting on the console.

"Fritz, will you unlock my door?" she asked. "Frisardi! Please!"

The driver ignored her. He stared straight ahead. Shortly afterwards, Sebastian climbed in beside Fritz. He was speaking sharply to the director. Rika heard something about "needless alarm" and "old man's vapors."

Over Wu's continued protests, they lifted off. She pressed her hands against the window. For Sebastian, it was as if the director had ceased to exist. He turned to Fritz and said, "I just received notice *that person* showed up at the retreat to see her family. You were supposed to monitor them. Where her brother goes, she goes. Head to Elysian Fields next."

Fritz winced, but his giant thumbs orchestrated the flight pattern. The vehicle heeled over and changed direction toward Elysian Fields. "Flight time, one hour," he told his employer.

"Sebastian," Rika said and placed a hand on his shoulder. "Thank you both for coming to my rescue. I can't believe what happened back there—"

"You should rest," Sebastian interrupted. When she began again, he cut her off with a raised hand. "After today's trauma, I insist you sleep."

Both men remained tight-lipped and focused on the sky traffic. Rika closed her eyes, not to rest, but to search data on the Homenaje Labs. The information either proved so old it was irrelevant or she came up against "classified information: security clearance required."

Hacking into Order archives would be dangerous. If alerted to an intruder, the Order daemons of Novis Orbis could be relentless. Rika definitely wanted to have all her wits about her for any data heist. Her headache made concentrating difficult. A good meal and a full night's sleep would take care of that.

Her stomach growled loudly as they landed on the heliopad just inside the retreat and again when a guard poked his head in Fritz's window and scanned them to ensure they were on the scheduled visitors list.

"This won't take long," Sebastian said, surprising Rika. "Please rest. We'll go get something to eat as soon as we return."

His solicitude took her by surprise. "Don't you want me to investigate the retreat?" Rika asked.

"I did, but you'll never recover if you keep pushing yourself. Experiencing the labs was enough for one day," Sebastian said. He scowled at Fritz who immediately became preoccupied with the heliovan console. "Besides this will be quick."

Sebastian motioned to the driver. They got out and headed off at a jog toward the series of white box buildings. Rika laid her head back for a few seconds.

"This is too much," she said out loud. For the third time in one day, she'd been ordered to stay put. First it had been Fritz, then Wu and now Sebastian. "What is it with these guys?"

Rika got out of the heliovan and started after Sebastian and Frisardi. If they'd truly wanted her to remain there, Fritz would have locked the doors. She'd never visited a refugee center and decided to call up the retreat's schematic. It showed her that the two men were heading down one of the many temporary streets that radiated out from the central square. As she loped after them, she realized with relief that it would be impossible to become lost. She passed Order regulars stationed at every corner.

Otherwise, the place was desolate, completely drained of evacuees, until she approached its center. That turned out to be wall-to-wall people who were unkempt and stank. The way the men jostled each other in front of her and their harsh jeers disturbed her.

Despite her small stature, when she stepped back from the sweaty mob, she could see the platform and an enormous half-floating device spewing candy. Three people dodged around the stage. The center of attention was the easily recognizable host of a popular news program, Lydia DeLydia, who was neither agile nor fast.

Still, every so often Lydia managed to corner the two others on stage for a few seconds to ask a question. The pair — a tall athletic man and a skinny nimble woman — refused to answer. The woman ducked and dashed about the stage like a trapped mouse looking for a way out, even risking coming dangerously close to the workings of a floating contraption that dispensed candy. The man was also quick on his feet and obviously looking for an escape route. Neither could easily jump off the stage, because Lydia's crew was down on the ground and stabbed at them with long poles. Through all this, the crowd roared with laughter. The host was definitely playing it for laughs in her elevator shoes and out-of-place schoolgirl outfit.

With a gasp, Rika recognized the two unfortunates as Noah the Spider and Cricket the gardener. At that moment, the cat-and-mouse game abruptly ended. A series of whistles caused Cricket to glance in one direction offstage. The gardener froze, staring. Everybody else — Lydia, Noah and the crowd — naturally followed her line of sight. Instantly, Cricket took a running leap off the opposite side of the platform. The crowd caught her and quickly lowered her to the ground so that she was out of sight. Following her example, Noah took the same leap and disappeared into the throng.

Standing still for a split-second, Lydia stared out at her audience. Deprived of her interview subjects, the host recovered like a show business veteran. She took a bow and said, "Goodbye Los Angeles Hello, that's all for tonight," then signed for her team to cut the media stream. Lydia started for the stairs.

Already on the outside of the throng, Rika dashed between buildings to the next street in the series of spokes that led off the central area, saw nothing and repeated the maneuver to the next spoke. She came out between two buildings to see a large crowd surrounding Noah and a group of Magi monks in their chameleon habits. The monks took the young man by the shoulders and forced him to crouch. There was a flurry of indistinct motion and suddenly Noah was not to be seen.

"I want one of those cloaks," Rika said to herself as she studied the Magi monks. Their robes made them seem no more than a blur against the stark backdrop of the retreat. Maintaining tight formation, the Magi separated from the crowd and moved off down the street.

Lydia's crew with their headgear and glowing logos had left the stage and were chasing after the evacuees who'd caught Cricket and Noah. The suspect group raced swiftly away toward Elysian Fields' main entrance.

"After them!" Lydia said.

Rika stepped back between the buildings. To her astonishment, she saw Fritz and Sebastian following the news crew. The two were so intent on the pursuit that they passed by the DeeJee without seeing her.

That has all the earmarks of a diversion, Rika thought. Not sure if she was making a mistake, she followed her hunch and watched the Magi and a stream of evacuees file into the last building in the row that lined the street. Rika caught up and managed to join the evacuees. A moment later she found herself in the building's great hall.

There was a broad staircase the Magi were climbing as a tightly knit group. Only one stayed behind, and from the way he looked at Rika, she was sure he was acting as a sentinel. As the monks went up, the crowd filled the stairs. They sat, pulled out snacks and drinks. Some started evening games of Go. Rika knew she must look out of place, but she made for the stairs. The Magi monk blocked her way and took her by the shoulders, which reminded her of Noah's dramatic way of getting her attention. His cowl slipped back and she recognized him.

"Jeremiah," she said. "I need to go up there."

He dropped his hands from her shoulders, but continued to block her path.

"Rika, what are you doing here?" he asked.

"I'm … I'm with your brother."

The news travelled up the stairs, passed from mouth to mouth. It was two long minutes before an answer came down the same way: "Let her pass."

A narrow path opened up that provided just enough room for Rika's feet. She climbed the stairs. The way closed behind her as she reached each next step. Rika was hoping she'd done the right thing by following her impulse. After all, Noah might still be the target of lethal violence by Heartlanders or by whomever had really murdered Senator Ortega and wanted the only witness out of the way.

And yet, it couldn't be a coincidence that Cricket and Noah had come to Elysian Fields the same day that Sebastian had scheduled her to see it. Something in her strange, enhanced psyche had pushed her to follow the trail of Magi monks protecting Noah and Cricket. Besides, she was sure that Cricket knew a lot more about the senator's death. Rika hadn't had the chance to question her. Cricket might even know about the labs and Circle Tide, too. The gardener had been an enigma from the start, and was even more so now that Rika had seen Sebastian and Fritz so intent on following her.

There was also another factor at play although Rika was not yet ready to examine it too closely. When she'd seen Noah up on the stage with Cricket, they'd looked like a couple, and the DeeJee had felt a sudden tightness around her heart. Everything inside her had sped up. Every step she took had seemed too slow. The previous night at Order headquarters, Rika and Noah had been mistaken for a couple. While preposterous, a part of her hadn't minded. Now she felt as if she'd been the butt of one of Noah's cruel jokes. He should have mentioned that he already had a girlfriend.

At the top of the stairs, Rika made her way through people sitting or leaning against the walls of the hallway. She passed several closed doors until she came to one that was open. Beyond was a particularly hushed room. Before Rika could register what was going on within, a Heartlander seized her arm and yanked her through the opening. The door slid closed behind her.

Inside, armed men stood at attention, lining the walls. They automatically moved their hands to their holstered weapons as she approached the room's center where Magi monks in their chameleon habits, their cowls drooping over their faces, knelt in a semicircle. Even up close, the monks managed to create a trick of the eye, concealing the three they surrounded. Rika immediately recognized the trio as Ochbo, Cricket and Noah. They sat in a row across from a woman who was surely the most striking, elegant person Rika had ever seen.

The woman rested on her knees, her body forming an S-shape. She had a dramatically narrow waist and slim legs neatly tucked beneath her. Her full lips and a perfect heart-shaped face stood out above a scarf that matched the deep color of her eyes. Rika blinked and the woman became a roguishly handsome man sitting in the same position with that scarf about his neck. He gestured for Rika to join them. Querying biostats, Rika bowed deeply to hide her shock at meeting a legend in the flesh.

"Lady Whisk-Away," Rika said. "This is an honor."

"Why don't you honor me by explaining why you're here?" the courtesan said. Her eyes glittered. It was rumored that Lady Whisk-Away, sometimes known by the Heartlanders who adored her as W-A, might present herself as either a man or a woman depending on the individual's desire secreted away in their biostats. To some in the room, W-A must be a man, to others a woman. To Rika, W-A personified the ideal of both sexes.

"I'm here because I followed Noah," Rika admitted and sank to her knees beside the monks. She bowed so that her forehead briefly touched the floor.

"I'll vouch for her," Noah said quickly and cleared his throat.

"You've already done that or she wouldn't be here," the lady said and smiled. Her men along the sides of the room relaxed a little. "Do you vouch for her, too, Cricket?"

"She's the DeeJee who breached OMM headquarters security from the Sanctuary library," Cricket answered. She was seated furthest from Rika. "She has many talents."

With a curt nod, the courtesan turned to the tallest of the group. "Noah, as I was saying, it's difficult to imagine you participating in the murder of the senator."

"That is a relief," Noah said.

"We unofficially represent the Heartland. We extend an offer to protect you when you travel in the retreats and across the Underground, as we did today."

"Thank you," Noah said. "Let me clarify that Lydia implied I had something to do with Soba's murder: I did not."

Lady Whisk-Away's lips compressed. "That reptile also blamed Heartlanders for skinning the Candyman, supposedly as an act of vengeance for his attack on the senator," she said.

Rika gasped. So the senator's murderer had been killed. She hadn't stayed current on the media streams all day. W-A's eyes flickered over her.

"Soba was a known assassin. Whoever hired him most likely tortured and killed him, counting on the media to make Heartlanders convenient scapegoats. Even though Senator Ortega did a lot to change groundsiders' misconceptions about us, it's all being undone. We need another Ortega." She gave Noah a considering look. "It's my understanding that Mari groomed you for a future in politics."

Noah shook his head. "I'm no Ortega. I've given up politics. Still, I appreciate your protection from the angry mob and from Lydia's cannibal crew. I'm in your debt, Lady Whisk-Away."

"Yes, you are. In return, we have a favor to ask." She unfolded her long legs from beneath her. "But first, let us eat."

Immediately, the door slid open and trays of steaming food were passed along. The same woman who'd pulled Rika into the room now served her a small bowl of crispy grown-chicken and baby bok choy on top of steaming rice with a side dish of pears for dessert.

Not having eaten all day, Rika immediately consumed her portion and could have downed several more had anyone offered seconds. Wishing she'd taken more time to finish her meal, she looked around the room at the diners. The Magi pulled back their cowls to eat. Every monk had dark half-moons below his eyes, as did Noah, Ochbo and Cricket. Rika imagined she must look tired, too. Noah took the longest of everyone to finish his meal as though he dreaded hearing the favor Lady Whisk-Away would ask.

"You've found your food passable," the lady said. Neither Rika nor any of the other guests had anything left in their bowls. Her eyes took on the inner-directed look that all MAM users knew as the sign she was receiving a communiqué. "So-so-so. I've been informed that the Order was tipped off that Noah could be hiding in the retreat. You're now wanted for the murder of Bartholomew Soba. Their search won't take long if we stay here. We'll discuss the favor you owe us later. Follow me."

"Don't worry," Ochbo slapped Noah on the back and said, "Jeremiah and I will find you and pick you up."

Lady Whisk-Away opened the only other door to the room and motioned to Noah. Cricket followed him. Rika rose and took up the rear.

"Cricket, you must see your mother," W-A ordered. Cricket nodded and moved out of Rika's way.

"You don't want to go where he's headed," Lady Whisk-Away warned Rika. "The Order isn't after you."

"Noah and I need to talk," Rika said.

"Suit yourself." W-A turned and hurried them through a string of dimly lit rooms packed with people. The earlier mood of pent-up aggression that Rika had sensed from the evacuees had changed. Many of the people who moved from their path wore strange facial expressions. At first, Rika thought the evacuees were smiling at them. By the umpteenth baring of teeth, she became suspicious. The look was more of a pained muscle spasm, a forced perma-grin that they had no way of controlling, than an actual smile.

"What's with everyone?" Noah asked W-A.

"We call it Happy Face. It's a side effect of the substance the Order uses to calm individuals who react assertively to the conditions here. Their biostats betray their state of mind, which means they get an obligatory dosing," W-A said. "Few survive long in here without experiencing Happy Face. We're just too many monkeys in a cage."

Rika noticed W-A's hands briefly curl into fists at her sides. At the last room, they took a stairwell down to the ground floor and peered out the glass panel in the exit door.

"Now, here's the hard part," the lady said. "You see the sewer grate. You have to get to it and climb down without being seen. Wait for a signal from the two boys over there; then run."

Beyond the door, Rika noticed the Order regulars were no longer at the street corners. They were probably conducting an overall sweep to find Noah. When that didn't work, because of his unregistered MAM embrace, they'd go door-to-door looking for hideaways. Rika and Noah bowed to Lady Whisk-Away in thanks. She hurried back up the stairs.

After several minutes, one of the boys stood and stretched. He made a nod towards them with his head. Rika gulped and Noah burst out of the door and raced for the grate. Always light on her feet, she sped past him. Together they pulled up the metal grill. Rika climbed down first. Noah pulled the grate overhead before descending as well.

Inside, the shaft that descended to the sewer smelled musty and wet. Slimy mildew grew on the sides of the walls. It rubbed off onto Rika's sleeve when she lost her footing and fell against it. In the floor at the bottom, another grate led directly into the waterway. An even stronger odor rose through its corroded slats. Rika gagged. They were stuck unless they wanted to brave the nasty water below them. Noah climbed down beside her. In the narrow confines, they were pressed together. Their height difference meant that her face pressed against his chest.

"You had to join me here?" Noah said, his voice raspy. "It couldn't wait?"

"Aren't you glad you have some company, here in this stink hole?" Rika countered. "Besides, I've got questions I want answered."

"So you said." Noah rolled his eyes. She could tell he took brief, shallow breaths through his mouth to avoid the brunt of the stench. She did the same.

"I hope Ochbo and Jeremiah come get us fast," Rika said. The light from the street filtered down to their level so she could make out his face and the mildewed wall behind him.

"Why don't you distract us?" Noah suggested.

"What's your relationship with Cricket?" she asked. "Are you two … together?"

He laughed and the motion made his chest move against her cheek. "You can't be serious. What are you, the DeeJee Stalker? That's the question that couldn't wait?"

"No," Rika said, her cheeks suddenly hot. She wondered if he could feel the change in temperature. "I care because my line of questioning changes based on if you are, or if you aren't, with her."

"Oh, that makes perfect sense," Noah said and shook his head. "If you must know, I met her for the first time today. Although looking back on it, I think I saw her the night of the murder."

"So you don't know anything about her relationship to Domus Restitio or if she's involved with Homenaje Labs?"

"What? No." Noah shifted his weight, pushing her against the wall.

"Hey watch it!"

"Look," Noah said and grabbed her by the waist. "I'm going to put you on one of the ladder rungs. That'll make us both more comfortable."

Rika swatted his hands away and climbed up two rungs by herself, which did give them a little more breathing room, and it put them face-to-face.

"What happened to your neck?" Rika asked. "That's a bad cut."

"It's a long story," Noah replied.

"Maybe I'll climb up a few more," Rika suggested. He stopped her.

"Rika, that'll have me talking to your … stomach," Noah said. "Let's just stay like this."

Suddenly, they heard a grinding noise and a thump. Their confines went pitch black as something covered the grill above them. The sound of the heavy grate moving gave Rika butterflies in her stomach.

"Are you two coming or what?" W-A hissed.

Relieved to hear a familiar voice and not an Order regular's command, Rika guessed each step up in the darkness. Noah kept one hand on her ankle to make sure he didn't climb up on top of her. They crawled up through the floor of a heliotruck. As soon as Noah cleared the grate, W-A replaced it. She went to the front and sat in the driver's seat, waving for them to duck down. They lifted off.

After Lady Whisk-Away cleared the retreat, she yelled back, "It's safe to come out now. I commandeered a ministry heliotruck for some donations for the retreat. That means I fly the no fly zone to the Ministry of Internal Affairs and to the Interplanetary Council. The Council tower is my first stop. You can spend the night where Cricket usually sleeps. She gave the okay. It's one place no one would ever think to find you."

"Thank you for getting us out of there so quickly. Where's my brother and Ochbo?" Noah asked.

"They've been taken in for questioning. Your mother has been notified."

"Will they be in trouble for being at the retreat?"

"No, the Magi often volunteer," said Lady Whisk-Away. "Any trouble they're in will be over you. Listen; since I recently became an evacuee, Jeremiah and I have discussed the retreat's overcrowding at some length. Your brother visits us daily."

"I didn't know you two were friends," Noah said.

"Yes. So … about the favor you'll do for us. Until this crisis is over, all the domus need to pool together and fund better conditions for the evacuees. Domus Aqua should lead by example."

Rika watched Noah. His spider tattoo crawled to the bridge of his nose and perched there. His moving tattoo gave away his nervousness every time — even though his face remained stoic.

"We need you to convince your family to help us and to commit more resources to stopping Circle Tide," the courtesan continued.

W-A's request for help from a wealthy domus made sense to Rika. Querying the domus' properties while she sat there, she saw that many of Aqua's buildings were listed as sick. Residents and workers had relocated to the retreats or were living with relatives or friends, which was all the more reason for Noah and his family to be obliged to help.

"Honestly," he said. "I would be glad to ask my eldest brother Daniel and my parents for you, but my influence over them is zilch."

"You have the power of a brother and a son. Give them what they want, and you'll get what you want," Lady Whisk-Away said. Her words carried a certain import that escaped Rika, but Noah reacted immediately by crossing his arms over his chest and refusing to make eye contact. W-A sat straight with her smile frozen on her face. The threat behind the lady's words made Rika feel relieved no favors were being asked of her. "I have confidence in you. As you are aware, lives are at stake including yours."

"I'll do what I can," Noah said.

"Promise on the honor of your domus that Domus Aqua will help."

"I promised myself not to make such promises. It gets me in trouble, but I'll do my best."

"Your best? We will be certain to match your best efforts," the lady said. Her forbidding tone sent a chill up Rika's spine.

Riding in the heliotruck reminded Rika of Sebastian and Fritz. She hoped they'd left without her, even though she was grateful they'd saved her life. It had been awkward on the way back from the labs. Rika wanted to figure out a few things before she saw Sebastian again. A pang of guilt caused her to take a moment to close her eyes and access the MAM.

<Sebastian, I—>

<We're almost done. We're looking for an old friend. It's crazy out here with all the Order regulars and crowds of evacuees. We'll be back at the heliovan soon.>

<It's too late.>

Shifting in her seat to face southwest in the direction of her apartment so that her next statement was true, Rika improvised.

<I got so tired I decided to head toward home. Thank you for rescuing me. Let's meet up tomorrow.>

Before giving Sebastian a chance to protest, Rika signed off. She would find out what she could from Noah. Tomorrow would be soon enough to share what she learned. Everything and everyone had become so tangled up in her head that she needed time to make sense of it all.

On the Council tower rooftop, Lady Whisk-Away let them out and said, "To keep your cover, you'll need to load the heliotruck."

They opened the back. Rika groaned when W-A gestured at the stack of supplies that had to be loaded into the cargo bay. By the time they'd finished, Rika's arms and shoulders were so sore she wanted to collapse on the heliopad. W-A poked her head out of the window. "Rika, I assume you don't need special privileges to access the gardener's quarters. I hear you can get in anywhere. Make sure no one spots you. Cricket would get in serious trouble. Someone will come for you in the morning."

Before either of them could protest, W-A closed the access door and kicked the heliovan into lift off. Rika looked around the rooftop, at the bamboo grove, at the crows perched above the tiered garden, all silhouetted against the moonlit sky. She sought a schematic for the roof. The visual played over the backs of her eyelids and she followed the rooftop pathway into the center of the bamboo grove. There she found a small door. It had no security or lock. Wondering if that was W-A's idea of a joke, she entered. A step behind her, Noah ducked down to come inside. The tiny room had no windows, but the roof was transparent so they could see the stars. On the floor were a discolored sheet and pillow. It smelled faintly of fertilizer. A tiny mirror hung on the wall along with some stained gardening clothes.

"There's no chance I could sleep outside in the grove without being seen, is there?" Rika asked. The space allowed them enough room to stretch out, but that was about it.

"It might be risky," Noah said. "There's more chance of getting seen."

Rika dropped onto the floor and rolled up against the wall. He lay down beside her and turned his back to her, taking the pillow. "Let's just hope we can make it through the night without something else going wrong, I'm exhausted."

"Noah?"

"What?"

"I'm going to examine what's on the datasphere," Rika said.

"Right now?"

"Yes, if I wait until morning, I may never have a chance to figure these mysteries out. The IEC director wants me to check into the sick ward. My friend wants me free to play detective," Rika explained. "First, I have to find out who I can trust."

Noah grunted.

"You're welcome to join me."

"You are a strange one," Noah said. "First you insist on sharing a drainage hole with me to ask me if Cricket is my girlfriend. Now you get me alone for the night, and all you want me to do is review the datasphere with you."

"Do you know that when you become upset, your spider tattoo parks on the bridge of your nose?"

"I wonder what I did wrong in my past life to deserve you," Noah said. He rolled flat on his back staring up through the transparent ceiling at the stars. "Tell me where to meet you in Novus Orbis."

CHAPTER 19

For the first time in years, Noah longed for home, specifically for the luxurious hot springs bathhouse beneath the Domus Aqua compound. A good soak would ease the ache in his back from hauling all those supplies onto the heliotruck.

Pressed up against Rika in the gardener's makeshift sleeping quarters, he felt unbelievably exhausted, dirty and frustrated. His fingernails were black with grime. His exposed skin had a gritty film. The stench from their musty hiding place beneath the grate clung to him, wafting over him every time he moved.

What struck Noah most about their hygiene situation was Rika's hair. It shone deep blue and gave off a mint scent that became stronger the filthier their conditions became. On every level, she baffled him, but then so did Cricket. Rika and Cricket were both extraordinary women, nothing like the girls from other domus he'd grown up with. All the girls who he'd known led sheltered lives, ate the best food, went to the best academies, knew all the right protocols and followed the destinies their domus laid out for them. His mother expected him to marry one of these well-bred daughters from a respected domus.

Rika and Cricket made his ex-girlfriend, Beatrice, the wildest of any of the refined girls he'd known, appear to be the model of propriety. Cricket, the neck-slashing gardener, had bravely followed him the night of the murder and had later manipulated him into going into the lair of a notorious assassin. This same rooftop gardener and grand manipulator would risk her life to bring a little light into her brother's dreary world. And then, there was Rika the DeeJee stalker and datasphere thief, a pipsqueak who teased him to distraction even when she was nowhere nearby. Being beside Rika for a second night in a row was starting to drive him mad.

To keep his sanity, he entertained her absurd proposal to investigate the datasphere even though both of them suffered from sleep deprivation. He had agreed to join her in Novus Orbis, now he waited.

Rika had stashed the datasphere in Jaa City and explained to him that he could not enter until she formally invited him. To add to the complexity, she herself had to be in the city first.

Lying on her back with her eyes closed, she appeared delectably innocent. Her mouth had dropped open and her fingers twitched. If Noah hadn't known better, he'd have guessed she had slipped into the first stages of sleep. Instead she was busy controlling the one piece of real estate that every hacker in Novus Orbis wanted to own.

No doubt, the Order had been searching for Jaa City and Rika, although they had yet to identify her, ever since she turned Seven Walls and Spookdom inside out. Unlike anyone before her, she'd flaunted the Order's security vulnerabilities by floating her city wherever she chose. In response, Order operators had gone to the extreme of permanently shutting down Seven Walls: one of Noah's favorite places in Novus Orbis — erased. Noah waited restlessly for Rika to contact him.

Her initiation lit up the backs of his eyelids as though lightning had gone off in his brain. He'd set his preferences to the dullest of pings, and she'd literally overridden them in the blink of an eye. If he didn't watch out, she'd infiltrate more than his Novus Orbis settings. She'd already hijacked his emotions.

Breathing deeply he carried with him the mint scent of her hair as he entered the virtual universe, experienced its initial vertigo and the whoosh in his ears. He engaged all his senses and the mint aroma disappeared. Rika stood before him all in black with the wind of the high city tugging at her clothes. She cast a long shadow in the Novus Orbis sun. It revealed the silhouette of her enormous crow wings even when she didn't sport them visibly on her back.

"You are a strange one," Noah said.

In response, Rika blew him a kiss and he felt her lips brush his. He made a show of wiping his mouth with the back of his hand and turned to focus on her city. They stood on ancient cobblestones just inside a gated stone wall. Outside the walled city, cumulonimbus clouds stood out against the blue. Those clouds protected the spires and steeples of Jaa. From the ground in the Valleys of the Future, it would be difficult to catch sight of the floating city.

The only word that sprang to Noah's mind to describe the Jaa's architecture was pastiche. Plunked down on his left was a ship from a half-century past that on its belly read "Home Sweet Home." To his right sat a squat shack with a bright red door. The hovel looked as if it might collapse any minute. Beside it, a towering helix twisted so far up that the clouds ate at its top.

Squinting at Rika with spots before his eyes from the sun-light reflected off the helix, Noah asked, "What exactly inspired the city's unique architecture?"

Rika laughed. "It's not a planned city. It sprang up. Every memory event that I recorded in my life up until I became a DeeJee is here, as well as some DeeJee memories that I siphon off from Institute archives. Those are so detailed that they take up a quarter of the city. Unlike other people, everything I see and do becomes a memory event because I'm so tightly knit with the MAM."

"I'm confused. What do your memories have to do with this city?" Noah asked.

"Everything you see is a trigger to help me remember, when it's important. This is my private archive," Rika said making a sweeping gesture with her arms. "After I became a DeeJee, I lost my own memory and gained access to everyone else's memory events."

Noah stepped back. "Do you have access to mine?"

"I have access to any public and private memory events that you formally record using the MAM."

"Say I recall making love to a girlfriend, do you simultane-ously recall that?"

"No," Rika said. "I can't read your mind. A memory that's just in your head is yours alone and no one can reach it."

Noah nodded. It fit with his understanding of cognition; that everyone's brain processed and stored memories with minute differences, so no one could read anyone else's memory. Still, something troubled him.

"So, what if I decided to record sex as a memory event, could you access it and recall it after I've made it private?" Noah asked.

"Yes, once you formally record something, it's readable and stored by the MAM so it's accessible by me," Rika admitted.

"That's invasive."

"What's worse is that when I'm interacting with others, any memory events that they're calling up can also enter my brain space," Rika said. "If someone is agitated or experiencing any strong emotions, then their memory events pop in and take up all the space in my mind."

Noah's queasy stomach turned over as he thought about how many memory events he'd recalled while he'd been around Rika. From now on, he'd have to be extremely careful in her presence.

"So have you experienced me experiencing an intimate moment with my ex?" Noah asked.

"You're really fixating on sex," Rika said and stuck her tongue out at him. "That would mean you formally record that stuff."

"No, no, no," Noah said quickly. He scratched his head and studied the cobblestone at his feet. "This city represents everyone's memories?"

"No, the city holds mine. My problem is that after the mind enhancements, my memories became no more immediate or real than anyone else's memories. To keep my identity intact, I protected and secluded them here. Jaa represents the sum of my memories: It's me."

"I am the city's curator," a gruff voice over Noah's shoulder said.

Noah froze. He watched Rika's expression soften, and she flashed a smile so wide even her gums showed. He hadn't seen her smile that way before and turned, dreading to meet the man who inspired it.

The avatar stepped forward to greet him. As tall as Noah was, this figure stood taller and had a face Noah least expected. He might be the twin of Creid Xerkler, the original inventor of the MAM. This figure was used in the official seal of the Order and throughout Earth as a symbol of advancement, the renaissance millennium of the MAM. No one would have permission to use Xerkler's avatar except the Order or the man himself, and Xerkler was long gone.

"Sir?" Noah said and bowed. "You bear a striking resemblance to the late great inventor. In fact, it would be almost impossible for anyone not to identify you as the famous Creid Xerkler. How is this possible?"

"I have a mole," the man answered.

"Excuse me?" Noah said.

"I gave myself a mole on my cheek that he never had. Noah of Domus Aqua, I am Prometheus," Prometheus said and bowed.

"Creid created me in his youthful image as a sort of surrogate son."

"Look here," Noah said, poking Prometheus hard in the chest. "I don't know what kind of game you're play—"

Rika stepped between them and tugged on Noah's tunic. "Noah, may I have a word?"

Glaring over her head at Prometheus, Noah nodded. He let her lead him away from the placidly smiling Prometheus, down the cobblestone street further into her city. Noah heard cawing above him and noticed that crows perched on every windowsill and branch. Their beady eyes and the way they cocked their heads in his direction made him uneasy.

"Rika, is that guy back there with the Order? What's going on?"

"Prometheus isn't a human avatar," she said. "He's a Smart Intelligence. I found him in a place that had been mirrored and trashed. It was a terrible limbo space and somehow he'd languished there for decades, in a kind of suspended stasis." She showed him that same ultra-smile. "We talked and he agreed to help me. Let me tell you, he's brilliant. See how I trust you? I'm showing you my deepest secrets."

"How can this be?" Noah said. "Xerkler was an eccentric, everyone knows that, but to create a Smart Intelligence in his image that no one has ever seen before? It's absurd. Are you sure you aren't being manipulated by the Order without knowing it?"

"Completely sure," Rika said. "I found him, remember? He's a rogue S.I. who managed to survive all the MAM overhauls. I brought him his freedom so he's helping me."

"Terrific — a freelancing S.I. That's just what I need," Noah said. "Between you and Cricket, I'll end up in a work camp for life."

"Prometheus isn't strictly illegal," Rika protested.

"Maybe not, but you must have slipped past Order security to access those trashed archives."

"You have a point, there." She frowned.

"Aish!" Noah said and pulled at his hair. "I'm in way over my head. Just show me that datasphere."

"That's not a good idea," Prometheus said. The S.I. stood beside them. Noah hadn't seen him arrive. "You open the datasphere or use that key, and Jaa will get tagged. The people searching for you will find you. If they suspect you have evidence against them, you could end up like the senator."

"Well then, we'd better look at the datasphere from where they can't receive a notification," Rika said.

"Where's that?" Noah asked

"We'll go to no man's land — Seven Walls. It's shut down. Nobody will be running searches for a sudden appearance of the datasphere there."

When Prometheus nodded, Noah threw up his hands.

"I thought Seven Walls had been erased," he said.

Prometheus corrected him. "The Order hasn't dismantled the gaming world. It still exists in Novus Orbis, but it's inaccessible and its functionality is disabled."

"We'll hop in, do the viewing and hop out," Rika said. "Give me a little time to figure this out. Maybe you'd like to explore the city."

"Fine," Noah said, but she was already walking away.

Noah watched Rika head deeper into her city until she turned the corner and he could no longer see her. Feeling his backache even in Novus Orbis, he walked back toward the gates, climbed the steps up to the wall and looked out over the valleys from the clouds. Noah sat on the edge of the wall and hung his legs off the side. Wisps of mist curled around his feet. Rika had floated her city into an area not yet explored by the gamers. He looked forward to riding to it or getting there via canoe. He'd stake out territories and make his claims early. It even looked as though a fairly large uninhabited island graced the lake below.

"Noah," Prometheus said. The S.I.'s sudden appearance sitting beside him jolted Noah from his thoughts, and he almost lost his balance. It was a far drop to the valley below. "May I ask your intentions?"

"My — my intentions?" Noah stuttered. He stared out across the valleys, but no longer saw them. He saw Rika, small and slight, fast and strong, and grinned at the old-fashioned question without answering.

His intentions were to clear his name and keep his domus and family from being further humiliated by the accusations against their son. He intended to get some sleep. He'd have left it there and thought no further except that Prometheus continued to stare expectantly into his face. The S.I. must have no sense of timing. A person would realize Noah never intended to answer the question.

Lady Whisk-Away and the evacuees at Elysian Fields Retreat needed help, but Noah had no intention of paying the price for it. The courtesan wanted him to go to his domus and make the necessary compromises that would ensure their help. He knew, his two brothers wouldn't do it. Jeremiah had become a novitiate in the Magi, and as such could no longer directly lobby his mother and father. And it would never occur to Daniel to help others, even if he visited the retreats and saw for himself the overcrowding and other inhumane conditions. So the lady had correctly targeted him, the youngest son. Noah could get his folks to do everything he demanded as long as he committed to becoming a career politician, married whom they chose for him and complied with a few other life-hobbling demands. Although he wanted to help Lady Whisk-Away, he was determined to find some other way.

By "intentions," Prometheus surely meant Noah's interest in Rika. Noah intended to spend more sleepless nights with her, not in Novus Orbis opening a datasphere and certainly not at Order headquarters. He wanted to discover her favorite songs and what she liked to eat besides breakfast, but mostly how she kissed. Voicing these intentions wouldn't impress Rika, let alone the city curator. Noah kept his mouth shut, and Prometheus kept staring.

Finally, the S.I. broke the silence. "My specialty, that is, 'what I was designed for,' was originally pattern recognition. I'm a futurist. I take all current data, find relationships, define patterns and extrapolate."

Noah made a point of yawning, but Prometheus continued. The S.I. definitely didn't pick up on social cues. Noah wondered if it was as advanced as Rika believed.

"When I take all the data available on Noah of Domus Aqua and the near-past interactions between him and Rika, there are multiple potential outcomes."

Now the S.I. had Noah's attention. Noah peered suspiciously at him.

"With you in Rika's life, none of the outcomes that I've calculated end beneficially for Rika, except one. That outcome ends very badly for you."

"Why are you telling me this?" Noah asked. He crossed his arms over his chest.

"By your history, you would call yourself a man of honor, a man of your word when it comes to everything except girlfriends. Am I correct?"

"How dare you judge me?"

"I state facts and trends. Another fact is that Rika is vulnerable. She is also important at this juncture in human history. Therefore, I plan to protect her."

"You do that," Noah said, pulling himself up on the wall.

"I'll make you a deal. Let's spar. If you win, ask any favor you like of me as long as it doesn't involve Rika. If I win, you must promise on the honor of your domus to stay out of her life in both Novus and Vetus Orbis."

Noah laughed and turned back to face Prometheus. "You want me to spar with *you*? In return, I get granted any favor I request? That sounds like a challenge it would be hard to refuse—"

"No!" Rika shouted and bounded up the stairs. Startled, Noah stepped backwards and lost his footing. He toppled backwards over the edge of the wall. Freefalling through the clouds, he turned himself around. If his avatar faced sudden death, he at least wanted to enjoy the view for the moments he had remaining. Below him instead of the valleys and the lake, he saw two rivers converging and a blank white rent in the fabric of the world where his island had been.

As he fell towards that strange white abyss, he wondered numbly if it were possible to land there or if he might end up in cognitive suspension, no longer in Novus Orbis, but never disconnected either. He'd be caught between Novus Orbis and Vetus Orbis. His heart raced. A flurry of black feathers enveloped him. Rika's tiny frame supported him and her wings struggled to lift him toward her city. She rose a little, dropped and flew a little higher.

Another flurry of wings and this time hundreds of them dove at him. Crows pinched bits of his tunic and pants in their beaks and raised him toward the city. They even caught hold of his hair and as thankful as he was to avoid that white abyss, he batted at them to leave his head alone. With the black wings beneath him and surrounding him, he was blinded. The sudden pressure of the cobblestones against his knees and elbows was a shock. Cawing, the crows flew off.

"Would you mind rolling off me?" Rika asked in a muffled voice from beneath him.

"Oh," Noah said and immediately jumped up, stepping on her wing. She yelped. "Rika, I'm so sorry. I—"

"It's all right," she said, getting to her feet. Her thickened scapula cracked loudly as she stretched. Her wings receded.

Noah was watching the crows wheel over the rooftops and towers. "Are those your pre-DeeJee memory events, too?" he said.

She turned to look and shrugged. "I don't know where they came from. They just appeared and never left. Prometheus thinks they're produced by my unconscious, by parts of my psyche that the neural enhancements never touched." Her expression turned stern. "Promise me something."

"What?"

"That you won't fight Prometheus."

"Why not?"

"Because you'll lose."

"Lose?" Noah said. He felt his face go hot. She had no idea he'd been a well-regarded fly gamer. "You think I'd lose to an S.I. ?"

"He's no ordinary—"

"I'm no ordinary—"

Her glare made him hesitate. She'd just saved him from some freakish oblivion down there. It made sense that she would underestimate him. He took a deep breath and glanced around. At least the horrid S.I. wasn't standing there, listening. Noah planned to spar with Prometheus after that comment. He'd demonstrate his fly-gaming skills to Rika. It was somehow vital to him that this pipsqueak see what he could do, but now was not a good time to be bragging about himself.

"Thank you. You saved me," Noah said and bowed. "While you were busy saving me, I noticed that the city has moved to Seven Walls. I guess it is time to crack open that datasphere."

CHAPTER 20

Rika had put the datasphere in the painted eye of the Redeye Café's sign and the key behind the bar in back. When she went to retrieve them, she found neither in its place. Suspiciously, Prometheus refused to answer her communiqués.

"Noah, enjoy watching the crows. I'll be right back," Rika said.

"You've already torn up the bar. Did you forget where you put it?" Noah asked.

"No, I know exactly where it is," Rika said and jogged down the street away from him, looking for Prometheus down each side road.

Prometheus' sudden disappearance reminded Rika how much she relied on him. Jaa City fell silent without him humming to himself or quoting long dead poets as he strolled down her streets. She'd caught the tail end of the conversation between Prometheus and Noah when the S.I. challenged Noah to a fight. For the first time, Rika doubted Prometheus' intentions.

As Rika had mounted the stairs to the wall, she had seen the S.I. stick his leg out so that when Noah stepped backwards he'd tripped, lost his footing and toppled over the wall. Tripping his avatar so that he would fall into the highly unstable environment that was Seven Walls under spookdom was no prank. If his avatar had fallen and become trapped in one of Seven Walls' fluctuating, damaged zones, Noah might have been trapped between Novus Orbis and Vetus Orbis. No one knew what kind of neural havoc that might have wreaked upon the fly gamer. Her curator's actions worried Rika. Either he'd calculated it and known she'd save Noah, or he'd intentionally risked a human life.

She spotted Prometheus down a side street, seated on a doorstep, and slowed to a walk. He ate chipped ice with condensed milk and sweet plum poured overtop in a cone — the closest thing to ice cream that wouldn't spoil in crushing, humid heat. Walking down the side street brought back her early childhood on the other side of the Pacific where she'd been born. Her mother had been patient back then, raising her for six years until the funds dried up and it became clear Rika's dad would never come home. After that, they'd moved to the Los Angeles Heartland where her mom pretended she no longer had a daughter until the day she died. Rika frowned.

"You used to eat these when you were a little kid," Prometheus said. "Recalling your memory event makes me taste the flavored ice now as you tasted it then."

"I suppose as a kid I chose silly things to record as my memory events, but seeing you eat that cone actually makes my mouth water. I'd entirely forgotten them." She sat down beside him and rested her head against his arm. "I've come for the datasphere."

"Not many people have someone like me who can extrapolate their future for them and give accurate advice," Prometheus said.

"Most people have parents," Rika said.

"Parents?" Prometheus waved the comparison away. "I've analyzed the potential outcomes. Sebastian and Noah are no good for you and one is worse than the other."

"Prometheus!"

The curator held up his hand. "I won't mention it again. Just promise me you won't destroy Jaa City for either man."

"Destroy Jaa City? I need Jaa to keep my identity intact!"

"Precisely," Prometheus said and reached into his pocket. He pulled out the datasphere and held it over the palm of her hand. "May I tell you a secret?"

"A secret?" Rika said and tugged on the datasphere. He had a firm grasp on it.

"Yes," Prometheus said and paused dramatically. He ought to have been a Smart Intelligence assigned to the theater. "You are not to blame for Circle Tide."

"What?" Rika asked. One lone crow cawed in the distance. The wind whistled through the shutters overhead and pulled at her clothes. Until Prometheus reassured her that she wasn't to blame for Circle Tide, it had never occurred to her that she might be. Her shoulders felt heavy with sudden doubt, responsibility and an irrational burden of guilt.

"Remember that," Prometheus said and released the datasphere into her hand.

The object burned against her skin. Rika wrapped her fingers tight around it. That was a mistake. It took hold when her mind was completely vulnerable and her guard down. Her DeeJee hand melded with the datasphere. She'd expected it to be encrypted, but Prometheus must have already used the key. The connection completed and threw her onto a wide expanse of plain white grid. She landed on her butt. Closing her eyes, she attempted to exit out, but bounced up against the hidden walls of the grid. Her only clear escape route forced her to walk through the transparent data cubes lined up before her. At the end of the third cube stood a door marked "exit." Leave it to a rogue S.I. to trap her successfully when no one else had.

"Why are you doing this, Prometheus?" Rika yelled. Her voice carried out over the grid and ricocheted off the three cubes. "This isn't a funny! Get me out of here!"

No answer. She stood alone. The fastest and easiest way out lay before her. Noah would be upset that she had reviewed the data without him. If she hurried, she'd get out quickly, and they could go back over it together. Cursing the Smart Intelligence and his sick sense of humor, Rika tapped the first cube.

The steely half-light of the inactive Seven Walls felt oppressive, as did the rents in the fabric of his favorite gaming world. Although Noah knew he had to be imagining it, even the wind smelled stale. To amuse himself, Noah focused on Rika's crows. After multiple raucous birdcalls, Noah gave up trying to communicate. They didn't shoo away easily either. He waved his hand at the crow on his table, and it pecked at his finger. When it suddenly flew off, Noah felt gratified and then he looked up to find Prometheus staring him in the face.

"Hey!" Noah said. He sat back as far as he could without falling over. "What is it with you? You're always sneaking up on me."

"Are you prepared to fight?" the S.I. asked.

"Where's Rika?" Noah said, looking around. He found this curator exceedingly annoying.

"She's indisposed," the curator replied.

Something in the S.I.'s expression made Noah uneasy. The fly gamer got up and started in the direction he'd seen Rika take.

Prometheus called after him, and Noah picked up his pace. He glanced down each side street as she'd done until he found her collapsed on a doorstep with her hand locked in a fist that pulsed red. Noah eased her slack body up from the doorstep so that her head and shoulder rested safely against the wall. Cupping her hand in his, he tugged on her fingers.

"What have you done to Rika's avatar?" Noah asked. Her fingers had cemented together. "She's lifeless, and yet she's still here. Is she okay in Vetus Orbis?"

"That's none of your concern," Prometheus said. He gripped Noah by the arm and yanked him away from Rika. The S.I. had an iron hold. With one swing, he tossed Domus Aqua's son against the far wall so hard that Noah saw bursts of light behind his eyelids. A sharp pain ran from his elbow to his shoulder.

"Wait a second," Noah said. He put his hands on his legs and bent over to stop seeing stars. The S.I.'s strength was astonishing.

Prometheus approached him and swung a hard, fast blow at his face. Noah danced away. He was familiar with the quick rhythms of expert fighters. The S.I. picked up his speed and his fists became a blur. One clipped Noah's jaw, another hammered his ribs, dropping the gamer to the ground. Grabbing Noah's arm again, Prometheus swung him bodily to bounce against the wall. His breath knocked out of him, the gamer collapsed.

He struggled to get his breath back. Rika was in trouble; he couldn't afford to lose this fight. He would never abandon her in this state. Noah spat blood and used the brick wall to leverage himself to his feet. "If you're challenging me to a fight, we need to have equally equipped avatars."

"You want me to reduce my superhuman strength to your level?" Prometheus said. "Why would I do that?"

"Or, you could increase my avatar's strength to superhuman," Noah suggested.

"No, we might end up destroying Rika's city of memories. Trashing cultural artifacts is not something curators do," Prometheus said. "You've been up against superior opponents. Accept it. Keep your promise never to see her again if I win."

"As long as I get any wish granted if I win," Noah said.

"Agreed," the S.I. replied. "Pick your weapon."

With a sinking feeling that the odds were stacked against him, Noah massaged his bruised arms. He studied the short and long swords, the daggers and knives that the S.I. displayed, and then it came to him. He tapped his head. "I'll use this, instead."

"What?"

"My noggin. You act like you know Rika so well, Curator," Noah challenged Prometheus. "Let's play question and answer. Whoever answers the question right gets to ask the next question. We'll do two out of three."

"Interesting."

"What does Rika's hair smell most like when it's dirty?" Noah asked.

"Mint."

"How did you know—?" Noah began. His heart raced.

"My turn," Prometheus said. "What was Rika's favorite passtime before she became a DeeJee?"

Noah thought back to the short time he'd been in her studio. There were her organo-pumps lined up by the door, which indicated she liked to run. Besides, she was really good at it. He'd noticed little else except an antique guitar that looked more ornamental than anything else.

"Playing guitar?" Noah said.

"Yes," Prometheus said. He slammed a fist into the palm of his hand and paced. Noah must have surprised him.

"My turn," Noah said. "What was the first question Rika asked me when she entered the drainage hole at the Retreat?"

"You know very well that she hasn't sent her most recent memories to Jaa yet," Prometheus' face contorted and after a long pause he said, "I don't know. My turn. If someone orders Rika to do something, someone who is not her boss, what are the odds that she'll do as she's told?"

Noah thought of her feisty style and her independent way of handling everything. "I'd say there's zero percent chance she'll do anything she's ordered to do just because she's been ordered to do it. Unless it makes sense to her or she already had plans to do it, she'll ignore any order."

Prometheus belted out a loud string of Latin that Noah didn't understand and then disappeared.

"Hey, was I right?" Noah felt a chill and the hairs on the back of his neck stood on end. He wondered if he'd answered correctly or if he'd be banished from ever seeing Rika again. The pipsqueak would never forgive him for abandoning her while she lay collapsed in Novus Orbis. It would rankle more after she'd saved him from a Seven Walls abyss, assuming she could wake up without his help. He returned to her side and held her limp avatar in his arms.

The first cube confounded Rika since it was simply a list of addresses from all over the world. Every address represented a lab. The Homenaje Laboratories in Santa Barbara caught her eye. She searched for relationships. Her stomach clenched when she found Domus Aqua and Domus Superna jointly owned them all. Every lab made herbal supplements and had been cleared for low biosafety levels of BSL-1 or BSL-2, except for the BSL-4-rated Homenaje Lab. When she dug further, she discovered that Domus Aqua leased out these properties. The slew of third-party lessees appeared to have no relationship to each other and no lessee rented more than two properties. Rika had difficulty getting details about any of the business entities besides the names listed on the leases — that was a red flag. These businesses might exist solely as leasing agents.

Correlating the Circle Tide breakout and the labs geographically produced no statistically significant factors. The first Homenaje Lab incident, which she'd learned about from Frisardi's memory events, and the second one she'd caused, both remained unreported, but both appeared to have been contained. No living buildings in Santa Barbara had been stricken with the fungi. So Circle Tide had not spread directly from the labs. And yet, Senator Ortega had included this list for a reason. It signified something. Rika hoped Noah would have some insights.

Frustrated, she hurried on to the next cube, tapped it and found herself soaring through the air toward two men on the ground. From the air, she glimpsed Cricket signing at her from a rooftop overlooking the men. She realized that she was seeing a view from a crow, which had been equipped with a monitoring device. From Rika's perspective, she might as well have been flying herself. The crow landed on a ledge above the men's heads. Immediately, Rika recognized the spot where Cricket had taken her to talk without being monitored. It was an Order blind spot without access to the MAM. The men must have assumed they could speak freely here as long as no humans were nearby. Rika identified the two men: one was Sebastian's driver, Frisardi of Domus Restitio; the other was Bartholomew Soba. The date stamp revealed the meeting had occurred over nine months ago.

Despite standing in a blind spot, both men were jumpy. Soba kept looking around and even stared up at the crow for a minute before continuing his conversation.

"They're delivering blackbase from Mars directly to Earth. Planetary Protection and Customs are oblivious. The MAM hasn't issued any alerts. That's what I'm telling you. Get it?" Soba asked. Soba's face was flushed red and he emphasized each point with his hands.

"No," Fritz said. He looked thin-lipped and pale.

"We could be dealing blackbase *right now*," Soba said. "I know who has the shipment and where and when they're moving it. I say hit them now. We turn and sell it before they know it's missing."

"Look," Fritz said. He shook his head. "I told you before this is a limited opening. They'll close the security vulnerability as soon as they have enough blackbase. Once it's closed you don't want blackbase anywhere near you. Order regulars will swoop down and take you and that stash in minutes."

"That makes no sense," Soba said. "The security hole has to remain open for a while because it'll take months for them to sell that much blackbase, assuming they can convert enough new people to Bluegrazers. Boy, those were the flush days, when we had half the Underground with blue-glow mouths."

"And rotting teeth," Fritz said. "This isn't about addicting Undergrounders to blackbase. It won't be divided up into hits. It's being modified so that it'll never be recognized by the Order, the MAM or anyone else. Besides, since when did you go back to stealing from smugglers?"

"Work has been a little thin lately," Soba admitted.

"I've recommended you for a job that'll make you a wealthy gentleman, rich enough never to work again. That is, as long as you stay away from betting on fly games."

"Sounds risky," the hitman replied. He'd leaned toward Frisardi, but kept his hands at his sides. "Details?"

"Let's just say you've got to scare off a mutt — the type that follows a trail no matter where it leads. She needs to be disciplined. Only someone with your caliber skills can provide the right sort of one-time training."

"They want it to hurt," Bartholomew said with a nod.

"Exactly and seriously. You up for this?" Frisardi asked.

"Sure. Who's the target?"

"You'll know when it's time," Fritz said.

"I can probably guess. Is Sebastian behind this?"

"Are you kidding, Sebastian the womanizer? He's too busy tying up his paramours and checking his investment portfolio."

"Honestly?" Soba said and wiped forehead with the back of his hand. "I swear that guy has it out for me."

"He's not the only one," Fritz said. They both laughed. "By close of business, you'll have your first of three installments. See if the amount meets your expectations, but don't get greedy."

Soba nodded soberly and gave a perfunctory bow. Frisardi left first. The crow flew overhead, circled over the rooftop where Cricket sat, and landed on the gardener's outstretched arm.

Rika exited the second cube with the knowledge that Senator Ortega had known about Bartholomew Soba's impending attack, maybe months before the actual event. Fritz and Bartholomew had set in motion the same plan to teach the senator a lesson. Rika needed to find out more about who had the power to terrify and subdue the likes of Bartholomew Soba.

A shiver of anxiety went through the DeeJee as she tapped the third and final cube. Again, a wealth of data bombarded her: forms and lists as well as the cargo manifests of vessels passing through the Moon Interplanetary Port and Customs. The tracking focused on shipments from Mars to an Underground address on Earth. Rika mapped the address to a place called Yuki's Otherworld Treasures. A notorious black marketer, who went by the name Gun, owned the place.

Stranger still, and seemingly even less connected, was a confidential list of participants in a clinical trial for a new drug called Complete. The Clinician's name at the top read, Ieda of Domus Concepcion. A brief note from the senator also caught Rika's attention.

> Goth, a private investigator named Sakoda and his team compiled this information for me at great risk to themselves. It's time to open a formal internal government investigation. After you've reviewed the files, I'll explain everything when we meet. I may even have the names of the top people.

So much new data with no definitive or clear relationships between them left the DeeJee feeling short of breath. Rika took a moment to compose herself, to breath in and to exhale, to slow her racing pulse before exiting the door that appeared as soon as she'd reviewed all three cubes of the datasphere.

Prometheus returned in his usual stealthy way, suddenly appearing and sitting so close beside Noah they brushed arms.

"Must you?" Noah asked and scooted over. He held Rika close. "Do I get my wish or are you going to argue that I lost?"

"You get your wish," Prometheus said.

"Bring Rika back to full health. Release her from the state she's in," Noah blurted out. He ran his hand over her soft blue hair.

"Done," Prometheus said and then he chuckled. Noah had no time to ask what was so funny because Rika shifted in his arms.

"Noah?" Rika said and struggled to sit up. "Why are you wrapped around me like this?"

After removing his arm from around her shoulders and easing her legs off his, he stood up and backed away from both of them. Prometheus looked tremendously pleased. His expression reminded Noah of the times he and his brother Daniel had gone fishing. When Daniel had reeled in a big one and Noah hadn't even gotten a nibble, his brother's face had betrayed the same triumphant smugness.

Rika slugged Prometheus hard in the arm. They both stood and faced each other.

"If you ever pull a stunt like that again, our friendship is done," Rika said. "That wasn't in the least bit funny."

"Not funny?" Prometheus said. He rubbed his arm where she'd struck it and grinned.

To Noah, Rika said, "Thanks to Prometheus, I got stuck running through the datasphere. Let's go over Ortega's files together now that—"

The buildings around them swayed, and the ground rocked so violently that both Noah and Rika fell to the ground. Only Prometheus remained standing. Rika closed her eyes for a moment and opened them.

"The Order must be dismantling Seven Walls," Rika said. "If my guess is right, operators just attempted a shutdown or some deletions and failed since Jaa city is still running."

She tried to stand, but another tremor knocked her off her feet. Prometheus took a step and helped her up.

"What can I do?" Noah asked.

"Man the front gates if you can make it there. I'll maneuver us out of this world," Rika said. "We may face an attack."

With a curt nod, Noah took steps toward the main gates. The rolling heaves across the ground threw him against the cobblestones several more times. When he saw the gates in front of him, he picked up his pace. The shack with the bright red door had collapsed, but the helix building beside it remained intact. It swayed above him with each successive shock. Narrow fissures formed across the cobblestone street.

Seeing no one at the gates, Noah thought Rika wanted him to man the gate tower. Before he reached the tower, a pair of red-gloved hands curled around the great gates' metal and then a shapeless mass of red and black poured through the spaces between the gate slats. Inside, it reformed itself into an Order Operator's daemon scout that had a human form, but with a black beak in place of a nose or mouth. It drew both its swords, long and short, as its attention focused on Noah.

"State your business in Seven Walls," the daemon demanded. It pointed its long sword at the center of Noah's chest.

For the first time in his life, a daemon scout confronted Noah. He hadn't summoned it to ask for assistance. It had shown up because he was someplace he absolutely shouldn't be. Noah thought fast. He put his hands on his hips and said, "Doesn't your Operator read his communiqués? This is a training exercise. If you attack me, you're effectively attacking your superiors. Inform your boss."

The daemon's blade did not waver. "You're running unlicensed here, which means this is most likely a pirate operation pilfering treasures from confiscated personal property in Seven Walls."

Noah raised his voice. "Identify your Operator. He's going to be written up if he doesn't recall his S.I. scouts and let us finish this exercise."

The daemon dove at him, thrusting. Noah noodled out of its way. Its jabs weren't very quick. Noah kicked at its wrist and put one of its swords out of commission, but another instantly replaced it. The daemon advanced again.

When Prometheus appeared beside him, Noah took his chance.

"See?" Noah challenged the daemon. "You idiot, we've got the holy seal in the virtual flesh! This S.I. proves we're official. Pirates don't have the Father of the MAM Creid Xerkler at the helm. Now scram before your Operator gets a demerit."

Prometheus stared serenely at the daemon. The beaked creature lowered its weapons as it evaluated Prometheus. It took several steps backward, turned and bolted for the gate, melting through the bars.

"Let's hope that Operator you tipped off doesn't look into the training schedule today," Prometheus said. "Impersonating the Order is a much more serious offense than piracy."

"You ungrateful hunk of code! I have had just about—" Noah began, when Rika walked up.

"Are you two at it again?" she asked and winked at Noah. "Notice anything different?"

The sun shown bright and a fresh breeze scented with prairie sage wafted over him. Some of the tension in Noah's shoulders eased as he stretched his back and arms.

"Are we safe in Valleys of the Future?" he asked.

"Not exactly," Rika said and bit her lip. "I took us to Domus Concepcion internal operations."

Noah looked from Rika to a grim-faced Prometheus and back. "Tell me you have legal access to their internal operations."

"Not exactly," Rika repeated.

As if in answer to Noah's concern, a large shadow fell over them. Above, an impossibly bloated, winged ship broadcast an ear-piercing alarm.

CHAPTER 21

In Noah's estimation, the ship might have been taken directly from some toddler's drawings, with its fluffy, pastel exterior and the way it bounced in the air above them. It definitely would come apart in Earth's atmosphere. Like Rika's crow wings, this ship's design would forever confine it to Novus Orbis. The sound of the intruder alarm resembled a baby's cry. When a hatch on the bottom of the ship slid open, pink feathers floated down on his head. One landed on Rika's nose. Prometheus promptly disappeared.

An incongruous metal staircase clanked open one step at a time until its bottom step was level with their heads. The baby cries stopped as someone appeared on the ladder's top step, someone Noah recognized as Ieda, a low-ranking daughter of Domus Concepcion. The woman's blonde hair stuck out in pigtails as she flounced down the steps in a very short, tiered-lace affair above baby-blue, thigh-high latex boots whose heels clicked on the steps. On the lowest step, Ieda sat and swung her legs back and forth. She perched precisely at Noah's eye level, and he had to resist looking up her skirt.

"You're in my private workspace," Ieda said. "It's three a.m. I find that odd. Either I summon an Order operator or you explain yourselves fast."

Noah hadn't a clue as to why Rika had chosen to come to this particular spot in Novus Orbis. He could do no more than turn to the DeeJee.

"If I were you, I wouldn't be in a rush to contact Order Operators or their scouts," Rika said. "Our business here concerns a confidential list of participants in a clinical trial."

Ieda's cheeks flushed a deep red. In a hushed voice, she said, "What do you want?"

"I'd like the participants' addresses. We're doing a follow-up on Sakoda's investigation," Rika said.

"Sakoda has already caused me enough trouble," Ieda said. "He promised to keep me out of this. That P. I. couldn't dig up anything amiss with the clinical trials on Complete. After he conned me into giving him that information, the domus demoted me. I'm little more than a filing clerk now. If I weren't the niece of the domus master, my punishment would have been much worse," Ieda said. "Why do you think I'm working nights?"

"I thought it was because you can dress and act however you want on the night shift," Rika pointed out.

To Noah's astonishment, Ieda laughed. "You have keen observation skills," she said and rolled her eyes. "But understand this, sweetie. Unless my boss orders me to do it, I'm not giving out more confidential information about those trials. I don't care who you represent."

"I represent the Institute for Enhanced Cognition. We're investigating the Circle Tide infestations. We've found a connection between Circle Tide and Complete."

Ieda folded her arms and stuck out her lower lip. "Nonsense. First you have Sakoda looking to show that Complete contained blackbase, and I proved to him that it didn't. Now he's going around saying Complete is to blame for Circle Tide? That's insane. Tell him that."

"I can't," Rika said quietly.

"Suit yourself," the woman in lace said. She stood and brushed off a few stray pink feathers. "Complete could be the next wonder drug of the century. So far, it's really helping the people in the trials and has no side effects. Don't interfere."

Hearing this, Noah's inclination was to side with Ieda. Domus Concepcion was a highly reputable domus. They would never have anything to do with blackbase. The domus would never risk spreading a deadly fungus, no matter how compelling the financial returns.

Rika appeared to be thinking about what the blonde woman was telling her, and for a few seconds she stood in silence, eyes closed. When she opened them again, she bowed politely to

Ieda. Observing Rika's mischievous smile, Noah suspected she was up to something.

"Ieda, my apologies for the intrusion into your work space," the DeeJee said. "Thank you for clarifying things. We will leave now."

With a dismissive nod, Ieda turned and clicked her way back up the metal stairs. Rika had her eyes closed again. Jaa City tore through the workspace. Noah wondered what it looked like to Ieda, maybe a shooting star.

One moment the sun shone, the next they were in darkness, and then a split second later, they stood in diffuse light. Noah felt a fine spray of moisture on his face. He looked up and realized that he was seeing the sky through a veil of falling water. Its constant motion refracted the sunlight better than a stained glass window. Rika had brought them through firewalls and across worlds to Sacred Mountain — Hidden Falls. They must be floating beneath one of the world's giant deadly waterfalls. Rika tapped him on the arm. He realized his mouth was hanging open. She really was a Novus Orbis force, this little blue-haired pipsqueak. If only he had half her abilities, he'd win over entire gaming worlds in Novus Orbis.

"Noah!" she shouted over the sound of rushing water. "Let's return to Vetus Orbis. I'll tell you what's on the datasphere."

"I want to go through the datasphere myself—" Noah objected. The sudden vertigo and whooshing sound in his ears informed him that Rika had ejected him from Jaa City, like it or not. It felt as if it took an unusually long time for him to exit Novus Orbis. The darkness and that whooshing sound went on and on until he abruptly disconnected. He opened his eyes to a room lit with candles.

The smell of rice cooking drifted over him. Noah sat up in the gardener's place. Cricket sat near the door behind a row of covered bowls that were steaming. Noah heard Rika humming softly on the other side of the wall.

Noticing that Noah was alert to the real world, Cricket beckoned him to come forward and eat. His stomach made loud gurgling noises. When he scooted up to the food, Cricket made a face.

"What is it?" he asked.

"You need a shower. Yuck, even your hands are filthy," Cricket pointed out.

Noah examined his hands and stuffed them in his pockets. Cricket handed him a smudged, filthy rag.

"The shower is on the other side of the wall. Rika should be out soon. Remind her that the floor is slippery when wet. She's used to taking dry showers," the gardener said. "I'll be sleeping outside to ward off any Orders regulars changing shifts. Please don't come out until I say so. Ochbo and Jeremiah won't be here for a while."

"Thank you," Noah said. Through the transparent ceiling, he could tell they were still hours from dawn. He got up and headed for the shower. Around the corner, he stopped. The shower had one spout, three walls and no door.

Why didn't Cricket warn me?

Rika stood naked in profile. For a femtosecond, her eyes remained closed and her back arched beneath the steady stream. Her trademark cotton candy blue hair turned a deep midnight blue under the water. And then, she looked straight at him and let out a tiny yelp. She stretched for the undersized towel hanging on the wall and lost her balance. Her feet went out from under her. Noah rushed in and grabbed her as she went down.

Slipping on the wet stone, he fell too, but managed to break her fall by twisting beneath her. That got him no thanks, but a flurry of fists and curses. He rolled up and away from her, his clothes soaked with soapy water. She wrapped the towel around her torso. As tiny as she was, it hardly covered her. Exhausted and wet with all his clothes still on, Noah laughed.

Her scathing glance made him cover his mouth and pretend to cough. Rika yanked her clothes from the hook near the door and scampered into the front room to dress. Noah pulled off his clothes and quickly showered. The grime created brown rivulets down his arms and legs into the water reclaimer. When he finished, he had no other choice than to dress in his damp garments.

Noah entered the front room and quietly joined Rika, avoiding eye contact. Together, they wolfed down everything Cricket had brought, even the beets and pickled watermelon rind that Noah normally wouldn't taste even on a dare. Cricket must have sensed they were hungry because next she delivered bowls of noodles and meat. For dessert, they ate red-bean pastries, crispy on the outside and crumbly inside with a soft, sweet center. Nirvana definitely existed on Earth. Noah's stomach puffed up so full that he stretched out on the floor and forgot all about Rika's fine naked form, his musty, clinging clothes and his embarrassment. He dropped off to sleep.

Sunlight through the clear ceiling shone directly on his face and woke him. While his shirt had dried for the most part, it remained sticky where he lay against the floor. Rika had unexpectedly used his chest as a pillow and his hand rested on her stomach. When she moved her head, he shut his eyes as though he were still asleep.

Rika sat up and rustled about for a few minutes. It became quiet. He opened his eyes and found her face close to his, which gave him a jolt.

"Good morning," he said.

"Don't ever grope me like that again," Rika said and poked him with her finger in his chest.

"Excuse me?" Noah said and sat up. "I saved you from a concussion."

"I fell because of you ogling me."

"As if there was anything to see," Noah said. He scrambled up and adjusted his clothes.

"Why, you pervert!" she said.

"Perv—?" Noah said.

The door to the hut opened and Ochbo walked in, followed by Jeremiah. Noah ground his teeth to avoid saying anything in front of the two men. His brother would never let him live it down if he learned the pipsqueak had called Noah a pervert. Jeremiah tossed gardening clothes to the two of them.

"You're less likely to attract attention dressed as gardeners," Jeremiah explained. "All we need to do is get you to the heliovan, but guards are stationed all over the rooftop since the Council is in session."

Rika started for the shower area to change and glared up at Noah. "You stay right where you are," she said.

"Aish," Noah said and ran his hand through his hair.

"More women troubles?" his brother asked. Noah took off his shirt, balled it up and aimed it at Jeremiah.

"Hey, this reeks!" his brother said, tossing Noah's nasty shirt into the corner.

Noah undressed and pulled on the gardener's clothes, which actually fit. That surprised him.

"I see the Order didn't mistreat you too badly," Noah said.

"How could they with Ma-ma breathing down their necks," Jeremiah said. "Ochbo can't get over it. He keeps telling me how lucky I am to have Lila for a mother."

"I expected a beating, but instead they fed us," Ochbo said and snorted. "No one wants to take on the Domus Aqua Master over her sons."

Dressed as a gardener, Rika emerged from the shower. She'd rolled up the pants and the arms. In the over-sized outfit, she looked like a little kid pretending to be a grownup. Noah couldn't help snickering. When her eyes narrowed, he rushed to speak before she could say anything that embarrassed him.

"Rika had a chance to go over the datasphere. Maybe she can give us a synopsis," Noah said.

Jeremiah's expression turned serious. "Wait. Let me get Cricket. She should hear this, too," he said. While he stepped out, Noah and Rika straightened out the mess they'd made and stacked the empty dishes near the door.

"It must have been quite a feast," Ochbo commented.

"Thanks to Cricket," Rika said. "At first, I thought I'd never get enough to eat, but she kept bringing more delectables."

Cricket held the door for Jeremiah who carried a pot of tea and cups. They sat in a circle. After the first few sips of tea, taken politely in silence, Rika described the datasphere's contents.

She began with the part that was easiest to explain — the conversation between Frisardi of Domus Restitio and Soba the assassin. Their talk indicated that the hitman had indeed been hired to seriously injure Senator Ortega, but not to kill her. That meant the person who'd hired Soba, and might be her real killer, was still out there. Since it went a long way to vindicating him, Noah experienced a sense of relief hearing that this conversation had been captured and saved. He leaned back against the wall and closed his eyes. Still, if only he'd stayed with the senator, she might still be alive. That regret would not soon go away.

Next Rika described the clinical trials of Complete with its list of participants. Rika surprised Noah when she said, "I gleaned the actual addresses of the participants directly from Ieda. When I requested the confidential information, Ieda called up a private memory event. That allowed me access to the addresses and some other confidential data."

This reminded Noah of how careful he needed to be about what memory events he brought to mind in her presence. The most advanced security systems were no more than an open door to the DeeJee. Her access to the MAM seemed practically unlimited.

Ochbo shifted wretchedly around as though his legs had cramped. Noah noticed his flushed face and remembered that the OMM guru had shown him a phial of Complete, which he had been personally testing on himself.

Rika failed to pick up on the guru's discomfort. The pipsqueak kept talking, telling them about shipping manifests that mapped to an Underground store called Yuki's Otherworld Treasures.

Cricket nodded. She knew the place. "Gun owns that store. He has a prior record for selling unsanctioned offworld merchandise that made it past Customs."

Rika paused to finish her tea and accept another cupful from Jeremiah. Once she'd drained the cup, she reached over to touch the novice's knee and then Noah's arm. The gamer saw concern on her face.

"I have one more piece of evidence that the senator kept on the datasphere," the DeeJee said. She brushed her wild hair from her eyes to study both brothers. "The senator had a long list of labs at locations on every continent. All of these laboratories, except for five, are owned jointly by Domus Aqua and Domus Superna."

Jeremiah grunted and Noah froze. *Daniel*, he thought. Ortega had called him back from the wilderness because she had needed to talk to him about his eldest brother and about a scandal.

"Domus Aqua leased the labs to third parties," Rika continued. "None of them appear to be legitimate businesses. There's no domus associated with them. None of them have any history prior to a year ago. Who's managing the labs and what they're doing remains a mystery along with the reason Ortega included the list for the Minister of Internal Affairs."

"That's troubling," Jeremiah admitted. "There must be a connection here to illegal activities. Senator Ortega didn't randomly add the shipping manifests, labs and clinical trial participants along with a conversation between two thugs plotting to hurt her."

Noah was surprised to feel the impulse to protect his domus. "Maybe the labs are important precisely because of their good research. Or, the senator included them accidently with everything else," he said.

"Come on," Ochbo chimed in. "Don't get defensive. No one is blaming anyone. Not yet."

"I'm committed to protecting our domus too, Noah," Jeremiah said. "This is a tangled web of relationships and if Domus Aqua is involved, we need to find out how. The more Circle Tide spreads, the more desperate the situation becomes for the evacuees. We owe it to them."

"If you fail as a monk, you'll make an excellent preacher," Noah said. "But you're right. You and I should follow up on the shipping manifests and do some investigation in the Underground. I want to know who's behind all of this."

"You need to formally meet Investigator Sakoda, then," Cricket said. "He'll help you understand what concerned Mari most in the Underground. I can take you to him if Ochbo drops us off at Elysian Fields. We can walk to his place from there."

"We're taking supplies to the retreat anyway," said Ochbo. He turned to Rika. "Why don't you and I chase down more details about the labs and the clinical trials while they do that? I'd like to discuss Complete with you."

"Tonight I could," Rika said. "First, I promised IEC Director Wu that I would go in to work today. I must also meet with a domus master who is collaborating with the Institute on Circle Tide. I'm going onsite to a sick building as part of an investigation."

"How about I drop you off at IEC. We'll talk until then, okay?" Ochbo said. When Rika nodded, he rose to his feet. "Everything is in the heliotruck except for a few boxes. Take one as we head over. Let's all look busy loading the back."

Order regulars had positioned themselves at each corner of the clearing and near the rooftop entrance. The five only had to pass directly in front of one regular. They'd nearly made it to the heliotruck when the uniformed man yelled out, "Hey, you there! Where do you think you're going?"

Assuming the guard was addressing him, Noah scurried past his brother and hefted the box into the back of the vehicle. It was only then that he heard the sounds of a scuffle and turned to see that the Order regular had seized Jeremiah by his cowl. The man yanked Noah's brother off his feet and onto the ground. The box that Jeremiah had been carrying tumbled out of his hands and across the roof to land near Noah's feet. The gamer hoisted it up onto his shoulder with every intention of throwing it at the guard's head, but Ochbo stepped in his way.

"You will keep cool," the OMM guru muttered. He held Noah and forced him back toward the heliotruck.

Reluctantly, Noah climbed into the back beside Cricket and pretended to be reorganizing the supplies for the evacuees. Teeth gritted, he watched what was happening to his brother. The guard had no qualms about attacking a peaceful monk in front of witnesses. Jeremiah did what he could to try to escape the Order regular without using force. The man hit him in the face several times; Jeremiah groaned. Noah knew Jeremiah could easily fight back, but his brother did nothing. He didn't even block the blows. When Noah made a move, Ochbo pushed Noah back among the boxes.

"Major Fingrif lost his job because of you! You worthless scumbag!" the guard said. He hawked phlegm into his mouth and spat on Jeremiah. The novice monk only turned his head and slowly wiped his cheek. Ochbo grabbed Noah by the arm and held him fast. The guard kicked Jeremiah in the gut. "I'm assigned security detail for the rest of my life because of a mama's boy."

Two other regulars, a man and a woman, came running. To Noah's surprise, they yanked Jeremiah's attacker off him.

"What do you think you're doing?" the woman said. She had her colleague by the arm, twisting it behind his back so he could no longer attack the novice. Jeremiah managed to lurch to his feet, hugging his stomach. "That's not even the one who caused you to get reassigned. It was his brother Noah who put his mother on us and got Fingrif fired. Besides, don't you know it's bad luck to attack a monk, even a Magi cult monk?"

"Wait," the guard said, obviously confused. "This is the son of Domus Aqua who was arrested last night, right?"

"No, he was never arrested," the woman said, refusing to let the regular loose even though he thrashed about to get away from her. "Hold still or I'll break you arm. That's Jeremiah. They only asked him in for questioning last night to find out if he knew the whereabouts of his brother, Noah."

The guard spat again at Jeremiah. "Doesn't matter to me. You better stay out of my way, monk. I'll beat the daylights out of you every chance I get, and when I get my hands on your brother, I'll kill him."

In response, Jeremiah brought his cowl over his head so that his face was hidden and bowed deeply. And then, he hit his chest hard with his fist and threw out two fingers, before turning on his heel and marching on stiff legs to the heliovan. The baffled guard watched the monk and forgot to struggle to free himself from his colleague's grip on his arm. She reacted with alarm, releasing him and stepping away from him.

"Now you've done it! You've been trouble since I started working with you," she said. She made the signs that warded off evil and bad luck. "Now you've been cursed by the Magi."

Pushing past her, the man started after Jeremiah, but a third regular, a big veteran with a scarred face, blocked his path. "You want trouble with the Magi," he said, "get it on your own time. Now back off, or I'll give you what you gave the monk."

The loudmouth went back to his post. By now, Jeremiah was seated in the back of the heliotruck. Ochbo quickly slammed the backdoors shut and climbed forward into the driver's seat. He lifted off. Jeremiah threw off his hood and used his sleeve to stem the blood flowing from his nose. He also had a swollen, bruised left eye and a big bump on his chin.

"Thank you, Jeremiah," Ochbo said from the front. "You kept them focused on you. That could have turned into a fiasco for all of us."

Jeremiah grunted and patted Noah on the shoulder.

"I wanted to punch that scumbag," Noah told his brother.

"Tell me about it." Jeremiah flashed his classic grin and added under his breath, "Me, too."

On the way to Elysian Fields, Ochbo told Rika that he'd gotten access to Complete as contraband and that others may have bought it, too. "Identifying the buyers will be more difficult. It's not the kind of information a supplier willingly shares, but I'll find out for you."

"Okay," Rika said. "We won't know if it's important until we put all the puzzle pieces together. I'd say if the senator treated the participants as significant then we should, too."

"Agreed," said Ochbo. Noah didn't want to think about what Pharmo would have to do to get the contraband supplier's user list. Rika glanced back and caught Noah's eye.

"Fingrif lost his job because he was nice enough to let us go," Rika said. She sat slumped in her seat. "Noah, if you talk to your mom, would she get him his job back?"

Noah flinched. Every day he felt more pressure to become re-involved with his family to aid the evacuees and understand Daniel's involvement in the labs, even to get Major Fingrif his job back.

"Mother is better at wrecking things than she is fixing them. Fingrif dared to challenge her," Noah said, his voice low and gruff. His noncommittal comeback made Jeremiah sit up straight.

"So," his brother said. "Is what that idiot-guard said actually true? You got someone fired?"

"It appears so. Mom ordered that I remain in custody because she's worried about my safety 'or there would be hell to pay', but the major let me go." Noah studied his hands in his lap.

"Speak to our parents about all this, Noah," Jeremiah said. "The damage being done here … I mean … it's crazy."

Noah shrugged and refused to meet anyone's eyes. So far, his only bargaining chip with his parents was to let them decide his future, which seemed like such an unreasonable price. There had to be another way. He refused to become another Daniel, in whom the business acumen and conniving of their mother was magnified a hundredfold. Daniel had become just what their parents had raised him to be: a very rich monster. Nor could he be like the pure-hearted Jeremiah whose religious calling dated back to childhood. Their parents had never pressured their middle son to do anything but follow his dream.

They pressured Noah to go to an elite, snobbish academy and then into politics. They even expected him to marry some intolerable domus daughter of their choosing and grow their empire. Noah slumped against the boxes and closed his eyes.

When they set down in Elysian Fields, so many volunteers came to unload that the five didn't need to help. Cricket spoke with Lady Whisk-Away and then returned to lead Noah and Jeremiah through the retreat. Bae came running and jumped into her arms the way he'd done before. As rail thin as she was, Cricket managed to carry him the entire way to the retreat entrance.

"We're headed for another rooftop," Cricket said. "It isn't too far from here, and he'll be expecting us. Lady Whisk-Away says we should trust you."

"What makes you trust me?" Noah asked, grinning over at Jeremiah and figuring his brother the monk had convinced W-A that he wasn't so bad.

"Lady Whisk-Away told me that your domus will make conditions in the retreats a lot better," said Cricket. Noah stopped grinning and looked away. "Bae is excited to have a playground for all the kids and not so many people to a room so that it's impossible to sleep."

"About that," Noah said and looked to Jeremiah for support, but his brother's cowl covered his face and he couldn't make eye contact.

"Please, there's no need to explain. She told me you're giving up a lot to help us," Cricket said and lightly touched his arm.

Noah's face felt on fire. He didn't know where to look to avoid eye contact with Cricket. He hadn't made a commitment to Lady Whisk-Away, and here she'd gone and given Cricket false hope. Jeremiah proved no help. With his hood pulled forward, he remained silent, his head bowed toward the ground so that neither Noah nor Cricket could read his face.

They walked the better part of an hour and came to a thirty-story living building uniquely adorned with Sakura trees growing out of its many windows. Noah's feet were sore from walking on the warm pavement in ill-fitting gardener's shoes. A communiqué from Ochbo brought him up short. Ochbo sounded unusually agitated and spoke fast.

<Noah, Rika has been picked up by a team from Domus Aqua.>
<My domus?>
<She didn't go willingly, either. She put up a good fight. I saw it from the air, but by the time I landed again, they spirited her off. I couldn't find them anywhere.>
<How did this happen?>
<Rika wanted to change clothes before going to work and asked me to drop her off at her apartment. I guess they were waiting for her.>

Noah groaned. Too late, he remembered that Cricket and he had overheard his mother order one of her thugs to keep Rika's place under surveillance. He should have known that Lila would do more than have the DeeJee watched. Noah knew exactly what the Domus Aqua Master wanted out of the kidnapping: him.

"What's wrong?" Jeremiah asked.

"Mother has had Rika picked up. She's under the false impression that Rika is my girlfriend. Kidnap the girlfriend, get the boy," Noah said and pulled on his bristly chin, trying to stay calm.

"What are you going to do?" Jeremiah asked, and Noah thought he could hear in the question his brother's expectation that he'd cut and run, the way he'd run off to chase butterflies in the wilderness.

"Do I have a choice? You know Mother. She'd hurt a nobody like Rika without a second thought if it meant getting her way. You two go see the investigator on your own." Noah dug his fisted hands deep in his pockets and squared his shoulders. "I have an unscheduled appointment with Mother."

CHAPTER 22

Waving to Ochbo as his heliovan left the rooftop, Rika heard gravel crunching under foot behind her. She turned to see a heavyset man with light curly hair and a pointed beard loping toward her.

"Rika Grant," he said.

"Yes?"

"We'd like to ask you a few questions," he said.

Rika nodded and checked his biostats, Szymon of Domus Aqua.

She dodged past him and leapt onto some tiered planters. The crows cawed loudly and dove at her as she navigated through the vegetable plants toward the rooftop exit. One crow nicked her arm. Another pecked her head. The planters creaked under her weight.

Szymon swiped at her ankles as she climbed a tier higher and covered her head with her arms to ward off the angry crows that dive-bombed her. Above her, Ochbo's heliovan swung around and re-approached the rooftop. Two Domus Aqua heliocars cut him off and landed so that there was no room to set down on the rooftop. His heliovan rose and circled the building. Two men got out of the vehicles and joined Szymon. They stared up at her, clearly unwilling to brave the planters.

"Come down from there, DeeJee," Szymon said. "It's too dangerous. You could fall, or the planters collapse."

In response, Rika climbed to the highest tier with the crows still cawing and pecking at her. She swung over the planters and dropped down into the gardener's room. Landing on the folded bedding softened her fall, but it still jarred her. Steadying herself, she reached down, tightened her organo-pumps and then tip-toed to the door. She heard footsteps pounding toward the stairs and also back toward the heliopad.

"Where did she go?"

"That crazy wench didn't just jump off the roof, did she?"

Rika heard their steps recede to the heliopad where the men could easily see over the side of the building. She opened the door to the gardener's room and dashed to the rooftop exit. Taking the stairs in twos, she heard their yells and the echo of footsteps in the stairwell. Rika blitzed it out the ground floor door and ran straight into a tall woman with a pointy jaw and straw-colored hair who immediately seized hold of her. Rika pulled one arm free and struggled to free the other. Szymon and the other two men burst out of the building.

Realizing she couldn't escape all four, Rika did the next best thing. She collapsed. Without hesitation, Szymon picked her up and placed her over his shoulder, not bothering to hide the fact he carried the DeeJee like a sack with her arms and blue hair hanging down over his back. The other two men and the woman flanked him. Forcing them to carry her bought her time to send an emergency communiqué to Noah and also caused a stir on the street. So many commuters pinged her biostats, she felt certain her brazen abductees had been reported to the Order.

Back on the roof, Szymon dumped her into one of the Domus Aqua heliovans. He climbed in beside her and shook her until she cried out. The scarecrow woman joined Rika on her left.

"I knew you were conscious, you wench!" Szymon said.

Rika remained tight-lipped. The Domus Aqua thug slapped her hard across the face. She slammed into the woman beside her.

"Szymon," the scarecrow warned. "Show some restraint."

"Do you think this is a game?" he asked Rika, ignoring the other kidnapper. "Tell me where your boyfriend is."

"My boyfriend?" Rika asked.

"Domus Aqua's son," he said.

The windows of the heliovan had shaded black so that she could not see where they took her. If he quit his attacks, she could query the MAM and find out. Rika put her hand up to her cheek, which stung. Her neck also hurt from the force of his slap. She hurriedly checked their route. They were headed up the coast. And then she opened his most recent memory events. She whipped through a series of confrontations with his boss and finally landed on something useful — a smooching-fest with his neighbor.

"Szymon, do you realize I'm a DeeJee?" Rika asked. "That means I have access to your memory events, private ones like you cheating on your wife."

"Did you hear that?" Szymon bent forward and addressed the two men behind the glass in front. He laughed. "The DeeJee just threatened me."

His hand whipped across her cheek again, bringing tears. The force of the slap caused her to bite her tongue. "Where is Noah?"

"If you lay another finger on this young woman, I'll report you," the woman said. "Mae is waiting for us."

"Shut up," Szymon replied. "You forget I outrank you."

Swallowing the blood from her wounded tongue, Rika kept her expression blank. She expected another slap from the bully sitting beside her. For all his defiance of his colleague, he left the DeeJee alone. No one spoke again until the heliovan landed. The door on Szymon's side opened. A woman in a trim suit with a deeply etched face peered into the heliovan. Rika checked her biostats and learned that this was Mae, the personal assistant to Lila. The assistant studied Szymon for a long moment. She stood, and the heliovan door opened wider.

"Get out," Mae ordered Szymon. "You're fired."

When he hesitated to leave the heliocar, the man in front jumped out of the passenger's seat and assisted Szymon in exiting. Once he left, Mae slid in beside Rika. Lila's personal assistant steepled her hands and bowed her head to the DeeJee.

"I apologize on behalf of Domus Aqua for the treatment you've received," she said and repeated the gesture. "You must know that Noah's mother and our entire domus are worried sick that he hasn't been located. His life is in danger, but that is no reason to mistreat his girlfriend."

"Please understand, I'm not his girlfriend," said Rika. She inclined her head, still tasting the coppery flavor of her bloody tongue. She queried Mae's most recent recorded memory event — a communiqué directly from Lila about Noah — and her stomach churned. Domus Aqua had already discovered Noah's whereabouts and yet, Mae made no motion to set her free. Rika smiled a bitter smile and knew the blood on her teeth showed. Mae didn't blink twice. Lila's personal assistant had clearly become accustomed to seeing the blood of Domus Aqua's casualties.

"Would you be so kind as to accompany me inside?" Mae asked.

"Do I have a choice?" Rika asked.

"We can carry you," Mae replied. She slid out from the heliovan and glided toward the rooftop exit. Rika followed, the retainers closing around her. She found the personal assistant's movements exceedingly lithe and fast for her seventy-five years. Here was a woman who would easily reach beyond a hundred. And yet, Mae was as intimidating as her boss.

Calling up a map, Rika realized that she was traversing the roof of the exclusive hotel that Sebastian and she had cut through to get to an Underground bar. The knowledge offered her no advantage. The DeeJee had no chance of escape, surrounded by Domus Aqua personnel. A moment later, Mae plunged them into a dim stairwell and led the way down a half-flight of stairs to the penthouse suite. Its double doors opened instantly.

Sunlight streamed through the wall of open glass doors, a wide balcony beyond. The all-white décor glowed so that it momentarily overpowered Rika's vision. The penthouse was almost as stark and unadorned as the MAM grid. When her eyes adjusted, Rika noticed several people in the room. A pair of Domus Aqua employees bickering over something by the double doors, broke off abruptly as soon as Mae turned toward them. Staff bustled about, seemingly on important business, but everyone paused to bow to Lila's personal assistant, who barely acknowledged the deference. Mae took Rika through the main room then down a hall to a small, windowless room that contained only a dressing table and a fluffy, white stool. She left the young woman there. Rika's last view of the penthouse was the thin woman and the two men standing at attention with their backs to her as the door shut.

A penthouse suite would be perfectly attuned to the premier guest's needs, Rika knew. This one revealed a lot about Lila. She must be fastidious and expect an extra-hygienic environment. The DeeJee sank down on the stool and looked in the dressing table mirror. The haggard, blood-smeared face staring back startled her. Where the crow had pecked her just above the hairline, the skin was swollen and showing the first signs of an infection. Blood had matted her hair and turned it a darker blue on one side. One cheek was unnaturally pink and plumped out from Szymon's slaps. She sat lost in her oversized gardener clothes.

Would it be better for Noah if I escaped? she wondered. Rika tried to contact him and then Sebastian, but her communiqués bounced back. Before she could assess how to override whatever security this room had bound to it, Mae returned.

Lila's assistant carried a large sack out of which she wordlessly pulled a pale skirt, leggings, shoes and a flouncy blouse that Rika wouldn't normally wear.

"These will fit you. The shades will compliment your honey skin tone," Mae said. "Do you have any clothes this color?"

"No."

"I didn't think so. They're the finest designer materials available, our gift to you. Please prepare to meet Lila of Domus Aqua."

"I'm expected to be appropriately dressed in her presence?" said Rika. "Forget it. She and I have already met."

"Would you like my associates to dress you?" Mae asked in the sweetest tone with a slight grind on each last syllable that gave away her vexation. "Or if you prefer, I could re-hire Szymon for the task."

Rika took the clothes from Mae's outstretched hands, but waved off the delicate shoes — useless for any emergency sprint. "I wear my own organo-pumps."

"Fine, although they're hideous. There's a shower through that door and toiletries in the top drawer of the dresser," Mae pointed out. Mae turned her back, but remained in the room.

Rika took her time getting ready. Bypassing protocols, she attempted an emergency communiqué with Sebastian, but did not receive notice whether it reached him. Everything in the dressing room and bath turned out to be of exceedingly fine quality, including the meticulous dry shower that she swore cleaned her down to her individual pores. Her skin glowed back at her in the mirror. Only a tiny patch of blood darkened her hairline.

"I'm ready," Rika told Mae who kept her back turned and said nothing in reply.

Suddenly the door to the dressing room slammed open, and Noah waltzed in. He, too, was elegantly dressed in fitted clothing that showed off his broad shoulders and lean muscles. His dark skin stood out against the official white and blue of Domus Aqua. He'd discarded the Spider Zynx MAM embrace with its traveling spider tattoo.

"Mae," Noah said without inclining his head. "Leave us."

Without hesitation or surprise, Mae bowed and left, closing the door silently behind her. In a few short strides, Noah stood beside Rika and wrapped his arms around her. Her heart raced, pounding in her ears as though she'd just run a kilometer as fast as she could.

"I'm sorry," Noah said. He let go of her and stood back. "Your head is bleeding. Are you okay?"

Rika nodded.

"One of the drivers will take you wherever you tell him to," Noah said. "I'm fixing this so that you won't have to worry about Domus Aqua ever again."

"I want to walk out of here on my own," Rika insisted.

"Whatever you want," Noah said.

"What I don't want is to have a meeting with your mother," Rika said.

Noah hesitated. A shadow passed over his features. He straightened his shoulders and said, "Well then, you'd better allow me to see you out. You have to trust me no matter what happens between here and the door. Promise?"

"I'm not promising anything," Rika said. "This is a kidnapping. Some people think that's a crime."

"I'm on your side," he said, "but my mother is not going to give up until she gets everything that she wants. If she thinks you're in the way of me making 'the right choices,' she won't hesitate to destroy you."

"You people," Rika said. "You look down on everybody else, but you're horrible."

"Tell me something I don't know. I went to the farthest reaches of the wilderness to escape my family, but they've still managed to find a way to drag me back." He showed her a sad smile. "And they've dragged you here, too. I'm sorry."

"Sorry isn't good enough," she said. "I want out of here. I've got my own life."

"With Sebastian?" Noah said. "Think he's any better than the rest of us?"

"He's rescued me, twice. All you seem to do is get me into trouble."

The young man threw up his hands. "I said I'm sorry. Any second now, we're going to be up against my mother. All I ask is that you follow my lead, and I'll get you out of here. Everything will be all right."

Rika folded her arms. "All right for whom?"

There was a knock on the door.

"Just take my hand and don't let go," Noah said. "Okay?"

It was not okay, but Rika clasped his outstretched hand. The door opened and the thin woman stood in the doorway. She bowed and said, "Sir, your mother has asked that we escort you to her sitting room so that the three of you can talk in private."

"Step aside," Noah ordered.

"I can't do that, sir," she replied.

"We've known each other a long time. Yes?"

"Yes, sir."

Noah bent forward and spoke quietly to the woman. Rika stood so close she heard. "How is it you always know where my father is when no one else can find him?"

Rika heard the woman's involuntary intake of breath. "S-Sir?" she asked and briefly met his eyes with hers. She stepped aside.

Noah and Rika made it to the double-door entrance. Mae blocked them. Noah gripped Rika's hand so hard she winced. Otherwise, he wore an easy smile and casually turned halfway around, a spectacle for the employees who had stopped any pretense at work and stood staring at the confrontation. The silence must have alerted people in other rooms because a few poked their heads around the doors. Rika heard the click of fine shoes across the tile.

"Well if you insist, I'll do it here," Noah said. He stepped close to Rika, wrapped his free arm around her waist and bent down. Cocking her head, she looked up at him. His lips met hers. He sucked the breath from her in a long wet kiss, holding her tight against him. She dug her nails into his hand, but he refused to release her.

"Enough," Noah's mother said from the far end of the room.

Slowly, he let Rika go, though he held onto her hand, clinging to it as if it were a lifeline to their futures. Furious and red-faced, Rika barely resisted slapping him. She brought the back of her free hand up to her lips and vigorously wiped them off. Noah looked down at her and laughed before turning to his mother.

"Do you never tire of making a spectacle of yourself?" Lila asked.

"As this DeeJee once commented, I take after my mother," Noah said. Rika felt her cheeks go hot. She studied the floor and tried to free her hand from his without being too obvious. His grip tightened. At least he'd made her so angry she couldn't shed tears of embarrassment.

"I should thank you, Mother," Noah continued. "I never would have gotten a kiss from this little fool if you hadn't had our people kidnap her and knock her around."

Open mouthed, Rika brought her head up fast to stare at him.

"I see," Lila said and shook her head, as her eyes flitted over Rika. Her slow, curdling smile made Rika queasy. "Are you done having your fun so that we can talk?"

"Would you mind if I escort this one out first?" Noah asked and made a chin gesture in Rika's direction.

"Please," she said and waved to Mae to stand aside. To their backs, loud enough so that Rika heard, Lila added, "The DeeJee proved too easy a catch for my son."

Before Rika found her voice or managed to free her hand, Noah swung her around and thrust her out the penthouse door. Many curses sprang to her lips but not one escaped. Instead of taking the stairs, he marched her to the elevator. Mae followed, but left them to step into the elevator alone. She struggled to free her hand.

As soon as the doors closed, Noah let go of her.

"You," Rika spat. "You—"

He bent down and whispered in her ear so quietly she barely heard, "Before you call me names and make me angry, kiss me again."

"What? Kiss you?" she said, still burning from his laughter and his mother's dismissive smile. "Pervert is too kind a word for you!"

The doors opened and she leapt away from him dashing around the hotel guests and out of the lobby into the sunlight. She never glanced back. Although she detected neither Noah nor any Domus Aqua employees chasing her, Rika raced to the Institute of Extended Cognition. She bounced off every surface as hard and fast as her feet would take her.

At the gates, the on-duty guard stopped Rika to tell her that Medic Vasil expected her to check into the sick ward across campus, as soon as she arrived. Rika shivered at the mention of the medic. The second guard countermanded the first's message. Sebastian of Domus Restitio was meeting with the director and Rika was to go straight to the director's office.

"The director trumps the medic every time," the woman concluded. Rika bowed and then continued up the path.

Her first destination was neither the sick ward nor Director Wu's offices in IEC Silver. After the fiasco at the lab in Santa Barbara, she needed to apologize to her boss, Angela, and discuss what had happened. That way, Rika could assess what to expect from Director Wu. She headed directly to the Bolsa Complex. Once inside, she found the place even more frantically busy.

Huifeng spotted her and said, "Rika, thank goodness you showed up. I need your help."

"I'm actually looking for Angela—"

"Angela has been over at IEC Silver all morning with the director. It'll only take a teensy bit of time," she insisted. Raising her hand to Rika's bloodied forehead, she asked, "What happened to you?"

"A crow attacked me," Rika said. Huifeng raised an eyebrow. "Don't ask. Lead the way."

"We'll use the office upstairs. Everyone is crowded into the lab." Looking Rika up and down, she added, "That's a classy outfit."

Rika groaned. "Don't expect to see me in it again anytime soon. I haven't had time to change."

Upstairs, Rika found the quiet of the small office reassuring. They sat across from each other and linked work grids in Novus Orbis. Huifeng's virtual space was softly lit and littered with data blocks.

"Rika," Huifeng said. "You recognize patterns no one else sees. I've been at this since last night, and none of it connects."

"You're so thorough, I doubt I'll be much help."

Huifeng flipped through interfaces and organized her findings to show Rika. The blocks unfolded in overlays on the map. They highlighted a concentration of serious security breaches reported by domus and government agencies in the Los Angeles area. Rika turned to Huifeng.

"Do these security breaches relate to Circle Tide?" Rika asked.

"I assume so. Angela asked me to look into them. Since she and the director returned from Santa Barbara, I've only talked to Angela once. Otherwise, they've been holed up in Wu's office so I haven't heard their take on it yet," she said. "Here is what's weird. Look."

The snippets of reported problems that Huifeng pointed to all came from complaints lodged with the Order by confused security personnel. The first and oldest complaint came directly from the Ecumenical Union Center Hospital in Santa Monica. It concerned a communications breach and the unauthorized re-purposing of a nurse-in-training interface. The next emergency notifications originated from Seven Walls administrators just prior to the Order closing the world down. The Sanctuary librarian in Pasadena lodged another complaint when he found that the private top-security door leading to the OMM had been compromised.

Expressing fears of sabotage, URT safety engineers went to the Order when the main hospital stop's URT access gate inexplicably came crashing down and couldn't be re-opened. The reports continued, but Rika dodged away from the data blocks as though she'd been bitten.

Applying her DeeJee skills would be unnecessary. In every case, Rika had initiated the MAM security breaches dating back from when she'd communicated with Yori at the hospital up until the closing of the URT entrance gates that had blocked the Order regulars so that Noah and she could escape.

To Huifeng, Rika said, "I admit there're a lot of security breaches, but it's normal for employees to report security issues. If my trusted security system failed, I'd report it to the Order."

"But look how the MAM responds to these security failures," her colleague insisted.

Huifeng aligned the complaints with the system logs and Order responses for each incident. The MAM reflected normal operations during those times. No alarms. A small spike in internal activity proved the only anomaly. This tiny, consistent and distinctive blip had caught the scientist's attention.

"Once these heavily secured subsystems have been compromised, they return to normal," Huifeng said. She spoke fast and breathlessly. "Take the URT gates malfunction. The MAM accepted this security breach — represented by this blip, whatever it actually is — as part of normal operations and suddenly the gate came crashing down. People could have been seriously injured. Within an hour, the URT safety engineers raised the gate. It's never malfunctioned before or since."

Rika gulped. "You're definitely onto something here. Do you want to know the root cause? How this could be happening?"

Huifeng nodded and gestured with her hand for Rika to continue. The DeeJee rubbed her neck. Rika looked hard at her before continuing, "Even though I don't know how or why this is happening, I can tell you the cause."

Her friend's eyes opened wide and she leaned in toward Rika in anticipation. After a long pause, Huifeng said, "You're killing me. What is it?"

"The root cause is … me."

"Honestly, this is no time for joking around." Huifeng stood straight and put her hands on her hips. "Let me give you more time to look at this."

"I'm serious," Rika admitted.

"You can't be." Her friend's eyes narrowed.

Rika nodded.

"Let me give you some advice. Even if you believe that, keep it to yourself."

"Why?"

Huifeng studied her for a long moment, then said, "Isn't it obvious?" She actually stamped her foot for emphasis. "Angela told me Vasil wants you checked into the sick ward because you're unstable, which I told her politely was bunk. If you go around blaming yourself for MAM malfunctions completely out of your control, you'll give the Institute no choice. Vasil will get his hands on you."

"I'll stop scaring you," Rika said. She laughed, but her friend's serious expression remained the same. The laugh sounded tinny even to her ears. "Give me some time alone to process the data if you don't mind."

"Sure. Either you're too good at teasing me or I've lost my sense of humor," Huifeng said.

The implications of Huifeng's discovery frightened Rika. *Why is the MAM treating my security breaches as part of its daily operations and the offworld, modified fungus as though it's a native species?* Rika wondered.

As soon as Huifeng left Novus Orbis, Rika called up a map of the sick buildings. These evacuated dead husks showed up as orange squares on the map and littered all the largest cities on Earth, but she focused on the first; the worst struck city and the only one she knew well, Los Angeles.

Careful to be perfectly accurate about her dates and locations, Rika mapped Huifeng's security breach reports in green against the sick buildings and then added in red the addresses of the mysterious labs from the senator's datasphere. The Circle Tide incident at Homenaje Labs had occurred before her first security breach. None of the sick buildings were places she'd been prior to their outbreaks. The labs on the senator's list were nowhere near any sick buildings. Based on Frisardi's memory event, the Homenaje Labs had had an internal outbreak, but no buildings around it or anywhere else in Santa Barbara had suffered from Circle Tide. Nothing correlated.

Rubbing her temples with trembling hands, Rika ran through the data again. Orange squares, green diamonds and red circles speckled her 3D map blinking in or out to match her timeline. No pattern emerged. She had yet to add the most recent pieces of the puzzle — the addresses of the participants in the clinical trials of Complete that she'd pilfered from the clinician Ieda of Domus Concepcion.

After adding the last layer of clinical trial participants' addresses in blue, Rika sat back and studied the city geography from a high-level perspective. The map shone immediately purple when she overlaid the addresses. Almost every place where a clinical trial participant lived or worked marked in blue matched a Circle Tide outbreak, marked in orange. Other sick buildings existed where no participant lived or worked. Thinking about her conversation with Ochbo, she guessed if, once he obtained the list of illicit Complete users and their addresses, the source of the sick buildings would be fully explained.

When Huifeng returned to their linked workspaces and touched her shoulder, Rika jumped. She'd been so focused on her work she hadn't noticed her colleague.

"Return to Vetus Orbis, Rika. Hurry!"

Exiting V. O., Rika found Huifeng standing over her, cracking her knuckles one after the other.

"I've found some interesting correlations," Rika said. "I left our workspaces linked so you can go over my findings. Let's review it."

"Not now. Vasil found out you're on campus and came to the labs looking for you," Huifeng said.

"Oh, no," said Rika. She stood.

"He's got another medic with him," she said. "They'll head here next."

"How can he force me to check into the sick ward when there's clearly nothing wrong with me?"

"I don't know. He's acting pretty cocky," said Huifeng. "I bet he's alerted the front gate to detain you. I don't see how you can talk your way past them, but I'll run interference if you want to try."

"Thanks. On the MAM blips you identified, look for one in the IEC grounds exterior security system logs in about..." Rika paused to calculate, "Six minutes."

Huifeng's brow furrowed. "Whatever you're planning," she said, "be careful."

Huifeng took a stack of new sample kits. They reached as high as her chin. "Help me pile them up."

Rika added more kits until her friend couldn't see over the top. "Okay, that should do it," the scientist said. "While I distract them, take the stairs."

Bending down, Rika adjusted her organo-pumps and pulled at the short skirt's hem. Voices from outside the office door made her friend nearly lose her grip on all the kits. Huifeng headed out first. The medics ran straight into Huifeng, and the sample kits scattered across the hallway floor. The scientist screeched and dramatically activated her hazmat anzug, hood and all.

"Activate your hazmat anzugs!" she ordered. All three men backed up immediately since they weren't properly equipped.

"Hang on, these are new kits, aren't they?" asked the medic. He bent down.

"Step away from the sealed kit. What if it's been compromised?" Huifeng said. He sprang backwards knocking Vasil off balance.

Rika didn't wait to hear more. She bolted for the stairwell.

"Hey," Vasil said. "That's Rika. Stop her! Hey, someone stop the DeeJee!"

Several people dodged out of her way, and she made it to the stairwell. Vasil charged up, gaining on her. She took the stairs a few at a time, but on the final riser, she tripped on an uneven tile. Her head slammed against the exit door. Vasil was on her in a second, lifting her to her feet. Rika struggled to free herself. The man only more tightly held her. A minute later, the second medic came running out the door. Instead of helping to restrain her, he gazed past the struggling pair and slid to a halt.

Rika turned and saw Sebastian striding toward them. Frisardi's intimidating bulk followed close on his heels. The domus master said, calmly, "Ah, Medic Vasil, you're just the man I needed to see."

Sebastian bowed formally to the medic. Protocol, ingrained in Los Angelinos since birth, required Vasil and his colleague to return a deeper bow. When Vasil let go of Rika to bow, she bolted.

She ran in the opposite direction from the front gates, crossing the expansive grounds toward an overgrown exit in the far hedges. Behind her, the medics shouted for her to stop and raced after her.

She glanced back and ran straight into a guard who was headed toward her at an angle. At that speed, their collision sent them both into the hedge. He grasped hold of her.

A high-pitched alarm sounded. Momentarily startled, the guard loosened his grip, and she tore free. Rika sprinted for the exit, so close now. The medics had narrowed the gap to no more than an arm's length. Two steps from the gate, Rika shouted,

"Open!" The hedge parted slightly, just wide enough for her to squeeze through the branches. The moment she felt the prickles tug at her arms and legs, she yelled, "Close!"

The hedge sealed itself behind her. She could hear curses and shouts of "Open!" from the other side. The barrier remained intact, as Rika sprinted away.

CHAPTER 23

Noah paced the terrace that ran the length of the hotel pent-house and worried about Rika. He would now have to give up seeing her, or his mother would certainly go after the pipsqueak. This outcome alternately saddened and enraged him. No matter how much he strategized, there didn't seem to be a safe alter-native for Rika other than his strict avoidance of her. *It's not as though Rika is likely to ever want to talk to me again anyway,* Noah thought.

Most of all, Noah wanted to escape the hotel and his mother, but he was forbidden to leave the premises. Since the Order's public statement linking Noah to the notorious Soba, Lila had lived in fear that some Heartlander, outraged that Noah might have played a role in Senator Ortega's assassination, would kill her son. He discounted the risk. Heartlanders were more skepti-cal of Order proclamations than anyone else on the planet. Out on the balcony with the ocean breeze and any food or drink available for the asking, he should have been grateful. Instead, these luxuries further agitated him.

Crows landed on the veranda and peered at him, calling to mind Rika and her Jaa City. Not only the crows reminded him of her. Looking down into the street outside the hotel, he kept noticing the many girls in short pale skirts similar to the one Rika had worn the last time he'd seen her. Apparently, pale rose was the color du jour. While he'd never remarked on the style before Rika wore it, now it seemed that far too many women sported similar outfits. For some reason, he was reduced to noting every single one.

On his umpteenth tour of the terrace, Noah turned from staring out over the railing and its view of the sidewalk full of Rika lookalikes. He groaned and plopped down in a chair that reformed around him. He put his feet up on the railing. If anyone had told him when he came to L.A. that he would witness his mentor's murder, become a suspect and fall so hard for a DeeJee that he would sacrifice his future for her, he'd have considered it absurd. *No,* he thought, *impossible.*

Mae stepped out into the sunlight and came to stand beside him. She leaned her elbows against the railing and looked out over the sea. He'd known her ever since he'd turned twelve, the day his brother married. Throughout his life, Mae's loyalty to his mother had always been extreme and unquestioning, which had sometimes proven problematic for Noah.

"I'm curious. Why did you come to us in the end if it wasn't for the girl?" she asked, still facing out toward the water.

"That's what I'm here to discuss with Mother," Noah said. Watching her, he shifted slowly to sit straight in his chair, removing his feet from the railing and weaving his fingers together in his lap. Mae was expert at reading any telling gestures.

"Are you in love with her?" Mae turned to face him.

His eyes widened; he couldn't help it. Noah flashed his mother's smile.

"I don't want to lie to you," Noah said. She'd catch him if he did. Instead he had to figure out how to distract her and keep her distracted. "I don't want to come off as heartless, either. Rika and another girl I met recently have helped me get over Beatrice."

"You're over Beatrice?" Mae asked. She pulled a chair up close to his and checked his biostats. The notification made him chuckle.

"Yes," Noah said. "I didn't think it'd ever be possible, but I am over Beatrice."

"That will make Lila very happy," Mae said. "So about the DeeJee—"

"Yes," Noah said. "About Rika. Let's see. This will surprise you. Since Beatrice and I broke up over a year and a half ago, I've been with a lot of women. It became a kind of habit. Whenever our science crew finished a project reinstating a once extinct species, we'd celebrate for a night in the closest city — take a shower and get …. I always met someone. It was a pleasant diversion, but Beatrice was always in the back of my mind."

Mae nodded. His mother kept such close tabs on him. He knew Mae must have a list somewhere of all the girls he'd met.

"When I got back here, I found out that Daniel and Beatrice were having an affair."

Mae visibly paled. He waited, but she remained silent. He couldn't tell if he'd surprised her with the news or if her shock came simply from hearing what he knew — that Daniel still lived.

"After that, I got to know the DeeJee and this other crazy girl. They're so different from the privileged types I grew up with, even from Beatrice. They've helped me define what I want and what I don't want. That's about it."

"You aren't romantically involved with the DeeJee?" she persisted.

"Mae, listen to me," he said. He made an effort to keep his hands in his lap and remain composed. "Today was about me keeping Mother from doing something stupid to an innocent person in order to control me."

"She only acts to protect you and the domus," Mae said, frowning.

"Politics are unforgiving," he said, revealing his hand. The question remained: if he showed interest in politics, would she refocus on that breakthrough? That's what he needed Mae to do when she talked to Lila. "If we misstep this early in my career, it'll come back on me. Don't you agree?"

"It's a relief to hear you're thinking this way," Mae said. "Well my dear, we always have good talks, don't we?" The color had returned to her weathered cheeks. She said, "Let me see if Lila and Achilles are finished."

Noah had seen the Order Elder Chief Chiron's entourage take off from the roof a half hour ago, but he said nothing. For once, he wanted to give Mae a chance to tell his mother everything she'd learned from their discussion. The Order Elder and his mother had most certainly discussed Noah. He understood that it had cost Domus Aqua and his mother a lot to clear him. As a result of this and to protect Rika, his mother owned his future.

Noah didn't have to wait too long for his mother and Mae to finish their conversation. When Mae returned, he followed her inside and couldn't help noticing the many curious glances aimed in his direction as the domus employees bustled about their tasks. He went directly to the back room and sat across from his mother. Mae immediately took her leave.

His mother poured a cup of her special tea concoctions and offered it to him. He had not sat down with her to share a cup of tea in years and savored the first bitter sip.

"This brings back memories," he said. "Now that we're alone, I want to apologize for all the worry I've caused you."

Her head came up and she arced an eyebrow. He reminded himself not to act too nice or she'd become suspicious.

"Chiron has agreed to make a statement exonerating you, which eases my worries," his mother said.

"That's extremely good news," Noah said.

"From what Mae tells me, you've finally come to your senses."

Gritting his teeth, he took a moment to reply. After all these years, it amazed him how easily she pushed his buttons. This time he couldn't afford to get angry. He managed only to say, "Yes, you might say that. Not everyone would agree that my decision to return to politics indicates that I've come to my senses."

"And I would be one of them," said a voice from behind him.

Noah turned and was startled to see the man in the doorway, tall like him though with Daniel's light complexion. Noah stood, bowed low and said, "Father."

The older man advanced into the room. "*You* return to politics? That's idiocy." Mae trailed behind him making helpless, nervous gestures with her hands.

Although Lila's frown demonstrated how unhappy she was about her husband barging in, she sat up and made room for Isaac next to her. "I wouldn't call it 'idiocy'," Lila said and coughed delicately into the back of her hand. "However, both Noah's name and the domus have been tarnished by these allegations. A political career may be impossible for you now."

"It's often a short step in either direction between infamy and a hero's acclaim," Noah said. "I've become a household name and plan to stay that way."

"And just how do you expect to do that?" his father asked. He slapped his leg as though Noah had made a joke and guffawed. "By winning the fly-gaming championships?"

"No, by winning the hearts and minds of the Heartlanders," Noah said.

Lila sat back on the couch and cradled her cup in her hands, studying him.

"Listen," he went on. "We know that over seventy-five percent of the Circle Tide evacuees are Undergrounders who relocated groundside as part of Senator Ortega's improvement projects. Now their buildings are sick." He looked from one parent to the other.

"Go on," Isaac said.

"The retreats are all desperately overcrowded. Only a few high profile ones like Elysian Fields are receiving proper supplies," Noah said. "Domus Aqua should lead the other domus in improving conditions in the retreats. It's good public relations."

"Do you know how much that would cost?" his mother asked. "We're already footing the costs to ensure proper cleanup of our sick buildings and to help with relocation."

"The Order is close to an answer on the cause," Noah said. "The scientists are coming up with effective treatments for the living buildings and afflicted humans." He spread his hands, the image of the reasonable man. "The emergency is nearing its end. If we move quickly before the Order resolves the crisis, we'll come off as heroes, and it won't cost us much."

"Ridiculous," Isaac said, crossing his arms over his chest.

"Wait a second," Lila said, touching her husband's arm. "I just met with Achilles and he sounded unusually optimistic about Circle Tide. Maybe we should consider Noah's proposal."

"No: absolutely not," Isaac said. He stood and stepped toward Noah who jumped to his feet. They glared at each other. Nothing had changed. His father seized him by the front of his shirt and twisted it. Noah balled his hands into fists, but kept them at his sides. And then, Isaac astonished him by winking. Lila missed it since she couldn't see her husband's expression from her vantage point on the couch. His father roughly pushed him backwards so that he fell against the armchair. "I strictly forbid it."

With that, Isaac marched out of the room. Wringing her hands, Mae followed behind him and locked the door so that no one could barge in on Lila and Noah a second time. Noah heard reassuring bleeps from the activated MAM security.

Lila resituated herself on the couch and poured them both more tea. "Lately," she said, "your dad has been barging in on meetings and making a lot of proclamations. I don't understand what's up with him, but I always do my best to do the opposite of what he insists. His intuition is always wrong." She sipped her tea and went on, "If we were to go ahead with your plan, you'd have to work directly with the retreats. Because of our excellent reputations and relations, Daniel and I can lobby the other domus to contribute. Still, the gulf you must cross between hero and elected politician is not a short step."

Noah nodded. He told her that for the next five years he planned to spend time in different areas of the government making contacts and learning what he needed to while making a name for himself as a philanthropist. He sketched out his future for her, the one she'd planned for him ever since he could remember, and he acted as though it was all his own idea. He saw a satisfied smile overtake her usually stern expression. He concluded, "Unfortunately, this is all moot now that Father has forbidden it."

"Since when has he made decisions like that?" she bridled. "Where do you want to go first to gain experience?"

"We're wasting our time. I might as well just have dinner with you and take the next flight out to the Revillagigedos Islands," Noah said and shook his head. "Come to think of it, I do miss my crew of scientists."

"Nonsense! Tell me," she insisted.

"Well, I thought perhaps the Ministry of Internal Affairs," he suggested. Forcing Gothardi Lotte into doing something to expose the person who hired Bartholomew Soba would be gratifying.

Lila shook her head. "Too dangerous. You could end up stepping on the wrong toes. How about working directly with Our World Emissary Falkenrath?"

"That's more than I could ask for," he said. She certainly did not lack ambition for his political advancement.

"We also need to forge strong alliances with other domus, such as the up and coming Domus Concepcion. That brings me to another topic. The eldest daughter of the domus is a year younger than you, attractive and very intelligent."

He looked out the window. A crow crossed his line of vision, cawing plaintively as it passed. Turning back to Lila, he said, "Of course, I'll consider it, but my future wife must fit my true ambitions. Since I'm too young to run for elected office immediately, I'd prefer to take my time deciding."

"Mae will set up a date for the two of you once you've been exonerated," his mother said, as though he'd agreed. "She is anxious to meet you…. Just a moment, Noah, it's Mae, and it's urgent."

Lila shut her eyes. The urgent communiqué from Mae to his mother saved him from having to respond. All of a sudden Lila's pinched look transformed into an easy smile. She stood and glided toward the door. Puzzled, Noah stood, too. The door opened, and Jeremiah came in with Isaac walking behind him, his hand on his son's shoulder. Jeremiah always brought a smile to his parents' faces. The novice monk bent over his mother and kissed her on the forehead.

"You look so beautiful, Mom," Jeremiah said. Lila actually leaned into him. Noah wondered if he'd been adopted as a baby. How else to explain his own stilted relationship with Lila and Isaac? When one brother melted their hearts as soon as they saw him, and the other, Daniel, left them feeling secure about leaving a wealthy legacy. "It's been too long. May we all eat together tonight?"

"That's an excellent plan, "Isaac said. "We could even eat now. I skipped lunch."

"I've got to talk over a few things with Jeremiah," Noah said.

"Okay," Jeremiah agreed, before his father could object. "I sense we've got a lot to pray about, as they say."

When his father unquestioningly accepted that statement, Noah snorted. If he'd said that, they would have interrogated him until he made up an answer that satisfied their view of him. Maybe that was his problem.

"Are you still enjoying being a novice?" Lila asked her middle son.

"Always. I've really learned how to fight," Jeremiah admitted.

Both Isaac and Lila glanced at each other and chuckled. Noah was about to clarify that his brother wasn't joking, but Jeremiah shook his head. After a little banter, Jeremiah had their parents laughing and even holding hands. His brother was a walking miracle. When Jeremiah waltzed out of the penthouse front door with Noah, everyone they met bowed pleasantly to the two brothers.

"How do you do that?" Noah asked. "It's so irritating."

"What?"

"You make everyone feel good without even trying."

"It's easy. Your problem is you always distance yourself. You even refer to them formally as Mother and Father."

Noah changed the subject. "Look, I need you to ask Daniel to come here. It's urgent."

"Is he even in Los Angeles right now?" Jeremiah asked.

"Definitely, he's here," Noah said. He twisted Daniel's emerald ring back and forth on his finger.

"Okay. I'll contact him. Let's go to the hotel bar," Jeremiah said. "I asked Rika to meet up with us there if she could, but she said she was on the run."

"On the run?" Noah asked.

"Yep. Funny, she actually sounded out of breath. Since she can't make it, we'll keep our midnight appointment with her. If you can sneak away, that would be great."

"I'll try," Noah said. "The place is full of plainclothes guards."

"Luckily, no one here knows Spider Zynx," his brother replied.

Downstairs, the hotel restaurant was empty except for Domus Aqua security. While Jeremiah contacted Daniel, Noah walked toward the privacy booths at the back of the bar. Ducking behind the curtain, he ordered some food and waited until Jeremiah slid into the seat opposite him.

"Daniel said he's already on his way over. He has to discuss some business with Mom and Dad," his brother said. "He'll a be here any minute, now."

"I'll be right back," Noah said. "There's food coming."

He wanted to get out of the booth before Daniel arrived. When he pulled back the curtain, he stood face to face with his eldest brother. Without a word, Daniel turned to leave, but Noah maneuvered around him and blocked his path.

"It's time for us to talk," Noah said in a low voice, "and not just about Beatrice."

Noah pushed his brother in the chest and Daniel backed up toward Jeremiah.

"What's wrong?" Jeremiah asked.

Noah used his fighter's skills to control the space around them, which kept Daniel backing up until he had to sit down opposite Jeremiah. Noah slid in beside his eldest brother so that he couldn't easily escape.

"Do you even like Beatrice anymore?" Daniel asked Noah.

"What's going on?" Jeremiah interjected.

"Whether I like or love Beatrice is beside the point," Noah said. "How could you sleep with my ex-girlfriend, especially when you're married?"

"Honestly?" Daniel asked. He smirked.

Noah nodded.

"Curiosity."

Launching onto Daniel, Noah shook him hard and then brought his fist back and slugged him. His brother yelped and fell backwards. Holding his nose, Daniel glared at Jeremiah. Blood streamed over his hand and down his chin.

"You better not have broken my nose," his older brother complained in a nasal voice. "Jeremiah, you're trained as a monk to stop violence."

"That's not violence," Jeremiah replied. "That's an honest response to your 'curiosity'."

For some reason the exchange between his brothers made Noah laugh. He laughed so hard and long that his brothers joined him. Daniel snatched Noah's sleeve and used it to wipe his bloody nose. Somehow it cleared the air, and Noah found he could get down to the matter he needed to talk with them about.

"Senator Ortega was investigating our properties before she died," Noah said.

Daniel did not even feign a look of consternation. "I know."

"You knew," Noah said. "How did you know?"

"One of my wife's cousins, no, a second cousin told me about a month before the senator was murdered," Daniel said.

Noah and Jeremiah looked at each other and back at Daniel.

"Someone from Domus Superna worked for Ortega?" Noah said. The domus had done so many things to thwart the senator's initiatives. He found it hard to believe the senator would have hired anyone who came from Domus Superna.

"No, Gigi works for the Minister of Internal Affairs," his older brother said. "She contacted me because Goth Lotte feared Domus Superna might have gotten involved in something unethical, but I checked it out."

The image of Rika flattening Gothardi Lotte so that Noah could give him the datasphere flashed into Noah's mind. So the weasel had known about the senator collecting fishy, incriminating data and had warned the suspicious party.

"What did you find?" Jeremiah asked Daniel.

Daniel's brow wrinkled. "At first, I thought it was strange. We'd hired another domus to handle leasing our lesser properties. Between Superna and Aqua, we've got many properties over every continent and offplanet, too. Well, everything checked out except the senator's list of labs. None of the leasers for those properties that the senator was looking into were legit. They existed in name only. I mean they don't do anything. That had me worried, knowing the senator."

"You figured it had to be serious and she'd expose anything illegal," Noah prompted him.

"I knew she would, but it ended up being nothing," Daniel concluded.

"How can you be so sure?" Jeremiah asked.

The eldest brother shrugged. "I confronted my property handler. He explained it. Apparently, a prestigious domus has been working on a new groundbreaking herbal supplement and didn't want any competitor domus to find out what they were up to and steal the idea. He arranged for all these labs to be under separate names so that no one became suspicious and look into what they were doing until they were ready to go public."

"A groundbreaking herbal supplement," Noah said. Turning to Jeremiah, he added, "I wonder if any of the ingredients were derived from blackbase."

"Bl-Bl-Blackbase?" Daniel said. His mouth remained open for a moment and then he vigorously shook his head. "There's no way. Blackbase hasn't been seen on Earth in over a quarter century. It'd be destroyed in minutes by the MAM if anyone managed to get it past Customs."

"Who is developing the herbal supplement?" Noah asked.

"That's confidential," Daniel said. He threw up his hands, but Jeremiah simply repeated Noah's question.

"It's a highly reputable domus," Daniel said. "They would never have anything to do with blackbase. Their new head has been at the helm all of five years. While he's much more ambitious than his father, he wouldn't risk it."

Five years, Noah thought. That gave him a clue. "Domus Restitio," he said.

"You didn't hear that from me," his eldest brother said.

"Were they successful with it?" Noah asked.

"How should I know?" Daniel said.

"Come on," Jeremiah tag-teamed with Noah. "You're too good at business not to follow something that might end up with an enormous payoff."

"Fine," the eldest admitted. "My sources tell me Restitio cut a deal with Domus Concepcion. It's an additive in a new pharmaceutical that has been highly successful in clinical trials. Everything has been first rate and fast-tracked. It'll only be approved for centenarians initially, but the application is touted to become much broader for practically any age."

Turning to Jeremiah, Noah said, "That explains why Mother wants me to date the eldest daughter of Domus Concepcion."

"I recommended her to Mom," Daniel said with a curt nod. "She's beautiful and a handful, just like you."

"It was you?" Noah said. The eldest covered his swollen nose.

"If we're done here," Daniel said, "I'm going upstairs to have the medic take a look at my nose."

Always demonstrative, Jeremiah gave Daniel a hug as soon as they were out of the hotel restaurant in the lobby. When he let Daniel go, the eldest turned to Noah.

"For what it's worth, I'm sorry about Beatrice," Daniel told Noah.

"There's one way you can make up for it. No matter who it is, when I choose the woman I want to marry, you must support me and convince Mother and Father on my behalf," Noah said.

"On the honor of our domus, you can depend upon it," Daniel promised.

"Count me in, too." Jeremiah said. "Considering Noah's eclectic taste, he's going to need both of us to lobby for him. Yet why do I have a feeling he already has someone in mind?"

Noah shot Jeremiah a warning glance and Rika's name went unmentioned.

Upstairs, the five of them ate dinner together as a family for the first time in many years without the obligation and ceremony of a domus function. Noah appreciated how Jeremiah kept the banter light yet still managed to make the conversations meaningful. For his part, he didn't say much, but he laughed more than he had since he arrived in Los Angeles. After dinner, Daniel and their parents retired to another room to discuss domus business.

Before Jeremiah took his leave for the night, he pulled Noah aside. He inclined his head politely as Mae passed them and then said in a low voice, "Cricket and I met with the private investigator Sakoda, whom Senator Ortega hired. He gave us some interesting info that I want to go over with you later."

Noah nodded. "He compiled the information on the datasphere."

"Right. Now we've got him hiding out at the OMM headquarters in the catacombs and he has additional information," Jeremiah said. "But he needs someone to convince him it's safe to share what he knows."

"I could—" Noah began, but now here was Mae coming back. He waited until he was sure she was out of earshot then said, "We need somewhere to talk where there aren't so many ears."

"Let's just meet as planned in the catacombs," his brother said.

"I'll see you at midnight," Noah replied.

After Jeremiah left, the penthouse grew more somber for Noah despite the familiar hubbub of the domus staff. Preferring the outdoors, he sat on the balcony. A crow hopped along the railing. He had a sudden flash of memory: Rika, swooping down to rescue him when he fell off the outer wall of Jaa City. Instead of shooing the bird away, he went inside and came out with bread crust for the crow and a bowl of cherries for himself. He crumbled the crust and tossed it on the veranda. The crow swooped down and pecked at it but lost interest and returned to the railing. Then, as soon as Noah's hand left his bowl of cherries, the crow flew to the table and stole one.

"Aish! You are just like her," he told the crow, pushing the bowl of cherries toward it. "So irritating!"

Noah's mind returned to the conversation with his brothers. Something Daniel had said nagged at him. His brother had been certain that Domus Restitio wouldn't risk its reputation by using an illegal substance. For once, Noah agreed with him. However, a respectable domus might be tempted if key government officials sanctioned the substance as part of a clandestine project. Hypothetically, if the senator had uncovered the operation and threatened to expose it, then Ortega would have become a huge liability.

On the night of the senator's murder, Cricket had seen Bartholomew Soba and the Order — a captain and two Order regulars — whom Noah assumed had shown up because of his emergency call. Now he wondered if they hadn't already been sent to finish off the senator on the heels of Soba's attack, using the hitman as a cover.

The weight of a hand on his shoulder made Noah jump so high he almost toppled out of his chair. Daniel stood back.

"You okay? I didn't mean to startle you," his brother said. "I'm heading out now and wanted to say goodbye since I'm not sure when we'll see each other again."

Noah stood, but he didn't have Jeremiah's easy way about him and hesitated to hug his older brother.

"Give my regards to Beatrice," Noah offered.

"That I won't do," Daniel said and touched his nose. After the medic's careful administrations, it wasn't even swollen.

"Why?" Noah asked.

"Honestly?" Daniel asked and moved so that the table was between them, too far for Noah to reach across if he had the impulse to punch his brother.

The fly gamer calculated the split second it would take to knock the table out of the way.

Daniel said, "I have a feeling Beatrice will be finished with me the moment she finds out you don't care. She just wanted to make you jealous — payback for your preferring giant sea turtles to her charms." His shoulders sloped a little and he became very interested in watching the waves in the distance. "The only one who's jealous turns out to be me. What is it with you and Jeremiah?"

"What do you mean?" Noah asked.

"Jeremiah ends up with all the charm. You get all the girls. What does that leave me?" his brother asked and chuckled.

"All the business savvy," Noah said. Suddenly, the weight of Daniel's rotten arranged marriage and his endless tactical maneuvering to keep afloat a domus with millions of employees worldwide seemed too heavy for any human to bear. All this while one brother prayed and the other played the idealist in the wilderness. Noah's idea of a daily challenge was how to scale a rock face or remove ticks. The goal of repopulating the planet with diverse species had proven much more gratifying than the daily grind in a city filled with human pettiness. "None of us would be anywhere without you and your business savvy."

His brother groaned and turned to go. In a few short steps, Noah moved to block him. Only a sliver of air divided them, but crossing that distance seemed harder than bridging a giant chasm with a walking stick. He reached out his hand. Daniel hesitantly raised his palm as if expecting another blow. Noah took his brother's hand, gently turned it over, and dropped the emerald ring in Daniel's palm.

"Remember your promise," Noah reminded him.

"Now I have this to remind me," Daniel said and slid the ring onto his pinkie. He bowed and left.

Noah thought his brother was probably going to spend time with Beatrice, but found he didn't care.

Not much later, Noah's parents came and bid him a civil good night. When they had gone to bed, Mae also retired.

Noah told the night security staff that he was going down to the hotel bar for a nightcap. Courtesy required that they leave him the privacy of his own elevator; they took the stairs. Moments later, on the ground floor, Spider Zynx left the hotel while increasingly worried domus security combed the lobby and the bars.

Still, as Noah rushed down the back alleyway behind the hotel to the Underground entrance, he couldn't help but feel that someone had followed him. He thought he caught a glimpse of a shadow cast briefly in the light of an open door behind him and heard the occasional scrape of a shoe against the pavement. Yet when he looked back, he saw no one.

CHAPTER 24

Sebastian grabbed Rika's hand and squeezed it while he ordered Frisardi to fly to the El Segundo Blues Lab. She checked and found it on the senator's list stored in Jaa. Still out of breath from sprinting to the parking platform where the two had picked her up, she put her free hand to her chest. The domus master put his arm protectively around her and pulled her close.

"I paid off her debt and still they came for her," he addressed Fritz in the front seat.

"You paid off my mind enhancements?" asked Rika. "They were a fortune!"

"Congratulations, Rika. You're free!" the driver said. She slipped from under Sebastian's arm and pulled her hand from his. Maybe she should have felt liberated. Instead, she thought cynically that her debt had transferred to a new lender — one who's terms she hadn't heard yet.

"With the contract done, how can they expect to keep her?" asked Fritz.

"That director threatened to bring in the Order. He maintains that when he closes that damnable security exploit, our DeeJee will either implode or do so much damage escaping that it'll take years to repair. He wants that hack Vasil to rollback her mind enhancements."

"Reversing DeeJee neural-knits means guaranteed brain damage," Rika said. She slid her hands under her thighs to hide their shaking. "Severe trauma."

"Precisely," Sebastian said.

"I wouldn't be of much use to you then," Rika said.

"No," he answered.

"Sebastian, we can't go up against the Order," Fritz said. His voice had dropped an octave and his fingers stalled over the heliovan controls.

"I know that," the domus master said. "Wu is bluffing. He doesn't want the Order involved anymore than we do. Besides, we have our insiders there."

"Unless Rika poses a serious threat to MAM security," the driver said.

"Hey," Rika piped up. "Would the two of you stop speaking as though I'm not here? Fritz, I have no plans to destroy anything no matter what Wu does."

"You hear that?" Sebastian said and laughed. Fritz only shook his head.

"It's good you escaped from the Institute," Frisardi said, but it sounded to Rika that he worked to convince himself as much as her.

They touched down on a building that overlooked the sand dunes and the water. Frisardi remained in the heliovan while Sebastian and Rika climbed out.

"I'm going to give you a tour of this facility. It's a secret within the domus, but I trust you. As of today, you're part of Restitio. I'll take care of you," Sebastian said.

"Wait a minute. I never asked you to take care of me or to pay off my debt," she said.

"Don't get defensive," Sebastian replied, "or feel obligated to me for what I did. Sometimes good things happen, especially to people like you."

He patted the top of her head, and she shrank from his palm. Rika had never been this lucky. Winning a trip to Mars or the lottery were things that happened to other people. His smile that had so charmed her now seemed predatory. He took her by the elbow, and they left the roof. His carefree fashion, so meticulously selected, seemed contrived and his words calculated. Ever so subtly, he was changing in her estimation from a potential boyfriend to a dangerous stranger.

She also saw that he was overconfident and assumed an instant familiarity with her. He acted as though she would welcome his unhesitant hand: steering her by her elbow, with a palm against her waist, or the brush of his fingertips across her neck. These caresses were not for her benefit, but acted as a reminder that he now owned what he touched.

In the elevator, she bent and tightened her organo-pumps. When the door opened, he moved her toward a viewing area walled in by thick glass. Down below, Rika observed the gray expanse of a lab with the same large domes that she'd seen in Homenaje. Three technicians were on the floor in hazmat anzugs monitoring the domes and the web of interconnected pipes and gauges. The two entrances that Rika could see were each air-locked.

"This lab has been upgraded. It's a BSL-4," Rika said. "This is a safer and more secure version of the Homenaje Laboratory. The question is: what are you manufacturing?"

"Very good," Sebastian said. He stood behind her and gently arranged her hair. "What we have here is a farm that replicates the cave ecosystems on Mars with some major modifications and enhancements."

"In other words you're growing fungi to make blackbase," Rika said. She ducked under his arms and paced the length of the glass wall more to keep him from touching her than to study the domes.

"No, this isn't for making blackbase. We started by importing and replicating a Mars fungal ecosystem unique to one of the Martian caves. Let me tell you supporting the ecosystem continues to be a challenge. First off, it thrives only if extreme temperatures are maintained in the domes. Lately, all our labs have been doing great, but then this farm suffered a system-wide blight. The crew down there is working round the clock to bring the ecosystem back, but I plan to start over."

The data that Yori had shared with her came to mind. Martian isopods cultivated *M. somnis* for their food supply, but no overabundance of food ever occurred. A parasitic fungus also lived off that supply. The isopods carried bacteria that killed the parasitic fungus, keeping its growth in check. Another parasite survived off the bacteria, and around the circle went, one living off another living off another. It was a society of hosts and symbionts maintaining a delicate ecological balance in the deepest caves of Mars.

"So this isn't about processing the *M. somnis* fungus to make blackbase," Rika said. They'd gone to a lot of trouble to replicate its ecosystem not to harvest and process the fungus for blackbase.

"No," Sebastian said. "Blackbase is illegal, addictive and debilitating. We wanted to create something much more sublime. *M. somnis* inspired our scientists. Even though starting with its complex ecosystem made our project possible, it's become our bane. Our workers stole these miniature ecosystems in the hopes of producing blackbase, which is why we ended up with Circle Tide spreading everywhere."

"What?" Rika said. She studied his face, but detected no intentional deceit. "That isn't how Circle Tide has spread. At least it isn't the primary transmission vector."

"Unfortunately, it is," the domus master said. He reached out to catch her hand, but she stepped back as though she hadn't noticed. "Don't feel bad about it. Director Wu is the one who played god."

Rika felt the cool glass hit her heel and realized she couldn't back up any further. The room tilted one way and then the other. She sank to her knees.

"Rika?"

Abruptly, her mind flooded with memory events of Director Wu. Sebastian had purposely called up these events, knowing they would overwhelm her. The director's discovery of the security vulnerability barreled into her thoughts. Next she witnessed his creation of an exploit that allowed smugglers to import the *M. somnis* ecosystem onworld without the fungi being identified or the smugglers caught. The memory torrent ceased, and Rika refocused outward on Sebastian. "The director did more than create a security exploit so that the MAM would accept the fungi as a native species, didn't he?"

"Yes," Sebastian said. She felt certain he'd planted those memory events so she could access them every time she tried to access Sebastian's events. "Wu dreamed of going beyond the IEC's domain-specific DeeJees. Leveraging the MAM's vulnerability, which the genius Wu discovered, allowed for the dawn of a new breed of the great generalists with limitless MAM access. You're one of three DeeJee Eye-47s."

In response, Rika hid her face in her hands. The unique and unbounded MAM-human relationship had destroyed the other two DeeJees' personal identities. Vasil had them in his care, human husks. They lay unmoving in their beds, dead to the world.

Only her forbidden Jaa City had let Rika maintain her identity. Oblivious to the implications, she had multiplied and morphed Wu's exploit so extensively that the security vulnerabilities might never be completely fixed. She had seriously compromised the MAM security systems. After everything she'd manipulated, adjusted and changed, she doubted if Wu could ever close the security vulnerabilities and destroy all the exploits without her help.

"Rika!" Sebastian said. He had dropped to his knees beside her and held his hand to her forehead. "Talk to me."

"You gave me a shock even though it's been in front of me all this time. I'd ignored my connection to Circle Tide," Rika said.

He gave her a hand up. Rika looked out over the gray domes once more.

"Sebastian, the workers may have caused Circle Tide at Homenaje Labs, but they're not the main culprits. The primary transmission vectors for Circle Tide are the clinical trial participants. Everyone who's taken Complete ends up living in a sick building."

"How is that possible?" Sebastian said. It was his turn to recoil from her as though she'd slapped him.

"Spores may be released through human waste and grow to overtake the reclamation system of the living building. Yori and I went to one of the first sick residential buildings. Its elevator shaft was completely overgrown with Circle Tide. The reclamation system runs in the walls along that same route."

"Whom have you told this to besides me?" he asked. The cold look on his face made Rika think twice about mentioning Huifeng. She hadn't explicitly told Huifeng about the clinical trial participants, but she'd left the evidence on their linked workspaces at IEC.

"No one, but it's clear from the data," Rika rushed to explain. "I won't be the only one who will figured it out."

"I've got to get back to Los Angeles and do damage control. If this becomes public, it'll destroy everything. Complete is positioned as the next biggest drug for improved cognition. There's nothing like it." He took her by the hand despite her protests and practically dragged her with him back up to the heliovan.

"We've got a problem, Fritz," Sebastian said. He opened the back door for Rika, but sat in the front beside the driver. "Take us to Hotel Kenzan. I must get an audience with the Domus Aqua family."

Leaning forward, Rika felt her heart race. "Are they involved in this, too?"

Preoccupied with his own worries, he noticed neither her tone nor her stricken expression.

"Yes," Sebastian said. "They just don't know it yet. I need their clout. Daniel's man leased all the labs for the 'herbal supplement' to me through nonexistent third parties."

"So Domus Aqua is innocent of wrongdoing," Rika said.

Pivoting back around, Sebastian's expression looked as though he might spit on her. "Let's get something straight. No one did anything wrong. We bent some rules, that's all."

"Murdering a senator is not just bending the rules," she said.

"That wasn't us," the domus master said. "Lynnfield took the initiative when Ortega wouldn't give up the datasphere."

Frisardi glanced over at him. "Is it wise to tell her everything?"

"Shut up," Sebastian said. "Rika needs to understand. She's a member of our domus now." He turned to her. "We started with the *M. somnis* because of its euphoric properties and optimized its ecosystem in our labs to create something new. We added our own set of parasites and modified the fungi. It's no longer simply organic. It has synthetic properties, too. The end result is HMS — what my scientists nicknamed Holder, Molder, Scaler. The active ingredient in Complete makes it such a successful cognitive enhancer because it temporarily molds to the brain, holds stable existing cerebral cortex connections, and yet scales to grow new neurons. It literally extends neurites making new connections in a mature brain."

"And then it gets flushed out?" Rika asked.

"Exactly, after twelve hours it's flushed out. There's no trace left of it, only the positive impact on the individual's cognition."

"So centenarians will be a lot smarter, but none of us will have any place to live," Rika quipped.

"Not funny," Sebastian said and turned back to the driver. "Maybe you're right, Fritz."

Rika stood frozen in place at the center of the Hotel Kenzan's lobby. It was one of those moments when what she felt most like doing would be most ill advised — throwing back her head and screaming for help from the hotel employees and guests until her vocal chords gave out.

Sebastian insisted that he put the three of them up in the penthouse across the hall from the Domus Aqua family. He had business with the eldest son, and this was a rare opportunity for them to connect in person. "Besides," he told her, "this will be a chance to make them pay for how they treated you this morning."

"I want to go home," Rika said. She'd had all she could take of Sebastian's condescension.

"Do you think you'll be safe there?" he said, dismissing her protest with a casual wave. "Weren't you kidnapped from your apartment rooftop this morning?"

"Yes," she hissed, "by them!" She indicated the white and blue livery of the many Domus Aqua staff in the lobby. "I don't want to be in a hotel room across the hall from Lila and her minions." *Or*, she thought to herself, *from the son of the domus who humiliated me in public.*

"Fritz and I will take care of you, and you'll have your own room," Sebastian promised. He put his arm protectively around her, clearly misinterpreting her twitching as fear. In actuality, she struggled with her impulse to punch him and bolt.

Frisardi and Sebastian steered Rika into the elevator, out and down the hall to the penthouse across from the Domus Aqua guests. As they neared their suite, the opposite door opened and out stepped Mae. A jolt of adrenaline shot through Rika, but the older woman didn't so much as glance at Rika or the two men. Instead she hummed to herself with a tiny, preoccupied grin on her face.

As she passed Rika, Mae's most recent recorded memory event overwhelmed Rika's mind: suddenly, she was on a balcony with Noah sitting across from her, talking. The memory event shook Rika. She stumbled through the entrance to Sebastian's penthouse, and Fritz had to catch her. He carried her to the settee in the wide, open room and brought her a glass of water. This penthouse mirrored the one across the hall, except that the décor was awash with indigo blues, purples, reds and brilliant oranges, along with the heady scent of cloves. Popping from each wall were chattering, 3D media streams, news from around the world about Circle Tide. The sensory bombardment rattled her and deepened her growing sense of helplessness.

At least Sebastian wasn't demanding her attention. He disappeared into the adjacent room and locked the door. Fritz opened the wall of glass doors so that they could enjoy the ocean breeze and fresh air.

"Is there anything you'd like from your old place besides clothes?" asked Frisardi. "I don't think you should go home any-time soon."

"My guitar," Rika said.

"I'll get it for you."

"I'd appreciate that," she said. "Would you mind if I spent a little time in Novus Orbis?"

"Not at all. In fact, we need a few bits of information," Fritz said. "There's a draft contract rumored to have been drawn up between Domus Concepcion and Domus Aqua. It concerns exclusive offworld distribution of Complete, pending its approval."

"All right," Rika said and sighed. "I'll see what I can do. What's the other 'bit of information' you need?"

"Daniel of Domus Aqua has supposedly taken a lover. Knowing who she is, and where and when they meet would be very helpful."

"I'm not sure I understand how these two correlate," Rika said.

"You don't need to. It's part of how Sebastian negotiates. Knowledge is power. You ought to know that, DeeJee."

Rika let her head drop against the settee head cushion and studied the ceiling. There was no sugar coating to what Frisardi had told her. Now she knew why Sebastian had been courting her and had paid off her debt. She was a new source of knowledge that would give him power, which was clearly what Sebastian craved. The idea of getting him confidential legal documents and potential blackmail material added butterflies to her empty stomach. At least, the mystery of his interest in her was solved. Still, she had to wonder what other plans he had for her.

"Are you okay?" Frisardi asked.

"Oh yes," she said. "I'm fine if you don't count being hungry, tired and terrified about the Circle Tide spreading while we sit here strategizing backroom negotiations."

"Food is on its way. Come. I'll show you your room," he said. He gestured for her to follow and led her to the door farthest from the entrance. When it slid open, she saw herself reflected in the walls, ceiling and floor. The message hovered above the bed: *Try me. I'll become anything you want, including sand.*

"Oh boy," the driver said. He glanced at the décor and added, "I'll check on the food delivery."

"Nasty," Rika said, looking up at her face repeated in the ceiling and reflected from all the other mirrors. Below the window, a large wooden box with *Toys* inscribed on its top attracted her attention. She opened the window to air out the cloying scent, and then opened the box. Inside, she found handcuffs, crops, long lengths of rope, masks and fanciful garments, all made of leather. She slammed shut the lid and placed her hands on her hips.

"He's got to be joking," she said. She turned and addressed the room, "Mirrors off. Walls black. Bed … turn to stone."

The bed hardened. Rika sat down on its rock surface. *Time to think*, she told herself. She would never become Sebastian's plaything. And yet, it might not be safe for her on her own. She worried about how Lila of Domus Aqua perceived the world. If there was the smallest chance Noah was sweet on Rika, it might cause the domus master to have the DeeJee removed from this world for good.

She briefly considered staying under Sebastian's protection until the Circle Tide ecocatastrophe had been stopped, but knew Director Wu and the rest would need her help to succeed. And yet, as Frisardi had said, knowledge was power. She would see what she could learn about her temporary protector. She entered Novus Orbis and went to her workspace.

First, she attempted to access Sebastian's recorded memory events or any private data that he had archived on Domus Restitio. Immediately, her feet sank deep in wet, rotting muck that pulled her down. Fireflies rose up around her, blinking in dreamy succession. Mesmerized, and unable to move, she stared at the winking, ascending orbs and forgot what she'd come to find. Her feet sank deeper into the trap. Time stopped. Out of the dull, lifeless sky, a crow swooped down, opened its beak and cawed in Rika's face. The bird's raucous caw shattered her concentration on the lights. Rika pulled herself together and returned to her own workspace.

Rattled, Rika focused on Sebastian's requests.

Locating the draft contract between Domus Aqua and Domus Concepcion proved far more difficult than she'd imagined. She started with Aqua's legal counsel. This led her to a wealth of encrypted documents named and organized through a mysterious labyrinthine system in which she quickly became submerged. When she finally succeeded in locating and deciphering the draft contract, she saved it to her workspace. Exiting their system felt like coming up for air after being under water too long.

Returning to the hotel room in Vetus Orbis, Rika physically gasped. That brought on a coughing fit. She was glad to find that while she'd been working, Fritz had brought in a small table with water, a teapot brimming with tea, a bowl of strawberries, as well as shortbread and chocolate truffles on the side. She ate everything, even the strawberry tops and stems as well as the last crumbs licked from her thumb. Afterwards, she re-entered Novus Orbis to hunt down Daniel's lover. Picking through Daniel's recorded memory events brought her no closer to the man himself. He recorded only his business dealings. Not one family moment had been captured, not even his own wedding, yet he chronicled every domus business meeting in precise detail. Finally, her head swimming, she gave up and went in search of Fritz.

"Are you sure Daniel is having an affair?" Rika asked Frisardi, who had his back to her in the kitchen. He was busy pulling an enormous slab of newly grown prime rib from the meat grower and arranging it on a platter. Fortunately, over the aroma of steaming rice and cloves that filled the room, Rika couldn't smell the raw slab.

"No, I'm not," Fritz said. "Sebastian was tipped off that Daniel had been seeing his brother's ex-girlfriend, Beatrice of Domus Phrack, but they've never been seen together."

Rika brought her hand up to her face and rubbed her temples with thumb and ring finger.

"Is something wrong?"

"It would have helped if you'd mentioned that little detail a couple of hours ago," Rika said.

She headed back to her room where she found she had to reset the mirrored décor to her preferences. Although she had never met Daniel or Beatrice, she accessed the woman's private memory events about as easily as she had Daniel's. Beatrice's cache proved the polar opposite of her supposed lover's memory archive. For this daughter of Domus Phrack, nothing important enough to record and keep had to do with her domus duties. Instead, Beatrice scrupulously organized her events by the many people she'd known.

Her most extensive memory set was archived under the simple name: Noah. Rika sidestepped that altogether, afraid of what she might discover. With Daniel, Beatrice's first recorded event began years earlier with the discarding of garments in a building stairwell and ended on the woman's kitchen counter. Rika dipped into several recent events and decided that if the two were simply friends with benefits, the benefits had become more frequent and extensive over time.

Since becoming a DeeJee, Rika had known easy access to recorded memory events from practically everyone on the planet except for the events expressly protected by Director Wu and now Sebastian. Thrown into another's M. E., as she passed by or interacted with the person, Rika had gained a clinical view of lovemaking coupled with the sense that she'd personally accomplished each of these intimacies.

In the real world, the furthest she'd ever managed had been a few passionate kisses and that all-nighter cuddling with Noah after he'd passed out from exhaustion and overeating. Those were her accessible memories carefully saved in Jaa City. She was not sure what experiences she'd had before the mind enhancements. Rika might have led a life as exciting as Beatrice's, but she doubted it. Besides, it didn't matter. Anything not saved in Jaa or the IEC's repository, effectively had never happened.

"Time to eat," Frisardi said. He shook her shoulder as he spoke rousting her from her thoughts and her workspace in Novus Orbis. "Sebastian is at the table."

On the veranda, Sebastian stood when she came out and sat only after she did. He wore formal domus robes and the table was set for two.

"This morning I wasn't very gracious about your having paid my debt to the Institute," Rika admitted. "Thank you. It's such a relief. While I promise to avoid acting like your debt-slave from this point forward, I did get you the draft contract and investigated Daniel. The gossip about him is true. He's seeing Beatrice of Domus Phrack."

Sebastian had just placed a big chunk of meat in his mouth so instead of talking he chewed and patted her knee under the table. Rika looked down at the thick, rare lump of meat. It soaked in a red pool of its own drippings and was surrounded by an indeterminate mash of unidentifiable *edibles*. It destroyed her appetite.

"Sebastian, I have to be honest. I've been a data thief since I became a DeeJee. At first, I did it by accident. Private data just invaded my head when others were around. Lately, I've accessed stuff or gotten around MAM security to save myself or someone else from trouble."

Watching her, he put down his fork and dabbed his mouth with his napkin. "I'm not sure I like where this is headed."

"Please hear me out. Until today, I never accessed data to give one domus an edge over another. It feels wrong," she said. "I don't want to do this again."

His expression hardened. "I'm sorry it bothers you so much to help me out. Listen, data bandit, before you draw your moral lines in the sand informing me of what you will or won't do, take a good look at yourself. Is this a moral conflict or have you developed a schoolgirl crush on the handsome — though sadly ridiculous — Noah of Domus Aqua?"

Rika felt her cheeks go hot.

"You have!" Sebastian said. When he laughed, she could see a scrap of meat between his teeth. It made her stomach roll. "I see from your expression. Besides, I've had you monitored. I know where you've been and how you spend your free time."

"I can't help how I feel," Rika said, studying her lap.

The man laughed again. "Noah would never give you the time of day. He's started building a career in politics, and he'll need a wife who can carry the load. Even if he wanted to be with you, his dragon of a mother wouldn't let him." He took a mouthful of wine and swilled it around. "Sure, they'll use your DeeJee skills, once they find out about them. When your abilities fade, you'll be out in the street or they'd kill you to keep you quiet. On the other hand, here I am, willing to share everything with you, even after Wu destroys your mind."

"What do you mean 'even after Wu destroys my mind?'" Rika asked.

"Figure it out yourself, little bandit," Sebastian said. "I'm fed up with these childish games."

Whipping his arm across the table, he rose. His plate cracked against the tiles and the food splattered in every direction. He strode out the door and was gone without a backward glance.

Calculating how many steps it would take to get from the terrace to the front door, Rika bent over and tightened her organo-pumps. The too-short skirt had ridden up again and she yanked it down. At least the outfit self-cleaned so that its pale rose tint remained unblemished no matter whether she sat on the floor or kicked up dirt in a sprint across the IEC campus. Frisardi came out on the veranda and sat down where Sebastian had been.

"My dinner turned out to be a big hit," Fritz said. He gestured to the plumped up tiles that were absorbing plate shards and food. "At least, the terrace cleaned the mess before the crows got into it."

"I'm leaving."

"You know I'm here to protect you."

"Will you stop me?"

"Don't make me into a bad guy." Fritz placed his palms on the chair rests and slid his feet under him. "The penthouse is locked tight inside and out. It's not safe for you out there. If you need to go someplace, let me take you."

"Is it too dangerous for me, or am I too valuable to lose ... or do I know too much to be out on my own?"

"All of the above, my dear."

She'd never make it to the outer door with Frisardi chasing her. The attempt would mark her last moments of partial freedom. The terrace offered another option. It was too many stories high to jump to the ground, but she was confident she could override the security barrier, climb over to the Domus Aqua terrace, and go up. No one could follow her without a security override, but she'd have to keep Fritz wondering where she'd gone or she'd find him waiting for her on the rooftop.

She closed her eyes to enter Novus Orbis, reaching for the security controls. Fritz launched himself from his chair and pounced on her. "Whatever you're planning, quit it," he said.

Rika came back to Vetus Orbis, cursing and struggling to free herself. He carried her under his arm through the glass doors to her room and shut her inside. From the other side of the door, he said, "I'm sorry, Rika."

"Let me out," Rika yelled. Frisardi failed to respond, but she knew he was standing right outside her door. She could read his biostats. Next she went to the window and tested the opening. It wouldn't have accommodated a normal-sized person, but proved large enough for her. One misstep, though, and she'd fall. It was a long way down. Returning to the door, she hoisted the armchair in front to block it. If Fritz or Sebastian decided to make a surprise entrance, she'd have a few seconds warning.

She opened the toy box and pulled out the ropes. *Not exactly climbing rope or a harness,* she thought, *but it should get me down one floor.*

After attaching the rope to the window frame and testing her weight, she edged herself out the window and down. She used the mottled hotel façade as footholds while she alternately slid and climbed down from the penthouse. Someone noticed her and shouted. A small crowd gathered on the ground. When she'd reached the end of the rope, she'd gained confidence in the façade. Its decorative surface offered natural handholds and she was soon rhythmically descending the wall. One story above the ground, the façade ended and instead, she faced slippery glass. The crowd was on her side now. A couple of big men stood right below her, looking up.

"Jump," one of them said. "We'll catch you."

She did. They caught her to grins and cheers.

A frowning woman pulled one of the men away. "Next time," she told Rika. "You should wear pants. Even with the tights, it's a bit much."

The second man laughed and said, "Please don't."

Rika smiled and bowed in thanks to them. And then, she was gone, a last cheer sounding from behind her as she sprinted toward the nearest Underground entrance.

A quick call-up of a map showed that the entrance was down an alley on the other side of the hotel. Her route would take her past the hotel entrance. As she neared it, she saw a tall man with spider tattoos crawling over his arm leave the hotel and turn toward the alleyway. She followed him.

CHAPTER 25

Changing trains across the Underground, Noah couldn't shake the feeling that someone was following him. On the second train, he scanned the passengers in his car. After disembarking, he ducked behind a structural beam and studied the crowd for anyone suspicious. No one stood out.

Noah arrived at the Sanctuary's public library in the Underground on the far side of the catacombs. The library served as one of the few places in the Underground where one could access Novus Orbis anonymously in safety as a reliable, free service. He passed a solid row of patrons accessing Novus Orbis. More people stood in reserved meeting cubicles while still others reclined cross-legged on pillow chairs arranged in concentric circles. One librarian worked with students gathered around him in Vetus Orbis. His authoritative voice carried across the floor. Another librarian sat silent in a corner with her back to the room, probably answering reference questions in Novus Orbis. Neither librarian noticed the man with spider tattoos. At the end of the hallway, he stopped in front of the high-security OMM emergency exit.

From behind, Noah received a tap on his back. A shock went through him. The gamer whipped around only to see Rika with her jacket's hood pulled up over her head. The fuzzy trim framed her blue hair and sparkling eyes. Tilted upwards toward him, her face sported a self-satisfied smile.

"I've been behind you since you left the hotel," Rika said.

"It was you?" Noah said. "I can't believe I didn't spot you in that getup."

"You are totally oblivious."

"I'm not."

"You are."

The emergency exit door slid open to reveal Ochbo's bulky frame. "Ah, the two antagonists have arrived. You're always arguing, unless you're asleep or too busy stuffing your faces with food."

The OMM guru's warm expression turned stony as his eyes shifted from the couple to over Noah's shoulder. In one swift move, Ochbo yanked Rika inside behind him. He attempted to protect Noah, too, but the gamer already had a glock-goku digging into his back.

"Move along, Spider Zynx, a.k.a. Noah of Domus Aqua. No sudden moves, Ochbo, or I'll hijack this young friend of yours," said the man. Noah recognized the voice, but couldn't immediately put a name to it. He checked biostats: Fingrif.

"Major!" Noah exclaimed.

"Ex-major, thanks to you," Fingrif said, grinding the weapon into Noah's back.

Noah grunted, but didn't dare complain or move away for fear of Fingrif firing his glock-goku. Inside the OMM offices, Noah found the walls still seared by the earlier blasts from the Order and not yet renovated. The only vestige of the old clutter that remained was piled high on either side of the library entrance. Where there'd once been a doorway into the next room there hung a soiled tarp.

"I knew I'd catch you if I tailed Rika long enough. Down on the ground. Hands behind your heads," Fingrif ordered. With his glock-goku, he motioned for Rika, Ochbo and Noah to kneel in the middle of the room. He had his back to the tarp. "Rika Musashi Grant, you're an interesting case. Did you know that you don't exist? It's a mystery how the IEC finagled it, but the MAM systematically expunges you from its archives as some type of redundancy."

"What do you mean?" asked Rika.

"Just what I said," he replied. "I went to review surveillance of your time with Noah at Order headquarters and it was as though you didn't exist. No record. You can't hide from human eyes though, especially mine."

"It's because of my DeeJee enhancements. Everything I experience is captured in minute detail and archived at the Institute. Additional surveillance might be redundant." Rika gestured at his weapon. "You must be very angry to come after me like this."

"Keep your hands behind your head! Relieved is more like it. Discovering you're involved with scumbags like Sebastian and Fritz makes turning you in feel good. Not to mention that the Order has been searching for something tangible on the OMM for years," Fingrif said. Ochbo snorted in response, and Fingrif nudged him with his boot.

"You've got it all wrong," Rika said.

"Oh, really? What part do I have wrong? The part where you went to El Segundo Labs where they're manufacturing suspicious substances under maximum security? Or, the part where you got a hotel room with Sebastian across from the Domus Aqua folks?" Fingrif asked. "Do you plan to negotiate with Noah for a bigger share of the Complete distribution revenue or blackmail his unscrupulous older brother?

"Rika, is it true?" Noah asked. "You got a hotel room with another man?"

"Honestly — you're focused on that detail after everything he said?" Rika shot back. "Major, you have this all twisted around and—"

To Noah's surprise, the tarp covering the doorway suddenly billowed out toward them, then tore loose from the wall and enveloped Fingrif. Noah scrambled up off his knees pulling Ochbo back with him. Rika barely avoided getting trampled by the flurry of movement beneath the tarp. Noah tried to join the fray, but the confusing series of under tarp-yells, kicks and punches made it impossible to tell where he should step in. When Fingrif broke free and rolled out from under the tarp without his weapon, Noah pounced on him while Ochbo snatched the glock-goku that skidded across the floor.

Throwing off the tarp, Jeremiah stood up and rearranged his rumpled Magi robe. After tying back his long dreds, he grinned at Noah who held Fingrif immobilized with Ochbo's help.

"I see you made it past Mom's guards," Jeremiah said.

"Yes. You know, Ochbo was right. You're really fast," Noah said. He focused on Fingrif. "Major, no matter what you think you saw, Rika is working with us to find out who actually murdered Senator Ortega and stop Circle Tide."

"I don't believe it," the major said.

"Well then, believe this," said Jeremiah.

He pointed to the doorway. A squat, nondescript man in a rooftop gardener's uniform appeared. His biostats said his name was Sakoda.

"Major," the man said, "you know me."

Fingrif's face clouded. "What's going on here?" he asked. "Sakoda-san, I've been trying to locate you."

"I've been in hiding since Captain Lynnfield came after me with her goons. All my people are dead except my youngest operative, a roof gardener who goes by the name of Cricket. I have her to thank for my life, but that's a story for another day."

Fingrif's face darkened.

"Let me tell you what I know, major, and the reason Lynnfield wants me dead," Sakoda said. "There's been a lot of activity around Yuki's Otherworld Treasures over the past few days."

"That's Gun's place," Fingrif said.

"Right," Sakoda said. "Cricket knows a guy who operates a food cart down near Yuki's. She's been manning it for a couple of days to keep an eye on the place. I'm fairly certain that's where the contraband is stored after it arrives from Mars."

"What kind of contraband?" asked Fingrif.

Rika answered him. "It's the Martian fungus that was used for making blackbase. It's being smuggled here to make a new cognitive-enhancing drug called Complete. The manufacturing process modifies the fungus so it becomes much more dangerous and volatile. It spawned Circle Tide."

"Who's behind it?" Fingrif wanted to know.

"Domus Restitio," she said. "Master Sebastian himself."

Sakoda nodded. "He's covered his tracks well. Cricket was watching yesterday when a guy showed up to give Gun his orders. It was Sebastian's driver, Frisardi."

Fingrif stared hard at Sakoda. "Have we got anything else to go on besides the word of a roof gardener?"

"A bit. Unlike Circle Tide, the natural fungus is delicate stuff," Sakoda said. "It requires special handling. They've set up a holding area at Yuki's and are dealing with extreme temperatures. That means drawing energy from the grid. I've been tracking that. Also, they've got to use one-of-a-kind equipment, including a custom-fitted heliotruck."

Fingrif turned to Ochbo. "Let go of me. I'm convinced."

The monk set him free and said, "The question is what's our next move? We can't just go to the Order — they've been infiltrated. There aren't enough of us to tackle Gun's place. He'll have thick walls and blast-proof doors, not to mention that all of his thugs will be on guard."

Sakoda said, "If only we knew where the stuff was going. Once Gun ships it out—"

"I know that," said Rika. They all turned to her. "El Segundo Labs. The 'farm' there had problems, and the lab is starting over. That's where the new shipment will go."

"How do you know that?" Noah asked.

"I'm a DeeJee," she said. "Knowing things is what I do. You know, like the privileged son of a domus master treating people no better than disposable clothes."

"Hey!" said Noah. His brother nudged him.

"Here's something else I know," the DeeJee went on, "Sebastian has seen the contract between Domus Concepcion and Aqua for distribution of Complete after it's approved. He's also meeting with Daniel of Aqua right now to blackmail him into keeping quiet about the deal that had Aqua leasing the labs which manufacture Complete."

"Blackmail Daniel?" Noah said. "Over what?"

"Over leasing the labs and his dalliance," Rika paused. "That is the word people of your rank use, isn't it? His dalliance with his brother's girlfriend." She made a face of refined disapproval. "If such a thing ever got out, how could we live with ourselves?"

"That's enough," Fingrif said, as Noah opened his mouth to respond. "Have your lovers' spat on your own time." He stroked his chin. "Rika is right about one thing. If we want to stop Sebastian and his crew, we'll have to do it at El Segundo."

"How?" said Ochbo.

The former major thought about it. "I didn't serve in the Order for twenty-five years for nothing. There are friends in the Order I can call on; people I trust and who trust me."

"I think I've met one," Jeremiah said, rubbing the bruise on his chin.

"And if this works, I'll get my job back."

"Better yet," said Noah, "you'll get a promotion. That, I swear on the honor of my domus."

"Keep your honor," said Fingrif. "I prefer my own. Sebastian is no fool. He won't be anywhere near the delivery. We might round up his people and the Martian shipment, and still not be able to lay a legal glove on him."

"We need to lure him in," said Noah. "That means we need bait he can't resist and someone to dangle it in front of him."

Having been quiet a long time, Sakoda said, "Daniel. Sebastian thinks he's got him under control. Suppose Daniel tells Sebastian he knows the identity of a spy in his operation. Daniel says he'll name the name in exchange for the damaging evidence about him and Beatrice."

"That might work," said Fingrif. "How does Daniel convince Sebastian he's got solid information?"

Rika had that part. "His tall, handsome little brother has been making a fool of a first-class DeeJee."

"Wait a minute!" Noah said.

"That's good," said the major. "Noah coaxed the information out of you and told it to Daniel: family loyalty?"

The DeeJee laughed. "More like a jealous younger brother taunting the elder about how his grand scheme will blow up in his face. It's Noah's revenge on Daniel for stealing his girlfriend."

Fingrif nodded. "It sounds like the kind of thing that goes on in domus families," he said. He ran his hand through his already tousled hair. "So we've got the set-up and the deliveryman. Now, who's the bait?"

Ochbo interrupted. "Trouble!" he said. He closed his eyes and raised his hand to his temple. "Captain Lynnfield and two Order regulars are at the library entrance."

"It's my fault," said Fingrif. "I notified the captain that I was holding Rika and Noah. You need to disappear. I'll go tell her that I was jumped, and you got away. We'll reconnect later."

"Let's get out of here," Ochbo said. "I don't think Lynnfield will take the major's word." He closed his eyes for a moment and the debris on either side of the door began to move, forming a thick lattice across the library entrance. "That won't hold them for long."

Rika said, "I've got to access Novus Orbis. I need somewhere safe."

Jeremiah snapped his fingers. "The Sanctuary's private library upstairs," he said. "No one will be there at this hour."

"Wouldn't it be better if you came with us, Rika?" Noah asked.

She gave him a cool look. "No, thanks."

An alarm sounded, and a series of clicks. "Time to go!" Ochbo said. He led the way through the inner doorway, then through a maze of tunnels and a series of tarps. After a minute, Noah realized that Jeremiah and Rika were no longer with them.

The OMM guru turned toward him as though he'd read the fly gamer's mind. "Jeremiah knows the labyrinth of the catacombs better than anyone except me. He'll get Rika safely upstairs to the Sanctuary." He closed his eyes briefly. "Hurry. They're in."

The catacombs smelled of dust and decay. The dim lighting and narrow passageways reminded Rika of many places in the Underground, but everywhere she turned, she encountered abrupt dead-ends, odd corners and nooks with inscriptions in Latin, and carefully-tended tombs and altars. Many were decorated with domus emblems, heraldic designs or human bones. She stayed so close to Jeremiah that she stepped on the hem of his Magi robes several times. They made it to a small fountain at the confluence of several passageways. Behind the fountain, hidden by an outcropping of rock, a narrow staircase wound upward into the darkness. Noah's brother turned with a finger to his lips. They took the stairs as fast and as stealthily as their legs could carry them. Her breathing sounded loud in her ears.

At the top of the stairs, a landing offered four doors. Jeremiah stepped aside and motioned for her to try the one door covered in cobwebs and dust that looked as though it hadn't been opened for decades. "This one leads to the library, but only Sanctuary elders have access and I've never seen them down here. Maybe you'll have more luck than I would."

Willing herself to relax, Rika placed her hand over the deceptively ancient latch. She felt the peculiar vibrancy of the Sanctuary's living building, its complex security weaving among sacred scriptures, so many believers seeking truth, simplicity and understanding. She let the mechanisms of the door meet her furiously protected spirit, clenched against anything that didn't bear the familiar stamp of secular logic. And then, she let go.

With each breath, the DeeJee opened a little more of herself to the ways of the Christians, the Hindus, the Muslims, the Buddhists and so many others. Using her enhanced, data-gathering generalist's abilities, she found their common ground. New concepts, insights and epiphanies crowded into her uniquely organized brain. At last, the door's internal mechanisms whirled into motion and the barrier opened inwards. She and Jeremiah stepped through. Her mind was still singing as she closed the door behind her, as if a light filled her from the profound depths of her being. She was conscious of a new bond formed between the Sanctuary and herself; a new strength unfolded deep within her.

Her spiritual buoyancy evaporated as soon as Jeremiah brought her to a specific spot in a hallway that had a built-in trash receptacle. He opened the receptacle as wide as the door would allow and gestured for her to look into the trash chute. It ran vertically inside the wall.

"Do you see the receptacle door directly on the other side?" Jeremiah asked. "We need to cross this narrow chute to get from this hallway into the library."

Peeking inside the chute, Rika thought it smelled so rank she might be sick. She saw the closed door on the other side of the chute. The distance across wasn't more than an arms length. "You can't be serious."

"Every library entrance has a novitiate manning it at all times," Jeremiah whispered. "Besides, I've always wanted to try getting in this way."

"You're a sick man," Rika whispered.

"I'll hold onto you as you cross over so you don't risk falling. Are you ready?"

"Yuck," Rika answered with a shudder. Holding her breath, she put her head and shoulders through the opening. Jeremiah had hold of her waist and fed her through. She had to snake up and around until she had pushed open the receptacle door on the other side. Now he only had hold of her legs. Bugs flitted from beneath her fingers as she leveraged herself horizontally across the stinking gap from one receptacle opening, through to the library trash receptacle door on the other side. Her hands slipped on the grimy surface, but Jeremiah held her steady until she gave the signal that she was ready to pull herself through the door. She tumbled in a somersault onto the library floor.

Jeremiah followed. He easily twisted his body like a contortionist to fit across the gap. But when his hands latched onto the library door rim, he flailed about a bit scaring Rika. His shoulders were almost too broad to fit through the opening. Rika used her legs to wedge the receptacle door open as far as it would go while wrapping her arms around his chest. She yanked and he wriggled. He moved his shoulders one way and then the other. Finally, he pulled himself free with such force that he toppled out onto the floor with a loud thump, and Rika barely had time to jump out of his way. Jeremiah brushed a stray roach from his chest. Looking up at her, he laughed at the expression on her face.

"The religious life isn't for everyone," he said.

He led her down the narrow passageway. She checked the Sanctuary schematic in her head and found that they were just off the domed great reading room that was off-limits to the public, but as holy a place as a data gatherer could imagine. She fought a mischievous urge to dash through and take a peek. She would probably never get a chance to see it, now that she had made up her mind what she had to do. Afterwards, Rika would almost certainly not have a mind to make up, ever again.

"Come," Jeremiah said. He opened the door in front of them to a tiny, austere room with one light, a multidenominational altar and a kneeling pillow. "No one uses this study room because it's so close to the trash receptacle. It's nicknamed the Stink Room."

Rika bowed deeply in gratitude.

"Back at the OMM offices, you whispered that you had to close a Circle Tide exploit," Jeremiah said. "Won't that be dangerous?"

"It'll be worse if I do nothing," Rika said.

"What I'm trying to get at is that I'd like to go with you and help in anyway I can," Jeremiah said.

"Believe me," Rika said and smiled, "I'd beg you to come if it'd make a difference, but my plan requires me to do this alone."

"Okay, if you need me, I can be in Novus Orbis or here in a few blinks of an eye," he said. As he slipped out the door, he added, "It wouldn't do to have something bad happen to the love of Noah's life under my watch."

Hearing love, plus Noah and Rika, referenced in the same sentence made her eyes sting. She wondered if it was a pang of emotion or the garbage smell emanating from her clothes as she sat on the kneeling pillow.

Closing her eyes, the DeeJee accessed Novus Orbis. The familiar whooshing sound and vertigo carried her to Jaa City.

This time, Prometheus did not greet her. Instead, rows of zombies stepped forward from the side streets onto Main Street and marched toward her in unison. Like the Operator scout that had slipped through the gates and attacked Noah, these were Smart Intelligences of every type, size and shape, lurching forward, in step, as if in a parody of military order that had been repurposed.

"Halt," she ordered, trying not to panic. "Where's your leader?"

One zombie stepped forward from the troop. It wore a gold lamé jumpsuit and had cones for eyes. The DeeJee took a quick step back in surprise at seeing Director Wu's discarded S.I. cataloguer, the one she had microsized and confined to an endless looping session. It pointed and moaned, "Aaaaaaah."

"Prometheus!" Rika shouted.

"Yes, my dear?" the curator asked, materializing beside her. He put his hand on her shoulder, but she shrugged it off.

"Why is my city filled with zombies?" she said.

"We need an army," Prometheus said. "So far, I've turned all MAM processes that have directly threatened the city into zombies and then repurposed them into daemon-eaters for city security. Director Wu keeps attempting to close the security vulnerabilities and destroy the exploits that made possible your extraordinary mind enhancements. If he succeeds, the MAM will attack Jaa."

"I left Huifeng all the necessary information so he could succeed. I guess I have to send them more explicit directions," Rika said. She wound a strand of her hair around her finger for a moment before calling up an interface. From the city, she pulled examples of each of her exploits. She included all the methods she'd used to bypass the MAM's security and detailed even the smallest modifications that she had made to each subsystem.

The curator poked his head through her interface. "Do you realize that without Jaa City your sense of self will be destroyed? You'll become like your two colleagues watched over by Vasil."

"Yes, I'll be reduced to a persistent vegetative-state. Kindly remove yourself from my work," Rika said. It took her many more minutes to document explicit instructions so that Wu and his team wouldn't miss anything. After marking the package as urgent, she sent it off to Wu. "There, that should do it. I don't even like Wu, but at least he's fixing what he started, unlike Sebastian."

Prometheus wiped a tear from his cheek. "I told you, you mustn't blame yourself for Circle Tide."

"That was an excellent clue," Rika said. She kept her shoulders back and her chin up. Internally, she thanked her curator for the zombie army. As creepy as it was, she appreciated him giving her a few more moments for herself.

"You forgot one exploit."

"I did?" Rika said.

"It's one that neither Director Wu nor Sebastian and his crew can use for their own means to circumvent the law. Too bad you won't be around to take advantage of it."

"Prometheus, you're speaking in riddles," said the DeeJee. She searched her mind for an answer, but the MAM offered nothing. "What exploit?"

"Me, of course," the curator said and bowed theatrically. "I'm the oldest exploit there is, as old as the MAM itself."

"I could take your place in the MAM. If I were re-designated as you, Prometheus, the MAM wouldn't attack me," Rika said and then shook her head. "That wouldn't be any good for you, and the city will still be destroyed unless we divide it into parts, hide and mirror it. That's the way I found you. We'd have to reassemble after the exploits were destroyed."

"It might work," Prometheus said. "I don't mind sharing the same namespace with you, but everything would change for you. You wouldn't have access to people's private memory events or be able to get past security anymore. The only extra access you'd have would be mine in the Order's high-security clearance archives. They're extensive and dull unless you like family dramas. The Order collects everything about everyone."

"It's better than lying in the IEC ward for the rest of my days," Rika said and laughed. "No more memory events to pop into my head and get me into trouble! Now that's progress."

"Rika, we don't have much time," the curator said. "I'd like to turn a few more S.I.s into zombies and deploy them where they can be useful."

"Don't forget the crows," she said. "Since they represent my unconscious mind, they're always here. They've got to be good for preserving something."

CHAPTER 26

By the time Rika and Prometheus had finished deploying the zombie defenders, crows had gathered in numbers she had never before seen. They perched on every windowsill, every tree limb and every doorway. They lined the city walls and flocked on the rooftops in such numbers that the roofs might have been made of black iridescent wings.

Gesturing wide, Rika turned to Prometheus in the city square and quipped, "Birds on alert."

"Daemon-eaters ready," the curator said and bowed. Rika shivered at the sight of zombies standing many deep along the entire circumference of the city wall and filling every side street.

Suddenly, Rika felt part of her mind go blank. She clutched her head and sank to her knees. "Prometheus, they're closing the exploits. I just lost access to the Institute archives."

Her chest constricted and pain shot down through her arm.

"Stand up," her curator ordered. "You can do this. They will try to take everything from you, but they can't take your will."

Rika waivered as another part of her mind shut down. "I'll fight until the end, until every last crow has escaped."

Prometheus blew her a kiss and headed for the gates. She decided to go out with her trademark wings and activated them. Her wings unfurled, Rika leapt into the air and flew to one of the highest spires, where she could look out beyond Jaa. She had floated the city into fair weather over the sunny Valleys of the Future, but the skies were now turning black with the Order's winged daemons accompanied by strange machines manned by the MAM's most ardent S.I. protectors. As hungry as the zombies were for daemons, Rika could see the numbers of her defenders were dwarfed by what already filled the sky.

And now, here they came. Daemons poured through the main gate and over the wall, swarming everywhere inside Jaa, even the center square. Ranks of zombies obediently trudged to do battle. Outclassed, they were cut down. Some zombies managed to get close enough to grapple. They bit and ate, but they were far too slow to prevent the daemons from destroying the city. It was time for Rika to join the fight. Screeching at the top of her lungs, she swept down on great black wings into the center square. She had given herself long and short swords, and when she brandished them whole squads of daemons came for her. She lunged, cut and ran, turned and stabbed, careful not to be wounded by a poison-tipped dagger. One thing worked in her favor. As soon as a daemon fell at her hands, it rose as a zombie and attacked its former fellows. As fast as she swung and as quick as the daemons died and rose as zombies, more kept coming.

Bellowing from across the square, Prometheus joined the fight. He downed dozens in one swoop of his arm, cutting through their flesh as though slicing through butter. Splattered daemon blood sizzled across the curator's chest and ate holes in his clothes. He joined Rika and they fought back-to-back, protecting each other and Jaa as its streets and towers were inevitably overrun.

As Rika's strength ebbed, the crows that had been watching from atop walls and eaves began to fly. Their beaks opened and they cawed. The raucous sound came at different pitches, but together it made a terrifying noise — and a heartening one. For a few seconds, an iridescent wall of black feathers rose into the sky. Rika saw that there were strands of crimson among the black. In every beak, a crow carried a ribbon the color of blood. The embattled DeeJee saw that every ribbon was a piece of her city. As though Jaa had been made of ribbons all along, it came apart in streamers that rippled, twisting behind the huge flock of birds as they swept into the sky, wheeled, then flew out and away in every direction.

The daemons swiftly fell back and regrouped, giving Rika a respite from battle. She expected no victory. Still, she stared up at the fading distant dots with their tiny strings trailing behind them. Around her, the city had been reduced to rubble, but at least the crows had taken the scraps out of reach.

The daemons, too, looked up and Rika followed their gaze. She saw an enormous balloon in the shape of a spider floating down to hover in front of her and her curator. Its fluttering legs moved in a rhythm that fascinated her. It looked so enormous and yet so light for such a deadly bomb. The DeeJee herself had never felt so heavy-footed; so exhausted. More spider bombs landed around them. *No more daemon attempts to gain control,* Rika thought. *The MAM plans to destroy everything.*

Prometheus stood tall, raised his fist toward the sky, and shook it, she raised hers with him, and together they yelled out, "Jaa City!"

The spider balloons exploded in a blast of melting heat and white light.

Noah and Cricket stood waiting on the sand dunes looking back at the lab. The sound of the waves on the other side of the dunes calmed his nerves.

"One day, we'll bring back the El Segundo blues," Noah told her.

"Huh?" Cricket said. She peered at the heliotruck headed toward the lab rooftop.

"A blue-winged butterfly used to inhabit these dunes before it went extinct. The science crew I work with — *did* work with — plans to return them to this habitat."

"Stay focused," Cricket admonished him. "Chatting when you're nervous only leads to mistakes."

"Fingrif says he has his team covering us from all angles. Sebastian can't get away with anything," Noah said.

"Hmm. If I know Sebastian, it won't be that simple. He likes to surprise," she said.

"You really want me to make like I'm handing you over to him?" the gamer asked.

"We've been over this. Sebastian has been trying to corner me ever since my dad died at Fritz's lab in Santa Barbara. He knows I know too much. I'm the perfect choice to be the bait."

"I don't know, Cricket. It's putting you in harm's way unnecessarily. Everybody else seems to see it, but having you here worries me."

"Worry about yourself," the gardener said. She gestured at his neck, a reminder of her first introduction to him when she sliced his neck with a glass shard. "Here he comes, and Fritz is driving. I hope to get a moment alone with Frisardi."

Noah gave her a startled glance and shook his head. He had an uneasy feeling that Cricket had her own ideas about how this encounter would play out.

The heliocar landed close to them in a stinging spray of sand. Sebastian opened his door and gestured for Cricket and Noah to climb into the back.

"Daniel has already contacted me so I was surprised that you wanted to meet in person," Sebastian said from the front seat. Noah bit his lip to stop himself from expressing shock over Daniel. Sebastian went on, "Your brother expects me to hand over our recipe just because you brought me Cricket? She may be an informant who deserves to die, but business is business. There's a lot of money to be made here."

Fritz had been concentrating on getting the heliovan up in the air and on course for the lab. "Sir," he said. "Cricket isn't an informant."

"She most certainly is," the boss replied. "Lynnfield warned me I had a spy in my operation. This little sneak is the one who talked to Ortega's snoop, Sakoda."

Sebastian pulled out a glock-goku and pointed it at Cricket's head. "I've had this weapon upgraded. It will do more than hijack you."

Noah tensed. Cricket turned her head toward him, as if she was frightened of the weapon, but her eyes flashed him a warning: *Do nothing!*

It was Frisardi who reacted. "No!" Frisardi yelled and pointed the heliocar into a nosedive for the ground. "You can't discharge that in here!"

"Fine," the boss said and lowered his weapon. "Calm down. I'll wait until we're safely on the roof."

The driver moved his big shoulders as if something was crawling up his spine. "Cricket never talked to Sakoda," he said.

"How do you know?" Sebastian asked.

They circled over the lab complex. Groundside, Noah could see a custom-fitted, oddly top-heavy heliotruck backed up to a loading dock. People in hazmat anzugs were taking containers out of the back and passing them inside. Fritz brought the heliovan to a gentle landing on the roof of the complex and turned off the engine.

Fritz shifted around in his seat, and Noah couldn't help but be aware once more of the size of the man. One solid blow with the weight of those shoulders behind it could smash all the bones in the gamer's face. If it came to a fight, Noah could only hope that Fritz's mass made him slow.

"If I tell you how I know that Cricket didn't talk to Sakoda, you'll let her live?" Fritz asked, still focused on the gardener.

"What do you care?" the boss asked.

Frisardi swallowed and explained himself, looking directly at Cricket rather than his boss. "I was responsible for the death of her father. When we pulled the stunt at the lab to get our hands on the Martian fungus, he was one of the staff. He was trapped by the Circle Tide. By the time I got to him, it was too late." He unclenched his fist. To Noah, it seemed an act of supplication. "Cricket, I tried to save him. I did."

"So," Sebastian said, "That's how she got around you? She's been playing on your guilt, tapping you for information? She must have turned around and sold the info to Sakoda."

The driver didn't seem to have heard what his boss said, as if he was listening instead to something inside his own head. "Ever since that day, I vowed I would protect her and her family. It was the least I could do."

Cricket regarded him coldly. "Who asked you?" she said.

Sebastian had not become a domus master by failing to make mental leaps. Now, as he watched his driver and the thin gardener, his eyes widened. "I get it!" he said. "She's not the spy. You are!"

Fritz nodded still keeping his eyes focused on Cricket. Sebastian raised his supercharged glock-goku, pressed it against Fritz's head and fired. The bones of the big man's skull seemed to vibrate like shaken jelly. He slumped in the driver's seat.

Where's Fingrif? Noah thought as he went for the weapon, but Cricket was in his way and moving faster. With a screech, she launched herself at Sebastian, the edge of one toil-hardened hand knocking the glock-goku from his grasp. In her other hand flashed a long glass shard. She slashed at the domus master eyes but his head snapped back and she gouged a long furrow across his face.

Sebastian swore a string of foul syllables as he dove for his weapon on the floor. Cricket went after him, the glass dagger rising to strike again. Noah yanked her away from the man, out of the heliocar and onto the roof.

"Remember what we came for!" he said. "Proof — not to kill that man!"

Stumbling out of the heliocar, Sebastian held one hand to his bleeding cheek and aimed his weapon with the other. He was